AGAINST *the* GLASS

Dear Robyn,

Bless you in your travels through this life. I hope you and your family find grace, peace, + happiness!

Linda Halik

Against the Glass

a novel

LINDA M. HABIB

© 2021 Linda M. Habib

All rights reserved under Title 17, U.S. Code. International and Pan-American Copyright Conventions. No part of this work may be reproduced or transmitted in any form or by any means, electronic or mechanical, including but not limited to photocopying, scanning, recording, broadcast or live performance, or duplication by any information storage or retrieval system without prior written permission from the publisher, except for the inclusion of brief quotations with attribution in a review or report. To request permission, please visit the author's website lindahabib.com.

ISBN 978-1-7375560-0-8

DISCLAIMERS

This novel is a fictional dramatization based on real events and was drawn from a variety of sources. For dramatic and narrative purposes, the book contains fictionalized scenes, composite and representative characters and dialogue. The views and opinions expressed in the novel are those of the characters only and do not necessarily reflect or represent the views and opinions held by individuals on which those characters were based.

Medical information should not be considered complete or up-to-date, as it is of the story's timeline. It is not intended to be used in place of a visit, consultation, or advice of a medical professional.

Dedicated To Women Everywhere

LIST OF PARTS AND CHAPTER TITLES

CHAPTER 1—First Cut 1

Part I — *Gathering Pollen*

CHAPTER 2—Moth to a Flame 14
CHAPTER 3—"What a Tangled Web We Weave..." 27
CHAPTER 4—Flag on the Play 40
CHAPTER 5—The Mating Call 42
CHAPTER 6—Final Entry 46
CHAPTER 7—Something in the Air 48
CHAPTER 8—Denial is a River 58
CHAPTER 9—Blood, Shit, and Tears 63
CHAPTER 10—Masked Men 73
CHAPTER 11—Eyelids of the Heart 75
CHAPTER 12—Kaleidoscope 79
CHAPTER 13—A Leathery Leaf 84
CHAPTER 14—The End of Her World as She Knew It 87

Part II — *Into the Jar*

CHAPTER 15—Snowflake Marble 100
CHAPTER 16—Time Machine 104
CHAPTER 17—Feme Decovert 113
CHAPTER 18—A Soupçon of Joy 117
CHAPTER 19—To Be or Not To Be 124
CHAPTER 20—L'Air du Temps 127
CHAPTER 21—Tête à Tet 134
CHAPTER 22—Gross Anatomy 140
CHAPTER 23—See Change 147
CHAPTER 24—Surren-dipity 156

CHAPTER 25—Lilium Candidum 165
CHAPTER 26—The Handwriting on the Wall 172

Part III — *Wings Beating Against the Glass*

CHAPTER 27—The Threshold 182
CHAPTER 28—Waived Away 186
CHAPTER 29—Vile Loss 192
CHAPTER 30—Nexus 196
CHAPTER 31—Exposure 213
CHAPTER 32—Autumnal Fall 221
CHAPTER 33—All That Glitters 226

Part IV — *Off with the Lid*

CHAPTER 34—L'Étranger 238
CHAPTER 35—Les Âges 246
CHAPTER 36—La Madeleine..252
CHAPTER 37—Fontaine des Mers 256
CHAPTER 38—Au Revoir 262
CHAPTER 39—Candy and Goliath 268
CHAPTER 40—Take Two 275
CHAPTER 41—Light in March 282

Acknowledgments 292

About the Author...294

> "One is not born, but rather becomes, woman."
>
> —Simone de Beauvoir

CHAPTER 1

First Cut

NEW YORK CITY, 1983

Sounds of shovels scraping snow, exposing sidewalk and steps, shot to her brain. No. Her solar plexus. Dr. Madeleine jumped up to go outside and motivate the men.

She placed a hand on her abdomen to counter her distress as she left the desk. Atop the neat pile of paperwork lay a list of more than a hundred names. Snow would not thwart this opening.

In the lobby, she pressed a hand against one of the double glass doors and pushed it open. The scene outside The Harkness Pavilion, facing Fort Washington Avenue in Manhattan, was gloomy and gray. Sideways-blowing snow beat the buildings, the sidewalks, the begrimed ice. Not a flash or dash of color — not a yellow cab, a red delivery truck, a glistening semitrailer, a pedestrian with a colorful umbrella — nothing cut the gray.

Snow fell as fast as the men worked. However grateful for the sound of their progress, the long-buried memory it stirred continued to eat at her, like acid. Through the partially open door, she waved to the janitor and his helper. "Good job. Thanks." Her breath, a haze, clung to the air.

"Don't worry, doc, we'll get 'er done," the older man yelled down to the plaza.

"Please join us for hot beverages after the ribbon-cutting." Her voice rose above the scraping of metal on concrete. "And of, course, cake."

A thumbs-up from the older man. The younger chipped away at a mini-glacier as he began to calve it.

After she released the door to return to her office, a backward glance revealed the imprint her hand had left on the glass panel. Ignoring her instinct to go back and wipe it clean, she instead turned away, moved forward. Momentum. She had dared him. Now an in vitro clinic would finally open in the Northeast, after two additional years of delays. Even if Manhattan were snowed in, what infertile couple wouldn't shovel their way to its opening? Opposed to the nay-sayers, opposed to a government that refused funding, opposed to a chief who protected his other funding, here she stood, a reproductive endocrinologist with a clinic she conceived, guided, built. She couldn't be readier and more anxious to help.

Like a mother in the last throes of labor (witnessed while delivering countless babies as an ob-gyn), she sought distractions. Back in her office, she circled the room, inhaling the smell of untrodden carpeting, gray, and fresh paint, blue, which hadn't yet witnessed tears of joy or sorrow. Their synthetic scents swirled with the fragrance of the stargazer lilies her husband had sent. She removed the anthers with tissues from within the flowers' newly-opened petals before the reddish pollen could stain anything.

Dr. Reed tapped on the open door and entered. Her gaze stopped at the wrapped gift on the coffee table. "You haven't opened it yet."

"A bit superstitious. Don't want to jinx the inauguration when we're this close." *The sooner the better.* An imaginary whalebone corset tightened around her ribs, impinging on her organs. How much longer could she hold her breath?

"One last thing. Help me fluff the pillows." She walked to the pink settee, a reproduction of the one in Paris, and tossed a down-filled throw pillow to Dr. Reed. A butterfly on each of the three pillows was painted with scientific accuracy — a monarch, a swallowtail, a cabbage white. Each butterfly thrust its proboscis deep into the center of a favored bloom. "A little touch of softness and resilience for a bit of comfort." The science came first, but considerate touches couldn't hurt. As with every ovum she ever studied, details were crucial. In her patients' time of deep need, she wanted them to feel cherished.

Then she clutched Dr. Reed's gift and forced herself to open it. Having donned the new physician's coat, she smoothed the folds with long, nervous strokes. When her eyes caught the gold script that spelled out her name, her identity, she traced it with her finger. The gold lettering was extravagant. She stared at Dr. Reed.

"The gold. You don't like it," Dr. Reed said. "We can switch it out later, but today is your crowning glory, regardless of what the chief may think."

"You're always stirring the pot, aren't you?" She loved Dr. Reed like a little sister. "I don't want to hurt your feelings, but I don't want to call attention to myself. Today is about the institute and all the women, couples, it'll serve. It's not about me."

She strode back to her desk and clutched the list of patients interested in exploring the option of in vitro. She bit her lip. "Which couples am I setting up for failure? Over a hundred names already."

"What are you really worried about?"

"I'm one hundred percent certain that the in vitro success rate won't be one hundred percent. I'm worried about the dark disappointment of those I'll inevitably fail." She placed the list back on the desk. "I don't deserve gold." The pitch of her voice rose. "Who am I kidding? I'm doing this work for myself anyway. I'm a fraud." She wrung her hands. *Would the first pregnancy she enabled redeem her?* She had to get on with it. "It is all about me, isn't it?"

Dr. Reed shot to the desk and popped the collar of her friend's new white coat. "I won't enable this doubt. You've always known there'd be a high failure rate."

"But now it's real. I do see why the chief wanted to wait until there was at least one successful American in vitro baby. But that was two years ago." The wait was like being in labor, cervix fully dilated, fetus ready to drop. A complication. "I can't wait another minute. What other obstacles are out there?"

"Today is the day," Dr. Reed said. "He was right to wait. You and the chief don't always have to be at odds. Let's see—." Exuding positive energy, Dr. Reed bounded through the office with the grace of a deer. "I think you need to set your water pitcher right there on the coffee table, on a tray, of course." She removed the Waterford crystal from the shelf behind the desk. "Your anxious patients will appreciate a sip of water." She circled to the lab in the rear to fill the pitcher, then returned to set it on the coffee table with the glasses and napkins she had gathered.

About to leave, hand on the doorknob, she surveyed the room. "Perfect. Focus on the couples who will have children because of your years of labor." She drew a smile in the air. "It's time," she said. "Give me ten minutes to set up the ribbon."

"You've got five." At her desk, Dr. Madeleine lifted the twenty-inch ceremonial scissors from its mahogany case. *International Institute for the Study of Human Reproduction* was engraved along one blade, with *January 1983* along the other. The carbon steel glinted in the light streaming in from the garden-facing window. The sun warmed her. It had broken through as she practiced opening and closing the ungainly tool with both hands, so different from her delicate surgical instruments. She laid the scissors down.

Another box awaited her attention. Relieved Dr. Reed hadn't noticed it and anxious to conceal it before going back outside, she lifted the cedar cigar box, its colors and brand long since faded. She removed a key from the drawer and clicked open the padlock. This day would begin the final phase of her unburdening. She rubbed the back of her neck and turned her head from side to side hoping to release some tension. Her neck crackled.

Her stomach churned. After opening the lid of the cigar box, she took up the bundle of papers wrapped in yellow ribbon. She sniffed it, nestled it back in, locked the box, and secreted it under a false panel of the bottom drawer. She dropped the key into her breast pocket. Scissors in hand, she left. Although she'd be cold, she didn't take her coat from the stand. Would the chief even notice the gold thread?

Regaining her composure, she marched to the lobby and out the glass doors to the applause of those gathered on steps and plaza. Reporters with cameras and pads. Smiling faces of family, friends, staff. The unknowns — prospective patients? And among them, arranged on tall stands, hundreds of spring flowers — tulips, daffodils, primroses, crocuses. Where there had been snow, there were now flowers. How had they materialized so quickly? Her family, staff, Dr. Reed? She tasted tears and smiled through them. Fingers to her lips, she sent a discreet kiss to her husband.

The Chief of Obstetrics and Gynecology at Columbia moved in close beside her behind the ribbon. "Your name in gold. I made you co-director, not queen, and the ungodly flowers." He patted the hand holding the scissors as though she were a child who had eaten her broccoli. "'Uneasy lies the head. . . .'" He forced a smile toward the crowd and waved.

He'd never change, but she'd rise above it. Too many years and too many setbacks, with him in particular. She wouldn't allow him to defile this moment. She also smiled and waved. Inside the smile, like a ventriloquist, she said to him, "I'm the one with the years of research, training, and knowledge for the position. Otherwise, there would be no co-director, or institute. It's not about me." The lie burned. She swallowed the cold air. "Thank you for securing the funding."

"My charm and charisma."

She opened the blades of the scissors and rested the upper blade against the entwined blue and pink ribbons Dr. Reed had strung across the entrance. The ribbons were embossed with colorfully-patterned Easter eggs. *Must've been hard to find in January.* She glanced down at the red plastic handles that lay in her hand, like a little pool of blood, clashing with the pastels the scissors were about to sever.

She brought the blades together with both hands. There — in one instant. Change, potentially for millions, joining the Joneses in Virginia, the only other IVF clinic in the country. Change whose seeds had been planted far back as 1944, with Miriam Menkin and Dr. Rock. Change that could have begun at these very doors ten years ago, but for the chief's intransigence. *How many children could have been?* With words of welcome, she said she was honored to usher the questing couples down these steps and through the doors to a new era, a hard-won battle, an era she wished could have begun here a decade earlier. It was too cold to keep them out here long. She was brief.

The gathering applauded or raised their gloved hands in the air and cheered. Ready to enter the building, they each picked up the nearest stand of flowers to take inside, as requested. She and the chief held open the doors to the Institute. "IVF is now available right here and it is as affordable as we can make it," she said. Curbing costs had been one of her demands. She'd do her small part to give any woman this choice. For families.

Swallowed up by the group, she wended her way to the refreshment table in the lobby. The stands inside, flowers bloomed everywhere. With a blade of the ceremonial scissors she had carried in, she cut the cake, made to resemble a microscope (no pink and blue plastic trinkets, no storks; she had been clear with Dr. Reed — never anticipating the ribbon), and handed the first slices to the janitor and his helper, Fred and Tom. The chief bypassed the table and entered the elevator.

Dr. Madeleine shook hands and shared cheek-kisses, hugged her family, smeared icing on her husband's nose, and cleaned the scissors. "The flowers were too much. Love you," she said to him. "I don't know how late I'll be." She then excused herself to get on with the real work of the day. "I appreciate your kindness and enthusiasm," she said to the gathering. "We have a long waiting list, and I've already spotted our first patients. Thank you all. And please help yourselves to the flowers."

She entered her office suite and placed the scissors, wrapped in napkins, on the white marble counter where her receptionist, June, was labeling dozens of stiff, new folders.

"This is it," Dr. Madeleine said to June. Her past was the scaffolding she had scaled to construct her future, this present. Blessed with a unique gift for recognizing the most mature and viable oocytes, she would help create families.

Her muscles relaxed. She strode into her office, pulled her chair out from behind her desk and assembled a sheaf of papers, which she attached to her clipboard. June rapped on the open door. "Ready for your first couple?"

Gasping, she could hardly utter a simple "yes." She had already met this couple, primary donors to the Institute. But she was no more anxious to help them than any others. Every woman had the right to overcome obstructions to her desire for a biological child. The desire. The frustration. The heartache. It lived in her.

June escorted them in, and Dr. Madeleine crossed the room to welcome them.

"We've waited and prayed for this day," the woman said. She removed her coat. "Thank you for giving us this opportunity. And the chief assures me all of our records will remain anonymous. No one needs to know our intimate affairs. I don't want our child labeled a 'test-tube baby.'"

Dr. Madeleine smiled, giving way to a tension-relieving laugh. "I wish the press would use scientific terms, in vitro, IVF." They shook hands. "But it is I who must thank you for the extraordinarily generous donation that got this institute off the ground in the first place. I can refer to you and your husband as 'Patient X' for our paperwork, if that will do." With unwavering eye contact, she said, as eagerness overtook her, "IVF can work. We'll adhere to strict protocols, which I'll review with you, for its best chance. What I can't offer are guarantees." She released the woman's hand.

"But the chief assured us you're the best. He urged us to wait for you, rather than go to Virginia. You have the gift. We'll give anything."

The longing ache she wanted to quiet.

The woman clenched her hands, then squeezed her husband's arm. He rubbed his wife's shoulder, then rubbed his thighs as he stood to take her coat to hang with his.

Time to get them to relax. She led them to the cozy settee beneath the garden window, and she sat in the green wing chair opposite them. The woman settled back, picked up a pillow, the monarch, and hugged it to her chest. Her husband grasped her hand.

Dr. Madeleine explained how his sperm would be tested first, as testing for fertility issues with the woman was always more complicated, even painful. When the tech, Joe, approached from the rear lab, she introduced him. The husband poured himself a glass of water. Coughed. "Could sure use a shot of scotch in this." He kissed his wife before Joe led him away.

She continued her conversation, reviewing Patient X's records as she explored possible reasons for the infertility. Her expertise delved deep into infertility's innumerable causes. She had invested nearly every waking hour of decades in research and training.

"The chief has been my gynecologist for years," the woman said, "and he couldn't find a problem."

"Some conditions aren't readily apparent. I have to be thorough." They worked up a schedule for a pelvic exam, testing, shots, and monitoring, all of which would have to be completed long before they could harvest ova. The husband was doing his part and might not have to return, except for moral support. "We're embarking on a long-term relationship." The clinic had its heartbeat.

When the husband returned, she accompanied the couple to the door. She took the opportunity to peek in and thank the couples in the waiting room for their patience.

Warmth radiated through her body. Adrenaline was pumping. She'd ease many aches, but not all. She planned to stay until she had seen every patient. This one day was an overwhelming open-house schedule. She was grateful to have seen over twenty couples of the hundred on her list. They had made it through the snow. A healthy start.

June appeared at the door with a young woman whom she introduced as the last patient of the day. *A would-be single mother?* There was nothing in the literature about such a case, but why not? She was intent on helping women. She wasn't concerned with society's arbitrary rules. There would be sperm donors. Why hadn't unmarried women had access to birth control pills, legally, until after 1965? Why wasn't abortion legal for all women until 1973? Why shouldn't single women have access to in vitro? Why was there a gatekeeper to women's reproductive choices? Hoping her eyes didn't betray her fatigue or her frustrations, she looked up and studied her patient.

"Brooke Diamond, doctor." The woman held out her hand and drew closer. Her perfume was strong, the familiar scent of Shalimar.

She led the pretty brunette to the settee. "Please make yourself comfortable while I get my forms."

Returning to sit opposite the young woman, her back was to the door. As it was already dark outside, she caught her own reflection in the garden window. She was spent, outside and in. Angling for information, she asked, "Will your husband be joining us?" She hoped it wasn't rude. She clicked her ballpoint a couple of times. "Sorry for the long wait. It won't be like this on future visits."

"Yes. He waited with me for a while, but had to leave. I'm sorry he's not back yet," Brooke said. "It's always something." Her eyelids fluttered. She hid her hands under the coat on her lap.

"We'll begin with your history, then." Dr. Madeleine asked Brooke for her records, if she'd brought any. Papers in hand, they discussed Brooke's sexual history, her past use of contraceptives. She mined for details not in the paperwork. Methods of contraception? Perhaps Brooke's use of an IUD had caused uterine perforations, inflammatory pelvic infections. Brooke's intake indicated she'd been sexually active for years, so sexually-transmitted diseases could be a cause of infertility. She'd schedule a thorough pelvic exam, after testing the husband. "Don't worry. We'll do everything we can to give you the family you want, but I admit, I can't make promises." Wide-eyed and thin, the girl looked young and vulnerable, a fledgling bird. She reminded the doctor of herself at that age. "Your sheet says you're twenty-two?"

"Is that a problem?"

"Not at all. Your age is a positive factor. How long have you been trying to get pregnant?"

"Since we married, almost two years. My gynecologist recommended you when he learned about this institute. I really want a baby, whatever the cost. My husband can afford it, and he's desperate for an heir." Brooke poured some water, then dabbed her eyes with a tissue.

"I really do understand." She reached across to Brooke to offer a reassuring touch.

A knock on the closed door. Dr. Madeleine turned in her chair. "Enter," she said. At the door, June said, "The husband poked his head in. Giving the car keys to the janitor, he said. He'll be right in. Should I leave this open?"

"Please." She turned back to her patient. She did want to test the husband today.

A thunderous voice penetrated the sober atmosphere of the room. "I finally made it. I need a disguise to get anywhere in this city." He brought in cold air, and a smell she couldn't quite place. She turned. The coat tree wobbled, its three legs thumping against the floor, when he tossed his jacket onto it. With quick reflexes, he steadied it, preventing its fall.

The blood drained from her face.

Brooke leaned toward her. "Are you all right?" She poured her a glass of water.

The doctor waved it away. "No, thank you."

The husband sprawled on the settee next to his wife, oblivious to his jarring impact. "I'll take some." Speaking to his wife, he lifted the pitcher, never looking across the table. "How are you going to help the doc?" he asked. He raised his arm, lifting the pitcher higher. "We're here for her to help us." The pitcher slipped from his hand and shattered on the stone floor. "I told you it was a bad idea coming to a woman doctor. This is a sign." He never took his eyes off his wife.

Brooke knelt to pick up the large pieces of the crystal and placed them on the table. "Sorry, doctor." Then Brooke said to her husband in mellifluous tones, "Now, honey, please."

It seemed Brooke was accustomed to calming him. Had she, herself, ever been that naïve? Dr. Madeleine stiffened and said, "Leave it. We'll take care of it." Her nostrils flared, seeking more air, and she took a deep breath. "Excuse me, please." She held on to the arm of her wing chair, lifted herself with some effort, and made her way out the door to June.

"Call Dr. Reed. I'll wait out here till she comes. The day must have caught up to me. I can't treat them."

There it was — the dead-on shot to her solar plexus.

PART I

Gathering Pollen

CHAPTER 2

Moth to a Flame

SEVENTEEN YEARS EARLIER:
STATEN ISLAND, 1966

Cocooned within the carrel fashioned from bookshelves and her desk in the corner of her tight bedroom, Candy wrote under the heat of the lamp clipped to the shelf above her. With her calligraphy pen and black ink, on fine Clairefontaine Triomphe tracing paper, she wrote without stopping, *Lampyridae*. She was lost in the fine work and details as she prepared to dissect and label the insect before her.

Her mother barged in. "It's time."

"I'm prepping a specimen for my group tomorrow." Proud of her work and pleased that the insects ignited the children's interest in science, she lifted the paper, blew on the ink, then showed her mother. "I'll mount the firefly above this label and ask the kids if they see a clue to the insect's common name in its Latin name." She paused, the paper mid-air. "Time for what?"

Her mother scowled, squeezing her brows together.

What had she done now?

"You're out of high school, done with the nuns' protection. Now's the time to meet someone to marry, time to leave home, time to have babies, like everybody else," her mother said. "That's what time. Babies, not bugs."

"This again?" She went back to working on her lightening bug for her little museum group. "I'm happy right here, working, alone, in control."

"You can't continue to hide out in this room, away from boys. The clock's ticking." Her mother's voice tightened, almost a shriek. "What man, tell me, is going to want a girl who handles dead things, bugs, dead bugs?" She snatched the firefly from the desk, flicked the specimen to the floor, and stepped on it. "Worthless."

Her mother's criticisms used to cut more deeply. Since her father's death, her mother was increasingly emotionally frail. Candy hardened herself to the insults. "Don't fret, Mother. I'll get another specimen at the museum tomorrow, before class. I'll take an earlier ferry." She pulled a tissue from the box on her desk.

"A museum," her mother drew out the word, "full of dead things." She slammed her hand against the bookcase. "You're getting old. You don't even date. Why can't you understand that right now you're the last woman, our family's last chance, to keep our ancient tradition?"

Candy clicked the lamp off and stood, face-to-face with her mother. "First, I'm not 'old.' I'm only nineteen. I'd truly love a dozen kids, not only a January baby, but not yet. I have plenty of time." She knelt and slid the tissue under the firefly, creating a hammock to lift it, careful not to damage it further, though it had been dead before her mother took out her frustration on it.

"I was married at your age."

"I know, Mother."

"Many of your classmates married right after graduation. I read the announcements in the *Advance*. They know what's important. Enough of this bug nonsense. It's time you start dating." She stomped out of the bedroom and pushed the door open into the room so hard that the doorknob dented the plasterboard wall.

"Are you harboring an eligible boy in the living room?" Candy asked after her. Twelve years of nuns in all-girls schools. At least her friends' parents let them socialize, but not hers. "By the way, that was an insect. Not all insects are bugs. But it is the other way around," she yelled out to her mother in the hallway as she crossed her room to discard the firefly. She removed the torn screen and dropped the firefly into the tall grass of the backyard. "Do you smell something burning? Wood?" She followed her mother to the living room.

Her mother shook her head and sighed. She pulled a pack of L&Ms and a book of matches from her apron pocket.

Start fresh. Stay fresh with L&Ms. The jingle made no sense. Could her mother burn away her anxiety? She hoped so. Candy tried to remain calm. "I have plenty of time. Our women have kept the tradition for a thousand years. Trust me. I won't be the one to extinguish it. Grandma gave me all the secrets. No cause for alarm."

Her mother repeatedly struck the match against the thin black strip on the matchbook cover. She dropped the failed match and tried a second.

Without the firefly to work on, Candy had packed her portfolio for the morning.

"I can be an entomologist and have a family. I want to do both. Read Betty Friedan." Her mother batted away the book Candy had pulled from her bookcase before leaving her room. Before she really angered her, Candy fished for the pendant snug between her breasts and pulled up the two-thousand-year-old Janus coin attached to the chain. "I embrace my obligation. There's nothing I value more. When the time's right, I will bequeath the coin to my January baby." Clenching the coin of the two-faced Janus, she said, "I look back to the traditions of our past, but look to the future as well." She tucked the coin back into her bra. "What suddenly brought this up?"

Her mother finally lit the third match, ignited the cigarette, inhaled, and threw her head back. The cigarette tip burned as red as her mother's cheeks. She blew out a cloud of smoke. "I don't understand why you have to go to college in the fall. College is men's business. Your job is to find a nice boy."

Then she latched on to her daughter's hand and dragged her to the living room window. She grabbed her shoulders and positioned her directly in front of the picture window, facing the beach. "This is what I'm trying to tell you. Look across the street. That's what's burning." Cigarette in hand, she pounded the air, the cigarette smoke creating trails around her. "See all the cars in the parking lot? There's a bonfire starting on the beach. You might have noticed it if you'd get out of your room." The vein at her temple protruded.

She hadn't seen her mother quite so agitated before, especially with so little cause. She was getting worse.

"Out on the beach like that, I bet they're college kids," her mother said. "Make yourself attractive and get over there and see. Change either the red shorts or the pink blouse. You can't wear red with pink."

"Who makes all these rules?"

"At least make an effort to look attractive and talk to a nice boy," her mother said. She sang, "'First comes love...' Just be home by midnight." She snuffed out her cigarette against the sole of her kitten-heel slipper.

"And exactly how would getting home by midnight help me meet a boy? He'd think I was ridiculous." Again, she'd have to tolerate the constraints and obey. It would be a good time to get married and leave home, but she couldn't afford it and her mother needed her. "The summer solstice. I'd forgotten. I'll go across and check it out, but I'm not looking for a boy. I'm not ready for that sort of thing. And, I'll go like this. I like red with pink." She didn't change her shorts or blouse, or fix her hair. "Besides, what would you do without me if I left home to marry?" She slid into her sandals and, without as much as a wallet or comb, strolled out the door and toward the beach.

Between the boardwalk and the water raged a fire that could have been set by Hephaestus himself. Flames stretched, threatening the dubious sky caught between light and dark, teasing at it, now towering above the boardwalk. The smell of burning wood overtook the saltiness of the air, and the crackling of the flames drowned out the lapping of the waves, a worthy opponent to the riotous music.

Annoyingly, her mother was right. They were college age. Those wearing togas made the crowd resemble ancients out in nature celebrating the longest day with drink and dance. That was a strong attraction for her, to be one with an ancient ritual, but she struggled with her inhibitions. Inching closer to the festivities, she procrastinated as she unstrapped one sandal and held onto it, aware that she didn't belong there. She hadn't been invited, after all. Although it was still daylight, the sand had cooled. Pressing her bare foot into the damp granules deep down grounded her at the fringe of the group. Finally, she tossed both shoes into the pile.

The latest songs from the player on the picnic table drew her in: Beach Boys, Rolling Stones, Diana Ross and the Supremes. She loved music and dancing — with her girlfriends. Here a hundred or so collegians of both sexes gathered, in shorts, bathing suits, and togas, mingling, drinking, dancing around the fire. Some, already coupled off, lay on blankets in each other's clutches. Her antennae were up.

"Hey, doll, I don't recognize you." The friendly male voice overtook her from behind, from under the boardwalk.

Who was this person who believed he knew everyone — and from behind? Caught. She turned. Eyes lowered reflexively, she gazed at his bare feet and stammered, "The fire lured me. I crashed. I'll leave." Before she turned to collect her shoes and go, she stole a glance at his face. Smiling blue eyes. The music vibrated in her body. A couple of dances. What harm could that do? She hesitated, mid-turn. Besides, Mother wanted her to meet someone.

"A sweet thing like you, leave?" he said. "No way. I'm inviting you. Join us." He caught her around her back with one arm.

Although she bristled at his touch, she admired the carefree style of his madras shorts and untucked polo, his Elvis-like hair loosely falling onto his forehead, but not the liberty he had taken in touching her. The type to break rules. The type the nuns had warned against. "Remove your hand. I don't even know you." She stepped back. Her cheeks warmed and she hoped he didn't notice. She'd have to get accustomed to socializing with boys, as her mother called them. She wasn't prepared. There was no textbook. How was she to navigate the space between interested and loose? The nuns' advice was not helpful. Don't cross your legs. Keep your knees together. Don't wear patent leather shoes. Save yourself till marriage.

"Fair point. Let's get to know each other. Wayne Woods." He extended his hand. "Come closer. Don't be coy. Peace offering." He dug into his pocket and drew out a purple foil packet, like Lifesavers, but square. He squeezed a purple candy into his palm. "Want one?"

"This is a mistake. I don't know any of you. I'll get my shoes and go."

"Don't be like that."

She could retreat to her safety zone, her room, her books. The music snaked itself up through her feet, carried by her blood, out her fingertips, leading her hand through the air between her and him, a brick wall, now breached. Palm open, she accepted the Violet sweet he squeezed into her palm. "Candy Krzyzanowski," she said and waited for a comment.

"You are a sweet thing."

There it was.

"Formalities out of the way," he said, "let me loosen you up. A lot of dancing, a little beer. You didn't crash to gawk." He clutched her waist to maneuver her closer to the heat and sparks of the fire, to become part of the writhing swarm.

Resistance was futile. Suddenly, she craved to belong, to forego the safety of her room, to be like everyone else, like him, friendly, attractive, confident — qualities she lacked. She moved his arm from her waist and took his hand instead. She'd practice interacting with this boy who showed interest in her. Virgin territory. "I'd love to dance."

As they neared the ring of dancers, they skirted the many blankets positioned on the sand. "That one's mine." He pointed to a red blanket with a team logo she didn't recognize. "We'll save that for later," he said.

Like nails on a blackboard. She was already on guard. Should she be concerned? All she had to do was walk away. Cross the street. Back to safety. She gritted her teeth, but restrained herself from over-reacting. She was here to dance. To celebrate the solstice. The bit of dancing she and her friends had done in their living rooms throughout high school, watching *American Bandstand*, as they rated the songs' dancing quality, would now pay off. She let him lead, not that he gave her a choice. She rarely had choices.

To a Lindy, Wayne pulled her close and swung her out. "I haven't seen you around campus."

"I start Staten Island Community in the fall." When he pulled her close, she asked, "You?"

"Staten Island University. So, the introduction wasn't a formality? You don't recognize me?" He let go of her and raked his hair with both hands.

Egotistical. Still, hands free, she shimmied in front of him, a brazen move she and her friends had practiced, but one she'd never used in public. Her parents didn't allow her to attend the dances with the boys' schools. But here she was, thrust into a college crowd.

"If you read the *Staten Island Advance*," he said, "I should look familiar. My picture is always in the sports section." He tapped his chest. "I'm the Wild Boars' star quarterback."

Brazen self-confidence. Quite her opposite. "I flip right past the sports section. Sorry."

"No problem, doll." As they danced to "I Can't Get No Satisfaction," "Under My Thumb," "You Keep Me Hangin' On," their clothes, glued by sweat, outlined every bulge of their bodies.

"'You Can't Hurry Love.' Very true, don't you think?" she asked Wayne. "I try to tell my mother—" He wasn't listening. Couples slammed into them like bumper cars rounding a curve. Everyone danced closer and closer as more joined the crowd.

Someone elbowed her, and a female voice whispered, "Stay away, if you know what's good for you. You're just a notch in his belt."

When she looked over her shoulder, she couldn't pinpoint the culprit. A friendly warning? A rival? She frowned. She wasn't about to compete for him. A tightening gripped her chest. This might be more than she bargained for. She wanted to celebrate the solstice and dance. That was it. But she convinced herself not to flee at every sign of conflict.

Dancing with his eyes closed, Wayne didn't seem to notice the brief interaction, but finally chimed in, "What? I don't think about the lyrics, but I dig Diana Ross. I'd definitely do her." He shouted over the blasting music.

She clenched her teeth. Was that how he thought of making love? But the music was so good. She'd dance a few more dances, then leave and be done with him.

The next few songs echoed his attitude, or fed it: "Baby Love," "I Get Around," "Fun, Fun, Fun." They danced without missing a beat until the music paused for a cassette change. "Ready for a beer?" he asked.

"Great idea," she heard herself say, thirsty, even though she'd never had a beer, just a touch of Chianti in black cherry soda with Grandma. She didn't want to ask for soda. This guy was putting her through the paces. Headed to college in the fall, even if she was commuting, it was time to try new things, and after all, beer wasn't liquor. She pushed strands of matted curls from her face, settling them behind her ears.

Wayne wiped his brow with the hem of his shirt, exposing his tight, tanned abs.

A visual signal to attract a mate? Patrolling for receptive females? Had she, like the firefly, flashed her light with the code that said she was interested in mating? What had her mother pushed her into?

He walked her to his blanket. "Make yourself comfortable. Be right back with some brews." She watched him walk to the bartender at the cooler. As she tracked him making his way back to her, she envied his confidence and ease in the crowd. They patted his back, touched an arm, like they wanted a piece of him. He was the god here. What was he doing with her? Intrigued, she couldn't look away.

With one hand, Wayne carried the two bottles by their necks, waving them overhead, swaying and punching the air to the beat of the music, which had restarted. He danced back to her, jostling his way through writhing couples. When he reached the blanket, he proffered the beers in her direction. "Take a brew, nice and cold." He licked the condensation on the neck of one bottle.

Suggestive. Her shoulders shuddered. But she reached for the other bottle, took a sip and smacked her lips. "I needed that," she said, aiming for bravado. Maybe she did want to impress him, certainly not signal him. Just hide her naïveté. She pressed the cold glass to her chest, then rolled it along the skin exposed above the neckline of her blouse. The bottle bumped over the chain of her necklace. Her mother's words blared in her head, "It's time."

Wayne plopped down to the blanket and sat hip-to-hip with her. She didn't flinch. Perhaps the exercise had relaxed her. She stared at the Coney Island Parachute Jump, visible across the bay, and felt that very dropping feeling in the pit of her stomach.

"We should go sometime," he said.

"I've been, with my best friend. The Jump was frightening, but I enjoyed the carousel."

"That's a little tame for me." He nudged his thigh into hers. "What about that Cyclone? We'd have to hang onto each other for dear life."

"I'm not that adventurous." She stretched her legs out, away from his, partially into the sand. It was hard to talk, so they drank, and sang, out of tune, laughing at themselves. Her heart pounded as she considered a plan to have fun, keep him interested, and keep him in check. She was doing well.

Fun was something her life was missing. She didn't want her mother to be right, but her ambivalence toward Wayne was waning. A one-night thing, though now he hinted at more. A boy like him definitely wouldn't want a girl who handled insects. If he got to know her, she wouldn't be able hide it. Then he'd flick her off the way her mother did the firefly.

When they had drained the bottles, he stood, holding the empties. "After I toss these, we can dance a little more. I'll ask Joe for some slow songs." He walked to the trash.

On her side, resting on her elbow, she observed him, the crescent moon smiling in the background, over the necklace of lights on the Verrazano Bridge. She had to force herself to leave, boyfriend material or not. With this experience, however, she was more confident there'd be others.

"Time check?" she asked when he returned. Slow songs played now, and couples ground against each other, pretending to dance.

Before he sat down, Wayne glanced at his watch. "A quarter to midnight."

"Got to go," she said. "Happy solstice." When he extended his arm to pull her up from the blanket, she took his hand, relieved he hadn't made a move on her. They'd never be a good fit. But she was inclined to agree with her mother that it was time to consider a long-term partner, not necessarily Wayne. Even fireflies had the code.

"Home? What? How old are you?" he asked.

"Nineteen. Mother wants me home at midnight. Besides, I've got to get up early to make my way to Manhattan." When she stood, she brushed the sand off her calves. "I'm always running for that ferry."

"Don't get to Manhattan much, myself." They headed toward the pile of sandals. "So, you work in the city and go to school? The girls I know don't work."

"At the Museum of Natural History. I'm somewhere between a docent and an instructor. Nothing big. Small groups of kids from the public schools come through the museum, and I help make science interesting."

"You lost me. Too bad you have to leave so early. You're a good dancer." Having peeled his wet shirt from his skin, he flapped the shirt a few times. "I don't usually hang with the community college crowd, but, for you, I'll make an exception"

Did community college lock her into a lower tier? Surprised his interest continued, she swallowed the barb. They walked toward the boardwalk where he sorted through the pile of shoes and dug out the pair she pointed to. "Come here, Cinderella. Let me slip them on for you." He knelt holding the shoes, and she slid each foot in. Unnecessary though it was, she accepted it as a gallant gesture.

Having no point of reference, except in books, movies, and songs, she didn't know what to make of him. How would she send and receive signals? It couldn't be that hard. Glad to be walking home, she'd soon be safe in her room. But she'd have to begin somewhere if she ever wanted to have babies, and she did, after her education. Was he a means to her end? They'd just met. *Stop thinking.*

"Finally found my loafers," he said after being gone several minutes.

Into the dark beneath the boardwalk they sauntered. She moved away from him, signaling him, she hoped, not to try anything. Of course, she couldn't come out and say she was a good girl. There was the shimmying and the beer, evidence to the contrary, and she believed in evidence.

"You said you walked over." He waved his arms across the parking lot. "How far do you live?"

"Right across the street."

"I'll walk you all the way home, if your parents won't mind." They crossed the parking lot, crushing weeds that grew through the cracked asphalt.

"Only mom and me. I promise you, she won't mind." She touched his shoulder. "Warning, she'll be watching from the window." They waited for a single car to creep by before they crossed the boulevard to her driveway where she said, "Good night. I'll track you in the sports section."

As if they were still dancing, he reached for her hand and pulled her toward him. "Not so fast. I'd like to see you again. *The Endless Summer* opened last week. I'm a surfer, so I'd like to see it. Come with me. Definitely work it to get you home before midnight."

Caught off-guard, she wasn't sure how to react, which seemed ridiculous, but he did respect her ridiculous curfew. He waited for an answer. She'd go with the truth, omitting, however, that it would be her first date. "I'd like that, but I should tell you, I know as little about surfing as football."

"That's my doll. Who knows, if you play your cards right," he said, "I might take you surfing down the Jersey Shore one day. I'll teach you." He stroked her hair. "You don't seem like one of those screaming girls afraid to get their hair wet, or their mascara smeared," he said.

Future date suggestions. A budding relationship? The prospect made her a bit jittery. Or, maybe that was the beer. He hadn't released her hand. She squeezed it and let him pull her in until their bodies hit. She didn't fall apart. Knees together. Legs not crossed. "Still want my number?" she asked, giving each of them a last out.

Either way, however, she'd lose. She wasn't looking forward to an "I told you so" moment with her mother if he called, or to her own disappointment if he didn't. She gave him her number. Would he go back to the party? Signal another girl? She didn't need this disquietude in her simple life.

He had turned to go back across the street, then backtracked. "One last thing," he said. "The color of your house. Is it pumpkin, or is the color a trick of the moonlight?"

"It is different from every house on the block."

"Reminds me of a nursery rhyme Pop recited over and over: 'Peter, Peter, pumpkin-eater, da, da, da, there he kept her very well.' You must know it. 'That's what you do with women,' Pop said. 'Keep 'em in their shell.'"

A sinking feeling in her chest made her blow her cheeks out and release the air. Is that what his father taught him? "You can't possibly subscribe to such a theory," she said.

"Me, of course not." He shrugged his shoulders. "That was Pop."

She saw her mother watching as they said goodnight. One evening wasn't sufficient to decide whether or not he was a 'nice boy.' One date, if he called. Insects didn't have to overthink anything, yet they reproduced very, very successfully. And they pollinated the food supply.

She'd have to gather and analyze evidence on him. In her room that night she decided to conduct a personal version of the scientific method to determine whether he was long-term material. If he calls, if he treats me with respect, if he treats others with respect — she set her hypothesis and started with the evening's events. She'd have to publish. From her desk, she pulled out a sheet of Clairefontaine Triomphe and her calligraphy pen and wrote:

June 21, 1966

Dear Children,

I may have met your father tonight. My mother, your grandmother, sent me out to meet a nice boy. I'm great with insects, but don't know a thing about relating to boys, so I can't say if this one's the one. Yes, you're all laughing at me. He's probably not. A false start. But I promise, one day, there will be one. This is a first step.

Let's study this specimen for now. He made me laugh. We had a great time dancing. He wasn't beneath pulling my shoddy shoes out of a pile of shoddy shoes. He walked me home. He has lots of friends. He says he's a good athlete. Maybe a braggart. He touched my back before we even knew each other, but he let me set him straight. He didn't try to get fresh. But his father's interpretation of a nursery rhyme jarred me. But I can't blame him for his father's thoughts.

Do you all agree — respect? You have a better vantage point. These are my findings for tonight. Don't get too excited.

Love,

Your mom-in-waiting

June 24, 1966

Dear Children,

My first actual date. The movie was an adventure, boys chasing surf around the world. He enjoyed it too much, I'm afraid. Maybe he's not the type to settle down. Don't be too disappointed, there will be others. You must know that. Maybe your great-grandmother knows.

Love

CHAPTER 3

"What a Tangled Web We Weave…"

"Yes, yes, I'm coming," Candy yelled to her mother's insistent calls of "He's here. He's here. Hurry." Buttoning her beach cover-up, she walked out of her bedroom. "He can wait. I don't want to appear too anxious, do I?" She had picked up a couple of magazines that looked promising — *Seventeen*, *Cosmo*, and *Ladies' Home Journal* — for the advice not forthcoming from her mother, and already found that tip.

In the living room, she hunted for her sunglasses in the basket near the picture window where her mother sat watching Wayne in the car idling in the driveway. "Can I call him your boyfriend now that it's been a couple of weeks?" her mother asked. The first question she had asked about Wayne, having shut down any of Candy's questions about dating protocol with, "These are not topics for discussion."

Although Mother always wanted to know where they were going, sharing didn't come easy to them. "Not yet, Mother." She shrugged her shoulders. "I don't know how serious he is. He'll be graduating this year, and he wants to play pro football. It may not be in the stars."

"Invite him to dinner one night so I can get to know him, just in case." She handed her daughter her beach tote. "And remember, 'they don't buy the cow if they get the milk for free.'"

Mom and the nuns. That's all they cared about. She tugged the tote away from her. "Mother, that's disgusting."

"Where's he taking you this early in the morning?"

"Surfing down the Jersey Shore. I might give it a try." She ran out to Wayne in his candy-apple-red MG convertible.

"Hop in, doll." He patted the passenger's seat, but didn't get out to open the door.

She opened it and sat, knees together, lady-like, and pivoted in. Even if her mother hadn't been watching, she had been indoctrinated. Twelve years of nuns. She leaned over to skim his hand, pulled a kerchief from her tote, tied it under her chin, á la Audrey Hepburn, and added her large black sunglasses for effect, as well as protection. She rejected channeling Annette Funicello from *Beach Blanket Bingo* in favor of the more sophisticated look. Wayne's comment about community college kids the night they met had stung. "Don't we need a surfboard?"

"We have to go to Nana's to get it. She wants to meet you." He brushed her cheek. "Looking good, doll."

That was hopeful. He must be serious if his grandmother wanted to meet her already. She tilted her head and touched his shoulder. "Mother asked me to invite you to dinner some night." At nineteen, she was a virgin. Could she reject this boy? Would he ultimately reject her? Was he the one? She could call Brenda, who lived and worked in Manhattan, for advice. She'd play it by ear for now. There was hope.

They pulled into the driveway of a rambling Queen Anne Victorian with a sweeping front lawn bordered by a white picket fence. With its complex mix of robin's-egg-blue clapboards, intricate moldings and spindles, and gables to rival Hawthorne's. "It's a fairy-tale house," she said. Meeting his grandmother so soon. The quick pace of the relationship was the fairy tale, a true romance, perhaps. Cautious, however, she left space in her throat for disappointment to leap out.

"You'll fit right in."

"Into the fairy tale, or into the pumpkin shell?"

He ignored her question, or perhaps he had filed away and forgotten his father's vile rhyme, which would be a good thing. With a triceps dip, he hoisted himself over the door and out of the car and walked around to open her door. He held her close as they walked across the lawn hand-in-hand, up the stairs, and to the front entrance where Nana waved down to them. Upswept white hair framed Nana's Mrs. Santa glasses and smile. A kaleidoscope of colors in her housedress clothed her frail frame. With the exception of the glasses, Nana was very much her own grandmother, down to the housedress.

"My grandson's told me so much about you, dear." She reached for her cheek. "Aren't you cute as a button? Call me Nana. She saw where Wayne got his charming grin, and she was curious to know what Wayne had told Nana about her. This would be an opportunity for her to get background on Wayne. But Nana might not give away any secrets.

"It's a perfect morning to sit on the porch and get acquainted," Nana said.

"Wayne hadn't told me he lived with his grandmother till today." He pulled out a chair for his grandmother, and they sat on either side of her. "I guess there's a lot he hasn't told me."

"Since I was twelve," he said.

"It's a little cool out here. This house catches the morning breeze off the bay." Nana inhaled. She patted Wayne's hand. "Be a dear and get an afghan for my shoulders, my crochet bag, and a pitcher of lemonade and glasses."

"Sure thing, Nana." He hurried inside.

She'd use the visit to get to know Nana, but also to gather her date-data, mull it over, adding up pros and cons at the end of the day, then publish her conclusions in her "laboratory notebook," her letters, back in her bedroom that night, as she had begun to do after each date. She'd have a treasure trove of information by evening. This could be a turning point. She beamed. It was important to know if he was right.

Nana touched her arm. "You look like you swallowed a canary. Warm enough in that thin frock?"

"Quite." Time to enjoy the moment.

On his way into the house, Wayne called from the screen door, "You'll love Nana's lemonade."

Looking over the yard and bed of lissome purple and white cosmos swaying on the slope below, she said, "This is a beautiful spot, and Victorians have such personality. My house is a bland bungalow."

"My husband and I fell in love with this place the moment we saw it. Our daughter, Millie, Wayne's mother, was born in our bedroom, back in the day." Nana pointed to the stained-glass window above them.

With stories of her own birth in mind, she said, "That doesn't happen much anymore." Few people began and ended their lives in the same home, she remarked.

"Millie left home when she married her high-school sweetheart, Rob, the day after graduation. They were so young, seventeen and eighteen. At your age, you can't see it, but it is so very young."

"My mother would disagree." Wriggling in her seat, she said, "I just graduated and have no plans to marry anytime soon. College is important."

"That's a smart young woman. Take advantage of the changing times." She winked. "I keep up with the news."

On his way back, Wayne let the screen door slam shut. An afghan over his shoulder, that grin on his face, he walked toward them. The crochet bag hung from his wrist, and a tray holding a pitcher of lemonade, a dish of cookies, and two glasses balanced on his other arm. At the table, he placed the tray down, wrapped the afghan around Nana's shoulders with a hug, and set her bag beside her chair.

"Thank you, dear boy. Watching you two walk up before, I noticed how overgrown the lawn is." As she sorted through her crochet bag, she asked him if he'd mind mowing the lawn, giving her and Candy time for girl-talk.

"As long as you don't spill any embarrassing secrets."

Nana turned to Candy. "I can't make any promises." She laughed.

Wayne hung back, reluctant to leave, it seemed. Secrets? Candy poured lemonade for Nana, then for herself, and tasted. "You'll have some when you come back," Candy said to Wayne. He squinted at Nana and left. "Perfect lemonade," Candy said.

"What was that boy afraid of?" Nana shook her head. "The lemonade. I squeeze a dozen fresh lemons and sprinkle in a cup of superfine sugar. That's the secret." She winked. "Then I add ice, fill with water, and stir."

"Just the right balance of sweet and tart. I'll make it for mom as a welcome change from the tea we always drink."

"What about your father?"

"He died two years ago. Heart attack." She and Nana put their glasses down. "It's been very hard on Mom."

"Then loss is something you and Wayne share." Nana lifted her eyeglasses and pressed a napkin to the corner of each eye. "It still hurts."

More data. Something in common. Over the past weeks, they were too busy having fun to broach heavy matters.

The lawnmower choked a couple of times, then killed the quiet, even though Wayne started mowing at the bottom of the hill, away from the house. Candy raised her voice. "I'd like to learn more about Wayne."

Nana straightened the purple and salmon afghan on her shoulders. "There's something you should know, since you share grief. We'll get to it." She picked up her crochet bag. "I've crocheted afghans for Wayne since he was a baby. He still has some in his room."

She admired people, like her mother and grandmother, who could craft things out of fabric. Her father too, a carpenter, made furniture and built their house.

"I find creating useful objects fulfilling, and I have to keep my hands busy." Nana picked out a needle and yarn from her bag. "Fights arthritis, I think, and calms me. The repetition. Gardening too. Do you crochet?"

"Not good with my hands. Mom sews. And Grandma was a seamstress. Though they tried to teach me, I didn't take to it. I'll watch you." Wistfully, she considered she should have learned more from Grandma, rather than just focusing on the stories and the secrets of their tradition. She'd make an effort to learn from Wayne's grandmother.

Nana rummaged through her bag. "I happen to have an extra crochet hook or two and lots of yarn. All you need are your fingers." She raised Candy's hand. "Long, nimble fingers. Forget your past failures. You'll pick it up quickly."

Nana's can-do attitude was refreshing. No wonder Wayne was so self-confident. "Please pass that needle over."

"It's a crochet hook. Crochet is something girls should know, even today with all the new notions floating around." She lifted Candy's chin and stared into her eyes. A relieved expression washed over her features. "I'll teach you while I tell you what happened to my daughter and Wayne."

Nana dumped the contents of her bag and a rainbow of colorful skeins rolled out on the table. She handed her the purple. "I used my wool winder to make this pull skein. I can make one in another color, if you'd prefer. It's a lot easier than working from the store-bought skein — no tangles, knots, or lost ends." Nana handed her a hook and then demonstrated the crochet technique, emphasizing the tension of the yarn, creating the loop, and pulling the yarn through, repeated with rhythm over and again. "We'll make a motif, a square, together, the start of a granny-square afghan."

Dangling the limp yarn about a foot above the table, Candy asked, "How can I possibly make this into anything like the beautiful shawl you're wearing?" Less meticulous than her insect study, the work required attention to detail nonetheless.

As the sounds of Wayne's mower got louder, she squinted, straining to hear Nana.

"Like I said, the tension and the repetition, but you need exactly that slack to begin." Nana raised her voice. "The loops create a chain, the chain, a circle, the circle a small square which will begin a larger square." She demonstrated. "Start with the one small loop, keep working the hook, catching the yarn."

Mimicking Nana's deft movements, she created the loop, then six loops to form a chain which she edged into a circle with a slip stitch.

"All the chains are connected to each other and the first circle." Nana checked Candy's work. "The completed shawl begins with the first loop."

She picked up the loops and formed a small square. When she finished, Nana showed her how to tie off the final square.

"Now tie and cut the yarn here." She stopped to show Candy the spot. You created a perfect square."

"From a circle."

"Just repeat. Once you've sewn all the squares together, you'll have your masterpiece."

Candy studied her square and patted it out on the table. "I'd like to try another." She liked working to an internal rhythm. Even with the distraction of the mower, the crocheting exerted a calming effect.

"You're a quick study." Nana cradled Candy's face in her hands. "I so miss my daughter. You remind me of her. While Wayne is busy with the lawn, we may have time for one or two more squares, enough time for me to give you a better understanding of Wayne." They continued with the in and out motion of their cro-hooks.

The mower got closer.

Nodding along, Candy leaned in, thrilled that Nana accepted her and was about to reveal a family secret, confident she wouldn't reveal secrets to just anyone Wayne brought over for the first time. Had Wayne shared his intentions with Nana? She wasn't ready to settle down and have those babies just yet, as she told Nana — but it is what she wanted, tradition, marriage, even a dozen babies. She could please her mother, marry soon, but have children later. There was the small detail of having Wayne ask. And it was disconcertingly soon. She wasn't that naïve. Maybe Nana wanted to scare her away.

"Picture the scene as I tell it," Nana said. "I've heard the account from my daughter and from Wayne, never from Rob."

"You're sure you want to share this?" Wayne's mower got louder.

"Of course. I'm a lonely old woman who rarely gets company. Besides, Wayne likes you a lot. He's told me so, and that's a first. He tells me he dislikes the spoiled girls who fawn over him. He's had to work so hard for everything."

So, he really did like her, and it was more than just fun. He was being honest when he remarked on her being different. She thought it odd that Wayne and Nana had open discussions on his social life, while she had no such talks with her mother.

"Anyway, this story is history." Nana continued working the crochet hook. "Wayne's father drank too much, and it's still hard for me to admit, but he beat my daughter when he drank. She hid it from me, until this one night when Wayne got involved. He raced over here on his bike, with a broken arm, poor thing."

She was apprehensive about getting serious background information, but nonetheless Candy felt compelled to lean in as close as she could as Wayne's mower got louder.

Nana continued, "He sobbed inconsolably while he related his story:

"From his upstairs bedroom he had woken up to shouting, then glass crashing.

"'Know your place, woman,' his father had said."

The pumpkin shell. That was his father's philosophy in a nutshell. It was real, and it wasn't a harbinger of good outcomes, Candy feared. Now might be a good time to end this budding relationship with Wayne. Since the night they met, she vacillated. It would have been so much easier to stay in her room. But then she'd never fit into society, be like everyone else, with children — a family. She gripped the coin on her necklace. Her destiny was set.

Nana continued, "Wayne confided that he had soaked his sheets. He said he sprang from the bed and rolled down the stairs to defend his mother.

According to Wayne, his father reacted with few words, his fists punching his mother. Wayne said he tumbled with his father."

Candy couldn't understand this level of violence, but she admired Wayne's courage to defend his mother in the face of it. Perhaps he hadn't inherited his father's tendencies. To date, she had seen no signs of anger or violence, only grins and laughter, but she'd be wary.

"'A knight to the rescue, huh? What do I smell, boy? Did someone pee his pants?'" Nana imitated a gruff voice, like a pirate's. Nana's fingers worked faster as she continued the account. "Wayne related that with a single strike his father delivered a bone-crushing blow to his arm."

Candy dropped her crocheting. This was too much. Had eight-year-old Wayne suffered a broken arm in defense of his mother? She wanted to run outside and comfort him. The pain he must be hiding.

"And Wayne went on quoting his father: 'He thinks he's a tough guy, coming down here in his wet undies. If he wants to be a man, he'd better be tough. Learn to fight and keep score. No sissy sobbing in this house.' That's what Wayne told me."

The lawnmower neared the top of the hill.

"Things were never the same. It seemed I couldn't help them, dear." Nana continued crocheting, but Candy stopped.

Tears slid down her cheeks. She neither knew what to make of the event, or why Nana related it. To gain her sympathy? To scare her away? What is inherited? What is learned? Does it matter how behavior becomes the fabric of a person? The crocheting didn't alleviate her anxiety, as it seemed to for Nana, who must have become inured to the pain of the story after all these years. Deep in thought, Candy heard her continue.

"I had the parish priest talk to them," Nana said, "but once Rob started drinking, nothing could put the brakes on, and nothing could stop him from drinking. Millie wouldn't leave him. 'For better or for worse,' she'd say. I begged her to move back with us. At least Wayne said his father never touched him again after that night. Everything out in the open like that."

The mower got closer. The noise stopped. Candy had put her crocheting down, but clutched the needle, retreating inward to hide the secrets she wasn't sure she should hold. She considered how Wayne must feel living with that memory every day. She rubbed Nana's back.

Uncertain about what to say, she stammered, "I'm sorry for your pain and Wayne's. I would never have guessed. He's so uninhibited, confident, popular." She envied those qualities, but not his experiences.

"There's more," Nana said, "for another time." She cut the yarn from the square then picked up the plate of cookies, offering one to Candy.

They partook of the cookies, a sharing. But, she thought, Wayne had been living here since he was twelve, not eight. She wasn't able to absorb more.

"As you can imagine," Nana said, "he has nightmares. I think it's why he throws himself into football." She waved the cookie. "He wants the pain. He wants the glory. 'Keep score,' his father had said. There you have it." She took a big bite of the cookie.

"It's awful, for both of you." Candy got up from her chair and hugged Nana, holding on to her for minutes. She could feel her sobbing. She pulled herself away and sat beside her again.

"You're right for Wayne," Nana said, "warm and thoughtful. He's hardened. You can soften him. He told me you make him happy. He deserves happiness, don't you agree?" Nana squeezed her arm.

So, the story wasn't meant to scare her away. Wayne needed her. But did she need him? Should she be scared? It was time to think about what she wanted. "It's a lot for me to digest. He hides his pain well." Without taking a bite of her cookie, she crumbled it in her hand and brushed it into the plate. "How could you reveal all this?"

"Perhaps I've shared too much." Nana reached out to her. "Don't let me scare you away, dear."

"I think I understand him now." Could she choose to shower Wayne with love, keep him from alcohol, give him children to be a good dad to? A path forward. With this information, she could fight for him.

Wayne yelled from below, "I'm coming up."

"Show me your handiwork," Nana said to Candy. She stretched out the crocheted squares. "You've done a beautiful job with these motifs. Maybe, one day, you'll make an afghan for my great-grandchild." She brushed her hand over Candy's hair. "You are so much like Millie."

Although she didn't want to be a mother-figure to Wayne, the idea of being a nurturer appealed to her.

"Done with the lawn, Nana," Wayne yelled midway up the stairs.

Both women looked over to the porch steps, which Wayne took two at a time, racing up to them at the table.

"I'll have some lemonade, wash up, and then we have to go." After his refreshments, he loaded the tray and carried it back toward the kitchen. He kissed Nana's head and said, "Hope you didn't hurt my chances with her."

"I'm glad your girl and I got to talk. Don't let her be a stranger."

"She's a keeper, just like I told you." He held the door open with his foot, then it slammed behind him.

Words from his own mouth. Candy appreciated this more fully-rounded Wayne. Evidence of his attraction to her and his respect for his Nana bubbled over the surface. There was no need to deep-dive for it. Despite receiving the unsettling knowledge, she relaxed her shoulders. She swept her crocheting into her tote. Feeling like family, although she had revealed little of herself this morning, she embraced Nana and thanked her.

When Wayne came out from the kitchen, he snapped up the surfboard leaning against the doorframe, and tucked it under his arm. "Don't make dinner for me, Nana. We'll grab hot dogs or burgers with the gang at the beach."

She was impressed with how sweet he was with Nana. As he usually waited in the car when he picked her up, she had yet to find out how he'd interact with her mother.

She and Wayne skittered down the steps. "Nice mowing job," she said. At this moment, it was all she could bring herself to say.

He opened the car door for her, secured the surfboard to the MG and then jumped over the driver's door. She tied the kerchief back on, around her neck to secure it for the long ride. With the surfboard, there was little room for both of them, which forced her to lean on the door, with the window handle digging into her back.

Candy considered sharing the story of her dad with Wayne, though he had never commented on her father's absence from her home. Best to avoid old wounds. When would be a good time to bring up their shared grief? How? When he came to dinner?

Nana's revelation hanging in the air, she remained at a loss for words. She fumbled with the tote at her feet. Her posture stiffened. It was best to adopt a positive tone. "Would you like to see what Nana taught me?" She pulled out the squares.

"Just like Nana's," he said.

Without further evidence, she hoped he was "the one," especially since he was her first boyfriend, as it should be, and they hadn't done more than kiss. He was a complete gentleman.

Wayne flashed another one of his Cheshire grins, then dialed the radio volume far right, blasting the AM stations, and he didn't stop tuning until he heard "Surfin' Safari." With the beat at deep bass throbbing in the car, they took off toward the Staten Island Expressway for the New Jersey Turnpike.

Although she found it disconcerting to go back to the carefree singing and laughing at the bonfire, Wayne didn't, belting out the lyrics. His hand rubbed along her thigh, to the polka-dot bikini under her cover-up. She flinched.

"I'm going to teach my honey to surf."

For him, nothing had changed. Of course, he didn't know what Nana had disclosed, and she was uneasy about deceiving him. For her, the sudden break in mood was jarring. Despite her deep sadness for Wayne and Nana, she decided to sugarcoat this moment with the distraction of singing. Thinking about all she had learned, she stuffed the motifs back into her tote and sang along, ready to be tossed into the surf of the Atlantic for the day.

July 9, 1966

Dear Children,

This day started out so well with an invitation to his Nana's house. Wayne gained points for mowing the lawn while Nana taught me to crochet as she narrated a story from his past. Wayne and I share a deep grief, but his is far more complicated.

However, I'm wary of his father's influence, alcohol, anger. How deep could the influence be? For me, a sunny morning turned cloudy. I believe I can help him, but not at the risk of hurting any of you as he was hurt.

Love

CHAPTER 4

Flag on the Play

Rubbing her scalp vigorously, Candy shampooed her hair to rid it of the clinging odor of cigarettes, just as she had done on other nights they spent the evening dancing at house parties or the packed local college hangout. Her fingers lathered up an antidote of perfumed foam as she stood in the shower, mulling how quickly July had dissipated into sand, surf, and smoke. His drinking. The tips of her finger scrubbed into the bone of her skull. Although her entreaties for Wayne to drink less were fruitless, she continued to coax and cajole. But for Nana's revelations, she might not have noticed the drinking at all. She chose to abstain from alcohol. Tonic water with a twist looked like a drink, enabling her to fit in.

Other than Wayne's use of alcohol, she enjoyed a perfect summer with her first boyfriend. He taught her to surf on rented longboards, and she was soon paddling out with the guys, leaving the beach bunnies on the sand. Although she suffered rubber arms, sinus drain, and wipeouts, the waves didn't intimidate her. The challenge was exhilarating. Wayne was a pro, pigdogging and shooting the curls.

Endless fun, including trips to Coney Island, with terrifying rides on the Cyclone, and one tame session on the carousel, didn't interfere with her insect work (which she hadn't yet disclosed to Wayne) or his football practices. They continued to visit Nana (though Wayne hadn't yet accepted her mother's invitation) and she completed an entire granny-square afghan. Wayne was always a complete gentleman, although they did engage in what her magazines called "petting." Those first steps from her bedroom to the bonfire had whipped her through an exciting month.

Wrapped in a towel, she sat at her desk as her hair dried under the heat of the desk lamp. Calligraphy pen in hand, she visualized her future as Mrs. Candace Woods, writing the name all over the page. Of course, he hadn't mentioned marriage yet. Nana had hinted at a great-grandchild, though. The flimsiest hints fueled her fantasies to make this relationship work, to marry, to add another link to the thousand-year chain of January baby girls. For now, she was the last. Setting aside that sheet of paper with her name paired with his, she pulled another and wrote:

July 30, 1966

Dear Children,

It's more fun than I ever dreamed I could have, but is it love? The tests in the magazines and the horoscopes say it is. Nana hints at it. You certainly know.

Regarding my hypothesis, he's been very respectful. I often initiate the kissing out of the sheer joy of being near him. But the drinking. Will he end up with anger issues like his father? I would never want to bring his father's violence into our home. Not for anything. You all deserve more.

Love

CHAPTER 5

The Mating Call

August triggered earlier sunsets. The darkening sky outside Candy's bedroom window reverberated with the mating call of the male cicadas. Her peace, as she completed staging the *Megatibicen auletes*, the northern dusk-singing cicada, was broken by the familiar sound of her mother calling her, and she headed for the living room. She plucked the straw tote from her mother's hand and slung it over her shoulder on her way to Wayne who had come to the door for the first time. "Good night, Mother. Don't wait up," she said.

Wayne held the door for her. "I didn't hear anything about midnight, Mrs. K."

"The bugs must have drowned me out."

"Mother, you got that one right."

"Don't forget our dinner invitation," her mother said to Wayne.

"Sure thing, Mrs. K."

The screen door slammed shut and they walked down the porch steps to the driveway.

"Pick a night to come for dinner." He reached for her hand and clutched it. "Mom wants to get to know you now that I've been visiting your grandmother." They each went to a side of the car and slid in. "And I've pointed out your picture in the paper. She trusts you." Although she knew her mother was watching, she leaned over and wrapped her arms around Wayne's neck as she gave him a long kiss.

"You trust me, don't you?" Without waiting for an answer, he said, "Let's do something different tonight." He moved her arms from around his neck, then brushed his hand across her breast and down to the gear shift. "How would you like to go submarine-race-watching?"

"I'm pretty sure there aren't any submarines around Staten Island. Besides, how would you watch submarine races?" She rolled her eyes. "Mother would like you to believe I'm not smart, but really." She pulled the car door closed.

He turned the radio on. "Something else I'll have to teach you."

They drove along Seaside Boulevard, parallel to the unlit boardwalk, and away from the lights of the Verrazano Bridge. The wind tousled her unrestrained hair. The rows of summer bungalows, interspersed with overgrown lots, lined the street opposite the beach until the fields overtook development at the boardwalk's end, a few miles down the road, where the dirt beach-side parking area abutted the sand. On this stretch, there was little artificial light; however, tonight, there was a full moon, a blue moon.

Wayne parked at the far end of the lot where there were no other cars. He opened her door, then whipped a blanket from the trunk. They slipped off their sandals and dropped them into the convertible. Barefoot, they stepped from the lot to the sand, naked feet in touch with the crushed vestiges of earth's rocks, seashells, and marine life. They walked down the sand to the shore, dropped the blanket, beach tote, and radio just above the wrack of the high-tide-line, and waded in knee-deep. The spray of the waves wet their shorts. Bumped rhythmically, they braced each other against the force of the incoming water. They waded back out. Laughing.

Holding hands, with no words to mar the purity of nature's discourse, they headed to their spot on the deserted beach. They kicked up sand, which stuck to their damp legs. With opposite corners of the blanket, they brushed off the sand. Wayne then lifted the blanket and snapped it clean. It sounded like a sail in the wind. She caught the other side, and together they floated it flat down. He put his transistor radio on one corner and dialed for a clear AM station.

"Don't turn it on. I prefer the quiet, don't you?" She did her best imitation of batting her lashes. More tips from the magazines.

"Okay, doll. Anything for you."

"And what is it you're going to teach me about submarine races?"

"You got me." One of his big grins filled his face.

He sat on the blanket first, then pulled her down to him. Such a graceful fall. They lay back gazing into the deep sky. The language of the surf pounded the silence, and the blue moon created a wavering path from the sky, across the waves, to them. She turned onto her side toward Wayne, who was staring at her. His fingertips traced her eyebrows, cheeks, and lips, then swept through her curls. She moved closer and rested her head in the crook of his arm, safe. She slipped an arm under his back and held him close as they kissed.

No music. No dancing. No surfing. It could have been any time, any beach, any couple, lying within reach of the sand and the ocean, both having witnessed the beginning of time. Primeval. Someone to love. A line from a song? He had been a complete gentleman. She had to stop now, before she slipped. She had to stay a good girl. "We should stop now. We don't want to ruin everything."

He ignored her as he wiped stray grains of sand from her calf, then massaged her leg upward with easy, slow strokes. She twitched when his fingers insinuated themselves beneath her shorts, and under her panties. She had to stop him, get up, walk back to the car. But his rhythmic touch lulled her into some soft, sacred place where she seemed to be floating, untethered, uninhibited. She'd do anything to honor her family obligation, why not this? She rationalized. Once they were intimate, he'd never leave her. *But the cow and all that.* She could go just so far, a little more delicious pleasure, and then stop him. "Wait."

He didn't. With his free hand, he held her face, then kissed her, lips parted, his tongue tasting hers. He rolled over on her, his body, hot, strong, muscles tight under his shirt. She opened her eyes and wondered how many couples this sky, those hidden stars, this moon had spied on having sex on beaches the world over. Her heartbeat and breathing accelerated. Time to stop. She couldn't…move…away. Lost control. Trapped.

He captured her hand beneath his, and guided it to his waistband. *Stop now.* He helped her unbutton and unzip his shorts to fondle him. She never thought to wonder how a penis would feel. No time to think. Succumbing to hormones. Chemicals. Animal lust. Inhibitions melted into sweat. Drowning. She helped him remove her shorts and panties. He had her remove his briefs. She participated. She felt wet, not from the surf. "But—"

"I love you," he said. "That's all that matters."

CHAPTER 6

Final Entry

August 31, 1966

Dear Children,

I hope you weren't witness to this night's events. I take out my notebook before slipping into bed and write with a burdened conscience. I'm glad Mother was asleep when I came home. Would she have seen the change in me?

I fear the experiment may be over. It wasn't his fault. I was weak. I lost control. I didn't act soon enough.

But he did say he loves me. If he wants to marry me now, now that I am ruined, it will end with a happily-ever-after.

I'm closing my laboratory notebook. I've acquired all the evidence I need, and as it turns out, I am the guilty party. This is my final entry, unless you know otherwise. I don't know what will happen. I don't know how I will face him in the light of day.

Love

CHAPTER 7

Something in the Air

She had every reason not to trust Wayne.

The bustling airport startled her senses, the drive from Staten Island to Queens not a sufficient buffer through early morning darkness. Adjusting from the twilight ride, the pupils of her eyes constricted to filter the vastness of the terminal, the lights, the rushing crowds, the blaring announcements. All of her senses alert, the scene was dizzying, like the carousel, calliope music blaring, the startle-eyed horses, reigned-in, bridled, bits holding their tongues, their pole-impaled bodies moving up and down in pointless circles. She and Wayne had gone around and round. He convinced her this was the only solution. Overwhelmed, she bit her tongue. She had allowed emotions to run roughshod over her intellect, again. She had agreed to his plan.

Tickets in hand and no baggage to check, she and Wayne evaded encumbered passengers at the counter and pressed on to the departure gate.

Keeping pace with his athletic stride, the stilettos she normally wore to her job at the museum, the museum of dead things, screeched on LaGuardia's hard, polished floors. It was her heart that screeched. Not ready to capitulate to Wayne, she was battling all the way. She was buying time.

He was focused. "We have to hurry," he said, squeezing her hand. "I didn't expect such heavy traffic on the BQE this early in the morning. Not to mention the time we wasted parking."

Amid the frenzied crowd, something bumped her leg. When she pivoted, her gaze traveled from the man's worn loafers and white socks to the veined, gnarled hand around a cane, to the gray whiskers darting in different directions, much like her grandfather's. Releasing Wayne's hand, she fell out of step with him as he continued on. She'd catch up.

"Sorry, bambina," the man said, wobbling. "My sugar must be low."

After taking his bag, she steadied him, her hand on the back of his threadbare coat. "Would you like a wheelchair?"

He nodded, wisps of his yellow-white hair fell across his forehead down to his eyes, which welled up. "Bless you," he said. *Yes, she needed blessings.* Crowds had swirled past this lone man, all intent on their journeys. Would she have noticed him had he not made physical contact with her?

She led him to a bench, rummaged for the juice he told her was in his bag, then forged through the mob to the ticket counter for help. When the agent spotted the distressed man, he rushed a wheelchair to him.

Assured he was safe, she squeezed his hand, left him, and raced past a variety of fluorescently-lit shops where she stopped at a newsstand long enough to snap up the latest issue of *Cosmo*, a blond actress on the cover, "Fifteen Ways to Manipulate Your Man." Yes. She stuffed it into her bag. Maybe there was still a way to have him see things her way.

Although her stomach grumbled, the aromas of grilling hot dogs, pizza, donuts, and coffee were too conflated to be tempting, and actually upset her. Well-practiced at running in her heels, she reached Wayne at the gate in time to hear the boarding announcement for Isla Verde. She could simply miss the flight. It was so clear.

When she reached him, he raised his chin, curled his lip. "Why do you have to put your nose in other people's business?" He pushed her hand away. "Focus on our game plan."

She didn't even want to think about his game plan. She hated it. Her back against the wall to keep her from shaking, she said, "I couldn't leave him there, befuddled, alone." She squeezed her hands and pulled at her fingers until she heard joints pop. "You couldn't go without me."

"No, but I should leave you here."

Moving away from the wall, the couple lagged to the rear of tourists jockeying for boarding positions. She surmised they were eager to reach their destination. They flaunted their resort attire, the tropical colors — red, green, yellow — shouting their way out from under the unbuttoned, predominantly black, New York winter coats.

She gazed beneath her unbuttoned coat at the embroidered roses in full bloom cascading over the fitted bodice of her crisp, white graduation dress. Floral, not tropical. Unlike the other travelers, her destination wasn't an exotic escape, but an escape from her dilemma. She had chosen her most flattering dress hoping to beguile Wayne, as women's magazine articles advised, to soften him after weeks of relentless arguing.

Although he promised marriage, she knew his football prospects were uppermost in his decision-making. Marriage and family were her goals, or her mother's, not his. With the arguing, the deal-making, she couldn't get him to regard her as he had that August night on the beach, almost two short months ago, when he said he loved her: his pupils dilated, laugh lines radiating from the corners of his eyes, the dimple, the parted lips, the invitation to his heart. That was the Wayne she probed for. She never dreamed she'd have to fight for him like this, desperate. *Where had she gone wrong?*

Moved to stroke his arm, she instead jabbed her hands into her coat pockets, her fingers widening the hole of the satin lining in one, shredding the used tissue in the other, as she avoided touching the boarding pass. Despite misgivings, she dug for the courage to confront him, and breathed in deeply, sending innocuous words out on the exhale, "Won't you reconsider?"

"This is Coach's best plan," he said. He brushed her cheek with the back of his fingers. "Once I go pro, I'm all yours. We have to be rational adults," he said. "Trust me."

There, the long-hidden dimple appeared with his grin. But the look in his eyes was off. His voice, a shriek of a scowl remaining. Tempered with apprehension, her hollow joy faded, like hot tea mixed with too-cold milk. "I wouldn't be here if I didn't," she said. Bland words.

A layer apart from the outer commotion, opinions sparred in her mind's ear — a chorus of the old guard, tradition, nuns and Mother, countering the verse of new ideas, like those of Helen Gurley Brown and Betty Friedan — the chorus and the verse offering conflicting visions for her future. It was time for her to leave home, set up a household. "Begin a family," the never-wavering old guard sang. Her mother wouldn't allow her to leave home until she was married, not even for college, as many of her classmates had done.

The new voices of Brown and Friedan challenged women, her, to be independent, neither men nor children essential. A jolt to everything ingrained in her. Was she destroying the very thing she was trying to salvage? Here she balanced, on the rail of a speeding ferry, in danger of tumbling into the roiling tide of change.

She had only a few hours left to convince Wayne that marriage, sooner than later, would work. It wasn't feminist Brown's goal, marriage, but Candy needed strategies like Brown's to accomplish her objective. Manipulation could be a means to her end of budging the intransigent Wayne Woods. She'd read the article in Cosmo and find a way to convince him that marriage now was their best choice. Her last hope.

A tug on her arm. He snapped his fingers in front of her face. "Your ticket," he said. "Take it out of your pocket. Give it to the agent." Then he motioned her to walk ahead of him.

Where was his respect now? All of her options, if she had any, were bad. The evidence against him was mounting. He was like his father. Or was he just as nervous as she was?

Pulled by the momentum of the jet bridge's pitch, she proceeded. The walkway curved left; her feet followed. She eyed the entrance to the jet. Naïveté and optimism, hand-in-hand, led the way.

Her first flight, she paused and lifted the handles of her carry-on over her shoulder. She rubbed her throat, sucked the saliva around in her mouth, and swallowed. She wished she had one of those Violet candies now, recalling its calming lavender scent and taste. A candy with a girl's name, a pretty name. Wayne's hand on her elbow ushered her over the breach between jetway and threshold, into the galley of the Eastern DC-9.

"Welcome." A stewardess in a mini-skirted suit greeted her into the stagnant acridity of trapped cigarette smoke and Lysol spray.

Wayne followed Candy up the aisle. She considered he might block her if she attempted to leave the plane, leave the plan. Could she do that? And what then? After this, they'd be together — he'd promised what she wanted, marriage.

"This is it," she said when she reached their row over the wing. She removed her coat and dropped it on the seat, baring her shoulders. After taking the magazine out, she lifted her black-and-white striped weekender to the open bin, steadying it on the edge. Wayne stepped behind her. He reached up and pressed against her back to slide her bag over the lip. She blushed, and slipped out from under him as he tossed his duffle in. She wouldn't let him trap her, not again. Yet, here she was.

She chose the window seat, unsure whether she wanted to see what she was leaving behind or heading toward. After raising the center armrest, she slid across the bench to the window. Once in the air, she assumed she'd see only clouds, but she didn't want to feel trapped. She wanted to see beyond the interior of the fuselage. Already, she envisioned the tube as a metal corset about to tighten around her ribs. She was sick, physically sick.

Wayne sat, and snapped the armrest down between them. She had to make him amenable to the change of heart she would declare once she worked up the courage. Her opinion on the matter had for weeks incited his fight response and she hoped to avoid conflict.

The engines revved, compounding the uproar in her head. And cries from a screaming baby cut through the ambient noise. Her shoulders itched against the seatback as the jet pulled away from the gate, and she was pinned back by gravitational forces beyond her control. Every rut in the runway, and every jerk, as the they turned and taxied for several minutes, jolted her.

When they began their ascent, she watched the ground peel away like flayed skin. Flying south along the Eastern coastline, she inhaled the aerial view of the Verrazano. The plane flew parallel to the span, tracing Staten Island's coast. Her eyes focused to pinpoint the location of the house she had left behind, near the bridge, not far from the beach where she and Wayne had sex, where he declared his love for her. Having ascended above the clouds, she closed her eyes. The air was cold. She maneuvered her coat onto her shoulders taking comfort in its warmth. The Easter coat reminded her of spring and Grandma's stories, and her obligation. That was the other piece. Was she meant to sacrifice her happiness, to prevent this disaster, and dive into what appeared to be a disastrous marriage?

She returned to her struggle and flipped through her magazine to the article, "Boost His Ego." Discuss things he loves. Show your admiration of his fine qualities.

"Good morning, ladies and gentlemen. This is your captain. On our flight from LaGuardia to Isla Verde, we expect turbulence. Keep your seatbelts fastened."

Wayne hunched over and made a guarded sign of the cross.

Boost his ego. She smoothed her hand over his back, her fingers sweeping the short nap of his varsity jacket back and forth. "With all the flying you do for games, I'm surprised you get nervous."

"I'm not the one calling the plays up here." Wayne took his arm back as though passing a football. "I visualize the fuselage as a pigskin hurtling through the air, me tightly curled up inside, until touchdown, when I pop out through the lacing."

"You always have a game plan." She reached over and brushed his cheek.

He flinched.

"Have you given any thought to Nana, how alone she'll be rumbling around in that old Victorian when you leave to join the pros? Wouldn't she love great-grandchildren to visit?"

"Pro or not, she knew I wouldn't be living there forever."

Fingering the coin dangling from her necklace, she sighed as she recalled making pasta with her grandmother. As they fashioned a well in the pile of flour and broke eggs into it, Grandma would tell her how the married women in the family "got busy" in April, hoping to get pregnant, each hoping to be the first to deliver a girl, the Janus baby, to inherit the coin. To hear Grandma tell it, there were so many women back then. Now she was the only one.

As she and Grandma kneaded the flour, the mixture fattening her fingers if she had failed to flour them, Grandma recounted the secrets, as well as the exploits, of women who, for over a thousand years, had become notable for their accomplishments, like Grandma's fearless emigration to America, alone on a ship, as a child. Candy never tired of hearing the tales told while the dough chilled and as they cut it with sharp knives into ribbons to slide into the boiling water to later enjoy with a rich, meat gravy.

Whatever her legacy, her actions had brought Wayne into it. Her light touch on the coin tightened. What would her story be?

"Anything to drink, sir?" the stewardess asked.

The voice pierced and deflated Candy's musings. She opened her eyes to the present to hear Wayne order.

"Johnnie Walker Black, neat," he said, "two."

"And for you, miss?"

Wayne answered for her. "She'll have—" He shifted his gaze from the stewardess. "Coffee or tea?"

"Apple juice," she said, her mouth still dry.

The stewardess smoothed napkins over the cup indentations of their tray tables. "Be right back with your beverages."

When she returned, she reached across Wayne to place the juice on Candy's napkin. The stewardess's black hair fell into Wayne's face. Her forearm brushed the "8" on his varsity jacket. "A quarterback, I see."

She placed his order on the tray. "Yep. And I'm going pro." He twisted the cap off a mini-bottle, poured, and gulped.

"Should I get your autograph now?" She winked and moved on to attend to the next row.

"Boost His Ego." Whatever was at stake, she couldn't deny that he wasn't marriage material.

Wayne took a pencil and a notebook of what must be football plays — letters, circles, lines and scribbles — from his jacket. He scratched notations as he studied the pages. The blare of the plane, combined with the air blowing from the overhead nozzle, made conversation difficult. Or he was totally ignoring her.

She read. So far, the magazine advice was unsuccessful. There was more. Be seductive. Greet him at the door, naked, wrapped in plastic wrap. Not suitable for her current situation, but did women have to do that? What had she gotten herself into?

Why did she have to work so hard for his attention? When they met, she didn't care if he asked her for a date. Then, it was he who worked for *her* attention. She curled her knees in her arms under the full skirt of her dress, covered herself with her coat, and faced the window, the armrest biting into her back. Marriage wasn't an option. Her choice was clear. She'd go through with this, then have a blank slate.

Wayne turned toward the aisle. He waved his empty glass at the stewardess several rows behind. "I'll have another."

More alcohol. Would it make any sense to say anything? She tapped his arm. "I'd like to use the restroom." She flipped her tray table up and handed her half-filled glass to Wayne. "I can't finish this," she said. It was over for them.

He stood in the aisle to let her by.

Toward the rear of the plane, where the roar of the engine was deafening, sat a mother with a baby in her lap, probably the one who had been screaming earlier. The baby waved her arms, chubby fingers losing hold of the pink rattle's heart-shaped handle. It rolled under the seat. Although nauseated, Candy knelt on the floor to retrieve it; grit on the carpet dented her knees. The rattle was monogrammed, Cynthia. She handed it to the mother. "Pretty name."

"Thanks, sweetie," the mother said.

She patted the baby's hand and moved on.

In the lavatory, she felt the pressure; her stomach contracted. She vomited, then splashed cold water on her face and patted dry with a brown paper towel, which irritated her skin. The juice had been too sweet. She had no idea what to expect. She'd have to face the inevitable. Helen Gurley Brown couldn't possibly know what she was writing about. There would be consequences. She was relieved to escape the barbs of Wayne's attitude and remain shielded within these four walls until landing. There she hid, weeping, when an announcement blared, "There's turbulence ahead. Return to your seats. Keep your seatbelts fastened."

Despite several attempts, she couldn't open the latch. She panicked, then paused, studied the structure of the latch, regained her composure, and slid it open.

Mentally fatigued, she wasn't ready to confront Wayne, but she lumbered back to their row where he merely moved his knees aside to allow her access to her seat.

When the stewardess came by for the glasses, Wayne asked her if she could do anything about the screaming baby in the back of the plane.

"You won't notice it once everyone's screaming," she said, and left to buckle herself into the jump seat.

"The baby is so cute," Candy said. "I saw her on my walk to the restroom."

"I don't want to hear, see, or talk about babies," he said.

"I never thought to ask how you felt about children." She wrapped herself in her coat.

The plane pitched, dropped, and shook. She couldn't feel worse. Everyone screamed. Baggage fell from bins. A woman hit her head on the ceiling. A cart rolled down the aisle, spilling items in its wake.

Wayne leaned over and made another sign of the cross. He ignored her.

After interminable moments of tumult, the plane stabilized. "This is the captain. Sorry about the turbulence, folks. We flew through some cumulonimbus clouds. You were troopers. We should have smooth sailing to our destination. Press the overhead call button if anyone is injured or if you need prompt assistance."

Not long after, the plane began its descent. Patches of color gained definition as trees and water. A thump jolted her.

"The landing gear," Wayne said. The plane thudded down and taxied to a stop. When it was safe to unbuckle, he stood, retrieved the bags, and carried both. "Ready?" he asked. He motioned her to exit ahead of him.

She wrestled her bag from him. "I can take care of myself." *Could she?*

CHAPTER 8

Denial is a River

Ominous clouds gathered in the humidity of the late morning. Pulling her behind him, Wayne dashed toward the sinuous line of Chevy sedans, white taxis, awaiting arrivals at the curb. A driver in a short-sleeve guayabera, linen pants, and Panama hat burst from his cab patting his cheeks with a handkerchief. Eager to greet the couple, his arms open wide, he approached them.

Oblivious to their body language, he began, "Bienvenidos, señor y señorita. Taxi?" He tucked the handkerchief into a pocket, freeing both hands to shake Wayne's. "Welcome. No baggage? Only one pequeño (squeezing his thumb and finger together) bag por la señorita? Milagro."

"This is everything," said Wayne. "Gracias."

The cabbie settled the duffle under his arm, looped the bag over his wrist, and with a flourish, opened the passenger door for her. He gestured Wayne to follow her into the cab, then tossed the bags into the trunk.

All windows were rolled down, yet a hint of Bay Rum lingered, covering the odor of the remnants of rice and beans left in a container on the dashboard, not far from the half-smoked cigar resting in the ashtray, channeling smoke curls her way.

The pressure in her head was near its limit, like a dam about to give way. She rubbed her temples and caught the driver's eyes in the rear-view mirror.

"Okay señorita? Muy bonita." He handed her a clean handkerchief.

She took it and patted her face. "A bumpy plane ride," she said. "Thank you. Gracias." She squeezed the handkerchief in her palm.

Away from the traffic, the car stopped. The driver faced them, resting his arm over the seatback. Ignoring her, he faced Wayne. "Señor, permit me to introduce myself. I am Miguel, owner of this taxi. I will be your host this afternoon." He removed a business card from his pocket. "Please take my card, por favor, and call me, day or night, anytime you want a ride to the sights, the bars or the chinchorros, to the best nightclubs, the hotels, shopping, anything. I am Miguel, at your service."

"Thanks. We won't be here long." Wayne put the card in his pocket and removed a folded sheet from the playbook in his jacket. He handed it to Miguel. "We're going to this address. Do you know the way?"

"Por supuesto, señor, but no big hotel, no sights? Are you sure this is the right address?"

"Let me see the paper again," Wayne said.

Miguel handed it back to Wayne. "Coach's handwriting is chicken scratch," he said and read it aloud.

"Querido Dios." Miguel made the sign of the cross. "I'll show you sights on the way. Okay?" he asked.

As they proceeded to their destination, her lips quivered and she couldn't control her fluttering eyelid. Wayne wrapped his arm around her shoulder. Another glimpse of the old Wayne. "It'll be fine. Trust me. How long, Miguel?"

"Maybe twenty minutes, señor."

She sensed Wayne seemed worried. Her eyes widened, taking in the details of this foreign place. If danger lurked, she'd be helpless.

On these large streets, which Miguel identified as Ponce and Infanteria, homes appeared as dots in the green of the hillsides. Horns blared. Hints of distant music harmonized with the sweet fragrance of the trees.

When they reached the smaller streets, alleyways, wide enough for only one car, the environment invaded the cab. Vendors rang bells hawking their wares. Strains of Spanglish circled in one window and out another. Music blew in from the parks. Miguel identified the aromas of the fried plantains, carne asada, comida criolla, and mofongo, the pungency sickening her further, the litany of names increasing the tightness in her gut. On the sidewalks, the stuccoed buildings' cramped walls were green, yellow, pink, and purple pastels, like a sideways roll of Neccos.

The heat, the sounds, the smells ultimately overwhelmed her. Beads of sweat formed at her forehead, temples and cheeks, swelling like water balloons, gathering momentum, rolling down her face, the salt stinging her eyes. Her coat having fallen from her shoulders to the seat, droplets of sweat slid down her bare shoulders, between her breasts, around her necklace, and down to her belly under the flared skirt of her dress, which she ached to tear off. She closed her eyes and covered her nose with the handkerchief for a moment's peace. "We have to stop the car."

Miguel checked the mirror. "I know a place you can rest under a ceiling fan at a little café, si?"

"Just stop the car," she cried.

"Good idea. The señorita needs a break, brief," Wayne said. "We can't stay long. We have an appointment to keep."

A display of empathy. "A fan and water, please," she said.

Miguel parked and helped her from the car. Wayne sat her at a table near an open floor-to-ceiling window, where a breeze flowed through the café.

Miguel followed them in. "I'll order. She needs a cold piraguas," he said. "Trust me. And you, señor? A Barrilito, made only in this country."

"You're a winner, Miguel," said Wayne. He slapped a twenty into Miguel's palm and sat with Candy.

"We're so close, minutes away. Don't ruin everything now," Wayne said. He dipped a clean edge of the used handkerchief into the glass of water a waiter had just placed on the table, and dabbed her cheeks. "I don't see as you have a choice."

Miguel walked back to the table and handed Candy a bright pink piraguas.

"I can't go through with this," she said to Wayne.

"What? Eat a snow cone?"

That grin. He was making light of her distress. She reached for the confection Miguel offered. At first lick, the ice cooled her tongue, her lips, her mouth, her throat. *What was she in for?*

"You look better already, señorita," Miguel said. "I'll stay nearby," he said to Wayne, then walked a few tables away to watch men playing dominoes.

She and Wayne sat at the table beneath the spinning blades of an overhead fan. "I've changed my mind," she said.

"It's too late for that," Wayne said. "A lot of the team have come here over the years. There's nothing to worry about."

She formed her lips around her snow cone. If she went through with this, she wouldn't marry him anyway. Not with the lack of respect he had shown. The ice had cleared her mind. She'd deal with her mother, most likely leave home. The words she wanted to say froze, the snow cone rendering her tongue numb.

"What's worrying you?" Wayne asked.

"Everything." Even one word was hard for her frozen tongue to form. She drank some water. "I don't care about your promises." She forced the words. "I won't marry you. I'll suffer the consequences." *Why wasn't this clear while they were safe at home?*

"It was never up to you," Wayne said. "Let's just get it over with."

With the paper cone on her lips, point in the air, she caught the last dregs of ice. She crushed the paper, wrapped it in a napkin and left it on the table. She had been drained, crushed.

Almost finished with his drink, Wayne signaled Miguel, who walked over. "Ready, señor? I'll bring the car around."

"We're ready." Wayne smacked his lips. "Time to do what we came to do."

Miguel pulled up at the curb and got out to open the door and help her back in. They navigated the narrow alleys.

"These drivers really lean on their horns," Wayne said. "How much longer?" He wiped his brow with the hem of his shirt.

"Cinco minutos, señor," he said. "Don't worry. I'll get you to your address."

From the front seat, Miguel picked up a brochure and handed it to Candy. "This is a historic place, a fort, Castillo de San Cristobol."

She scanned the humidity-drenched pages of the brochure promoting La Garita del Diablo, the Devil's Checkpoint. Within minutes, the cab stopped and blocked the narrow street. "Ah, we are here, señor." Miguel got out and pulled the door open, releasing them into the heavy air about to gush with rain.

"How much, Miguel?" asked Wayne.

"Fifty dollars, señor. This is good, si?"

"Yes." Wayne folded three twenties and handed them to Miguel.

"Muchas gracias, señor. Call me."

Wayne carried both bags with one arm and, with the other, took her hand.

She stared at him, blankly, acknowledging defeat, for now.

CHAPTER 9

Blood, Shit, and Tears

Lightning. Exploding raindrops faded the pastels of the buildings to gray. The upbeat music devolved in the relentless beat of the downpour as she tasted the metallic smell engulfing her. She and Wayne, sweating bodies now drenched, awaited access to Ladies First. After countless minutes, in response to their several strikes of the old-fashioned knocker beneath the iron-caged window of the crimson door, tumblers clicked.

A stooped woman, dark hair pulled into a loose bun, inched the door open. "Si, señor?"

"We're here for José." Wayne spoke through the sliver of space between the door and its frame.

"We're expecting you." After admitting them, she latched the door, then led them into a dim waiting room. "Dry yourselves with these." From her armful of ragged towels, she gave Wayne two. "I'll be right back."

Candy's pupils dilated to take in the details of the shuttered room. Dust motes floated in slow motion within the strips of light created by the louvers. The rays exposed the scuffed floor and wooden chairs, with missing rungs and torn rush seats, set around the perimeter. On tarnished brass stands ashtrays were filled with cigarette butts smoked to varying lengths. This wasn't a doctor's office. She moved close to Wayne, and though repulsed, wrapped an arm around his waist. "Let's leave," she said, "please. How could you bring me to a place like this?"

Her legs were about to give way. Her words carried no weight. Her stare was the painted stare of any Barbie doll, or the crazed stare of the glass-eyed carousel horses. The windows were shuttered. And the door was locked. The stench was the smell of danger.

"We've come too far. So it's not the Ritz. This isn't a vacation," he said. He moved her hand and gave her a towel. "Dry off." They sat and waited, saying nothing. The scene purged her of any delusions she may have tried to cling to. This was her only path away from Wayne to a fresh start, damaged goods as she might be. The moment would be her secret to keep.

Another door creaked open and a man, with the silhouette of a running back, addressed Wayne. "The cash, señor?" He stepped within arm's reach.

Wayne stood, routed around in his duffle, then snapped an envelope into the waiting hand. "It's all there."

In his black T-shirt and black pants, the figure blended into the background. He licked his thumb and counted off each bill. "Call me José," he said. "Another Jane on the DC-9 express. Follow me. Both of you." He unlocked a door at the far end of the room. "Go through here and wait for my assistant."

The woman who had handed them the towels reappeared. "I'm Marta. Señorita, por favor, remove your clothes, everything, and put this gown on, open in back." She cast her eyes down, and left. The lock clicked.

With the door closed, this room, with only one tightly shuttered window, was even darker than the last. The strong odor of bleach and ammonia forced her to put the damp towel to her mouth. How much bleach was needed to eradicate one mistake?

Wayne raised his hand to cover his nose and mouth. "Whoa. That is strong."

One bare incandescent bulb hung in the center of the room directly over the stainless-steel stirrups. Her eyes swept the surroundings. One sturdy but scraped wooden chair sat in a corner. Over the peeling paint on the walls hung pictures, randomly placed: Our Lady of Guadalupe, eyes down; Madonna and Child, Mary holding the unclad baby on her lap; and a ghostly St. Catherine of Siena, crowned with thorns, the stigmata visible on the backs of her hands. They watched her, these familiar icons of her Catholic school classrooms, their presence disconcerting. Nailed to the wall by a long black spike, above the examining table she'd be lying on, hung a foot-tall wooden crucifix.

Opposite the wooden chair squatted a porcelain toilet minus a toilet seat. She resolved to avoid using it. Crushing the frayed gown Marta had given her to her chest, she walked toward the iron-stained basin with a dripping faucet and no soap. She delayed changing. After splashing water on her face, she said, "I want to leave." But she had no say, no voice. Wayne had already told her.

He stomped his foot. "Stop asking, already. We discussed this again and again. I call the plays. You just started SICC. Besides, I wouldn't have time for you and a kid." He swaggered from her. "Football is my one commitment. I've always been up front about that."

She pursued him. "The night we had sex," she said, "you said you loved me. I thought we'd always be together. And Nana told me I made you happy." Evidence that he cared, that she could trust him. "How could you put me in this danger?" No one knew she was here. Her knees buckled, and she leaned against the table for support. She saw herself fall from the ferry railing into the whitecaps below. He wasn't about to throw her a lifeline.

An arm's length away, he pushed her into the table. "You should've been on the pill."

"I had no intention of having sex so soon." Her words sputtered. "And I read that doctors only gave the pill to married women."

"Smart girls know how to get them." A now-familiar look of disgust overtook his expression. "Or you should've made me use a rubber. Girls do that too. Water under the bridge." He marched to the opposite side of the room, his back to her.

It was her fault. She wouldn't compound the mess by taking on the costume of victim. She'd own her mistake. Get out of here. Never see him again, whatever the cost.

He bellowed across the quiet of the empty room. "I'm here with you, paying the price, setting things straight. I didn't have to come."

"Leave now," she said. "Leave me Miguel's card, money, and my plane ticket." *It couldn't get any worse.* Back in the center of the room, captured by the dangling light bulb, she stood, more isolated and alone than ever, without energy to fight.

She buried her face in the tattered hospital gown and retreated to her corner. Without further procrastination, she peeled off her sullied dress and underwear, moved to the chair and threw the clothes there. She inserted her hands through the gown's armholes. When she tied the string on the neckline, her fingers brushed her Janus necklace. She held it and cringed at the thought of the price she was about to pay. She tore the necklace off, breaking the chain, and zipped it into a pocket of her bag.

The bulb holding him in the spotlight, Wayne took her place in the center of the room.

The latch clicked. Again, the door opened a sliver. José's disembodied head appeared. "Ready?" He turned toward Marta. "Go in."

She found Marta's presence comforting. Perhaps she had an ally who would at least keep her safe.

"I have some pills first," Marta said. She pulled a bottle from her apron pocket. "Take these to calm you." With a maracas-like sound the contents shook in the bottle as Marta spilled two white pills into her palm. "I'll be back. Cigarette, señor?" she asked Wayne.

"A few," he said as he paced the room.

Within minutes, Marta returned and approached Wayne first. "Cigarettes and matches, señor, and, señorita, for you, painkillers." After Marta measured off and cut a sheet of brown butcher paper from a heavy roll stored beneath the table, she spread the piece over the stainless table. "It's time for you to rest here, señorita."

Candy burned to lie down. Marta held her arm and helped her climb up. Then, like a guard, Marta positioned herself in front of the door.

Wayne slid Candy's soiled clothes off the chair to the floor, then sat and lit a cigarette.

José entered, took his place beside the patient, then placed his foul cigar in the ashtray on the instrument stand near Candy's head. The smoke circled up to the light bulb. Looking down the length of her body to her feet, she followed José as he moved toward the stirrups. His calloused hand tugged on her ankle as he thrust one foot into the cold metal loop. He repeated the action with her other foot. Pressing hard, too hard, against her inner thigh, he inserted something into her vagina. She felt his putrid breath as he neared her head and spoke into her ear.

"You had your fun. I'm here to do your dirty laundry. Remember that. You did this." He turned to Marta. "Everything here?"

"Por supuesto, señor, everything you said."

Wayne had made the procedure sound clinical, routine, no details. Trusting him, she had failed to ask. Afterwards, he promised, they'd be together, happily ever after. She'd have a husband and, soon enough, kids. One, she hoped, would be her Janus daughter. She'd be indistinguishable from all the other housewives. And Mother would be happy. What she was about to undergo was the price she paid for her gullibility. Her only choice now was to irrevocably reject him.

When she turned her head, she saw, spread out on a white cloth, the several stainless-steel instruments Marta had laid out. Pain shot through her as José reviewed each tool, with the tinny sound the instruments made as he allowed their handles to jostle one another while reciting their names, pausing after each: "uterine curette...manual vacuum aspirator...syringe... forceps...embryotomy scissors...cranioclast...Smellie's double crochet... vaginal speculum...uterine dilator."

The metal-on-metal ting sliced the silence, along with her muffled sobs. Sadist. As muscle control drained from her body, like the last spurts of air from a deflated balloon, she mobilized intention from her every cell to raise her arm and sweep the instruments to the floor. The clatter confirmed her momentary success. Marta gasped.

José said, "I don't have time to sterilize these again. I'll pick them up and continue. You are a foolish girl."

"Enough!" Wayne jumped to his feet and faced the tableau, "Put out that cigar and be more respectful."

She waited for him to say, "Get up. We're going." And waited.

But it was José who spoke. "If I do, señor, it'll cost you, let's say an extra hundred." He snuffed out his cigar into one of the stainless-steel basins beside the instruments and raised his hand to Wayne. "Done," he said.

"You'll get your money," Wayne said.

What was that one show of gallantry? Pity? Conscience? She'd have neither. She could no longer turn her head. Her limbs became weak and her vision and hearing were distorted. Double images of ghostly figures in the room moved in slow motion. Echoing voices spoke with drawn-out vowels. The outcry in her mind was the worst it had been all day. The drugs amplified the pandemonium. With the weight of it all, her head fell to the side as the distorted voices continued. It was as if her eyes were painted shut. The doll. The horses. But she could hear.

"What happened to her?" Wayne asked.

"The drugs, the nerves. She's okay," said José. "I have to do a D&C."

"Shouldn't you be wearing gloves?" Wayne asked.

"Do you want to do this?" asked José. "You can leave now, but you won't get your money back."

"Get on with it," Wayne said.

She heard Wayne walk away, vomit into the toilet, and flush.

"Marta, gloves," said José.

A cold instrument entered her vagina, and warm blood oozed down her thigh onto the crinkling paper. Semi-conscious, she was too weak to protest, a prisoner of her own body.

"The procedure will set bodily functions in motion soon after I finish here," José said. "I've done thousands. Trust me." He continued poking instruments around inside her. Time stopped.

She had no idea how long it had been, but she began to regain control of her body, and she sprang up with a sharp scream, clutching her belly. Wayne sat beside the table, asleep. She reached over the edge and shook him. *How could he sleep?* She needed him to get her out of this place. "Help me to the toilet. Quick."

She couldn't avoid sitting on the bare porcelain rim. Again, she didn't have the luxury of choice, not even a private moment. Clots plopped into the water as severe cramps chomped at her insides. Diarrhea streamed, mixing with blood. The smell vanquished her. The loss of blood and tissue didn't make her feel lighter, but added a weight she imagined she'd never lose. Just as she prayed for the power to wish Wayne away, he draped a towel over her shoulders, and she was grateful for that scrap of concealment, that scrap of compassion. He soaked another towel in the stained basin and dabbed her forehead, cheeks and neck. She leaned back against the cold, sweating tank of the toilet, which she would have felt through ten towels, sweat again dripping down her jaw line. She pointed across the room. "I need that bucket," she said, lifting her hand to stifle the nausea.

Wayne bolted across the room, removed the blood-stained mop, setting it against the wall, and carried the empty bucket to hold it in front of her as she heaved into it. She tried to stand up long enough to flush. Wayne steadied her. The room smelled far worse than it had when they entered. *Yes, it's only right he should experience this to know firsthand the pain women can be subjected to.*

She was unaware of Jose's presence until he said, "Ah, good. She's on the toilet. It'll be over soon. After this, she can rest on the table," he said. "I'll let you leave when she's up to it. Knock when she's ready. I have others to attend to." He left and locked them in again.

"There's nothing left inside me," she said to Wayne. "I have to lie down." She wiped her mouth with the towel.

Having pulled more towels from the shelf, Wayne walked her to the table, ripped off the butcher paper. Throwing it to the floor, he replaced it with the towels, and helped her up. She yearned to push him away, but needed him now. She was both shivering and sweating. He covered her with more towels and rolled another under her head. He stroked her forehead. "It's over," he said. "We'll be okay." Wayne sat back in the chair, smoked a few cigarettes, and closed his eyes.

The coquis sang outside the window. She invited sleep.

Someone shook her. She opened her eyes to Marta showing Wayne to a shower in a cubicle not far from the sink. She couldn't wait to feel running water on her skin. Wrapped in a towel after his shower, Wayne walked over, then helped her to the shower.

"It's cold, but you'll feel better," he said. "There's no soap."

She stepped in and braced herself with her hands against the walls. She was in pain and bleeding steadily. He didn't leave. *Guilt?* He held her and washed her with bare hands and the trickle of cold water as she focused on the stained grout. Wayne helped her out of the curtainless shower, cloaked her in a towel, and patted her dry. She was again powerless. How could she have been so naïve?

Leaning against him, she stumbled her way to the chair. She sat while he pulled clothes from her bag. He dressed her, like some doll, bending her limbs to his will, with fresh panties, bra, skirt, and top.

"Everything's pink. Don't you have anything dark to hide the blood?" He went back to the shelf for a sanitary napkin and handed it to her. She placed it in her panties. He removed her red patent heels from the bag, continuing to hunt in there. "I hope you have some sensible shoes."

"Only those." She remembered the night of the bonfire, when he called her Cinderella and slipped her sandals on. The summer solstice. They had barely made it past the autumnal equinox.

He knelt beside her and jiggled her swollen feet into the heels. "What were you thinking?" he asked.

She had wound herself into a desperate tangle of knots.

Marta appeared and motioned to Wayne. She handed him an envelope and said, "Give her these pain pills whenever she needs them. I shouldn't tell you, but José said something about maybe a tear in the uterus." From the shelf beside the toilet she took a few boxes of sanitary napkins and gave them to Wayne. "She'll need these for the trip." She refrained from making eye contact and never looked Candy's way.

"Will she be okay," Wayne asked, "for the plane?"

With head bowed, she lifted her eyes to meet Wayne's. "I think, yes. But take her to a doctor, a hospital, when you get home," Marta said. "I shouldn't speak." She put her hand over her mouth, lowered her eyes again, and left.

Wayne added towels from the shelf to Marta's collection.

"What's all that?" Candy asked, still seated in the chair.

He bent over her, cupped her face in both hands. "A few things from Marta. We have to leave your old things behind to make room, except for your coat."

"Marta said I'd be all right. I heard her."

Despite the heat and humidity, he hung the coat over her shoulders. "Good thing you have this to cover up," he said. "There's still time to make our flight. When you're up to it, I'll call Miguel to get us to the airport, and I'll order you a wheelchair so you won't have to walk."

"I don't need a wheelchair." She tottered when she stood up. Not quite ready to stand on her own, she sat back down.

Wayne knocked on the locked door and asked José for a phone to make a local call. José demanded the promised hundred first. Wayne got it from his bag, handed it over.

When Wayne returned, Candy asked for help to get back up on the table to rest until Miguel came for them, and she lay there until Marta came in to tell them their cab had arrived. Marta and Wayne supported her on each side as they led her through the labyrinth of dusky rooms to the exit.

Outside the crimson door, Miguel eased her into his cab. "Ladies first," he said.

CHAPTER 10

Masked Men

"Husband dropped her off and left. Blood's soaked her clothes. Been bleeding for some time."

"BP seventy over thirty, in shock."

"Get her to Room Four for a pelvic."

"Cut off her clothes, quick."

"My God, she's bleeding like a stuck pig."

"And cut that talk."

"Type and cross her. Transfuse a unit into her, stat."

"A rubella miscarriage?"

"Rubella pandemic was over last year."

"More likely an illegal abortion with perforation."

"We've got to get in there."

"Start a liter of Ringer's lactate."

"Get her to the OR, stat. Who's the ob-gyn on call?"

"Thompson."

Under anesthesia and bright lights Dr. Thompson performed a vaginal exam, then a laparotomy, found a perforated uterus, and attempted a repair.

"Let's sew her up. Such a young girl. What a pity."

CHAPTER 11

Eyelids of the Heart

In a patient bay of the maternity ward, the candy striper resettled her stiff white cap in front of the mirror above the sink, then tugged up her white stockings and reset her garters. The curtains hid Jessica from view as she squared away her uniform, tucked her blouse, and tied the sash of her striped pinafore into a perfect bow.

Having changed the bedding and tidied the area, she stood back to observe the patient. "This is bad," she muttered to herself. The tip of her tongue ran over her upper lip. Not much older than herself, resting nearly upright on the inclined pillows of the hospital bed, lying still, her eyelids drawn closed to the world, this patient began her third day asleep. Beneath the newly-tucked bedding, only the neckline of her printed gown showed above the folded sheet, her arms at her sides atop the covers. An intravenous line penetrated a vein in the back of her hand. The hospital band on her wrist read, "Jane Doe."

From the day Jane Doe had arrived in the maternity ward, unconscious, with no belongings, Jessica had become curious about how someone so young found herself in this predicament. She watched over Jane as though she were one of the precious collectible Madame Alexander dolls posed on a shelf in her bedroom — her favorite the vintage Red Cross Nurse. Unlike other dolls' painted eyes, Madame Alexander dolls were the first to have sleep eyes, which opened when the dolls were placed in a sitting position. With childlike faith, she wished that when she sat Jane up against the pillows, her sleep eyes would open too.

Only sixteen and only a candy striper, she stood behind Dr. Thompson when he walked in, surveyed his patient from the foot of the bed, and flipped through her chart. The patient was stable, though she had not regained consciousness since orderlies had rolled her into the ward from the recovery room.

"I've spent as much time as possible with your patient," said Jessica, who had kept watch like a mother hen. She raised her brow, shook her head. Her starched cap shifted, not quite secure with only the one bobby pin she had used. She sighed. "I wish she'd wake up. It hurts me that she's so utterly alone."

"I'm hopeful she'll wake up soon," the doctor said. Jessica observed as he checked the patient's pulse, blood pressure, temperature, fluid output, and notated the chart, until he clicked his ballpoint, clipped it back to his pocket, and reattached the chart to the bed.

"She's the only one on the floor who hasn't had visitors. Do you think anyone knows she's here?" She swept the hair off the patient's forehead. She was accustomed to interacting with happy new mothers and their babies. Jane was her first experience in the maternity ward with an unconscious woman, one who didn't have a baby in the nursery.

"An ER doc told me a young man carried her in," the doctor said, "and after they got her onto a gurney, he disappeared. He knows she's here, but he might not know her. Maybe he was just a good Samaritan." The doctor walked out past the curtains, leaving them open as Jessica followed him through the ward and patients greeted him along the way.

Before he walked out of the ward into the corridor, Jessica said, "I wish he'd come back. I bet he knows her. She might respond to a familiar voice." She stopped to face the doctor. "Do you think she can even hear me?"

"Hard to say, but studies of patients who've awakened from comas concluded some patients heard others talking to them, even though they couldn't respond," he said. "It can only help."

She wished she could do more than talk, straighten up, and deliver books and flowers. She ignored the happy patients in the ward, busy with the babies in the basinets beside them and with their visitors, and she revisited the patient she regarded as her personal charge again and again. From her position at the head of the bed, she spoke to Jane. "It's Jessica again. I hope you can hear me so you know I care about you." She twirled a few ringlets of Jane's hair.

"I bet we like the same things, like The Beatles and The Beach Boys. The Beatles can be a little cryptic, but fun sometimes. The Beach Boys are always fun, and I love their surfing songs. I love the beach. *The Endless Summer* was great. I'm rambling. I'll go to the book cart and find something to read to you."

She walked to the book cart near the entrance to the ward. After perusing the rows of cookbooks, baby-naming and astrology books, thrillers, mysteries, and biographies, she lifted a title she had heard patients raving about.

Next to Jane again, she pulled out the arm chair at the head of the bed. It screeched after she sat, and she wiggled it closer to the bed. She checked Jane to see if the noise had affected her. No change, though she would have been happy for one. Settled in, Jessica planned to read to Jane as she read to her dolls when she was young, the way her mother had once read to her.

"I'm surprised I was able to find this for you. Came out in January, *Valley of the Dolls*." She leaned forward to check Jane's eyes. "The women here have said it's positively scandalous, but they don't put it down until they have to leave. No one's finished it during her stay. Of course, you can't see, but so many pages are dog-eared. I hope you'll wake up before we finish.

"I've been told the 'dolls' are drugs, and it's about three young women starting careers in New York City, like we will, right?" Not long into the book, she noticed Jane's fingers at work twisting the sheet. Jessica put the book down and stood to study Jane's face. Jane's eyes moved under her closed lids. "Jane, Jane." She paused. That's not even your name." Jessica pressed the call button.

Nurse Wilson was quick to enter, rustling the bedside curtains as she did.

"Jane's fingers jerked and her eyes darted under her lids," Jessica said. She wished she could stop calling her Jane.

The nurse took the patient's pulse. "I'll get the doctor."

As Jessica, her hands clasped in a prayerful gesture, stood over Jane, Jane blinked, then kept her eyes open. She pulled the sheet up to her chin and her eyes moved side to side and upward, then stopped at Jessica.

"Don't be afraid. You're in a hospital. You're safe. I'm Jessica. I've been spending time with you. Your doctor will be right here." She stroked the patient's arm. Jane released the sheet and grabbed at the girl's wrist. Then the patient's grip weakened as her hand rested on the bed.

The doctor dashed in. He studied Jane's glazed, reddened eyes. "Jessica finally woke you up. I'm Dr. Thompson," he said. "We'll take things by degrees. You're in Staten Island Hospital." He raised his arms to take in the space, himself, and Jessica. "Don't speak until you're ready." He turned to Jessica. "Your talk therapy may have helped our patient after all."

"Would you like me to leave?" Jessica asked.

"Not yet," he said. He turned again to the patient. "Can you tell us your name?"

She shook her head. She raised the arm with the IV, appearing befuddled at its presence. Her lips moved, but no words escaped. She drew a breath in and sighed out. An audible swallow followed. Her tongue moved in her mouth, pressing against her cheeks, then jutted out to lick her lips.

"Relax. You don't have to talk. There's plenty of time for you to remember," Dr. Thompson said. Jessica fixed the pillows, and helped Jane sit up taller. "After you've had time to acclimate to your surroundings, your name will come to you."

CHAPTER 12

Kaleidoscope

The three curtains around Jane's bed defined the borders of her immediate world. She knew where she was. She didn't know where she belonged.

The doctor removed the stethoscope from around his neck and motioned toward her with the chest piece. "May I?" he asked. As he neared her, she recoiled at the approaching touch. He stopped. "Jessica," he whispered, "stay with her while I get Nurse Wilson. My presence is upsetting her."

Jane closed her eyes again and slid down the pillows until she lay flat on the bed. She turned away from Jessica. She refused to give credence to this reality. She must be dreaming. She'd have to wake up again. The tug between sleep and wakefulness was strong. The pain was unbearable. The light seared, even under closed lids.

The curtain rings scraped along the rod. She kept her eyes closed.

"I understand you've been through a lot," the doctor's voice said. "We're here to help you. Would you let Nurse Wilson check your vitals?"

She couldn't let them in.

"Please help us help you. Find you."

She had to be found. She knew she wasn't Jane. As she wriggled her way back to a seated position, she opened her eyes, cleared her throat. Her questions were slow in coming, breathy. How long had it been since she'd spoken? When had she lost her voice? She stared at the curtains. Balloons. "How did I get here?" Behind closed eyes, again, she scrolled through her memory. Darkness. A verdict. Okay. "I was okay. I don't understand what I'm doing in a hospital."

"Tell us what you can and we'll fill in the rest," the doctor said.

"Pain. Then nothing until these bright lights. So much pain." She tugged again at the IV. Not flinching at the nurse's touch, she allowed her to continue her examination.

Dr. Thompson kept his distance at the foot of the bed while notating the chart. "It's the anesthesia, the drugs, the initial trauma," he said. "When some of the haze wears off, when we talk further, you'll get a handle on your situation."

She fought against the friction of the sheets in an effort to keep herself upright. Nurse Wilson leaned her forward and arranged pillows for support.

"I've given you hydrocodone, but I can adjust it," the doctor said. "We do know that a young man carried you in and left. Can I call him, or someone else?" He nodded to the nurse that it was okay for her to leave. Jessica stayed.

A young man. Like bits of colored glass in a kaleidoscope, pieces were coming together to create a pattern, something she could work from, but each fragment sliced her.

"He didn't give anyone your name or his," Dr. Thompson said. "We took you into the OR. You had lost a lot of blood. We operated. You're recovering." He kept his hands in his pockets.

"Thank God. So, I am okay?" After a deep breath, she brought one hand down across the sheet to her abdomen and rubbed it. "To think I trusted him," she said. Yes, Wayne. Another shard. Her hands shook. Still at the side of her bed, Jessica reached for her hand.

"We'll fight the pain, but I must be forthright," the doctor said. "You'll be here at least a few more days."

"Days?" she asked. "You just said I was okay. I want to get out of here, now. Out of this nightmare. I don't believe you." She shut her eyes tight and they sank between her brows and her cheeks. She pulled her hand away from Jessica and clutched her abdomen.

"Can you give us your name yet? You came in with no belongings," the doctor said.

"No. I want to leave." *A wheelchair. A taxi.* Fragments. She tugged at the edge of her bedding and tried to pull it off. It was tightly tucked. "I want to go home." *Where is home?* Jessica ran her hand over Jane's damp hair.

"It's impossible for you to go anywhere now," the doctor said. "We have to remove the stitches. You have a catheter emptying your bladder, a drainage tube in your abdomen removing blood under the wound, and dressings. Later you're going to need support beyond any we can give. Someone close." He kept his distance, remaining at the foot of the bed.

"Marta, I remember," she said.

"Is Marta your name?" Jessica looked into her eyes, which were now wide open with fear. Painted open.

"No. Marta said I was okay. She told Wayne." She shook her head away from Jessica's touch. *Someone close. Not Mother. Brenda. Bits of colored glass.* "It will come to me. I must know who I am. I know *Lampyridae*." She touched her neck. "It's gone. I must have had a bag?"

"As I said, we didn't see anything, no ID," he said. "We've been calling you Jane Doe. Describe the bag to Jessica. If it's here, she'll find it."

Jane described the black-and-white striped bag, the towels, sanitary napkins, crocheting, *Cosmo*, and the necklace.

"I'm on it," Jessica said, then disappeared beyond the open curtain, along with the doctor.

Those lucky ones could come and go as they pleased. She was stuck. But her world had just enlarged. For the first time, the three mothers in their beds across the ward, holding their babies, entered her reality. Flowers, cards, and *It's a Boy*, *It's a Girl* balloons bounced, tethered to nightstands. Visitors flowed past the curtain opening. Happy sounds, cooing and congratulations swirled, like the aromas into the cab, into her head. The colorful balloon print of the curtains, for her, didn't signal joy, but intensified her loss — *the abortion.*

The thought struck her like a rogue wave from behind, dragging her under, making it impossible for her to get her bearings. She didn't know which direction to swim, to escape, to find air. She'd jump up and close the curtains if she could move. She chose to shut off her senses with a pillow.

Something gnawed at her feet, dragging her to the depths. Glints of silver. The stirrups. The water's surface was just out of reach, only an arm's length above her head. She could remember fragments, but not her own name. *Lampyridae.*

She battled against the suffocating water and glimpsed a shard of light. One day, she'd return to this ward, a mother with a baby, and cards, and flowers, and balloons. *Do I have to decide to remember?*

"What are you doing with that pillow?" Jessica had already returned. She took the pillow and gave Jane the bag. "I hope this helps. It has to be yours, but no wallet, no ID." She got a damp washcloth and wiped Jane's brow and sat her up.

Jane found the necklace and clasped it to her chest. She turned the end of the kaleidoscope. The bits of colored glass fell together. A pattern emerged. *Candy Krzyzanowski.* Then she said it out loud.

With a scissors from her pinafore pocket, Jessica cut off the wristband. "If you spell out your last name, I'll make a new wristband, but I'll get the doctor first."

Within minutes, Dr. Thompson stood at the foot of the bed. "Pleased to meet you Candy Krzyzanowski. Good work."

When the candy striper returned, she handed Dr. Thompson the wristband, and he asked Candy, "Would you allow me to put on your new wristband?" When she nodded, he approached and lifted her hand. "You have one more task. You have to call someone tonight to be with you tomorrow morning when I discuss your prognosis, someone I can speak openly with."

Nurse Wilson walked in. "I have some Mogadon. It'll help you sleep." She handed her the yellowish pills and some water.

She'd slept forever. Now that she remembered, not remembering had been the better option. She swallowed the pills.

The nurse handed her the phone. "The doctor wants you to make that call before you fall asleep."

She knew her friend, her one-time babysitter and neighbor, Brenda, would come, unconditionally. When she lifted the phone, Brenda's number lit up in her memory. After Nurse Wilson walked out, she placed the call. Despite Brenda's persistent questions, Candy gave only the name of the hospital and the time she should arrive. She couldn't explain further just now.

A welcome grogginess overtook her. She focused on the hospital sounds engulfing her. The loudspeaker paged doctors. Phones rang in the ward. Voices of staff, patients, visitors melded as visiting hours drew to an end. Medical equipment whirred. An alarm sounded. Televisions competed with each other. Machines growled in the corridor. A cacophony. Above it all, babies cried.

A cart squeaked past the open door of the ward. It emitted a strong odor of ammonia and bleach in its wake. Another fragment. *How many bits were yet to fall?* The fluorescent ceiling lights flickered.

CHAPTER 13

A Leathery Leaf

With the morning light, Dr. Thompson checked in. "Rest well?"

"The pills helped," Candy said.

Her chart in hand, he said, "I'm going to remove the catheter and the tube."

"I haven't been out of bed."

"After I remove the catheter," he said, "You'll have to. You might have bladder and bowel issues — urinary tract infection, constipation." As he spoke, he arranged equipment and supplies from the cart he had rolled into the room and the nurse joined them.

So unlike José. More tiny glass fragments coming into view to cut her. Whatever she remembered she'd not forget, but force down, just beneath the surface.

Numbing herself to the touch of doctor and nurse, she said, eyes closed, "My abdomen is itchy. Everything hurts." She rubbed the bandage on her belly. "What's this? Wasn't everything done vaginally?"

Nurse Wilson repositioned Candy's hands away from their field. "Not everything. Not here," the doctor said. "There's an abdominal incision, which is horizontal. I kept it low, but it will scar."

It will scar. What incision? She'd bear physical scars, not only mental and emotional, of her ordeal.

Dr. Thompson's tie, its abstract pink and blue print, much like the patterns of her imaginary kaleidoscope, hung out from his physician's coat, and dangled close to her abdomen. "Your tie is too close to my skin." She swatted it away.

"Apologies." He tucked it into his coat.

"Do you always wear pink and blue?"

"Gifts from my patients. Some women are superstitious, as if the color of my tie could influence the gender of their fetuses, so I remain neutral."

Blithe. A non-response to a non-choice. She never had a choice. "And me?" she asked. "What do I have to be superstitious about?"

He removed the tie and rolled it into his pocket. "Insensitive of me. Maybe it's time I retire ties altogether," he said. "There. All done for now."

"For now? When Brenda comes, I want her to take me home."

"That won't be possible today. Be patient."

She slapped at the bed. "I'm tired of being patient. Being a good, obedient girl. I want to get out of here." She screamed, "Pills could hide my pain, but you could never remove my pain. Let me out."

With measured words, almost whispered, he responded, "We'll leave this ward. You and I will walk to the consultation room at the end of the hall. You must walk. I'll show you how to maneuver the rolling IV."

It was as though he hadn't heard her, he hadn't felt her pain. How much more emphatic could she be? She couldn't exactly run away. Brenda was her one hope. She'd drive her away from here.

Unable to shut out the stark reality of her circumstances — the corridor bright with buzzing fixtures this dark fall morning — she looked down and concentrated on moving her feet forward in hospital-issue socks, the door at the end of the hall a goal she might not attain. *How could she move on with the life that stretched before her?* Dr. Thompson held her elbow when she wavered. When they finally reached the room, she was relieved to fall into one of the cushioned brown chairs. The table lamps softened the drab morning light entering the picture window.

"It's so cold and stark outside. Sharp, angled shadows," she said. They, too, cut her.

"Suddenly dropped to fifteen degrees," he said. "They're predicting a long, cold winter."

His matter-of-fact tone annoyed her. Ignoring him, she studied the oak tree in the courtyard. Except for one last, leathery brown leaf struggling to hang on, twisting in the fall wind, the tree was bare. The image perched just beyond her own reflection on the glass. She was struggling to hang on. Twisting. About to detach. "I'm weak," she said. "I'd like to lie down. Why did we come all the way here?"

"For a good first walk," he said. "You called your friend, Brenda? We'll come back here with her." They left the private room and headed back to the ward. "You're managing the IV well."

At her bed, he asked if she'd like Jessica for company, but she couldn't face chirpy Jessica. Instead, she said the walk had intensified her pain, which was true, and she asked for more pills. He left and sent the nurse in with them. She planned to save the pills, along with others she would get, and take them all at once, to release her from this waking nightmare.

She pretended to swallow the pills the nurse handed her, distracting her by asking for her striped bag. She tucked the pills into the pocket that held her broken necklace, pulled out her crocheting, and began work on a new motif, monochrome, purple. The crocheting calmed her. Or was it having a final plan? She worked a partial motif and fell asleep.

CHAPTER 14

The End of Her World as She Knew It

The metallic rasp of the rings grating against the metal rod woke her as the curtain around her world was pulled open sharply. "Candace, were you in an accident? Why are you in the maternity ward?"

Ten years older, Brenda was like a big sister. They had spent childhood summers on Staten Island, where their parents had bungalows together. And, until Candy's family moved to Staten Island permanently, they had been neighbors in Manhattan as well. Brenda took her to the movies, to Central Park — ice skating, horseback riding, the carousel — and by subway to the thrill rides of Coney Island.

Her notebook indistinguishable from a body part, Brenda recorded the day's events and answers to her ever-flowing questions about the types of insects Candy caught and studied, field guide in hand. Always the reporter, in the park she interviewed skaters and equestrians on their techniques and experiences. Early on, the comic strip heroine Brenda Starr was Brenda's idol; currently, it was Helen Thomas.

Unlike her, Brenda had developed a flair for fashion. Her fitted fifties-style wardrobe and her long, wavy red hair channeled Brenda Starr. Whenever Brenda arrived, she made an entrance. Neither arrogant nor self-conscious, she possessed a confidence Candy envied.

"I need your help." Feeling the agonized expression on her face, she lifted herself toward Brenda and held on to her as though she would be torn from the earth's gravitational pull if she didn't. "I desperately need you to get me out of here. The doctor thinks you're here to talk to him."

"That's exactly why I'm here," Brenda said. She pulled back, studied Candy's face, and wiped her tears. "I told reception they must be mistaken when they directed me to the maternity ward." Still cradling her, Brenda asked, "What's going on? Does your mother know you're in the hospital?"

With Brenda out in the working world, Candy hadn't kept her updated on her sudden relationship with Wayne. She, herself, was dizzy from the chain of decisions that had spewed her out here. Her body would heal, and she'd move on once she was freed from this nightmarish ride, a cyclone of delicious highs overmatched by the current hellish low.

Brenda beside her on the bed, the scent of L'Air du Temps dominating the medicinal smells in the ward, she inhaled deeply, anxious to absorb the fragrance of freedom, and Brenda's confidence, an antidote to all this hospital represented. "Dr. Thompson said he'd tell me the whole story as soon as he had us together, but he's already told me more than I wanted to hear. I've had surgery. I can't even bring myself to tell you; I could never tell my mother."

"Where does she think you are?"

"A sleepover with you. You can't tell her anything he tells us. She'd be irreparably disappointed in me."

Anxious to have her questions answered, Brenda strode from the ward, her platform shoes slapping the hard floors.

Within minutes of her departure, Dr. Thompson walked in, Jessica following. "Smells like Bloomingdale's," he said.

Returning through the partially open curtains, Brenda extended her hand to the doctor. "I'm Brenda. I want to know everything."

Dr. Thompson stared, saying nothing for a moment. Brenda had that effect on men.

"Brenda Starr?" Jessica blurted, then quickly covered her mouth. "Sorry."

"Brenda Frank. Though I am a reporter, for *The New York Times*, not the *Chicago Tribune*. I want to know everything and how I can help."

"That's why I wanted you here, Mrs. Frank," the doctor said.

"Miss, for now." Brenda flashed her engagement ring.

Jessica excused herself. "I have other patients, but I've spent a lot of time with Candy. I'm happy she has someone now."

"Ready for our walk?" Dr. Thompson asked. He helped her out of bed and positioned her IV. Brenda took Candy's free arm and supported her. As the doctor walked alongside Brenda, he said, "I was the ob-gyn on call the night she was brought to the ER. Let's finish this conversation in private. Curtains have ears."

"Why a gynecologist? Did she sustain internal injuries in an accident?"

At the room they had visited earlier, the doctor opened the door and, with Brenda beside her, Candy sat and searched out the oak tree. The leaf had fallen. Dr. Thompson sat opposite them.

"We concluded that Candy, whom we were calling Jane Doe, had had a botched, obviously illegal abortion—"

There it was. She hadn't expected him to get there so abruptly. Her shame heated her cheeks. It was intended to be a secret she'd take to her grave. She studied Brenda's expression.

"Stop right there," Brenda said. "That's utterly impossible. Her mother absolutely shelters her."

Candy grabbed Brenda's arm. "It's true. I wish I didn't have to tell you, but better you than my mother." She stood, then paced the room, IV in tow. "What more is there, doctor?"

"A young man delivered her to the ER," he said. "Then she was rolled to surgery where we struggled to save her. I repair more abortions than you might think. I wish the damned things were legal again as they were in the mid-nineteenth century."

"Please don't hate me."

"You're lucky you got to a hospital, poor child. Who was the young man?"

"I don't know," she lied. Fragments of the previous days, like bits of glass, fell through the imagined kaleidoscope. Nothing stuck. The pieces fell so quickly. The patterns, like her life, changed. Dizzy, she sat back down and held her head in both hands.

"Dr. Thompson—" Brenda began.

"There's more, which is why I wanted someone to be here with her, and I have her permission to speak freely."

"What more could there be?" Brenda asked. She watched Candy, transfixed by the tree.

"Yes, doctor, what more? You've kept me in suspense a whole day now."

"This is the hard part," the doctor said. "She's had major surgery. An abdominal hysterectomy—"

Brenda jumped to her feet. The handbag on her lap crashed to the floor, spilling its contents on the carpet between her and Candy on one side of the oriental rug, and Dr. Thompson on the other. "Stop. I'm going to sue this hospital. She's nineteen, for God's sake. What have you done?"

Apparently taking her question literally, he continued, matter-of-factly, "We removed the uterus, but we managed to save her ovaries." He leaned back into the cushions of his chair and made a steeple with his fingers. "She needs six weeks to recuperate and six months for a full recovery."

Candy continued staring out the window, hands clenched, tears streaming down her cheeks, as they discussed her innermost anguish. "Why didn't I know any of this? Didn't you need my permission? I have my ovaries? At least I can have children."

"I'm afraid not," he said. Those few words created a final pattern in the kaleidoscope, the colored glass bits cutting her with the swiftness of the impersonal blade of a guillotine.

"We left the ovaries so you wouldn't go into menopause so young," he said.

"I'm nineteen." Springing to her feet, she ripped out her IV, rushed to the window and pounded it to set herself free. As hard as she banged, however, she couldn't break through. "I wanted love, children, like everybody else."

Brenda lunged toward her, caught her from behind, and held on to her.

The doctor rushed to the door, motioned a nurse over, and ordered a shot to sedate her. Then he sat her down and reset the IV. "I should have anticipated this."

Sedated, Candy again stared at the oak tree from her chair, Brenda's arm around her shoulder.

Dr. Thompson knelt on the rug gathering the notebooks, pens and pencils, lipsticks, make-up, umbrella, tissues, and sundry items disgorged from the purse.

Candy put her fingertips to her forehead, straining to comprehend everything she thought she'd heard as her whole life emptied out in front of her. "You're saying I can't have children, ever? Why did you bother to save me? I'm dried up, useless, ovaries or not." She wiped her nose with the back of her hand. "My mother thought I was worthless before. Now I've failed a thousand years of family."

Her plan to hoard the pills would now be more essential than she had imagined. It was her only way out. Brenda patted her face with tissues from the packet the doctor handed her. Candy tugged the tissue away. "I can't even blow my nose without pain. I want to go back to my bed."

"We fought to save you, and you fought with us. You're strong," the doctor said. "Your whole life is in front of you."

Spilled out in front of her, like the contents of the emptied purse. She felt she had no future.

Brenda held her tight. "Come and live with me. I can take care of you. We'll work it out."

"Mother would never understand. I'm a complete disgrace and utter failure. What's the point of anything?" The leaf had disappeared, and she would too, certain no one would miss her.

"I'll smooth things over with your mother," Brenda said. "She's too fragile to give you the support you need, and the least of your worries. I'll work something out. I'll pack up some of your things and tell her you've decided to move to Manhattan, to go to school there. How's that?"

"She won't let me leave home till I'm married." She went through the whole packet of tissues, squeezing the wad of paper like a snowball. "She's worried about what everyone will think."

"I left home, and everyone survived," Brenda said.

"Let's get you well and out of the hospital," Dr. Thompson said.

"How soon can she leave?"

"Four more days, so we can attend to her dressings, sutures, and other matters."

Brenda said she'd visit every day, bring her personal items from home, work out the move with her mother. They'd create a future.

But Candy was convinced she had no future and couldn't wait to swallow the pills. She could only look back, not forward. Wayne had left her, no ID, no uterus, no longer a woman, empty.

Dr. Thompson extended his hand to help her up. She ignored him. "Brenda can take you to your room. I am sorry. Call me, Brenda, if you have any questions." He reached into his breast pocket. "Take my card. I'm glad she has you." He left them, then entered a private patient room.

She and Brenda walked unsteadily back to the ward, past the open doors of private and semi-private rooms with patients' names posted in the hall. The crying of the babies clawed at her. Her socks slipped on the shiny linoleum and she stumbled over the IV pole.

"We're almost there," Brenda said. "Keep hold of my arm." They walked into the ward, past the book cart still parked there, and past other women in their curtained bays.

Brenda tucked her under the covers and kissed her. "Is there anything I can do before I leave? Call me if you want to talk. I won't pry."

She reached for Brenda's hand. The sedative was overtaking her. "Nothing.

Good-bye. I love you." Her words spurted, as if they were being squeezed from an emptying bottle. Brenda walked out. Candy placed her hands over her abdomen, fingering the wound through the dressing. Until that moment, she hadn't thought how disfiguring it might be, a scar branding her with the loss of her womanhood. Damaged goods. Who could love her? How would she find her place in the world? The weight of it made her sleepy.

One of her wardmates poked her head in. "I noticed they haven't brought your little one yet?"

There was nothing to cushion the blow. Except for the damn balloon curtains, all the encroaching surfaces, metal, plastic, linoleum, glass, were hard and cold. They absorbed nothing. Her disorientation hit hard, bounced around the room, down the corridor, echoed through the hospital. She heard a chorus of gossip on the other side of the thin cloth:

"Somebody said that girl isn't married."

"What's she doing in the maternity ward?"

The bright yellow walls shrieking with the mother-and-child pictures displayed on them, and the curtains, closed in on her. She burrowed into the pillows, wishing again to smother herself, shut out everything. A good time to dig for the pills, but, her eyelids heavy, she couldn't even get out of bed to reach her bag.

The following morning, Brenda's signature scent woke her, and Brenda wasted no time moving her to the private room she had arranged the previous day. "We're going headlong into the future. Time for being maudlin is over. We're looking forward, like Janus. Where is the necklace?" Brenda put her bag on the table, the weight of it hitting the plastic emphasized her determination to help Candy move on.

"I'd rather not look forward," Candy said. She ran her fingers through her hair. "I was so stupid. It's in the zippered pocket of my bag."

"I promise not to badger you with questions," Brenda said. "We can't change what's done, but we have to work from it." Brenda found the necklace, with its broken chain, among a handful of pills. "What's this?" She held the pills in her palm in front of Candy.

"I won't lie." Her head pounded. An aura of thorned lights appeared in her field of vision. "I planned to take them all at once."

Brenda took the pills into the bathroom and flushed them. "No more bad choices. And I'll have the necklace fixed when you're ready to wear it again."

"That's a reminder I don't need."

With her departure from the ward, she could leave behind everything, Staten Island most of all, Wayne and memory of him. In her own room, she could make her own choices, no balloons, no crying babies, no judging whispers. From a space wholly hers, she would choose to get better, choose to accept help, to look forward, not back.

All starched and chirpy, Jessica appeared at the door. "I hope I'm not interrupting. I followed the trail of perfume here from the old bed."

"Come in," Candy said. *To be that open and innocent again.*

"Wanted to drop off your book, in case your curiosity was piqued," Jessica said.

As she passed the novel to Candy, Brenda intercepted it. "*Valley of the Dolls.* Is this where you got the idea?"

"What idea?" Jessica asked. "I found it in the drawer when I was tidying up."

"I brought a book of my own," Brenda said. "An old LMU catalog. Are you in college, Jessica?"

"My parents will take me on the tour soon. Dr. Thompson has me interested in pre-med."

"That's a bold choice. I can't imagine there are many women in med school," Brenda said.

"Only nine percent, Dr. Thompson told me. What are you interested in, Candy?"

"Entomology. I was working with insects in a museum program to interest children in science."

"If Dr. Thompson has his way," Jessica said, "he'll encourage you to consider medicine. He thinks we need more female doctors."

"Medicine never entered my mind." Maybe the perky girl was just the company she needed.

"Dr. Thompson's point is that women don't see themselves as doctor material."

Brenda sat on the bed and Jessica worked her way to the windowsill. "What got you interested in volunteering here?" Brenda found her pen and notebook. "Do you mind? No names."

"We have a couple of elderly neighbors who need assistance," Jessica said. "I help out. And there's a little boy with polio next door. I go over when I can to massage his legs and spell his mother a bit. My mother read about this candy striper program and encouraged me to do it."

"Don't let a guy break your focus," Candy said. "If I could possibly become a gynecologist, after my experiences, I would empathize with women. Female doctors wouldn't deny single women birth control." She sat up a little straighter.

"Whether it's education, medicine, or something else," Brenda said, and placed the catalog on her lap, "consider this a conversation starter."

"I've lost my first semester at community." She flipped through the pages. "I wouldn't qualify, and I couldn't afford it." She handed the catalog back to Brenda.

"You're overqualified for community." Brenda searched the catalog for entrance requirements and handed it to Candy. "I believe you meet these. Prepare for next year, maybe not this private college, but City, which we could afford

"Too many hurdles, especially for medicine." She shook the IV pole. "I've made a mess of my life. Who could I help?"

"Don't choose medicine, but look forward. You need time. That's all."

Dr. Thompson entered to check Candy's vitals. "What's that LMU catalog? My alma mater. I still live in my college apartment in 'the Row.'"

"Quite a coincidence," Brenda said. "I live on Fifth, near the park. I studied journalism there a few semesters, got a great job and never graduated."

"How is this relevant to the patient?" he asked.

Brenda said that Candy would be staying with her, near the school, and met the requirements for admission, although she'd missed this year's deadlines.

"And there's the matter of money, and my recovery, and my impaired judgment."

"A goal could aid your recovery, get you out of your head," he said. He explained that if she were interested in medicine, and well-qualified, a couple of female doctors who were recruiting female students for pre-med could grease wheels and get her in for the spring semester, with financial aid, if she'd work in the dorms, Bellevue, or the cafeteria. But she'd have to act fast. "And you wouldn't need room and board since you're staying with Brenda." He offered to help prepare her at Brenda's, the school library, even Caffè Reggio.

"I did have fours and fives on my AP tests in calc, bio, chem, and physics."

Before leaving to visit other patients, Jessica informed the doctor of Candy's work in entomology. "You handle insects?" he asked. "I could dissect the fetal pig in bio lab, but my partner had to dissect the insects. You're a step ahead of me."

"Yesterday I wanted to die. I'm on drugs. I can't think straight."

"If she can get her records," he said, "I can arrange an interview." They spoke in front of her as though she wasn't in the room. "The only real problem will be the men who stridently object to women in their profession."

"Really," said Candy. "And how do they do that?"

"They freeze the women out, few as they are, marginalize them, humiliate them, as they did to Elizabeth Blackwell over a hundred years ago. You're probably too weak right now to handle that." He put his hands in his pockets and turned to leave. "Again, reverting to the 1800s with constraints that bound New York City women, barring all but a very few from most professions, even labor unions and public places like restaurants. Men cling to their power and fear losing it to women. Don't get me started."

"You get me excited about the prospect and walk out? That makes you like the men you're talking about."

He turned back. "Can you take it? Do you have what it takes to make it in a man's profession, to withstand the torrent of hostility?"

Alone for the night with thoughts of a far wider world, she studied the catalog, then put it into her bag to read *Valley of the Dolls*. She noticed an envelope tucked into the pocket of the bag. She read it. Wayne. Just when she was erasing him from her mind. Threats. She shredded it and strafed her sheets with the torn word-bombs. A clear pattern emerged. *Men won't intimidate me ever again.*

PART II

Into the Jar

CHAPTER 15

Snowflake Marble

Manhattan

Weeks after her release from the hospital, but not from her depression, Candy stood back for perspective, tilting her head to read the words above the lofty wrought iron gate confronting her. Snowflakes pinched her face, and she blinked away those that burned her eyes. "New York Marble Cemetery."

"Why are we meeting here, in the snow, or at all?" Her words clipped, her pitch high, she chided Dr. Thompson, who removed his glove, then retrieved an antique brass key from his coat pocket. Her fury with him was compounded by their meeting out on Second Avenue in the cold, but was not the cause of it. She stomped snow from her boots. Although grateful for his time prepping her at Brenda's for her upcoming LMU interview, she harbored anger at him for having taken her uterus. "There must have been another way to save me." She pulled her beret further down on her forehead and brought her scarf over her mouth and nose. "I'm not well enough for this weather. You should know that."

"I accept your resentment." He unlocked the gate and pushed it open, the bottom rail tracing a track in the snow as the hinges creaked. "I hope you'll come to appreciate this place as much as I do. The reason I became a doctor lies here. You'll have your own reasons. Be ready to articulate them with distraction-free passion tomorrow." On this quiet, winter-solstice morning, he tightened his coat's lapels against the wind. In front of the nondescript alleyway, in the Lower-East-Side neighborhood of inconsequential tenement buildings, they stood alone.

"I understood that the female doctors were anxious to recruit me."

"They've reviewed your records. But they want to know who you are, your level of commitment. And you never know who may be added to the panel. Don't count on a cake walk."

After they entered the alley, he locked the gate behind them, then dropped the key into his pocket. Following the tight path created by weathered-brick buildings on either side, they arrived at an open parcel of land bound by twelve-foot-tall stone walls. Snow-laden shrubs and trees slumbered behind concrete benches that they would shade and beautify in the warmth to come. "As you see, we're not about to get any shelter from the snowfall. In this hidden garden, there are no structures, not even tombstones." He adjusted his hat to keep the snow from his eyes.

"Doesn't strike me as either a garden or a cemetery." That this place had anything to do with her interview was puzzling.

"No headstones, and now only dormant plants." Their boots kicked up the ankle-high snow as they walked to the center of the plot. "It's not usually open in December, so I had to wrangle a key for our visit. Just over a hundred years old, this cemetery's always a respite from the urban hustle and bustle. No longer in use for burials, it's become a place to reflect and meditate, especially in warm weather, when it comes into its own as a garden."

"You've taken me here to reflect and meditate?" She considered everything she'd lost. No headstones for her memories, either, but she hoped to bury them. And move on.

"Yes, to reflect and meditate," he said. "There are rituals for dealing with loss. Cemeteries provide closure, a place, with others, to mourn." He explained that underground, there were one hundred fifty-six marble vaults, which held over two thousand bodies of those who died of the scourges of their time — yellow fever, cholera, malaria, measles once rampant in Manhattan, a reminder that medicine has come a long way in a relatively short time.

"Buried ten feet down are medicine's failures," he said. "The idea back then was to contain the diseases deep down in marble vaults so they couldn't escape to spread again. Some of my ancestors are buried below. As I child, when my parents brought me here, I determined I wanted to prevent such misery, cure illnesses, and I eventually decided to bring lives into the world."

"And how am I supposed to feel about that? My misery is that I can't bring my own children into the world. I can't bury the misery of that fact in a vault deep enough to keep it there."

He related that he had once hired a gravedigger to dig down the ten feet to the vault. Underground, the Tuckahoe, or Snowflake, Marble remained as pristine as snow. Above-ground, however, the same snow-white marble, used as indexes on the tablets of the stone walls, had weathered and darkened from its exposure to the elements. "The world has the power to silently foul everything it breathes on. Though the earth protected the marble, the marble vaults couldn't protect the bodies. The coffins within the vaults deteriorated, spilling their decayed contents, mostly dust, as I observed. I placed a gold family ring there, left, then helped the gravedigger shovel the earth back." He studied the intricate design of the key he took out of his pocket.

"The insects at work," she said into her scarf. "There's hope that the natural order of things will one day turn my emotional pain to dust." No matter how much perspective she tried to get on her experiences, her mistakes, she suffered under their weight. "Helping others in physical distress, facing medicine's future challenges are goals I can latch onto."

"The healing sun will bring flowers in their time," he said.

In the snowflakes that fell onto her fuchsia coat sleeve, she traced their archetypal crystal pattern, like those she had cut into folded white paper as a child. She could not reclaim her innocence.

Dr. Thompson had given her an antique brass key to her own vault — family name: LOSS. Interred: Pregnancy, Uterus, Trust, Innocence. She resolved to hide her secrets and have them decay within her. Unable to resist one last taste of innocence, she yielded to the urge to stick out her tongue and have a snowflake melt there — a communion between her and nature. "Thank you," she said to Dr. Thompson.

He put his arm around her shoulder, imparting a brief hug as they exited the cemetery, and he locked the gate behind them.

CHAPTER 16

Time Machine

She and Dr. Thompson walked west across Houston Street, hunching into the wind as whorls of snow danced to their knees. They joined arms for balance. When they arrived at MacDougal Street, he pulled right to the north side, but she stopped and tugged left. "I'd like to make a brief stop on the other side of MacDougal."

With no traffic on the snow-covered street, they ran against the signal as Dr. Thompson held down his fedora. The single-story façade she led him to was a throwback to the nineteenth century — a time before Otis invented elevators, and before Rosenwach water tanks sat atop buildings over five stories; a time when meat, cheeses, groceries, and baked goods were each sold in neighboring mom-and-pop shops; a time when milk was delivered to doorsteps in bottles; a time when produce was sold from horse-drawn wagons, or pushcarts; a time before the proliferation of grocery stores and supermarkets.

They stopped under the green awning intended to shield the plate glass window from the sun, the refrigerated display case enticing passers-by with a selection of cuts of meat. The awning sagged under the weight of the snow, enough so that it grazed Dr. Thompson's hat. "Fritz's Butcher Shoppe" was printed on both the scalloped valance and in a semi-circle of black-outlined gold lettering on the window.

"Suddenly remember Brenda needed meat for dinner?" Dr. Thompson asked, his mood lightening from that of the cemetery.

Between the hat and the scarf, her eyes smiled. "Fritz, the butcher, was my neighbor from the day I was born till the day we moved to Staten Island. I'd like to visit."

She pushed the decrepit door open into the shop without having to touch the brass doorknob, and the bell, strung above the door, tinkled. The shop hadn't changed in all the years she had known it. Long and narrow, it was probably once an alley that had morphed into a storefront. The odor of the sawdust, spread a couple of inches thick over the wood floor to sop up the blood, fat, and pieces of meat that inevitably fell from the cutting table, hit her nostrils hard. It had been a long time. She removed her hat and gloves, shaking melting snow into the sawdust, and she ran her fingers through her matted curls.

They followed the length of the narrow shop back to the stout, maple butcher-block, where Fritz had cleavered carcasses into manageable sections, or, with more finesse, had hand-trimmed cuts of meat: *Don't want so much fat? Don't need a bone adding weight to the scale? Want one split ribeye to feed two?* Adept with his knives, he worked fast, so neither chairs nor benches cluttered the shop. At the far end was the glistening steel door of the refrigerated meat locker where the butcher hung the skinned animals he had selected at market and shut them away from his customers' view.

As early as second grade, she had happily delayed starting her homework to skip the two blocks from home to the shop to purchase the meat her mother needed for dinner. "I'd like a pound of chopped chuck, please," she yelled out now, as she had as a child, before Fritz interrupted his task to look up. She wondered if he'd recognize her voice.

"Be right with you, ma'am. I'm about to close. Check the case for anything else you'd like."

Her smiling eyes blinked, and she sucked in her bottom lip. He hadn't recognized her voice singing out her most frequent order. Innocence lost, even in her cheery vocalization, and, in not recognizing her voice, she concluded, Fritz had detected the change.

The top of Fritz's grayed head bowed over the table as he carved a flank into smaller cuts. He straightened in his uniform of a freshly-stained, white-bibbed apron over his white shirt, long sleeves rolled up to his elbows. Looking up with a glint of recognition, he then leaned against the side of the glass case. "I thought that voice was familiar. You have a habit of catching me off-guard, young lady."

"Brings back so many memories." She touched his shoulder. She introduced Dr. Thompson. "We were in the neighborhood. I had to check in on you."

Fritz lifted the bottom of his apron and wiped his hands. "No need to shake. Give me a minute." He brought his knives to the sink and pulled down a couple of pieces of butcher paper to wrap the cut meat while he spoke. "Five, six years since you moved?" He tied each package with twine and printed a customer's name on it.

"Six. But I moved in with Brenda a month ago, not far from here, so I'll see you often."

"That Brenda's a beauty," Fritz said.

"She's engaged now, to a soldier training down South."

"Tell her I'd love to see her. Bring her by. And your parents?"

As they caught up, Fritz included the doctor in the conversation, noting that he looked familiar, relating what a good carpenter Candy's father had been, that he had supplied his shop with sawdust since Candy's birth until their move, and that her mother made a wicked meatloaf from mere chopped chuck.

Dr. Thompson rolled his hat in his hands. "We're on our way to Reggio. Join us and we'll talk there."

Fritz went around to the sink to wash up. He caught their reflection in the wall mirror as he spoke to them. "Like your family, a lot of the old families have moved, or died off. It's only a matter of time before I close up shop and go to work for some supermarket chain." He threw his apron into the hamper and grabbed his coat from the hook.

Candy put her arm in his. "At Reggio, you can regale the doctor with our tale."

The bell tinkled again as the three left.

Shielded from the snow by the dome-shaped canopy at 119 MacDougal, Dr. Thompson yanked open the heavy double-doors, and, when he removed his hat, what little remained of his red hair fluttered in the wind while he held the door and Candy ducked into the warm coffee shop, chasing the aromas of brewing espresso and baking pastries, followed by Fritz.

"Welcome to Caffè Reggio," a voice behind the dessert case called, but not the voice she knew from her many visits with her grandfather.

Crossing the threshold into the shop was like entering a scallop-edged, sepia-toned photograph from another age. The dusky ambience enveloped her. Music from *Rigoletto* or *La Traviata* (her grandfather would have known which) floated from ceiling speakers to the tobacco-colored stucco walls. Nothing ever changed in here. Renaissance paintings hung around the shop, the most famous a Caravaggio, a chiaroscuro, a dark composition with splashes of light. The dusty busts and bric-a-brac from the Old World had lived in the caffè since it opened in 1927. An authentic five-hundred-year-old bench from a Medici palazzo in Florence, unrecognized for what it was by most who sat on it, still hunkered against the wall. The espresso machine, brought over from Italy, a five-foot-tall, nickel-plated work of art covered with angels, demons, and scallop shells, hissed under the pressure of brewing coffee. The machine, which had served the first cup of espresso in America, nearly drowned out the opera and made conversation difficult. The caffè felt like home, connecting her to her grandfather, to her childhood, to her Italian roots.

"As Fritz knows, my grandfather brought me here often," she said to the doctor. "Grandfather taught me to enjoy espresso in a demitasse cup, black with a twist of lemon. He talked about the music, the art work, and the rich Italian culture of the Renaissance. Reggio was a taste of the Old World he missed so much." The tiny shop was a peek her grandfather had given her into her heritage, promising one day to take her to Italy, a promise left unfulfilled.

And her grandmother had given her the Janus necklace, another connection to her roots, a thousand years in the making. Riddled with anguish, she clasped the necklace, which Brenda had repaired, seeing no way to fulfill its legacy. Guilt and shame seeped up to infect her reminiscences. She hoped medicine would redeem her abominable failure.

"I had no idea you knew this place, but I'm glad the caffè holds memories for you," Dr. Thompson said. "It's an LMU haunt, where I've spent lots of time, interrupted by the espresso machine, in heated philosophical, ethical, and medical debates with colleagues. Enough of me, let's get to your story, Fritz."

Niso interrupted to ask for their orders — Italian pastries and espressos all around. Fritz leaned back in his chair, balancing it precariously on its back legs. "I don't drink much coffee, but I occasionally meet a customer or two here to deliver their meat and to socialize."

"I'm still trying to place you," Dr. Thompson said.

"If you live in the neighborhood, we must travel the same paths," Fritz said.

"Forget about that. I'm anxious to hear your story."

"And quite a story it is," Fritz said. "After the war, back in '47, in the middle of a January night quite like this, the quiet woke me. In my bedroom overlooking West Houston, I gazed between the dusty slats of the Venetian blinds. In the light of the shepherd's crook cast-iron street lamps, falling in a sheer haze, at least two feet of softly settling snow had already accumulated."

"I'm familiar with that fine snow, *tlatim*, the Inuit call it. It usually indicates a hefty accumulation to come," Dr. Thompson said.

Fritz continued, "I moved the alarm slide of my Westclox Big Ben wind-up, luminous hands both at twelve, to the 'off' setting, knowing I wouldn't have any early customers, and drifted into a deep sleep. Terrifyingly loud bleating startled me. I followed it to my shop and beyond, to an abattoir in the Meatpacking District."

"I know the neighborhood well," said Dr. Thompson.

"I don't," said Candy, "but I think Fritz is embellishing for your benefit."

"Follow along," said Fritz. "I took Washington Street north, cutting across Gansevoort, continuing on Washington to number 837, Lamb Unlimited. My bare feet grazed the steel-gray Belgian-block streets, my body gliding mere inches above. Although I'd made this trip countless times when awake, I was always startled by the red, rusted metal bins filled with blood-stained bones, most recognizable as distinct animal carcasses, cows, pigs, sheep, left outside the squat slaughterhouses for disposal."

"We are to understand this is a vivid dream," Dr. Thompson said. "I want to know if Candy fits in."

"Blood, gristle and flesh caked in the crevices of the cobblestones. The walls of the buildings didn't confine the stench of ammonia, hot blood, feces, and slaughter by-products. Following the sound of the bleating, I opened the heavy steel door to a kill room. In a pane of window glass, I caught the image of myself carrying a seventeen-week-old lamb across my shoulders, and I winced at the smile on its face."

Dr. Thompson interrupted. "If I weren't a doctor, familiar with these same substances, I wouldn't be able to enjoy my cannoli here."

"I've never related this dream before, but it's quite graphic. Stop me at any time."

"I plan to enter pre-med at LMU," Candy said, "which is why I moved in with Brenda. I have my interview tomorrow. And I've seen more than I care to share with anyone. I'm ready."

"I squinted," Fritz said, "and saw, instead of the lamb, my pregnant nineteen-year-old neighbor, Gloria, hung from a meat hook, head tilted back, body slit breastbone to anus, a river of extravasations flooding the floor. Sheared wool on the ground below soaked in the blood. Skin removed, muscles exposed, the carcass somehow writhed in violent spasms."

"Too unsettling," Candy said and turned her head away.

"Shall I tone it down, or present the dream as I experienced it?" Fritz asked.

"I'll take your truth," Candy said.

"As I shook off my dream state, stabbing, red shrieks of horror and fear followed the path of least resistance, up through the floorboards of my room, through my mattress and pillow, into my conscious mind, waking me more urgently than my Westclox. I reached for my red flannel robe. It flew open as I ran barefoot down the flight of wooden stairs to Gloria's apartment. In this three-family tenement we didn't bother to lock our doors, but I banged on the metal door to be heard above the screams, 'I'm coming in.'"

"How terrible. I had no idea," Candy said.

"Quite the opposite," he said. "It was the best experience of my life. 'Help,' Gloria screamed. 'Save my baby.' I opened the door, not knowing what to expect. The familiar smell of hot blood. Across the narrow hall from the entry door, the bathroom door was ajar, its ceiling bulb, the only light in the apartment, accentuated the blood, which bathed the grout of the hexagonal floor tiles. The glistening red-brown fluids breached the marble threshold, cutting paths through the grooves in the hall's oak flooring. My newly-wakened brain took a few seconds to process the scene. Gloria was seated on the toilet. I knew her baby must be slipping into the water."

"My God, man, I'm the obstetrician here," said Dr. Thompson. "It sounds like you're about to usurp my job. Maybe I've been recognizing the doctor in you."

The two sat rapt, listening to Fritz, pastries in mid-air, espressos cooling.

"Gloria was paralyzed with fear of harming the baby she was delivering in this ignominious manner. My dream had crossed with reality. I leaned her forward and peered into the toilet water to see the baby's bottom, not its head, in the water. I ran to the kitchen for a knife, praying I could command the dull kitchen utensil to save a life, or two. With her leaned against my shoulders and chest, her long hair, down the length of her crouched back, soaked in toilet water. I gathered her hair out of the way."

Fritz neither moved, nor sipped his espresso, nor bit his pastry. He didn't even pause when the espresso machine hissed away. Others at near-by tables leaned their heads in to get the drift of the story. It seemed Fritz liked being the center of attention. Candy thought, as a widower many years now, he must be very lonely. She determined to spend some time with him.

"'Cut it off,'" Gloria pleaded. The chunk of hair fell and mixed with the liquid around the toilet. I dropped the knife. Gloria's hand gripped the rolled rim of the porcelain, claw-foot tub and the nails of her other hand chewed into my shoulder. Blood, shit, water continued to overflow the toilet, as the baby, enclosed in its amniotic sac, floated into the water. The odor was worse than what I've nearly grown immune to."

Dr. Thompson cut in. "I can attest that the secretions of a woman's body at childbirth must certainly rise from the bowels of the earth, the humus, the minerals, the dhghem of Genesis, the hand of God reaching deep, scooping clay, the umbilical cord connecting this new human to every other knot in the umbilicus of humankind."

"When I repositioned the fetus and lifted the head above the fetid water, the amniotic sac burst. I pulled the baby toward me, resting the head in my hand and the body along my wrist and forearm. The baby was wrapped in a veil, which I pierced about the face and removed. I wiped the mouth with my pinky and blew air in, held the newborn upside down, slapped its bottom and waited for a cry. The baby wailed and pinked. I groped for the knife I had moments ago dropped, sliced the cord, and dropped the knife once more."

"Amazing job, my good man. And under such pressure. If you close up shop, I'll put you to work in the hospital."

"Turns out the baby was a month early and Gloria's husband was helping his dad in his Hell's Kitchen bar. I settled mom and baby, wrapped in a green wool blanket I pulled from the wringer washing machine in the hall, and called the hospital, then the bar."

"I inserted my shaking index finger," Fritz continued, "cuticle and creases caked with blood, into the 'GHI/4' hole in the chrome dial of the black Bakelite phone, pushing it all the way around until it reached the curved finger stop at the bottom where I released it, and it rebounded to its starting position. I entered the next digit. I dialed all seven digits of the hospital's number painstakingly, requested an ambulance, and placed the handset back on its cradle. The ambulance would be delayed in its short trip from Second Avenue and Sixteenth Street to West Houston and Sixth due to the snowstorm, but I yelled to the new mother, 'They'll be here soon.'

"I told her that her husband wanted me to go to the hospital with her and the baby. 'Your baby picked a helluva time to come into the world,' I said. Before I ran upstairs for some clothes, she wanted me to open the blinds. I'll never forget what she said, 'It's like there's a white curtain outside the window, with a light glowing behind it, like the moon came right up to the window to peek in. How pure and white the snow is right now. I'm going to call my baby Candace.'"

"Thank you, Fritz," Candy said, "for the details I've never heard. Having survived that birth, I'm prepared to meet any panel tomorrow, and even deliver a baby, if necessary."

CHAPTER 17

Feme Decovert

Met by a locked door, Candy knocked, then planted herself on the wooden bench where countless other interviewees must have waited, their hands sweaty, their throats dry. She popped a Violet mint, then checked her watch. On time. Certainly not the wrong day. Had they cancelled? An intimidation tactic? She fussed with her hair, removed notes from her bag, and flipped through a few pages before two women in physician's coats arrived, unlocked the door, and invited her into the office.

Smiles exchanged, the doctors sat at a table set with water and a stack of glasses, where they set out papers and pens, rather than their stethoscopes, prepared to examine her. Opposite them, isolated in the center of the room, in a wooden chair, with no place to relax her hands, she sat, exposed, like one of her insect specimens, parts labeled, on display, under glass. With ankles crossed, pleased with her decision to wear pants, she avoided eye contact, quite the opposite of Dr. Thompson's advice to look them in the eyes. Her bag and notes lay on the highly-polished oak floor, which looked as threatening as thin ice.

Both women were in their forties, plain, graying, in dark scrubs under their white coats. Stern-faced, like the nuns of mere months ago, they elicited a fearful response. After all, her new path depended on their opinion of her. Several wall-size windows made for a cold room. The radiators clinked. She shivered. The nipples proclaiming her womanhood hardened. She had left her coat on the bench.

"To get the obvious question off the table," the shorter one began. (They had not introduced themselves.) "Why do you want to be a doctor?"

Candy explained that she had experienced some life-threatening health issues recently and felt that a female doctor would have approached her situation differently. She felt that the men who dominated the medical profession didn't sympathize, for the most part, and could never empathize with female patients. She recounted what the two female doctors surely knew, that Elizabeth Blackwell, the first female doctor in America, was encouraged to pursue medicine by her friend, Mary, who believed a female doctor would have saved her a great deal of pain in dealing with her cancer.

"Yes, Elizabeth Blackwell. Isn't that the obvious go-to," bellowed a male voice from the back of the room. He came forward and insinuated himself between the two women at the table. "Don't worry, dear girl, this formality will be over quickly." With both forearms, he swept the women's notes and pens to the sides of the table, leaving the space before him clear. "Don't look so shocked, ladies. You had to know I wouldn't miss this for the world. Thompson, again? How many of his little chickadees will he send here to be plucked off by their male superiors?"

This time the taller of the women spoke to her. "This interview, is, of course, less about you as a pre-med candidate, for which you are highly qualified, and more about you as a woman." She stood, and although the room was small, she raised her voice, out of anger, or in an effort to dominate the previous speaker. She waved her arm toward him. "Do you think his nineteenth-century attire is unintentional? Born in that dusty century, our esteemed Professor Schweinfurt here clings to the expired laws, customs, and sexual order of that time when female subordination was deeply inscribed in the law and women were boxed in by their fathers and husbands, or free to live in disgrace, without a man, especially if they were unfortunate enough to have gotten pregnant out of wedlock."

Not having expected the interview to become so heated, Candy straightened in her chair and planted her feet firmly on the floor, reaching down to her family's deep roots. She clasped the coin of her necklace.

Daring to speak out, she explained that she knew that *feme covert*, in which a woman's legal identity was subsumed in her husband's, was buried deep in legal tradition and had proved hard to rout out, but the law had been changed, here, in New York City, in 1853. Since then, women have legally been able to engage in any profession, to own assets, to engage freely in the public arena, and to wear anything they wanted, including Bloomers, now pants. Amazingly, pioneering Elizabeth Blackwell had managed to earn her MD degree before that law. "More than a century later," Candy said as she rose to her feet, "I stand here for my rights, as have you women before me."

Professor Schweinfurt's face reddened, presenting a vivid contrast with his mane of white hair. He jumped to his feet, flinging his chair across the room. "You align yourself with these two antiquated, homely, lonely females?" He gesticulated toward them. "Why aspire to be like them when you have everything — the vote, the pill, your own assets, freedom in public areas. Why do you come here to insist on barging into one of men's last strongholds, here, our dissecting rooms?" He paused and poured himself water.

Since all the doctors on the panel were standing, she remained standing. "I am academically qualified. Like Elizabeth Blackwell—"

At the mention of that name, Professor Schweinfurt made the sign of the cross, as though she were an evil to be protected from.

Candy continued, staring him down, "I am attracted by the challenge. I, too, hope, one day, to be the best in my class, despite any opposition."

The professor walked out from behind the table and circled her, like a predator. "You're young." He touched her hair. "Reasonably attractive." He grimaced. "Get married. Take advantage of your child-bearing years. Live happily ever after. Don't take a man's seat, for God's sake. She, whose name I will not repeat, never married, or had children of her own. Is that really what you want for yourself?"

The shorter of the women demanded that the professor return to his place at the table.

Candy waved her off and stood face-to-face with the professor without flinching. "My marital aspirations and my gender are not issues. Many women since Blackwell, clearly not enough, have hacked this path, and I intend to do so as well." She demagnetized herself from the professor's eye-grasp and directed her feet toward the women at the table. "These two brave women already told me I'm academically qualified."

"Brava," said the professor. He crossed his arms over his bulging belly. "You put on a brave front here where men are outnumbered, but what will you do, how will your delicate female sensibilities be affected in the dissecting room, for example, where you're outnumbered a hundred to one with naked corpses in front of you? Think about what it is you're asking for, what you're in for. I'm trying to protect you — feme covert."

Faced with his rigid pig-headedness, she said, "I can take care of myself. I have a rich history to fall back on."

He was the first to leave the room, raising his coattails as he left, the stench of his patriarchal philosophy emitted in his wake. "You won't last long. I will bury you."

CHAPTER 18

A Soupçon of Joy

Late afternoon hail crackled against the window. Mesmerized by the sound, Candy stood alone in Brenda's kitchen in front of the open refrigerator door. "Beef, milk, eggs, ketchup." She had offered to prepare dinner for Brenda and her fiancé, Rick, who had managed a holiday leave from the Army.

Her recent visit to Fritz's stirred a desire for her mother's meatloaf. As a child, she loved to crack the raw eggs on the counter then slide them into the bowl. She relished the mess of mixing the milk, ketchup, beef, eggs, and bread together, squishing the mixture between fingers, like Play-Doh, until it oozed out, a brain-like mélange. Having listened to the details of Fritz's story, she especially missed her mother and teared up. It was too soon to visit, but when she had phoned, her mother puffed on cigarettes the entire call, angry at how her daughter had dared leave home.

"I bought the beef at Fritz's," she yelled out to Brenda who was in her bedroom changing from her work clothes. "He was happy to hear you're engaged. Maybe you and Rick can pay him a visit."

Brenda slouched into the kitchen in a cashmere robe, green, to match her eyes. "Are you sure you know what you're doing in here?" Brenda asked as she pulled an apron from the hook and rolled her bell-sleeves out of the way. "Heard anything from LMU?"

"Two weeks and nothing, not even from Dr. Thompson." She changed the subject. "Trust me. Rick will beg you to make this recipe after he tastes it. I think it's the touch of brown sugar." She stopped staring, removed the ingredients from the fridge, and placed them on the counter beside the ten-cup Pyrex bowl she had scoured the kitchen cabinets to find. "I have to do my share around here. I feel guilty being in the way while Rick is visiting."

"You bought the meat at Fritz's?" Brenda asked. "How is he? Did he remarry? He's one of the last old-time butchers." She pulled the roasting pan out of the oven drawer.

Brenda and her questions. "I'd like to buy our meat from him, if you don't mind. And, no, he never remarried." She cut the twine from the package of meat, turned the brown paper upside down over the bowl and dropped the beef in. It was red, fresh, and bloody. "Dr. Thompson thought he seemed lonely. Perhaps, wistful."

"We'll buy our meat there, even though the supermarket is so close."

"What if I blew the interview? Professor Schweinfurt is a misogynist." She smashed the eggs, one at a time, against the kitchen counter and slid the contents of the shells into the bowl. "I thought the two female doctors were on my side, as I told you that day, but what if his opinion held more power than theirs? What if I didn't show enough fire to stand up to all those men in the program?" She splashed the milk over the meat. "Does LMU have an entomology program? Where's the catalog? Or, I could apply to City for the fall. I should've gotten a little pork for the meatloaf, though Mother never used it."

"Now who has all the questions? Don't backslide. Look forward. Be patient." She turned the oven on to preheat.

"I feel the fire of wanting pre-med after dealing with Schweinfurt. Although I really believe that women would benefit from having more women in medicine, that isn't the point. If a woman has the brains for it, and she wants it, she shouldn't have to justify her choice." Like being in the kitchen with her mother or grandmother, she and Brenda worked together, adding the other ingredients, and she formed the mixture into a loaf. "Where's your aluminum foil?"

Brenda opened a drawer and handed her the box. Candy ripped off a foot of foil, twisted it into a braid, and created an oval that she used as a rack to keep the meatloaf out of the drippings.

"That's a neat trick," Brenda said.

"Mother was a meatloaf expert. Because she thought the pan racks were too shallow, she found another way." Candy topped the raw meat with the brown-sugar-ketchup mixture she had whisked together. "What time do you expect Rick?"

"Any minute, unless the weather delays him. My shoes and stockings were soaked when I got home." Brenda took a bottle from the wine rack under the kitchen island. "We'll relax with Chianti while the oven preheats."

"I'd rather not drink," she said as she washed her hands and dried them on the towel hanging on the oven door.

"I raise my glass to your coming to live with me."

At the kitchen table, she raised an air-glass to Brenda. "Thank you for giving me a home." She drew strength from Brenda's ability to march into the world, without fear or doubt, in search of answers. "Do you know what Rick has planned for New Year's Eve?"

"I wouldn't mind a quiet evening at home with both of you."

"I'd be in the way." Her scars were fresh, but not visible. It drained her energy to keep their impact on her womanhood hidden. The preheat signal on the oven dinged, and she got up to put the pan in the oven and set the timer. The doorbell rang, and Brenda ran to answer it.

The heavy door slammed shut. "What's going on out there?" Candy called.

"It's Rick. Stay there. We're coming to the kitchen."

Having left his wet things in the hall, Rick entered the kitchen carrying Brenda. After twirling her around, he put her down and greeted Candy. "I have something for you from the doorman." He gave her the manila envelope, then sat, kicked off his boots, and slid them under his chair.

When she felt the weight of the envelope from LMU, she sprang from her chair, tore the envelope open, wrenched the contents free, and spread the papers on the table. They leaned in. The baking meatloaf sweetened the room. The crackling hail was no longer noticeable. "They accepted me?" she mumbled, as more a question than a statement. It was her first shot of confidence. "There's a scholarship, and a list of courses for the spring semester. I'll choose the most challenging. Like Dr. Blackwell, I'll show them what women can do out of the kitchen."

Seated on either side of her, Brenda and Rick squeezed her hands. "This calls for a toast," Brenda said. "To the future Dr. Krzyzanowski."

For the first time since her eyes had opened in the hospital, she wasn't staring at a blank future. "I have to call Dr. Thompson."

On the way to the wall phone, she told them that when she bought the meat that morning, Fritz had told her he was going to work the Houston Street soup kitchen on New Year's Eve. She told Brenda and Rick she'd join Fritz so they could have the apartment to themselves for the day. Something rousing, like the scent of peppermint, sparked her spirit. By the time she had pressed the last button of Dr. Thompson's number, Brenda gestured that they would join her and Fritz. The doctor told her he knew she'd ace her interview, and he had sometimes volunteered at the Houston Street soup kitchen. He'd meet them there.

She made one last call to Fritz who said was dumbfounded and excited to have them all join him.

As the trio devoured the meatloaf, Rick told them of his promotion to staff sergeant and recounted his many responsibilities as mentor for new sergeants. His next step was warrant officer and helicopter pilot. Brenda winced. Vietnam loomed.

Candy ticked off some courses listed in her packet — organic chem, bio, pathogenic bacteriology, vertebrate anatomy. "Rick and I should enjoy this vacation. We'll both have our hands full soon." A short time ago, she thought the world had closed to her, but here she was opening doors and pulling loved ones into her vortex, catching them up in her renewed spirit of community. "We'll get our marching orders from Fritz. He'll meet us at the door, seven sharp tomorrow morning."

From blocks away, she saw a queue. Expecting to see men, like those she had often seen sleeping in subways, doorways, or on church steps in cardboard shelters, she was jolted by the number of women and children lined up as well.

She regretted the self-pity she had felt in the hospital, those days of drowning in darkness. Had Jessica, Brenda, and Dr. Thompson not thrown her hope, she would have drowned in a sea of bad choices.

Fritz beamed as he hugged Brenda and met Rick. "Like having family in the old neighborhood," he said. When Dr. Thompson showed up, Fritz led them to an office where they stowed their belongings before donning their aprons.

In the kitchen, Fritz orchestrated the cleaning and basting of the turkeys he had donated. Since they were making the stuffing in roasting pans, he instructed them to insert a whole Rome apple into each turkey cavity after removing the neck, liver, and innards for the soup. With gloves on, Candy reached right into the cavity for the innards, and, as the only one who displayed no ick response, she volunteered to do all of the turkeys.

Brenda joined the several men and women on the other side of the kitchen who were boiling and mashing vats of potatoes and filling roasting pans with bread stuffing made with sautéed celery, onions, and sage while waiting for the addition of the yet-to-come homemade turkey soup. Rick and Dr. Thompson opened cartons filled with cans of peas and carrots and creamed corn and poured the contents into huge pots. Dozens of strangers, under Fritz's direction, worked as a team, performing the sundry tasks of creating a multi-course meal for hundreds of guests. Early strains of "Auld Lang Syne" cut through the butter already thick in the air, and they hadn't even started on the fresh apple crisp.

Jerry, a volunteer, had brought bushels of Rome apples from his upstate orchard, and with a little sugar, flour, butter, cinnamon and brown sugar, he created apple crisp after peeling the apples with a commercial peeler.

Percolators brewed hot coffee to welcome the guests, and stations were readied with hot and cold beverages. Volunteers climbed ladders to hang banners proclaiming *Happy New Year* and *Welcome*. Rick and Dr. Thompson, among others, placed live poinsettias donated by local florists on the tables and on the serving counter. Candy caught up with them as Dr. Thompson was telling Rick how lucky Rick was to have a fiancée like Brenda. "I had come close to getting engaged to a nurse once, but my work always seemed to take precedence, and the relationship fizzled." It hit Candy that it was Dr. Thompson who was lonely.

When the institutional hall had been warmed with color, flowers, and the aromas of bountiful food, Fritz invited her to open the doors with him and welcome the guests.

She had improvised a lower counter for the children to select their own food and chose that for her station. To a scoop of mashed potatoes, she added pea-eyes and julienned-carrot legs. "Me too, me too," implored the next children, so she placed the peas and carrots on each plate for them to create their own spiders.

After all the children were served, she stopped by Rick, who hadn't worn his uniform, as he conversed with a group of vets wearing WWII caps during his clean-up rounds. Then she stopped by Brenda, seated within a group of women eager to be heard, eager to share their stories of the plight that had led them here. They shared stories of choices that didn't seem ruinous when made but had proved otherwise. "Perhaps an article, even a series in the paper," Brenda said.

She searched for Fritz among the dwindling crowd to thank him for the rewarding experience. In the kitchen, the last spot she checked, she found him crumpled on the floor beside a hundred-quart stock pot. She snatched a clean serving spoon from the counter and knelt beside him, placing the spoon under his nose to check for breath. Nothing. She ran to Dr. Thompson, who stopped at the office to get the stethoscope from his black bag. "Nothing. Go to the office and call an ambulance while I try CPR." When she got back to them, Dr. Thompson sucked in his lips and shook his head.

She dropped to the floor near Fritz, sat, and held his hand. With his head in her lap, she stroked his gray hair, startled at how hard she sobbed at his loss, the loss of someone whom, until days ago, she hadn't seen in years.

CHAPTER 19

To Be or Not To Be

"Miss Krzyzanowski, 'F.' Come up to my desk to collect your worthless drivel." Professor Porcelet made a show of circling the "F" with his red marker and waved the paper in front of the class as Candy approached his desk. "Your paper was supposed to address the theme of revenge in *Hamlet*. You took it upon yourself to write on Hamlet's misogyny. What misogyny? Rewrite. 'C' will be the ceiling for the rewrite. Fail to redo, fail the course. And remember, med schools require one year of English."

She didn't tremble as she stood in front of the sea of snickering male classmates. "Misogyny is the truth of what I saw in the play." She faced him down and took the paper. "I'm sure the rest of the class expounded on the topic of revenge ad nauseum, and you were probably bored to death. I wanted to present something unique."

"Unique it was and unique you are. I hope you're doing better in your science classes, since you need so many more of them than English. Will you rewrite?" He squinted and pulled his cheeks back as he emphasized each word, baring his tobacco-stained teeth with each syllable.

Standing soldier-like she said, "I'll give you my answer tomorrow." When she returned to her seat, the professor followed her up the row to distribute the rest of the papers to the students' desks. The two other women in the class shook their heads and flashed sympathetic, maybe empathetic, looks. As the class went on to discuss the topic of revenge, she had difficulty concentrating, but raised her hand and dared to ask if she could present some of her ideas on Hamlet's misogyny, especially with regard to Ophelia and Hamlet's nunnery speech.

One of the boys said, "We don't want to be defiled with thoughts from an 'F' paper."

Only her first semester, but every day was some kind of battle. True, she brought this one on herself. She knew better than to bring attention to herself. She shouldn't have strayed from the assigned topic, but their reactions were disproportionate to her sin.

As class dispersed, she and the other women, Maria and Liz, huddled outside the classroom door. "Will you rewrite?" Maria asked.

"Probably not."

Liz reached for Candy's arm. "But he'll fail you. The men, professors and classmates, are against us at every turn. I find I have to compromise."

"If we can't get through a first-semester English class, how will we survive the tough science courses?" Maria asked. And I'm the only woman in all of my science classes. She put her heavy load of books on a windowsill. "It's not the coursework, it's the men's attitudes, not telling me about assignments, avoiding me at social events, even study groups. Your misogyny theory is on to something."

Some boys walking by their little group catcalled as they passed. "Like shooting fish in a barrel," one said.

"That's another thing. I dress as conservatively as I can," Liz said. She buttoned the top button of her shirt collar and pulled her oversized cardigan closed over her breasts.

"Me too. I hope I fade into the background in my dark clothes. I rarely show skin, and never a leg." Candy lifted a pantleg to her knee. "My skin would like to breathe. So would I. So much for halls of academic freedom. I don't see how I can rewrite the paper and be untrue to myself."

"What are the odds that all three of us will make it through to med school?" Maria asked.

"It depends on how badly we want in and want to be doctors," Liz said. "And how much of our dignity and scruples we're willing to sacrifice. It seems we're all getting the same treatment."

"These men get their strength from the deeply-mired conventions of centuries," Candy said. *Perhaps she should come to school in a long dress supported by a hoop or petticoats to make her point.* She put her heavy load of science texts next to Maria's. Wiping her sweaty hands along the sides of her black trousers, she said, "In organic chem, we learn that life forms are carbon-based and the compounds get their identity from their structure and valances. They are differentiated by their properties and uses. They aren't demeaned or limited." Her voice rose.

"We get the point," Liz said. "Let's not make a scene. I have to get to bio lab anyway." She split off from the group to be swallowed up by the sea of men.

Maria said she had to get to physics, and Candy headed for organic chem lab. She wished interactions among people could be as predictable as those among carbon compounds. The decision of what to do about the *Hamlet* paper weighed heavily as she juggled her options. What if she had to repeat the class with Porcelet? If she stayed strong this time, would she compromise her integrity the second time around?

CHAPTER 20

L'Air du Temps

Spirited winter winds snatched the pillbox hat from Brenda's head, flinging the millinery like a graduate tossing a mortarboard, releasing Brenda's long red waves to the elements. Having reached up for the hat a second too late as it separated from the hatpin securing it to her hair, she watched it spin away.

From the direction of the wayward headgear walked her fiancé, dress blues, peaked visor tucked between upper arm and coat, blond crewcut motionless. Still several car-lengths away, he strode toward her as she waited at the doors of Dothan Regional Airport in Alabama.

He had parked his Jeep at the far end of the curb where the hat bounced toward him; he reached down for it, as if reaching for a shell caught in an outgoing wave. Like Brenda, he missed it by a second. He checked with his fiancée. "Should I chase it?"

She shook her head and called out, "No." She gestured him her way, dropped her bag, and hurried toward him.

Rick sprinted. Lifting her off the ground, he whirled her in the air, like a dance partner, and her black Ferragamo flew from her foot. "It's a miracle you could make it with such short notice," he said. As he put her down, he clung to her, wound her hair around his palm behind her head, and kissed her with a kiss reminiscent of *Life*'s sailor and nurse in Times Square on V-J Day.

They had had few visits since the soup kitchen drama two years earlier. Both were caught up in their careers and separate lives. This was an opportunity to reconnect. He lifted her from her awkward position. And here she stood, minus her hat and one shoe. She wobbled on one foot. "I'd rather not let go of you, but please find my shoe."

"And your hat? I bet I can still track it down. It wasn't my intention to undress you on the sidewalk. But I do have something intimate in mind for tonight."

"I'm intrigued. And don't bother with the hat. It's an old style and nothing I need." She leaned against his arm. "I'm afraid we're creating a scene." The couple was now blocking passengers who had begun exiting the building.

"Let me get that shoe before it gets kicked away." He stepped off the curb to retrieve it.

Brenda steadied herself, the toes of her stockinged foot touching the sidewalk.

Rick recovered the shoe and knelt beside her. She lifted her foot and balanced with a hand on his shoulder as he slid the shoe on and skimmed his palm up her seamed silk stocking. He stood and sniffed her neck. "Your perfume even excites me in my dreams. I can't wait till we're alone together." He held her face in the palms of his hands. Then he took her bag with one hand and clasped her waist with the other as they walked toward the Jeep.

"We've been apart too long," she said, thirsty for the intimacy she had missed.

"I plan to remedy that with a romantic evening at the Dothan Grande. We'll be there in under an hour."

"We're not going to Fort Rucker?"

"Mother Rucker. Absolutely not. I want this night to be memorable." He stopped at the car and opened the door for her. "Would you like a boost up? Not the right car for a lady dressed like you. I should've rented something."

"I've got it." She slid her pencil skirt from her calf to her thigh and raised one leg to the running board, then hopped up.

"How'd I ever get so lucky?" Rick walked around to the driver's side and tossed her bag into the back on top of his. "Didn't feel like you packed much in there." He jumped up and pulled his door shut. He put the key in the ignition, disengaged the parking brake, floored the clutch, nudged the key, shifted from first, shook it into neutral, released the clutch while accelerating, shifted to first, hit the turn signal, checked his mirror, and pulled out.

She studied his movements. It had been years since she'd driven stick. Automatic was lazy. What if she needed to step in here and drive? "Clotheshorse or not, I know how to travel light. Didn't think I'd need much clothing for a long-awaited night together." She had been counting the days as Rick was nearing the end of a thirty-two-week, rotary-wing flight-training program at Fort Rucker, preparing for an eventual helicopter tour in Vietnam.

He stroked her windblown hair. "So, the hat. I thought a lady wasn't dressed without one."

"I'm ready to let go of hats entirely. I'm glad it blew away. I probably could've caught it myself. Here I am climbing up into a Jeep. And why would I need a hat on the plane? What was I thinking?" She shook her head and ran her fingers through her hair to let it down completely. "And I'm not sure I'm content being a 'lady,' with all the restrictions it implies." She reflected on the group in the Oval Office, with JFK signing the Equal Pay Act, five years ago now, all proper ladies with their hats, gloves, and handbags. Their paychecks still weren't equal to men's. "I'm a career woman. I need functional clothes, like slacks."

She stared at Rick, his blond hair framing the strong, square jaw of his profile — his blue eyes, his straight nose and high cheekbones — the quintessential knight-in-shining-armor. Physically, she was attracted to him, but she was beginning to see him as such a traditionalist. They had both made unspoken assumptions in their relationship, but their worlds were changing.

As they drove north from Airport Road, a monotonous route, past tracts of pines, stronger winds than those that had stolen Brenda's hat buffeted the Jeep.

"The feminists make a lot of good points," Brenda said, "things I never thought about, just accepted as written in stone, passed down generation to generation. But attitudes can change if there's a will strong enough to change them. I recently joined the National Organization for Women." Brenda studied Rick's face for a reaction from his perspective in a male-only club. She should whip out her notebook. Her awareness of societal issues provided a new prism through which to study her relationship with Rick. She wondered how he'd take to her evolving views.

"Does giving up hats have something to do with feminism?" Rick asked.

"Who cares about hats?"

"I don't, but it seemed important for you to abandon yours," he said. "Promise you won't abandon me." He brushed her cheek, but stared at the road. Then he set both hands on the wheel. "I'll do whatever it takes to make you happy."

"The women's movement has unearthed serious cultural issues and is kicking up a lot of dust," she said. She'd have to clarify her own thoughts. "Women don't have to trade their hats for their rights. For Bella Abzug, an ardent feminist, hats are practically a trademark. I'm finding hats cumbersome, my choice. I refuse to wear them just because society dictates that they are the mark of a lady."

The women's movement articulated what she knew instinctively. Women could choose their own paths, rejecting pre-determined roles. Day-to-day living benefited from critical thinking. Critical choices. The pill had been major. She wouldn't be forced into marriage, as generations of other women had been. She and Rick could choose. Women could find fulfillment in work and gain economic independence even if they weren't born into money, or if they didn't have a man to support them.

"I want to marry you because I want to be with you, but that doesn't mean I want to be a housewife. You understand that I'm invested in my career?" The car swerved. She held onto the seat with both hands.

A pine bough fell onto the car's hood. Rick jerked the steering wheel and knocked the branch off into the middle of the next lane. "I have to go back and move it." He drove the Jeep to a safe spot and walked back to push the branch out of the road.

When he got back, Brenda said, "Always thinking about others."

"Just doing the right thing," he said.

"Feels like a storm's coming. Do we have far to go?" She was more uneasy about the topic she had broached than she was concerned about falling branches.

"I fly Hueys." He faced her. "I could give you a lift and drag formula or discuss aerodynamic force. I'll keep you safe. Almost there." He reached over to caress her thigh. "I hope you haven't changed your mind about children."

She wanted to enjoy this rare visit. It might not be the time to continue talking about her career, nor had she felt comfortable discussing her interest in the budding women's rights movement during their frequent phone conversations. Should she leave her views unmentioned — like tampons?

She never hid her independent nature from Rick. Not many women were unmarried and financially independent at her age. She had even learned to successfully invest her income. And she was nurturing Candy, supporting her move into a male-dominated field. "We'll have to find a way to combine children, if any, and my career. Our mothers never had to," she said.

"Mom was an Army wife. She followed the general all over the world."

"I don't want to do that." Being an Army wife hadn't even occurred to her. She wanted to determine where and when she went. Maybe she had allowed her physical attraction to blind her to important choices she'd be making by default.

She had met Rick, four years ago, at Fort Wadsworth in Staten Island, where she was researching a story on the completion of the Verrazano Bridge and its impact on the base. As she walked from the visitors' center to one of the barracks, a German shepherd charged her, either mistaking her fur-trimmed glove for an actual rabbit, or, off the beaten path as she was, marking her as a trespasser. She always believed the former. The watchdog tore the glove from her hand, along with a chunk of skin, tendons, artery, and vein, requiring hours of surgery. Rick witnessed the event, too late to intervene, but he had rushed her, a stranger at the time, to the base hospital, his instinct to protect taking over. "I'll never forget how gallant you were the day we met." She touched his hand. "Seems like a long time ago."

"If there's love at first sight, you were it for me. I don't know how I managed to convince you to marry me." The wind gusted. The car veered. The traffic signals above the road ahead shook. "Let me have your hand."

"I don't need rescuing right now. Pull over whenever you can."

With few cars on the road, Rick pulled to the shoulder, stopped, depressed the clutch, put it in first, and engaged the parking brake. "We're fifteen minutes away. What's wrong?"

Brenda unlocked her door, opened it slightly, and paused to consider Rick. "We're switching places."

"What the—" Rick said. Brenda was standing at his door. He opened it and scrambled to the passenger seat.

She boosted herself into the driver's seat. "I don't want you to think I'm afraid, or that you have to rescue me. I want to be an equal partner in this relationship."

"Your car's an automatic," he said. "Can you drive a stick?"

"Dad had a blue Olds '88, his pride and joy. Taught me to drive it. I watched you for a refresher. You can be my navigator. We'll get there together."

"I have been away too long."

"Very true," she said. Helicopter training had been intense. The war was intensifying, as were the protests. She was no stranger to the truth. She held the steering wheel with one hand and squeezed his hand with the other before wielding her Ferragamos to command the clutch, the brake, and the accelerator. "I'll get us to the Grande."

"It's time we set a wedding date, unless you've changed your mind," he said.

"I love you. I want you to be my partner, equals." At the intersection, she slowed the car to a stop with only a slight jerk. "I thought the wedding date may have been behind your urgent invitation. I'm not complaining about flying down. I couldn't be happier, but we could have discussed dates on the phone."

He squirmed in the passenger seat, fumbled in his pocket, pulled out his lucky rabbit's foot, and rubbed it. "Beauty, brains, and spirit. Keep your autonomy." He crossed and uncrossed his legs. He searched the glove compartment, pulled out a crushed pack of Lucky Strikes and shook one out. He groped for matches, found a cigarette lighter, and flicked it.

"Make a right at the next stop sign, then a right onto Resort Road. The place is almost four hundred acres on the lakefront. You can't miss it. I booked one of the private cottages."

She made the right and drove about a mile along a live-oak-lined lane, stopping in front of the hotel.

The valet came around and opened her door. "Welcome, 'er, ma'am."

Brenda engaged the emergency brake and reached behind her seat for her overnighter. Rick snuffed out his cigarette and got his duffle. He didn't offer to take her bag. She thanked the valet, tipped him, and walked in front of the car to meet Rick on the sidewalk.

CHAPTER 21

Tête à Tet

"Welcome to the Dothan Grande." The concierge took Rick Dean's name and searched a file box for the reservation. "The special," she said, then tore a map from a pad. Circling cottage six on the sheet, she showed Rick the map and drew a line from a lobby exit to the cottage. "Prepared, per your request." When she offered the key, Brenda swooped it up along with the map.

She read the nametag on the clerk's lapel. "Thank you, Lyza. I'm anxious to see this place."

Rick reached for his duffle and motioned toward Brenda's. "May I? We have a long walk."

"I'll ask if I need help." Determined to force Rick to accept her independence, she said, "I'll lead the way." As she risked finding his breaking point, she checked herself. Was she subconsciously trying to cause a break-up? "There's horseback riding, archery, golf, tennis, swimming, hiking, fishing. I didn't pack for any of it. Don't keep things from me."

"The weather's not cooperating anyway." He moved his bag to his other hand and held her around the waist. "I wasn't focused on the amenities when I booked, just time alone with you." As they walked, he unbuttoned his jacket.

Brenda pushed the exit door open to a paved path bound by budding azaleas, fading camellias, fragrant pansies and snapdragons. They followed the walkway around a fountain to a cul-de-sac. Number six was a cottage with a front porch. "Makes me nostalgic for my old Staten Island bungalow." She was about to insert the key.

Rick intercepted it and dropped his bag. "I'll get it, and allow me to carry you over the threshold."

"That old tradition." She laughed. "Pretending to kidnap the bride so I'll have an alibi for losing my chastity? It's a little late, and I'm not the bride yet."

"You never know what evil lurks at a threshold." He kissed her cheek. "I'm a big believer in tradition, and a bit superstitious."

Despite her protest, he lifted her. As he hoisted her, she relaxed into his body. "You'll always be chivalrous, and I'll always be countering to stand on my own."

Although she had been drifting away from following traditional female roles, he had remained anchored in testosterone. The rift between them was not only one of distance and time. Though he was thoughtful and madly in love with her, she had begun to doubt that marriage lay in their future. When could she speak up?

Rick carried her in backwards, so she couldn't immediately see the surprise, then spun her around to a darkened room with curtains drawn, the focal point the fire lit in the stone fireplace. A hundred candles glowed throughout the room.

The flickering light accentuated dozens of lilies. Their intense fragrance, along with the piano notes of "Claire de Lune" playing on the turntable, flooded her senses. She looked up from Rick's shoulder and they savored a long kiss.

"I wanted our night to be magical." With her still in his arms, he walked towards the fireplace, then let her down.

"I'm overwhelmed," she said. He had put a great deal of thought into planning this, and sex wasn't his only endgame. Even without the romantic setting, she was strongly attracted to him, physically, and he knew it. And they were engaged. Was there a common ground they could negotiate? Should she continue to drop hints or stifle herself? He had put real effort into planning a romantic weekend. She kicked off her heels and massaged her feet.

"I'm glad it makes you happy. You were a bit tense in the car." He sat beside her, buried his face in her hair, and kissed the back of her neck. He moved to her ear, the tip of his tongue tracing its interior curves, finding its way to the orifice. He reached under her bra to caress her breasts.

He was hard to resist, but she put her hands over his, then stood and adjusted her bra. "I need a minute."

But, with her in front of him, he undid her garters, peeled the stockings down her legs, slid them, one at a time, from her feet, then reached behind to remove her garter belt.

As difficult as it was, she twisted away. "We really have to talk."

"We really do, but let's enjoy these rare moments first." He took the bottle of champagne from the bucket beside the sofa and wrapped the folded white napkin around its neck.

She took hold of the bottle, ran her painted thumbnail across the foil, undid the muselet covering the cork, and wiggled it until it popped off, releasing foam that dripped over the top of the bottle into the napkin. She poured the champagne into the flutes Rick held. This didn't exactly suit her plan, but it gave her breathing space to delay sex, which she both wanted and didn't. Although they saw each other infrequently, she was glad she was on the pill, for spontaneity's sake.

"This wasn't exactly as I planned it," Rick said, "but let's toast to a winter wedding."

"We are setting a date?" She put her glass on the table and rubbed her thighs with long strokes.

"I picture you in a gown trimmed with the fur that was on those gloves that brought us together."

"Rabbit? I'm surprised you remember that. We really have to talk."

"Any white fur you like, then. I should be back by January."

"Back? From where?"

"I've been avoiding this conversation since the airport," he said. "My graduation and swearing-in ceremonies have been pushed up to tomorrow."

"You could have told me that's why you asked me to fly down."

"I wanted to surprise you." He poured them both more champagne. "Would you do me the honor of accompanying me to the ceremony and pinning the bars and wings on the newly-minted Chief Dean?"

"I'd be honored, but you really didn't have to keep me in suspense." Relieved to hear the news, she raised her glass to him, then put it on the coffee table and kissed him. "There's something else, isn't there?" She studied his face, stared into his eyes. "They're sending you somewhere. I trust you to tell me the whole truth."

His cheeks reddened and he loosened his collar. "Tonight's my last night in the States. I got details from my father, unlike the general to reveal sensitive info, so it's not for the record."

She wasn't sure she was prepared for the whole truth.

"The scuttlebutt is that General Giap, the North Vietnamese, and Viet Cong violated the Tet Lunar cease-fire when they launched a wave of surprise attacks. Westmoreland has been holding Khe Sanh but thinks the battle may have been a diversion." He reached for both her hands and held them tight. His were sweaty.

Tears welled up in her eyes. The dreaded moment had finally come, and just when she was wavering on their relationship.

"My unit is being sent to support the Marines there. I'm off to the 21st Replacement Station in Long Bin." His grip on her hands tightened.

"Tonight's leave is shorter than the traditionally too-short leaves prior to departure for 'Nam. Tomorrow, after the ceremonies, I deploy. I couldn't tell you on the phone. I wanted tonight to be special. I don't want to lose you."

She had closely followed the Vietnam War. She knew what she had signed up for with Rick. She had guessed he'd be deployed soon, without accepting the reality. She expected she'd have more notice. Pangs of guilt ran up her spine. "I heard rumors about an escalation." They locked onto each other. Knowing he had no control over deployment, she stifled her tears and any overemotional reaction, not wanting to add to his distress. They were parting, but he was the one flying into danger. She pulled away and lowered her head to her knees.

He brushed her long, red hair from her eyes and pulled her close. "When my tour's over, I promise I'll leave the Army. I won't be a career man like my father. You won't have to be an Army wife. I can get a job flying in the private sector, even in the New York area. We'll have one home. We won't move twenty-seven times like my parents did."

At a loss for words, she gasped. Although she was edging toward breaking off the engagement, circumstances had changed.

"One more thing," he said. "I want to give you this talisman, a rabbit's foot." He opened her hand and placed it there, closing her fingers around it. "It's the one my father gave me before he left for WWII. I was only eight, but I've held onto it. The general said it was 'the left-hind foot of a graveyard rabbit killed in the dark of the new moon,' and it was his promise to come home. He did. I will."

"How can I take this?" He was thinking of them as family, just as she was focusing on their insurmountable differences. In return for his parting gesture, she could return his ring, or give him the stopper from the perfume he loved, her L'Air du Temps bottle — a pair of entwined doves, symbol of peace and life-long loyalty.

"You give me something to fight for, a reason to come home," he said. He stared into her eyes.

She kissed him and got up to get her purse.

"I have to say this," he said. "It's perhaps the hardest thing I've ever said. You deserve a full and beautiful life, not one contingent on my choices, on my green Army blood." He got up and followed her. He turned her around to face him. "If I don't make it back, mourn me and move on."

He held her head with both hands, and she pressed her forehead against his. There the pair stood, arms wrapped around each other, even as the record finished and skipped, and skipped....

CHAPTER 22

Gross Anatomy

Mi. *Mi.* Two monolithic E-flat major chords penetrated the darkness and the silence of the auditorium filled to capacity. The shafts of sound introduced *Eroica, Beethoven's Symphony No. 3 in E-Flat Major.*

The students had settled into their seats in the lecture hall this first session of class before the space had gone black and the music began. After the second chord, a spotlight illuminated the lectern, which Professor Schweinfurt approached from behind, baton in his right hand, a sheaf of notes in the left.

The white mass of unkempt hair, and of his shirt and French cuffs, accentuated by the beam of light, rendered him incorporeal, his black cutaway receding into the darkness. As he lifted the baton cocked between his finger and thumb, the movement of his right arm cut into the music. Simultaneously, he raised his left hand, as though leading an orchestra.

Aiming the baton left, right, and center, in syncopation with the booming music, he commanded the lights of each section be turned on, thus pulling all of the auditorium to join him in illumination.

The music tapered to a background throbbing over which he delivered his lecture in a dominating bass voice. "We are here to study science, but what is science without music and art to inform it? No doubt you recognize *Eroica*, Beethoven's tribute to Napoleon. Eventually, his hero disappointed Beethoven when he intercepted the crown Pope Pius VII was about to hand him and declared himself emperor. Still, historians have linked the two, saying, 'What Napoleon did for society, Beethoven did for music. Both turned tradition on its head.'"

Candy worried where the misogynist was going with this line of thinking, but she was relieved that at least he wasn't discussing women. Perhaps he'd ignore her, rather than batting her around like a cat toying with a mouse. She settled into her seat. She had had no contact with him since the interview. She hoped he'd forgotten about her.

"Miss Candy Krzyzanowski, the one female in our anatomy class this semester, wants to develop her potential, exercise her freedom, transform tradition, and once more penetrate the gender barrier for women. She is one more female, trickling in among us males, who believes herself to be as smart as men, as she aspires to join a man's profession. Or does she wish to meet a husband among the many available men in the class?" He paused and waved the baton across the room, spreading laughter this time, rather than light.

She had relaxed too soon. Leaning forward in her seat, her fingers clawed into its burgundy fabric.

"We shall see if she's hero, or heroine, or a mere disappointment, as Napoleon ultimately was. Beethoven's *Third* inspires, and it is my introduction to the serious study of anatomy. In this course, we will dissect cadavers, study specimens and study each other, hands on. There will be days when you will not be able to scrub off the stench of formaldehyde despite the gloves and lab coats. These will be your petty sacrifices to a heroic profession. The courageous individuals who have donated their bodies to science have made the momentous sacrifices."

Professor Schweinfurt used his baton, body movements, and facial expressions to emphasize his words, again pointing to sections of the lecture hall — all the while holding her in his mesmerizing gaze. Enraptured by the professor's performance, the men, too, focused on her.

"In honor of our female companion, we will commence our studies with the female human reproductive system, the most important system, the reason women should stay in the home, to continue the human race." The lights dimmed. He clicked the slide carousel and flashed Gustave Courbet's 1866 *Origin of the World* on the screen. It elicited some gasps, but many more twitters.

"Those of you who eventually succeed in becoming doctors will deal with all aspects of the human body, in and out, flesh, bone, fluids, waste. You will examine naked patients, withholding your gasps and twitters."

She had seen nudes, but never one as revealing as this. Courbet's oil depicted a vulva. The painting was a life-size close-up of the lower torso of a woman reclining among the folds of a white sheet, shocking in that the model's legs were spread and nothing but her genitals, abdomen, and part of her right breast were visible — no head, no face, no shame.

She had emitted one of the audible gasps, and she squirmed in her seat. She had taken Schweinfurt's bait. She had always been subjected to small acts of discrimination. Her years with the nuns had actually strengthened her against the cruelty. And she knew better than to report the slights and abuse. Since her first day in the pre-med program, she had endured marginalization, humiliation, and isolation: Male doctors and fellow students pushed her aside; they hid meetings and classes from her; they stole her notes and instruments; they stained her lab coat with blood, placed to resemble a menstrual mishap; one professor hit her hand with a retractor while she performed a lab procedure; they kept her from joining study groups. But nothing had ever been this elaborate. The baton nailed her. Embedded in this hall of men, this theater, she experienced a public confrontation with in-your-face female genitalia, ten, or a hundred times, actual size.

"This painting is realistic," the professor continued. "It is not romanticized or shrouded in surrealism or mythology. It depicts the double-doors to life, the labia majora, the portion of the vulva protecting the opening to the uterus, the vulval vestibule, the introitus. Contrary to popular thought, the vagina is internal and not visible. This mons pubis is not shaved. This realism doesn't lie. The vulva, also known as the pudendum, literally means 'shameful thing.' Do you feel shame, Miss Krzyzanowski?"

This time, she held her gasp and held his stare. She'd withstand this onslaught.

Professor Schweinfurt advanced the carousel to the next slide, Sandro Botticelli's 1485 *Birth of Venus*. "In many artistic depictions, even Venus is shamed and covers her pudendum — like Eve with a fig leaf — with a hand or with long hair, as in this life-size nude. This female is not a Madonna, but a naked goddess, a statue on the verge of becoming human, an image of fragile virginity at the threshold of becoming a wife. Venus, venom. The fecund spring winds, the entwined couple, Zephyr and Chloris, in the upper left corner, blow Venus past the phallic brown rushes in the foreground, some of which lightly graze the white Vs, vulvas, on the translucent blue sea, while other rushes visibly penetrate the white waves.

"White roses, tinged pink with blood, float in the air. The scallop shell carrying Venus to shore has been a symbol of fertility since pre-historic times. An attendant, one of the Horae, clothed in rich robes, waits on shore with a billowing pink cloak, embroidered with floral representations of love and sex, including the clitoris which is represented by myrtle leaves. Venus cannot enter society naked. The cloak will enclose her uncovered body. Society has rules, Miss Krzyzanowski."

As much as she wanted to get up and leave, she forced herself to remain seated, hoping to make less of a spectacle of herself.

The professor pointed his baton at the painting where the handmaiden's right hand held the corner of the pink cloak in a loop. "She's holding the garment as I'm holding my baton, between thumb and index finger, creating not the realistic vulva of Courbet, but the secret image of a pink vulva. When Venus steps onto shore, she will enter the world of procreation and reproduction, the world where women belong."

The music stopped. The slides went dark. "Learn the female reproductive system, exterior, interior, nerves, veins, vessels, glands, bones, all of it. Next session in the lab, we will have specimens in formaldehyde and cadavers for dissection and prosection. I will distribute the syllabus and list of texts, your thousands of pages of readings. I must admit, I've never delivered such a theatrical first lecture. I'm now open to a Q and A session, and after you all leave, I'd like Miss Krzyzanowski to please remain behind."

At the end of the hour, the students filed out of the theater. Her sweater was wet with sweat. Thoughts of previous painful experiences spun in her brain like bits of glass in a kaleidoscope. Was today's the worst humiliation she'd face? It was a price she'd pay for the privilege of becoming another female doctor. She had read stories of the true pioneer female doctors. Society had exacted a heavy toll from them. They paved the way. She was no pioneer. It was 1968. She had believed times had changed.

Should she choose not to stay behind after everyone left? Slip out among the hundreds of male students? With her deep training in being submissive, obedient to elders, to those in authority, she walked to the far aisle along the edge of the auditorium. "You wanted to see me," she said. She walked up the stairs to where the professor was standing at the lectern on the stage.

Not giving her his full attention, he assembled his notes, striking the bottom edge of the stack on the wood surface to assemble a neat sheaf which he fastened, then placed in his briefcase. "I think you may wish to absent yourself next few sessions as this unit, the female reproductive system, may be too vulgar for the delicate female mind."

"The delicate female mind." That line, she had read, had been used on female med students in the distant past. Dressed all in black, she wished to recede into the background, but wrestled the impulse, raised her chin and scowled into his gray eyes. "I want to learn everything," she said, her bladder on the verge of release.

He showed her his back while he placed the extra syllabi into a carton under the table that held the slide carousel. "Do you, really?" He stepped down from the stage and headed to the rear of the theater where he padlocked the doors of the empty auditorium. He lumbered back to the stage.

She had time to escape, at least backstage. *Run.* Did he have something to teach her? Why weren't her feet taking her away? Was she trying to be polite, nice, liked, obedient?

He walked back up the steps back to the stage and faced her, giving her his full attention. He pointed his finger close to her face. "I will break you, and you will leave this honorable institution. Now, undress, everything, exactly like the paintings, and stand on the table. We'll see how heroic you are."

Every synapse in her brain fired. *Flee.* She could report him to the dean, or first, consult Dr. Thompson. She stood behind the lectern and removed everything but her white cotton bra and white cotton panties. She couldn't betray the support of Dr. Thompson, Brenda, Rick, or the commitment to herself. She hadn't noticed the chill of the air conditioning until now. She reached to the floor for the clothes she had dropped.

"Move out here." He pointed to the table with the baton. "Trying to be modest? There is no modesty in medicine. Doctors heal the body. Doctors see the body. They touch, smell, and listen to the body. How would you handle a naked male patient, or a female, for that matter, give an enema, check for venereal disease, check the prostate or the colon, with only a glove between you and the patient? Have you thought about the realities of the profession? Could you do it? Medicine is not book learning and theory. It's hands-on, examining, palpating. Now stand up on that table. Remove that childish underwear. Do you think I haven't seen a naked girl? We'll see how innocent you are."

She did as she was told, placing her left arm across her chest and her right hand over her mons pubis. She knew — felt — why the model in the Courbet painting had obliterated her identity, why Venus covered her mons pubis with her long hair. She clenched her jaw as her left hand clenched her Janus necklace. As if praying, she whispered, "As I prepare for this noble profession, I will be purged of my inhibitions and past damage. I can do this. If Simonetta could stand naked as Venus for five hundred years, I can do this."

"Did you say something?" Professor Schweinfurt asked. He picked up his baton from the lectern and approached her. "Ah, that's better. What's so difficult about being naked?" He stood below and directly in front of her, clothed in his three-piece tuxedo.

On the verge of one loud scream, she couldn't find her voice. She closed her eyes and transported herself elsewhere.

"I will come closer, and as I use the baton to point to parts of the exterior female reproductive system, I want you to name them."

He held the baton straight out, an extension of his arm, while she secretly wished the baton were longer than its twelve inches, to keep him farther from her. She wanted to jump off the table and run.

Tap. "Mons pubis."

Tap. "Pudendal cleft."

Tap. "Labia majora."

Tap. "Labia minora."

Tap. "Clitoral hood."

Tap. "Vulval vestibule."

Tap. "Perineum."

After the final tap, he struck the baton against the table, left it there, and removed a cigar from his vest pocket. Cigar between his lips, about to light it, he asked, "The abdominal scar, an abortion gone wrong, a Caesarean? You're not married, are you? Is all this false modesty a charade? But kudos for reading ahead in your text, or for paying attention during the lecture, a quick study."

He lit his cigar and puffed smoke her way, unburying in her a memory of Ladies First.

"For our first session in the lab, we have one prosection, a partially dissected female cadaver, an unusual specimen. A young woman who died during an abortion, illegal, of course. Parts of the fetus remain in utero. Get dressed. This is the course that separates the men from the boys and perhaps, the men from the girls as well. I have a whole semester to break you."

She glowered. "You will not deter me." *Two more years of this.*

"I have broken many."

CHAPTER 23

See Change

Shattered. Trembling. She lowered herself from the table, gathered her clothes and, shrouded by the heavy mahogany lectern, dressed behind it — although the professor, having moved on, never glanced back. Alternately puffing his cigar and jingling his keys in one hand, and carrying his briefcase in the other, his sinister shadow strode away toward the auditorium exit. He released the padlock, killed the lights, and disappeared, the theater once again plunged into darkness.

At the disappearance of the professor in the distance, and the slamming of the doors, she released her emotions and let loose with a scream of rage and pain and tears at the emotional cuts he had inflicted. The scream echoed in the vast auditorium, but was soon absorbed by the velvet stage curtains, the fabric seats, and the wall coverings. She groped for her belongings then followed the aisle to the back of the auditorium where a shard of daylight penetrated the crack between the double-doors. She pushed through them in a daze. *What had she done?*

Resolved to cutting organic chem and physiology, she walked around groups of students, ignored their comments about her straggly hair and disheveled clothes, focused on the travertine floor, and followed her faltering feet toward the exit, anxious to leave the campus and flee to the safety of Brenda's apartment and solitude.

"Miss K," a male voice called above the engulfing noise. A man, thirty-ish, left his books on a bench and jumped up to meet her. "Please, wait." When she didn't pause, he pursued. "I hoped I'd catch you. We're in the same anatomy class." He extended his hand, although she never looked up at him through the hair covering her eyes. "I'm Jonathan."

"Get out of my way," she said. When his fingers brushed her forearm, she flicked her hair aside to deliver a stare that screeched, "Don't touch me."

"Sorry." He pulled back and stepped away. "I can see how you'd be upset after that lecture. Hell, I'm upset." He continued after her, then jumped in front of her, causing her to gasp and lean back. "The professor's singling you out, ridiculing you, was inexcusable, deplorable. I don't see how any of those men could have laughed. I could understand if you're reluctant to report it, but I just wanted you to know that I intend to."

Her hand on the push bar, she stopped at the door. "Don't make trouble for either of us." Students jostled by.

Jonathan returned to his bench and books, beckoning her to follow him.

She jumped out of the students' way. "Don't."

"Too late."

With little strength to resist him or the oncoming crowd, she steered herself to safety between Jonathan's bench and the window. "You don't even know me, and you've ruined me." As though she weren't sick enough before, her head throbbed while her brain anticipated the flurry of events that would put her on trial. *"See what happens when we admit a delicate female. See what females incite. Off with her head. Out she goes. We dodged another bullet."* A wave of nausea overtook her.

He drew a book from his pile. "While you were behind closed doors with the professor, I also went to the lab and picked up your manual." Careful not to touch her, he added it to the books balanced on her arm. "We're in the same group with two others."

Anxious to find safety, she swatted the book to the floor and ran for the door.

He picked up the manual and his books and chased after her. "I want to help. Let me walk you wherever you're going, or we can go for coffee."

"You've done too much already." She covered her mouth, fumbled with her books and made her way through the rotating doors out to the sidewalk without him, relieved, however, for his sliver of compassion, and now, for fresh air. Though he had ruined everything, she shouldn't have been so brusque with — Jonathan. The blood in her body having risen like mercury in a thermometer was now covering her eyes; she was walking blind.

Grateful to find the apartment quiet, empty, she didn't expect Brenda back from her visit with Rick until late that night. Relieved, she didn't want to, couldn't, talk. Was this a shortcoming? Was she too humiliated, embarrassed, weak? Did other people talk about such attacks? Jonathan wanted to talk about the lecture. Hundreds of students had been present, but the lecture was nothing compared to Schweinfurt's actions which, of course, no one had witnessed. What did Jonathan want from her? She didn't know him, but she knew she didn't trust him.

Now to rip off her black turtleneck and pants, her white cotton underwear; to stand in a hot shower, scrub her skin with a bar of Lifebuoy until the soap faded to a red splinter; to soak in a tub of scalding water; to take her clothes to the basement and feed them to the agitator of a washing machine — all of which she did over the course of a couple of hours, followed with a pot of chamomile tea and a stab at a nap.

Unable to surrender to sleep, she resorted to her old standby, crocheting. With her supplies assembled, she curled up on the sofa in an ankle-length chenille robe, drawn tight around her neck, and wool socks.

Despite her perturbed state of mind, her stitches were tight. Her jaw was clenched. She wanted to keep from unraveling. As Nana had taught her, she didn't want to leave spaces in the design — no openings for evil to enter, she now considered. She focused. A thought of Wayne floated through. Tighter.

She wouldn't say much to Brenda, who would be gratingly happy — not that she begrudged her — having spent time with Rick. She resolved to cope, deal with this herself, continue class as if nothing had happened, take refuge in the work. How could she report something she had gone along with? Tighter stitches. Leave no spaces. No floppy motifs. Tight. Tight. Weave.

The whistling tea kettle roused her. The kitchen clock read 5:35, morning, but still dark. Having fallen asleep on the sofa, she woke to see Brenda slumped against the stove, one hand flat on the counter, whisk in the other extending from the kimono sleeve of her black satin robe. "I didn't hear you come in last night," she said. "What's wrong?"

"I didn't want to wake you, so I removed your crocheting and covered you," Brenda said. "Yesterday must have been a long day for you."

She threw off the blanket, cinched the belt of her robe, and shuffled to the kitchen table. "It's like the hospital all over again. I can't begin to tell you." She put her elbows on the table and dropped the full weight of her head into her hands.

"Talk to me." Brenda lifted the tea kettle from the stove and placed it on a trivet on the Formica counter. "I was daydreaming when I should've been watching the kettle." She extinguished the teapot's burner, and the flame under the frying pan, and poured water into her mug. "Would you like a cup of dandelion tea?"

"Sure. Looks like you need to talk."

Brenda pulled another mug from under the cabinet and brought both over, one yellow, one blue. Both read, "A woman is like a tea bag; you never know how strong she is until she gets into hot water — Eleanor Roosevelt."

"I wouldn't mind talking," Brenda said, "if you're up to it. I have a late interview today, so no rush."

She clasped the hot cup with both hands. With closed eyes, she leaned forward to steep her face in the dandelion steam. "I thought you'd be happy today, after your time with Rick."

Brenda bit her lip and shook her head. "Rick had arranged a romantic visit, but, for almost an entire day, refrained from telling me he had his orders. He's already left for Vietnam. It'll probably be a year before he's home. I knew this was coming. But you, I can tell you're troubled." Brenda got up, then carried the teakettle and trivet to the table.

The hot tea burned Candy's throat. At least she felt something. She poured more. "I'm sorry about Rick." Her hand on top of Brenda's, she said, "It'll be just one more long separation." *A feckless platitude. Rick could die.* In seeking to comfort Brenda, who had never needed comforting before, her own pain seemed like nothing.

"That's what Rick said. And he gave me his father's lucky rabbit's foot to assure me he'd be back. Enough of me. Don't be evasive. What's happening? I can hardly count the number of granny squares you crocheted and dropped in front of the sofa last night. We could use a few afghans around here. Why don't you start sewing the motifs together? Make them into something useful."

"I can't quite put it all together yet." She wasn't thinking about the squares, but about her experiences, her choices, her strength, or lack of it, her life.

"Are those pre-med men still harassing you, or is it the course work this semester?" Brenda poured her second cup of tea.

"The misogynist professor from the panel. He's teaching my anatomy class, and the intimidation has escalated."

"I was hoping you'd seen the last of that bastard."

"After nearly two years, you'd think they'd be used to the few women in the program. They're so threatened. Turns out I'm the only female in anatomy. Some days I have to reconsider if it's worth it. No need to discuss it. I won't tell Dr. Thompson either, or the dean. I'll face the consequences tomorrow. But I'll be the best student in class." She spoke without pausing. Her words were brave, but her glance into the hall mirror across from her reflected an unnerved expression, belying her resolve. "I fear I'm drowning in the hot water of this gender tempest."

"You do have the option of dropping out."

She saw through Brenda's strategy, raising a red flag for her to fight. She was up to the work, loved it in fact. "I won't let a few boors take me down," she said, "but I'm in need of a paradigm shift."

"You're right. You don't socialize with your peers, do you? Perhaps I should have encouraged you to do so from the very beginning. You do realize you can bring friends to the apartment, study here?"

"I've become more awkward with people. I don't trust them, or myself, anymore. I can't afford to get hurt again." Although she had been sheltered, she had taken strength from her ancient family connection. And she had had a few good friends in high school, and always Brenda, and confidence in her studies, to make her feel comfortable in the world, to rest assured there was terra firma beneath her when she ventured out, that she was on solid ground with each step forward — until Wayne.

He opened the flood gates. Now Schweinfurt. She had to keep herself from being sucked into this maelstrom. Keep from drowning. For almost two years, she had been guarded — behind her books, within her silence, under her dark clothes, hoping to fade into the background, escaping the notice of this sea of men, but Schweinfurt had lain her bare. "You're right. I have to make friends, besides the couple of women I occasionally commiserate with, and I know where to start."

"I've never pressed you for details on what happened before the hospital, but I wish I could get you to open up about whatever happened yesterday."

"I can't right now." She did, however, tell Brenda about Jonathan, and Brenda suggested she befriend him, make him an ally, invite him to Reggio for coffee before he asked; propose studying together since they were in the same lab group.

"Helping you, doing something I can control, will take my focus away from things I can't control," Brenda said. "Let's see if I can help a little by conjuring up a sea change," Brenda said, "and transform you 'into something rich and strange' to take your rightful place among the men." She raised her hands in her black kimono, giving herself the appearance of a wizard.

"As the only female in class, I'm strange enough, but I need something. What are you thinking?" After Brenda cleared the table and placed the cups and used frying pan in the sink, Candy said, "I'll clean up."

"When you're finished, I'll be ready for you in my room. Decide what you want, how you want to face the day, how you want others to see you. Not to make light of what's troubling you, but a quick fix might be a good start."

She washed the mugs. Her hands covered in suds, she paused. What did she want? To be perceived differently. To be stronger. To gain respect. To make friends. To become a doctor. To help people. She dried the clean items and put them away.

In the bedroom, Brenda had already removed her museum postcard of Botticelli's *Fortitude* from the side of her bureau mirror and handed it to Candy. "Some inspiration. *Fortitude*. Unlike most richly-robed female Renaissance figures, this young woman wears a breastplate over her sumptuous fabrics, metal coverings on her forearms, and holds a scepter across her lap. Prepared for battle, prepared to rule, the picture of confidence, calm, fortitude, she motivates me when I charge into a man's world."

True to Renaissance art, her features were delicate, belying the strength and potential beneath; she appeared ready to pounce from her seated pose. "She could motivate me too."

"Dressed as society expects a lady to dress," Brenda said, "I wear a sheathing of confidence and catch many subjects off-guard. They don't expect my incisive questions. They see a woman concerned about clothes as shallow. But I'm giving up hats, by the way." Brenda selected some items from her closet and draped them over her arm.

"We're starting with clothes, really?" *That was where the gods started when Venus floated to shore, with the billowing pink robe.*

"Yes, your wardrobe." In Candy's room, Brenda opened the closet. Hung from the cuffs on skirt hangers were several pairs of dark pants, most navy and black, both winter and summer weight, and a few dark A-line skirts. In her drawers were also a few deep-colored turtlenecks — blue, grey, plum, ruby the same in button-down shirts, and pullover and cardigan sweaters.

"I never noticed how monotone your wardrobe is. I guess shunning the light is your way of shielding yourself. What if we try something different? Move from defense to offense. Are you game?"

"Yes, new clothing, the antidote to nudity." Her dark clothes hadn't hidden her from Schweinfurt. Years ago, her prized dress hadn't helped her influence Wayne. But Brenda's clothes, like her perfume, were her signature. It couldn't hurt to accept her advice.

"What was that about nudity?" Brenda pushed the clothes to one side of the closet.

"Nothing." She again tightened the belt of her robe.

"Those men are making light of you," Brenda said, "and you're going to go along with it, hiding. Step out. Be bold. Here's another Rooseveltism: 'No one can make you feel inferior without your consent.' You are not going to cower and consent. Follow me."

If only she knew.

Brenda dropped her armful of clothes on the bed and handed her a string of pearls. "Wear these today." Then she picked an azure dress and jacket from the pile. "And these. You still have heels?" Brenda urged Candy to borrow her clothes to mix with her own, or use on their own, anything she would be comfortable in since it would be a drastic change in style for her, which was Brenda's point, for her to stand out, to play offense, to oppose their chauvinism.

She took the pearls and dress from Brenda. Leave it to Brenda to work in *The Tempest*: pearls that were eyes; dress the color of the sea. These times, as well as their personal experiences right now, were tempestuous. She'd have to summon practical, not magical, solutions. Brenda's solution might help, short term, if she hadn't already been expelled.

Schweinfurt had put her into the spotlight, and now she'd answer by making herself stand out in the group, at least until she donned her unisex lab coat. When she thanked Brenda, she warned her about the stench of formaldehyde, which might attach to the clothes. Brenda dismissed that as a problem for the dry cleaner. Candy felt she could attend class this morning, face down Schweinfurt yet again, and perhaps, gather the courage to approach Jonathan. She hung the outfit in her closet and laid the pearls on her bureau atop *Fortitude*.

As Brenda left her room to shower and prepare for her workday, she said, "I landed a plum sports assignment, rare for a woman, hence my earlier sports allusion."

"Defense, offense. Not your typical diction. I caught it."

"I'm off to Shea Stadium today. I finally got an interview with Wayne Woods. I was afraid the star quarterback would cancel when I asked for a postponement to visit Rick, but Woods was okay with it, and quite charming, over the phone at least." She stepped out of the bathroom, passed Candy's room, and poked her head in. "In my research I discovered that Woods is from Staten Island where he played college ball. Did you know him?"

The parachute drop. The roller coaster. Her stomach fell. She went numb. "You know I don't follow football, college or pro," Candy said. "I didn't know him."

CHAPTER 24

Surren-dipity

On a sub-zero February afternoon in Central Park, a couple, facing the icy whiteness of Wollman Rink, laced up their rental figure skates. Finger tips clumsy and turning blue, she crossed the laces and looped them around the eyelets, pulling tightly all the way up for a snug fit toe to top.

The swarm of skaters already populating the ice were a blur of color, like the dots of an impressionist painting. Children and adults skated, some exhibiting more skill than others in avoiding collisions and falls. It might be mortifying to enter the arena with the children, skating at their level, since she was years out of practice. But perhaps it was exactly what she wanted, what she needed, in fact: to be among children; to capture their innocence and lack of inhibitions (true, they were closer to the ground with less danger in a fall, less fear of falling, in fact, and less experience with falls — and pain). She lusted to fly into the face of the biting wind, and, with the perspective of an adult who knew the dangers, to surrender to the fear and do it anyway.

Images of the countless happy hours she had spent as a child came rushing back, learning, and then acquiring proficiency, in figure skating with spins, twirls, and figure-eights — following Brenda, exquisite on the ice, her long red hair flying with her speed into the wind. To again hear the crunch of the steel against the glassy ice, the swirl of voices in the air, to feel the breeze of the forms rushing past. That gliding feeling. To float without obstruction. To feel beautiful and calm. To remove the knit-wool cap over her short blond curls. To have long blond waves flying free with only ear muffs protecting her from frostnip.

At her elbow, Jonathan tucked his street boots under the bench and stood. "You're somewhere else. You haven't said a word." Having laced his skates, he knelt to help her. When she waved him back, he stopped. "Was this outing a bad idea?"

"Quite the contrary." She stopped daydreaming and finished with her skates. She loved the idea of skating again, but was she sending the wrong signals to Jonathan? "I don't know why I ever stopped skating. There were ponds on Staten Island I could have skated on after I left Manhattan, but no Brenda."

Jonathan clapped his gloves together and then tugged them on. "After studying, cooped up in the library and at Brenda's, I felt compelled to do what was in my blood, what Minnesotans do in winter — get out on the ice, get the circulatory system flowing. I miss it. And I hoped we could get to know each other better, an ice breaker, pun intended."

"I think we know each other well enough." She didn't want this to get personal. He didn't know she was damaged. That she wasn't a whole woman. She'd never be girlfriend material. But she hadn't considered him boyfriend material either, just a study partner.

He stretched his back, pulled his arms out, twisted at the waist, rolled his neck, loosened up. "I'm ready. Let's see what you've got."

She mimicked his stretches and removed the guards from her skates, not from her heart. "Ready." She stood up, and together they clomped on the blades over the rubber mats to the rink entrance between the boards.

The familiar scrape of the blades cutting the ice, encountering resistance, the friction enabling skaters to advance, one foot planted, allowing the other foot to move forward. On the edge. Exert a force from the edge into the ice. Get a foothold. Propel forward. Could she? Could she launch herself from her past and cut into a future? Would gravity pull her back? Jonathan was a classmate, not a friend. It would be a long time before she dared, or cared, to make any assumptions, ever again.

They stood at the gap between the boards. "I thought you were a woman up to any challenge."

"Do you hear that? Swoosh. What is that sound like?"

"A little like a fighter jet flashing overhead," he said. "You are procrastinating."

She closed her eyes. "No. It's more like ripping paper." In the hospital, seemed like only yesterday, she had shredded Wayne's threatening note. They were holding up the line of skaters behind them.

They stepped onto the ice together. "I think I can wow you, even on these unsharpened rentals," Jonathan said. "We'll glide along the perimeter for a while, and I'll hold you around the waist, if I may, and we'll skate with the music. Nothing fancy — at first." They usually had a desk, or the kitchen table, piled with books between them. When he held her waist, she realized it was the first time they'd touched. Pain coursed through her body. She stiffened and swallowed hard.

"Afraid?" he asked.

No. Close to the boarding, she skated the perimeter with him. They circled the rink once more, this time, farther from the edge and faster, narrowly missing skaters wobbling along with penguin steps, arms straight out. She gained her foothold. "I've never skated with anyone other than Brenda, but you're good."

"I've skated since I was a child. Growing up in Maplewood, Minnesota, where it gets truly cold — forty below, we had a house on Lake Superior in Duluth. There were skating rinks, indoors and out, but we loved the thrill of cutting the frozen lake when the ice was at least four inches thick and clear of snow. Most skaters hugged the shore, like those here hugging the boards."

She was comfortable near the boards, much as she liked to think of herself as brave.

"Some days the ice at the shore was crystal clear, and being shallow," he said, "it revealed the secrets of each cracked rock, abraded pebble, and chipped shell frozen in place and visible at the bottom. Brave souls skated far from shore, however, almost out of sight. Are you up for something brave?"

Was she?

Without waiting for her answer, Jonathan glided her to the center where there were fewer skaters. Letting go of her waist, he gently extended her arm and spun her, a quick two-foot rotation. She remembered how to balance just behind the toe pick on the balls of her feet. He pulled her close again, and together they cut a figure-eight in the center of the rink. The tempo of the waltz playing on the speakers facilitated their fluid movements. She leaned into the wind with him, and they laughed.

What was that sound? Laughter? It collided with her apprehension of the eight they had carved, which jarred her as her brain darted to the eight sewn on the varsity jacket Wayne had worn on the jet that fateful day. She lost her balance and fell, taking Jonathan down with her.

Hoping to kill the memory, she tried humor. "Maybe we'll suffer ecchymosis of the gluteus maximus."

"Or medius, or minimums," Jonathan said. "It's worth it just to hear you laugh."

After sitting on the ice a moment, careful to remove their fingers from the path of oncoming skaters, they knelt, then stood, brushed themselves off and resumed skating.

"You've recovered with aplomb." Jonathan added, "Here and in class, by the way, even before you knew Schweinfurt was gone."

"Strange how he took a sudden health sabbatical," she said. He had never returned after molesting her, replaced in anatomy class by the shorter of the two women on the interview panel.

Skating leisurely, they continued their conversation. "It was bold of you," Jonathan said, "to come back to class the day after the lecture, making yourself the center of attention in that feminine suit, pearls, and heels, to work on cadavers. You looked proud of being the only female, and you looked beautiful." With his hand at her waist, he squeezed her close. "I could hear the jaws of those twits in the room drop."

She removed his arm from her waist and skated solo. "I am the only female in the class, and I intend to surpass all of you. What of it?" She cut her edge into the ice. Shutting herself behind her eyelids, she wanted to feel as she did before falling asleep, to abandon all control, to stop struggling, to trust the dark and the unknown. She lusted for that exquisite moment of surrender. To sail effortlessly along the ice without having images frozen in the past rise up to haunt her. Trust was a distant star. "Time to go."

"Did I offend you? We were doing so well," he said. He looked exasperated as he smacked his lips together.

"I had fun for the first time in years," she said. "But I'm cold, and it's almost dark."

In the west, the skyline, dwarfing the rink set in this man-made valley, began to flicker with window lights. The late afternoon sun had set beyond the buildings, ostensibly into the Hudson River. The western sky streaked through shades of gray, pink, and pale blue to indigo as she and Jonathan plodded to the bench to remove their skates and change into their boots.

"We've put this cold weather to use." He blew on his hands. "Let's get these back quickly. Perhaps we should buy our own skates, or I could have my parents send mine, if we decide to make skating a regular thing."

Why was he always pushing ahead? If only he weren't so solicitous. She didn't want to like him, or feel obligated to him, or move into a future with him in it. She enjoyed their study relationship, in which she knew more than he did. She actually helped him. She held the power. She wasn't ready to cede it to him just because he was attentive. He must have an angle, to get her into bed. "I'd like to check the Currier and Ives print I noticed in the gift shop when we rented our skates."

They put their rental-returns on the counter and Jonathan handled the transaction while she went to study the print that had attracted her. *CENTRAL-PARK, WINTER. The Skating Pond.* had been painted in 1862, three years after the pond had opened to skaters. The natural setting then, the silhouettes of dormant deciduous trees and clumps of evergreens near snow-covered rock outcroppings in the foreground, appeared much the same then as now, facing the bridge at the neck of the pond, extending to the snowy hills beyond.

Lost in the idyllic landscape, she was suddenly jolted to see that little had changed in a hundred years, much like Schweinfurt in his nineteenth-century garb. Reassuringly, the views unseen from this perspective had changed radically, of course, with a profusion of skyscrapers. She fingered her Janus necklace: Glance at the past; advance into the future. Plant that steel edge into the glassy ice and push forward. The past was not the idyllic scene it appeared to be. Not until 1920 did women even win the vote. Walk through the doors.

Jonathan approached from behind. "You're somewhere else again. We're ready to go, but we can buy the print, if you'd like. We should hurry though. We need some hot chocolate."

She turned abruptly. *The incessant we.* "Stop saying 'we.' There is no 'we.'" She pushed her arm out and pressed her hand against his chest. "You and I are study partners. Maybe you and I are becoming friends. That's it." Their physical contact while skating may have telegraphed the wrong signal. She decided not to purchase the print. She didn't want to live in the past. She wanted to forge ahead, to be one more in the rare breed of female doctors. Her rebuke made Jonathan's cheeks go flaccid. He didn't deserve it. He had helped her find her laugh. "Let's go for the hot chocolate. What did you have in mind?"

"I know the perfect place," he said, bouncing back. "Up for a fifteen-minute walk?"

"For hot chocolate?"

"Even a hayseed from Minnesota knows the 'in' spots. Let's walk across Sixtieth."

"You sound like a New Yorker, with a Minnesota accent. I bet I know. It's the perfect place." Hands in their pockets, they walked out of the park.

At the narrow brownstone, Serendipity III, they stepped from the sidewalk, down the steps to the double door, into the primary colors of childhood delight. "It's odd that something about Serendipity reminds me of Caffè Reggio, even though they're complete opposites," she said.

"They're both tight spaces."

Jonathan asked the host to be seated under the skylight in the back of the café, even though it was dark. They followed him to the rear tables, running the gauntlet of display cases hawking kitsch. The box of the Red Riding Hood puzzle with its 365 red pieces caught her attention. It had one anomalous white piece. She identified with that piece.

Seated, they picked up their menus, which explained that Serendipity was "the art of finding the unusual or pleasantly unexpected by chance or sagacity." From its fairy-tale namesake, the three brothers of Serendip, to its whimsical décor, its decadent offerings, and its fantastical menu graphics, it was a magical venue.

Although they knew what they wanted, they pored over the menu. Jonathan glanced at the map on the back page. "I don't know if you ever noticed this, but there's a city named Kandy in the center of Ceylon, old Serendip."

"I knew I had a connection to this place." She laughed. Again. Feeling guilty about her earlier berating of Jonathan, she was beginning to let her guard down.

She turned to the back of the menu and read the history of the word "serendipity." Serendipity and Reggio both had a connection to Florence, and to the Medicis. Sharing their simultaneous serendipitous discoveries, they laughed again. Cutting into their playful mood, the waiter appeared and asked for their orders.

"I'd like The Catcher in the Rye," Jonathan said. "BLT with chicken."

"I'll have a High Heel Pump," she said. "Prosciutto and brie on pumpernickel."

"And now, what we came for," Jonathan said. "Are you all right with sharing a goblet of Frrrozen Hot Chocolate with two straws?"

Another form of "we," she thought, but relented, "Absolutely."

After placing their order, they continued to amuse themselves, using the menu for additional conversation starters. They learned that the recipe for Frrrozen Hot Chocolate was such a secret that the owners wouldn't even divulge it to Jackie Kennedy for a White House party.

"Since we're finally getting to know each other better," he said, "do you have any secrets you'd like to share?"

"Can't think of any. Why don't you start?"

"All right. I moved to New York to forget my fiancée, who broke my heart."

He was once engaged. He was older than the typical college student. More reason to fear him, feel sorry for him? Manipulation? She had let her guard down too much.

He looked her straight in the eye, all traces of laughter evaporated. He reached for her hand. She pulled back. He continued. "We skated on the lake as children. We grew up, got engaged, and she ran off with a doctor. Truth is, Mother never thought she was right for me, but Mother would love you."

Mother. She thought of hers, pushing her out to the bonfire. Creating that chain of events. And his mother had interfered as well. A reason to feel close, or a red flag to stay away? *Keep her secrets.* "No secrets," she said.

"You must have some secrets," he said. "Here's a big one. When I told you I had to work to save money for school, it was disingenuous of me." He wriggled in his chair, put his elbows on the table, and studied her face closely.

She, too, moved in close, anxious to hear this. Would it clinch her decision for her?

"Father made me work in the family business for a few years, but I wanted to go into medicine, so I left one of the largest, most successful businesses in Maplewood, which I stand to inherit." He sat back in his chair, balanced it on its rear legs, and let out a sigh. "Secret is I'm fairly wealthy."

"And to think I was going to offer to pick up the check since you spent so much on the skating." This didn't change anything for her. "Why are you trying to coax a secret out of me?"

"I told you. I want to get to know you better." He reached for her hand, placing his over hers.

She pulled away and sat on her hands. *Minus her uterus, was she still a woman?* "I'm really hungry." The waiter approached with The Catcher in the Rye and a High Heel Pump.

She had laughed today. He had pried her open and let the laugh free, but she was not willing to let anything else free, not because she cared about how he would react, or if he'd think less of her. She wasn't ready to trust. Even though she had resisted revealing her weighty secrets, this was the first time in the two years of pre-med, while she was dressing in black, isolated, and buried in schoolwork, that a spontaneous laugh had escaped her. A heaviness gathered within her, and filled an imaginary balloon that floated up and out of her body, through the closed skylight above, into the dark.

When the dessert arrived with two partially-wrapped straws sunk through the thick whipped cream into the chocolate ice, she removed a straw and blew the wrapper off in Jonathan's direction, like an impetuous child. They had another good laugh.

CHAPTER 25

Lilium Candidum

*t*hwok...thwok...thwok...thwok...

Having driven uphill, through the gates, and along tree-shaded lanes, Brenda and Candy emerged from the limousine. She remained at a loss for words, but kept a tight grip on Brenda's hand as her own knees wobbled. Late, they nonetheless took small steps across fragrant wet grass, through muddy puddles, to the gathering ahead of them, overshadowed by an ancient oak. From that group, a woman, followed by an officer in dress uniform, waved her white-gloved hand and walked toward them. Brenda shuffled toward her.

"Brenda," the woman said, now just yards away. They reached for each other and stood in a tight embrace, silent. Clasping Brenda's arms, the woman stepped back. "Rick always sent photos and clippings of your stories. He was so proud of your work. And this is how we finally meet."

"I'm sorry I didn't make more of an effort sooner."

The officer caught up to them and Candy joined in. The black veil, attached to Mrs. Dean's pillbox, didn't conceal her tearing red eyes. "It's not your fault," she said, "Rick kept organizing dates for a get-together, but we were always on the move. He must have told you how he grew up in twenty-seven homes." She sobbed, lifted her veil, and jabbed at her eyes with the tissue she had pulled from her glove. "You know how it is — you pin your hopes on tomorrow. As though there's always a tomorrow."

Even in her state of grief, Mrs. Dean took hold of Candy's hand. As impressed as he was with you entering medicine, he sent me your meatloaf recipe, knowing I'm a terrible cook. He loved you too." Mrs. Dean fell back into the general's arms. "You're both a reminder of Rick's joy." She resettled her veil.

Again, at a loss for words, an inept "I'm so sorry" was all Candy could muster. What would people have said to her if she had had a funeral for her fetus? An absurd thought, but a devastating burden no black veil or dark glasses could hide.

Still supporting his wife, General Dean leaned toward Brenda and gripped her hand. "I have much to tell you."

"I can see him in you," Brenda said. Huddled in their own clique carved into the throng of mourners, the four joined the fellowship under the tree.

The chauffer chased after Brenda to hand her the flowers she had forgotten in the limo. "A beautiful bouquet," Mrs. Dean said, "and so fragrant."

"Rick had these white lilies," Brenda said, "decorating our suite the night before his deployment. He loved fragrances — my perfume, flowers. He'll appreciate these." She clutched the bouquet to her chest and burrowed her face in it.

THWOK...THWOK...THWOK...THWOK...

The reverberations, the percussion, the disequilibrium, the rotary blades pummeling the air into submission, the periodic motion, the rapid oscillation, seemed to steal Brenda's balance. When she wobbled, Candy steadied her with an arm around her shoulder, and snapped out of her own self-pity. As she held her close, she felt the fast throbbing of Brenda's heart.

Meanwhile, the lone drummer of the military band countered as he tapped his measured beat, a beat that could be depended on for the next beat.

Yet again, Brenda faltered, as she stood ankle-deep in water. Brenda, her rock, was inconsolably shaken. She'd have to reach deep to find strength to impart to her, an unfamiliar role, since she had always been on the receiving end of Brenda's largess. The rare and frail perfection of Brenda and Rick's love had been so swiftly shattered. The odds were against successful couples, but the Deans seemed strong. Candy rubbed the timeworn Roman coin of her necklace and prayed for Brenda, who was oblivious to the mud she stood in. Candy called her name and pulled her away.

The helicopter, which appeared to have risen from the Potomac on its flight to Arlington, hovered in a tribute flyover, above the hearse and caisson, witnessing the transfer. The eight soldiers of the casket team, the honor guard, with their ritualized movements, carried the flag-draped casket from the hearse to the aged, black wooden caisson. Aside from the helicopter, the only sounds were those of the drummer and of the clicking heels of the soldiers' highly-polished black shoes. The helicopter, like the suddenness of life events, brought chaos. The rituals set out to restore order could be relied on, like the rising of the sun in the east. A foothold.

As suddenly as it appeared, the helicopter darted off, causing the new-green leaves of the oak to quiver. Brenda, Candy, and the Deans stood together, a phalanx against the engulfing sadness of loss, the loss of a selfless hero. Her cheeks reddened at the recognition of her selfishness. The four pressed hands and led the mourners in silence a mile or so, amid the hundreds of thousands of rounded white marble tablets engraved with the names, dates, wars, and religions of the fallen. *So many lost lives.*

The mourners followed the caisson drawn by six muscular white horses in black tack, the three horses on the left ridden by soldiers in ceremonial uniform, erect in their black saddles. She had lost herself in black for two years.

The rhythmic *clop...clop...clop* of the horses' hooves, the jangling of the harness chains, and the creaking of the caisson wheels made solemn progress to Ord and Weitzel Drive in Section 52. When the caisson stopped, the honor guard saluted, presented arms, removed the casket and, led by the military chaplain, carried the casket across the grass, past other graves, and placed it on the bier prepared for Rick. The caisson rolled on. Out of sight, the seven-man rifle party fired a three-volley salute of blank cartridges over their fallen comrade. The tradition, she knew from her Latin readings of the Gallic Wars, dated back to an army-on-the march burying the warriors of the Roman Empire with honor and efficiency, where a mere three handfuls of dirt over the fallen constituted burial. The lone bugler, at a distance, played "Taps." The final salute was given. *As though that were the end of it.*

And the rituals sucked up emotion as the honor guard, three on each side of the casket, stretched and centered the flag before performing the thirteen folds, stars pointing upward in the final fold; they enclosed within the folds three spent shell casings — *three laughs, three brothers Serendip, a shell of a life.* The Army officer-in-charge presented the flag to Mrs. Dean, who held it tight and cried into it, her veil catching on a corner. She kissed the flag and clasped it to her heart as her husband wrapped his arm around her and drew her close. Candy envied their love.

The team backed away to allow the chaplain to perform the service, and he introduced Brenda, who was prepared to read from the Old Testament.

Candy helped her to the bier, where Brenda removed her dark glasses, revealing swollen eyes and the absence of any make-up to gloss over her grief. Brenda reached forward to the casket, as her heels sank into the soaked sod. Water-stained notes in hand and the bouquet of pure white lilies against her chest, she said, "Verses from The Song of Solomon, King James Version, Chapters 2, 3, 5, 6 and 8 best express my feelings:

...the rain is over and gone. The flowers appear on earth...

...I sought him whom my soul loveth. I sought him, but I

Found him not...the chiefest among ten thousand...His eyes

Are as the eyes of doves by the rivers of waters, washed with

Milk and fitly set...his lips are like lilies, dropping sweet

Smelling myrrh. My beloved is gone down into his garden, to

The beds of spices, to feed in the gardens, and to gather lilies.

...love is strong as death. Many waters cannot quench love,
Neither can the floods drown it..."

Her notes fluttered to the ground. "These lilies symbolize my pride in Rick's heroism and his purity of heart." She touched her lips with two fingers, then transferred the kiss to the highly-polished wood of the casket, and placed the bouquet on it. The Deans and Candy joined her, then walked her back to the congregation.

"The reference to the lilies is especially fitting," the chaplain said. "White lilies are the flowers the Angel Gabriel presented to Mary at the Annunciation. And they are the symbol of Easter, of the Resurrection, full circle — birth, death, rebirth.

"We honor Chief Dean's heroism. In his helicopter, he had evacuated several troops, some of whom are here with their families today, troops who had been trapped by enemy fire. After delivering them to safety, on a trip to rescue more men, his helicopter took enemy fire and went down into the Perfume River in Hue, Republic of Vietnam. For his act of selfless heroism, a grateful nation thanks him.

"From the New Testament, King James Version, Revelations 1:4: 'And God shall wipe away all tears from their eyes; and there shall be no more death, neither sorrow, nor crying, neither shall there be any more pain: for the former things are passed away.'"

The chaplain drew back.

The military band played "America the Beautiful." An Arlington official pronounced the ceremony concluded. Brenda, Candy, and Rick's parents remained to accept condolences, Candy standing behind Brenda. *Not three handfuls, six feet, or ten feet of dirt could cover the enduring pain of death, the guilt of not having done more.*

Not one of the little phalanx was yet willing to leave Rick. As they stood near his final resting place, the general again held Brenda's hand. "After the crash, the military was able to secure partial remains and personal effects." He removed a small package from his jacket. "You must know why Rick had this little pair of glass doves in his pocket."

"The stopper from my perfume bottle." She accepted it from the general. "On our last night, I gave it to him as a token of our love, after he had given me your rabbit's foot." She took it from her purse. "You should have it back."

"He still had it?" General Dean asked. "I'd forgotten about it." His stiff composure crumbled. His eyes welled up. He caught himself as his knees bent. His wife slipped beneath his arm, which he extended over her shoulder.

She handed an envelope to Brenda. "Rick had sent us this letter after he arrived in Vietnam. It came with instructions to give it to you if he didn't make it home."

Brenda broke the seal and read aloud:

"My beautiful Brenda, remember when you told me not to chase the hat that had blown away in the wind? You said there were times you had to let go. Let this be the most important of those times. I know how much you love me, and you know how happy you've made me. Grieve, as I know you will. Support my mother if you can. The general is strong. But let me go. Rebuild your life when you're ready. Don't throw your future away."

Brenda embraced and kissed Mrs. Dean. "You raised a fine son, a fine man, and I'll never stop loving him."

"You'll always be a daughter to me. Remember that."

"The limo's here," the general announced. "It's time."

Brenda walked to the bier once more, knelt on the sod, bent over the casket. "I love you, Rick. I'll be back." When she stood, the black Ferragamo, which had flown from her foot at Dothan airport, stuck in the mud and came off her foot. Instead of picking it up, she laid it on its side, then laid its partner shoe with it. "You really don't want me to have these shoes, do you?"

Candy helped her shoeless friend up and brushed the mud from her skirt. As they walked to the car, a white rabbit bounded across their path. "Oh, Rick." Brenda laughed.

Candy rubbed her hand in circles on Brenda's back. "In my darkest hour, I had you and Dr. Thompson. Now I'm here for you. Dr. Thompson said he's ready to support you too. Although he didn't think it proper to attend the funeral, he'll meet us at LaGuardia, if you'd like."

Settled in one limo, Mrs. Dean said, "Let's go somewhere quiet where we can share a meal and remember Rick and all the happiness he gave us."

Candy wished she could find such happiness, but with Jonathan?

CHAPTER 26

The Handwriting on the Wall

1970

The taxi deposited Candy and Jonathan at the Plaza Hotel, a facet of the panorama the two had enjoyed from Wollman Rink over the past two winters. Unlike the uptown trips of those days, when they rode the subway or bus, today they had treated themselves to a cab. Today, she celebrated a victory over the ridicule, the humiliation, the ceaseless studying of her four years of pre-med.

In the lobby, Jonathan used a house phone to ring his parents. "I'm excited to introduce them to you," he told Candy as he waited for an answer, which never came. When he asked the desk clerk if there was a message for him, she handed him an envelope. He slid out a note: "Dear Son, I had a few last-minute errands. Won't be terribly long. Mother"

"Typical. Mother's probably at Bergdorf's shopping or getting her hair done." He floated the note into a waste basket. "First, they brushed off our graduation, and now they'll be late for the celebration *she* arranged. She's still peeved I left the family business."

Candy recognized the slack-jawed disappointment written on his face. "We'll wait." She stroked his cheek with the back of her hand. Whether or not she met them was of no importance. "Let's enjoy the sunshine." She led him out of the lobby by the hand. "We can relax at the fountain. If they show, we're sure to catch them from there." Cutting through the queue of yellow cabs and glossy limos, they crossed the street to Grand Army Plaza.

At the fountain, Jonathan removed the red square, which he had done into a puff fold, from the breast pocket of his gray suit jacket, and whisked light debris and moisture from the fountain's lowest tier. "I wouldn't want you to soil your dress."

Although pleased he had composed himself, she continued to find his attentiveness grating. But his affect read "hurt," not "anger." Empathizing with the reaction, she didn't want to compound it.

Jonathan slumped down beside her, their hips and thighs touching, and he wove his arm under hers and around her waist. "We've never talked about our future."

Having successfully avoided the topic these two years, she had not divulged the secret of her hysterectomy — not on their first date at Serendipity or since. Initially, she thought it too soon; suddenly, it had become too late. She was certain she never cared for him in such a way that children would be an issue. She had fallen into a habit of being with him without ever falling in love with him.

After Wayne, she had deprived herself of male companionship. But Jonathan was patient. With an imaginary scalpel, he had shucked her from her shell, raw as she was. They had sex. One lonely human cleaving to another. Hovering above their bodies, she witnessed the acts clinically, even though she made sure it was always dark. Laid bare, the ice encrusting her heart never melted, and she never melded with Jonathan, despite the fact that she dated no one. In her eyes, they never "made love."

After Rick's death, Brenda had been her primary concern. When Jonathan came to the apartment to hit the books, Brenda would join them at the kitchen table for dinner, then retreat to her room. Weekly dinner became a ritual, a thing that could be depended upon to set life right. But Candy found it painful to make her one dish, meatloaf, since the funeral. Brenda cooked less than ever. And Jonathan didn't know his way around a kitchen. They agreed they'd order in: Chinese, pizza, pasta, burgers. When Dr. Thompson came by to gauge the students' progress and offer his expertise on some arcane medical topic, he'd join them for dinner. Brenda brightened. She began wearing lipstick and mascara again. Dr. Thompson made her laugh. Candy had suggested the four make order-in-nights a regular event. Some nights they played Monopoly, Scrabble, or Canasta in lieu of studying. They eventually branched out to a movie night now and then. Or a walk in the park.

With Jonathan, she didn't recognize a bond like Brenda and Rick's, or the Deans', or—. Although she had opened herself to sex, she didn't want to open herself to hurt. Damaged goods, she was never meant to get married. But their studying together helped them fly through pre-med. She didn't need or want anyone in the way she feared Jonathan was about to suggest.

"Where do you drift off to?" He moved his arm from around her waist and pinched her cheek.

"Ouch," she said. She studied the staccato clouds crossing over the French mansard roof of the Plaza. "Of course we've talked about the future — med school." She rubbed her cheek. "And we've charted courses to different schools, separate futures, mine here, yours back in Minnesota." *He had never hurt her before.*

"I did say our future," Jonathan said, "on a personal level." He held her hand between his. "Mother will just love you."

She realized she should have encouraged Brenda and Dr. Thompson to hop in the cab with them after graduation to join them for lunch. But she allowed them to beg off, with the excuse they'd be intruding. *Had she learned nothing?* She had aced the MCATs with a 40, was accepted to Columbia med school, her first choice, but she still didn't know as much as those fireflies. Lingering on the bridge between feeling obliged and being honest, she faltered, then touched his knee. "I'm happy to meet them."

"You'll love Mother too. Just wait." He stood and began pacing.

"We are waiting." He couldn't possibly be planning to propose. How had she let this go so far? Should she speak up before she met his parents? Was she making unwarranted assumptions? Burned once.

"I'm going back inside, in case we missed them and they're waiting in the lobby. I should've left a note. Would you prefer to stay put or join me?"

"I'm fine here," she said from her spot on the fountain, where bronze Pomona bowed with the grace of a willowy flower twenty feet above her.

Pomona, the naked goddess of abundance, had herself stood defenseless — in the flesh of her model, Audrey Munson, a guileless girl who had caught the brass ring. Brenda had interviewed Audrey at Ogdensburg, New York, for her series on women's choices. In her day, the innocent Audrey had displayed no fear of being naked in the world, and, at fifteen, considered her ease with the "abandonment of draperies," as she referred to her nudity, an affirmation of her purity. *Can purity survive out in the world the way evil can?*

Audrey had arrived in Manhattan from upstate with her divorced mother in 1906. A photographer, taken with her classic beauty, introduced her to a sculptor, which was the beginning of her career posing for at least a dozen allegorical statues in Manhattan and countless others throughout the country. Audrey had no fear in abandoning her draperies and acted in the first non-pornographic nude films. Neither mother nor child could have foreseen the outcome of Audrey's good fortune. The naïve girl fell prey to her married landlord who, in 1919, killed his wife and later, himself, when Audrey refused his advances. Although blameless in the deaths, society turned on her. She lost her modeling and acting careers and her newspaper column. She and her mother retreated to Mexico, New York, where Audrey fell into depression and alcoholism and attempted suicide in 1922. In 1931 a judge sentenced her, at age thirty-nine, to Saint Lawrence Psychiatric Center, for life, where Brenda uncovered her. Feme decovert.

Jonathan crossed the street to the Plaza. He paused as he waved to a couple ahead of him. Candy stood, stuffed the pocket square into her purse, and made her way toward Jonathan, who cheek-kissed the woman in a yellow dress and a broad-brimmed white hat banded in yellow. Then Jonathan shook hands with the man, and they slapped backs. He wore a gray suit similar to Jonathan's, with a yellow tie and yellow pocket square in a puff fold. Even from this distance, and without the similar sartorial choices, his form and movements fixed him as Jonathan's father.

As they converged beneath the fluttering flags of the Plaza, she caught up with them.

Mrs. Crane spoke first. "I hope the delay wasn't too off-putting. It's so hard to gauge time." She touched her son's arm.

"Mother, Father, we're sorry you missed graduation. I wanted you to meet Brenda and Dr. Thompson. They've been my family here in New York, but they couldn't make it this afternoon. Most importantly, this is Candy."

"You've been good for my boy," Mrs. Crane said. "Just as well about the others."

"The others," Candy said, "are my family." She stared down Jonathan.

"This is Mr. Crane," Mrs. Crane said.

"Welcome to the family." Mr. Crane stepped in to hug Candy as the brim of his wife's hat intervened.

"Plenty of time for hugs later," Mrs. Crane said. "Congratulations to both of you on this marvelous achievement, and now on to the real business of med school." She searched for something in her purse. "Presents later. No need to carry them down. I left them in the room, room 719. It took a bit of doing, but I was finally able to book it." She took a compact from her purse and powdered her nose. "It's always so humid in Manhattan. We're going to see *Plaza Suite* at the Plymouth Theatre tonight. All three acts take place in room 719, as you must know," Mrs. Crane said.

"Mother always gets what she wants," Mr. Crane said.

"Certainly not the last time we were here," she said. "While I was waiting for Father, earlier, I peeked into the Oak Room and the maître d' invited me in. The last time we were here, I wanted to enjoy lunch and an old-fashioned after a morning's shopping at Bergdorf's, but the maître d' told me that 'unaccompanied ladies' were not permitted." She huffed. "Can you imagine?"

Feme covert. "I can explain the change in attitude," Candy said. "Last year Brenda covered a National Organization for Women protest against the Oak Room's 'men-only' policy. Betty Friedan and fifteen NOW members forced their way in and sat at a table. The staff physically removed the table, leaving the women sitting in a circle. They were forced to leave without service. The story circulated and four months later, the Plaza changed its policy. Women were allowed entry into that domain of men."

"So that explains it," Mrs. Crane said. "Good for them." She moved closer to Candy. "Was Brenda one of the fifteen?"

"No. She's a member, but she was present as a reporter, instrumental in bringing about the changes. One little choice."

"I hope med school is the limit to your feminist ideas." She centered her hat and reset the hairpin into the grosgrain ribbon of the band. "I've booked lunch at The Palm Court. Since we're out here, why don't we sit by the fountain and visit before moving indoors?" She took her husband's arm as they walked beside Jonathan and Candy. "I love the sound of the trickling water, here in the cacophony of car horns and traffic." Mrs. Crane adjusted the back of her dress, about to sit on the fountain.

Candy took the pocket square from her purse and fingered it into Jonathan's palm. He placed it on the fountain ledge for his mother.

"What is that tantalizingly sweet smell?" Mrs. Crane asked.

"The candied nuts cooking in the street vendor's cart on the corner," Jonathan said. "We've snacked on them after skating. I'll get us some." Father, why don't you entertain Candy with your Civil War trivia, sitting right here in front of old General Sherman?"

"The aroma masks the odor of the carriage horses," Mr. Crane said. "But I do enjoy the drivers' handsome costumes, top hats and tails, so nineteenth century. Jonathan knows, of course, I'm somewhat of a Civil War buff," he said. "The gilded-bronze equestrian statue across from us is General Sherman. The general moved to Manhattan some years after helping

Lincoln win the war. And Sherman rode his horse-drawn carriage through Central Park each day until his death in 1891, not long before I was born. In his honor, would you all like to take a carriage ride after lunch?"

"You don't speak often," Mrs. Crane said to her husband. "But you do drone on when you have an audience."

Jonathan returned with a bag of hot nuts. "Put your hands out, and I'll pour a few for each of you."

Mrs. Crane removed her white glove and opened her palm. "Just one or two, Son. I don't allow myself such indulgences, but the aroma is so tempting."

Jonathan distributed the contents of the small bag. Before he had a chance to sit or talk, Mrs. Crane stood and brushed off the back of her dress. The group followed her lead. This time she wrapped her arm through Candy's and slowed their pace so Jonathan and his father could walk ahead and talk, as she held a private audience with Candy.

"Jonathan mentioned you're thinking of gynecology," Mrs. Crane said. "I hope you don't mind if I speak frankly. As you see, we're older parents. I was afraid I would never conceive. One doctor was so bold as to suggest I suffered from psychosomatic infertility." She tugged at her white cotton gloves.

"I'm familiar with it."

"He suggested we adopt. We wanted our own child, but I was feeling guilty, despondent, angry. It almost destroyed our marriage. We stopped trying for some time, and then I got pregnant. Jonathan's name means 'God has given.' He was a gift. I don't understand how *Look* could have run that recent cover story, 'Motherhood: Who Needs It?' Did you read it? Pure drivel."

"I did," Candy said. "You were lucky to conceive. Not all women want, or can have, a child. If it makes you feel any better, Brenda knows the writer working on the counter-piece — 'The Test-Tube Baby is Coming,' an article on in vitro fertilization, for those women who want motherhood and aren't as lucky as you were."

"Before I became pregnant," Mrs. Crane said, "my gynecologist told me of John Rock's work with in vitro at Harvard, promising, but not yet a reality. Genetic Laboratories, the world's first commercial sperm bank, recently opened near us in Maplewood. I'm glad we didn't need it. Nothing's more important than legacy. Even with your education and career, you surely intend to have children."

As Mrs. Crane was now the one droning on, Candy's thoughts screeched to a mind-numbing halt. With a flash of lightning visible in both eye sockets, she relived the pain, physical, emotional, she had compartmentalized. As it burst forth, she extended her arms for balance. Mrs. Crane had thrown it out there. Just like that. That old parachute drop had been good training for reacting to life's stomach-dropping moments. She left the comment hanging between them. Mrs. Crane must not have noticed as she continued.

"We're anxious for our only child to father a scion or two. You would be a perfect mate with whom Jonathan could continue our family tree. With your specialty in gynecology, you could work with the genetics lab in Maplewood and stay close to Jonathan at home in Minnesota."

Candy couldn't imagine sitting through lunch while facing the handwriting on the wall. "Would you excuse me, Mrs. Crane? I have to speak to Jonathan."

"Of course, dear. I'm glad we had a chance to chat."

When she called ahead to Jonathan, he and his father stopped and waited for the women. Mr. Crane joined Mrs. Crane, and Candy and Jonathan moved off and talked. She explained that a relationship between them could never work, if that's what he was thinking, and this was a perfect time to end it. Unable to face his parents, she asked him to make her excuses. To her surprise, she read no protest in his expression nor did he deliver one. She gasped at how she had agonized over her doubts and her thoughts about hurting him.

No flaccid cheeks, no anger. "I surmise your chat with Mother didn't go well. It wasn't meant to be, then," Jonathan said. "Give my best to Brenda and Dr. Thompson. I'll miss them. You and Dr. Thompson got me through pre-med." He wished her well, shook her hand, and rejoined his parents.

All the blood drained from her body, yet she walked to the curb and hailed a cab. She didn't want to marry him, yet all of them would have rejected her for her fertility issues, issues his mother should have understood. As on the day she first met Jonathan, she felt a blindness welling up inside her, covering her eyes, like mercury rising in a thermometer. A golden tortoise beetle, the shell of a yellow cab, carried away the shell of her body.

PART III

Wings Beating Against the Glass

CHAPTER 27

The Threshold

Columbia University Medical Center, Manhattan, 1970

Beyond the Columbia University Medical Center campus, founded in 1754 in the yet-to-be-born United States, loomed the George Washington Bridge, which honored the father of the country.

It was not fathers who interested her, but mothers, one in particular, as she embarked on med school. At their single encounter, Candy had recognized in Jonathan's mother a proclivity to control her, which wasn't the sole reason she had ended her relationship with Jonathan. However, it was their showdown that indirectly planted a seed. It focused her drive to help women conceive through in vitro, an addition to her desire to keep women from suffering as she did in her illegal abortion; the first small step was to provide the option of birth control to women, married or not. Brenda and NOW, in 1967, began the long game, the repeal of anti-abortion laws. Government, men, fought to block women from crossing the bridge to making their own choices. And there were women opposed to legalizing abortion.

Mrs. Crane's pronouncements on legacy and the family tree reverberated within the bell tower of Candy's mind. After Jonathan, she wouldn't be letting anyone else in. What she had assumed in Staten Island Hospital, that her infertility would ceaselessly torment her and leave her without a family, had become fact. Families wanted babies, legacy, continuance. She would never get over ending her matriarchal line. There was no redemption for her. If there were a way to give the gift of legacy to other women, she'd pursue it. The guilt of failing her own family's thousand-year tradition tormented her. She wore her Janus necklace as penance, although she didn't need a concrete reminder.

One father she was interested in, however, a father of test-tube baby research, worked on campus. She scouted rumors that the doctor featured in the test-tube-baby article she had learned of from Brenda, the proposed title of which she had cavalierly lobbed at Mrs. Crane, was an attending at Columbia's department of obstetrics and gynecology. Although she also got wind of Dr. Landrum Shettles' reputation as a recluse, she sought him out.

At his lab, she knocked again and again, harder and harder, day after day.

"Go away." He cracked the door open to peer at her through his thick black glasses, then closed the door in her face. With the fearless persistence displayed by ants, she persevered. A slammed door was nothing compared to all she had endured. Beyond this threshold lay the brass ring. In the middle of the night, night after night, she fought to see him, knocked with bruised knuckles until the night he opened the door and engaged her. "Why do you insist on interrupting me?" The thick Mississippi accent was unmistakable. He didn't slam the door, but he didn't let her in. "I'm a busy man."

"I'm a med student, gynecology, offering my time." Her hands were sweaty. "I read *Look*'s article about your groundbreaking in vitro work." A little flattery to soften him. "I'd like to volunteer as an assistant."

"I work alone. I don't need an assistant." He let go of the edge of the door and raised his glasses to stare at her. "I have no budget. The chief doesn't approve of my experimental work." He pushed the door in her direction, shutting her out. "Anyway, it will stain you."

She stopped the door with her foot. "Hear me out. I did say 'volunteer,' as many hours as I can squeeze in. I'm driven to provide women more choices in fertility. Wouldn't a female researcher benefit your work? I've read widely. I need clinical experience, to pick your brain, to learn your techniques, to make babies."

"So, it's all about you and what you want. On the contrary, a woman would bog me down. You're young. Go make your own babies. You'll get involved with boyfriends after I train you. Like my wife, you'll go and have seven babies. I can't afford to waste my time."

The door with which they played tug-of-war shoved her foot. *Could she work with this man?* Her experiences inured her to intimidation, and she didn't flinch.

Although there was so much she didn't like about his attitude, she was determined to learn from this pioneer. In the hope of getting him to share his secrets, she shared hers. "My work is my only interest. I've had a hysterectomy, after an abortion, and will never have children, will never marry, but I want to provide options to women for whom artificial insemination is not viable." After a late night at the library and this confrontation, she was spent. Her eyes and mouth were dry, her knees too weak to hold out against his strength on the other side of the door. "Consider a trial period." She switched her books to her other hip. When he opened the door to let her in, she dropped her books and crossed the threshold.

"One week. I keep odd hours. Middle of the night. And I don't believe in abortion."

"I'm accustomed to late hours. I barely sleep." The threshold was her bridge. Over it, she stepped into the future, Janus facing forward with barely a glance back. With her assiduous research and meticulous attention to detail, she'd convince Shettles to keep her on as a research assistant, to be her mentor, to impart to her the minute protocols of collecting, studying, growing, nourishing, and fertilizing eggs, human ova — the mission of his lab, even if he didn't like babies, or people.

Following her break-up with Jonathan after graduation, she had resolved not to date or even allow herself a social life at Columbia. She too, became a recluse. The loss of social time afforded her at least twenty hours per week to work so she could supplement her loans and scholarships without impacting her studies, and left excess time to volunteer. Sleep was overrated.

CHAPTER 28

Waived Away

1973

In Dr. Shettles' sixteenth-floor lab in the Harkness Pavilion, the asynchronous ticking of his collection of clocks focused Candy as she observed follicular ova through the Zeiss phase-contrast microscope. At night, most clinical med students were asleep or partying. Darkness enveloped the lab. It cushioned the inflexibility of the tile walls, the stainless steel, the glass of the Petri dishes, slides, beakers, vials, needles, syringes and pipettes arranged in stands.

Shettles believed night the optimal time to collect ova, since it corresponded with the natural cycle. But she knew well that the night also hid his deeds from a hospital administration whose strict rules on human experimentation he ignored. Shettles often charged from the operating room at Sloane to his lab. His white lab coat flapped open, like the wings of the ghost moth, *Thysania agrippina,* as he raced the halls with the short-lived live fluid in his syringe.

In this latest night-time raid, Shettles had planned to aspirate follicular fluid directly from an ovary with sterile syringe and 20-gauge needle. When he arrived in the lab, he'd express the collected mixture into a sterile Petri dish. She awaited his arrival with the dish she had prepared.

Having warmed the petrolatum, she drew it into an 18-gauge needle and exuded it uniformly around a Petri dish. Outside the ring she added sterile physiological salt solution to prevent the evaporation of the follicular fluid in the center of the ring. Her work with insects and their minute components had served her well for this work. But these specimens were alive, with the potential to give life, personhood, family, legacy. The preparations were in order, and Shettles would soon arrive to add the contents of the needle he had carried from the operating room — a ritual the two had performed countless times.

He had called her earlier that night and, in the Mississippi accent he held on to despite having been at Columbia since his residency decades ago, he had instructed her to prime the dish. When he arrived, he expressed the contents of the syringe. Tired, he rested for a few moments on his cot. "I've studied thousands of eggs. You can handle this on your own." He grabbed clean scrubs from the chest and headed for the bathroom to shower and change. "I need rest for tomorrow. It will be a portentous day, the day I've worked toward all my life." He slammed the bathroom door, but spoke through it. "Either stay in the lab when you finish or come back at six."

She chose to remain at the bench in the round-the-clock glow of the fish tank, another lab incongruity, the only light other than that at the microscope. She surveyed the tank and the clocks. For a sweep of the minute hand, she too, felt incongruous in the lab. She was the stray white piece added to the 365-red-piece Red Riding Hood puzzle at Serendipity, the only female in her pre-med anatomy class; she, with a missing uterus, was in a lab dedicated to the study of eggs and embryos. Shettles came out of the bathroom, hit the cot, and pulled the covers over his head to fall asleep. Refocused on the Petri dish, with a glass micropipette, she added to a glass slide — also prepared with the petrolatum ring to prevent the cover slide from exerting pressure on the specimen — a drop of follicular fluid. With a fine glass needle, she opened the follicles. With past specimens, she had discovered up to three primary oocytes, or immature egg cells. Shettles had removed as many as sixteen oocytes in a single aspiration. Sometimes only one. Sometimes follicles were empty.

As Shettles slept, she examined this night's fluid for eggs mature enough to fertilize. In a mature ovum, the zona pellucida was completely free of the nourishing granules of the corona radiata and ready for fertilization. Shettles said she had an exceptional gift for recognizing such egg cells. When she found that egg, she would add donated sperm. Under the microscope, she'd watch the heads attack. The sperm, possibly a million in number, flagellated their tails synchronously, rotating the oocyte clockwise 360 degrees every fifteen seconds, continuing for as long as twenty to thirty hours, until one sperm penetrated the ooplasm. Not only had she read the description in Shettles' *Ovum Humanum*, she had witnessed it. David Rorvik, in the test-tube baby article that had steered her to this lab, had hailed Shettles as "the first man in the world to witness the drama of human fertilization...on the stage of his microscope...." Was she the first woman?

At about thirty hours after insemination, if kept at 37 degrees Celsius, a healthy mature human ovum reached the two-cell stage and continued to grow exponentially. The zona pellucida remained intact until the fertilized egg, as a blastocyst, could be transferred to a uterus and implanted in the uterine wall. No researcher had ever gotten that far in the process. It was Shettles' Holy Grail, and tale.

Again, she focused on the fluid Shettles had collected and found some immature eggs ill-suited for immediate fertilization. She incubated those at 37 degrees Celsius and would examine them periodically for signs of maturity.

Under Shettles' tutelage, she had also incubated embryos at 37 degrees Celsius and monitored them at thirty, forty, sixty, seventy-two, and one hundred twenty hours — the blastocyst stage at which embryos must be transferred to a human uterus, if it were possible, or perish. She savored the rigorous, repetitious procedures, despite which outcomes were unpredictable: With fifteen eggs, eight might mature, five might fertilize, and three of those could arrest after two, three, or four days, leaving only two that might have been transferred to a uterus — again, had that procedure been possible.

But Shettles claimed to have performed one experimental transfer from the lab to a uterus back in 1962. And two days later when he removed the uterus in a hysterectomy performed for cancer treatment, he said he had located the embryo in the removed uterus. He claimed it had grown to several hundred cells. He had no documentation. "Embryos die in the embryo lab," the mantra went. That embryo allegedly died in the excised womb.

The ethics of human research was an issue she grappled with, especially after her own hysterectomy. Guilt had even haunted her over the butterflies she had killed and mounted when she was a little girl. There was the continuing pain and shame of her abortion with its resulting infertility. She admired Shettles' fervent quest to shepherd the first test-tube baby into the world, providing a chance of fertility and motherhood to infertile women. She weighed the ethical arguments of the research raised by segments of society, the Church, the government, even the American Medical Association, which urged a moratorium on human IVF — where both fertilization and early embryo development occur outside the body.

Conservatives viewed IVF as an unraveling of the tight weave of traditional reproduction, of society itself. The revolutionary idea of IVF had been greeted with resistance, just as the notion of female doctors had been. She challenged the naysayers, doing her tiny part to assure that in time, both — female doctors and IVF — would become routine and unremarkable. Although the government wouldn't fund IVF research, support rained into fertility labs from private donors anxious to provide fertility to multitudes of women who ached to become mothers. It was still all theoretical and experimental.

The American Fertility Society urged research forward, having already come a long way since the first human artificial insemination in 1909, coincidentally the year Shettles was born. Like the handful of pioneering fertility scientists, John Rock, Howard and Georgeanna Jones, Patrick

Steptoe, Robert Edwards, she chose to work through the objections in order to serve the increasing number of infertile women — as many as one in four between age twenty and thirty-five was infertile. She played her small role as research assistant in Shettles' lab, preparing slides and Petri dishes, investigating eggs and embryos. She gripped her Janus necklace, then released it, allowing it to fall against her chest. She wanted nothing more than to become a fertility doctor, a reproductive endocrinologist, a practitioner of IVF.

Neither the sixty-four-year-old doctor nor the twenty-six-year-old med student socialized much, and never with each other. She relished the psychological space the lack of interaction afforded. He wasn't one for conversation. He rarely went home to his wife and seven children. His children, she understood, were the hundreds of ova whose photographs papered his lab walls, the photos from which he had culled the sixty-five for his groundbreaking 1960 publication, *Ovum Humanum*. Having remained in the lab overnight, she too fell asleep — at the bench.

When Shettles awoke, he shook her. "We have a big day." While he washed his face at the sink, he said, "Yesterday a couple flew up from Florida. The wife signed waivers allowing experimental in vitro in spite of no promised outcome." He snapped a towel from the hook and patted his face dry. He groped around for his glasses on the cot and put them on. "She's been admitted to New York Hospital and scheduled for surgery with Sweeney to remove eggs first thing this morning." He checked the thermometer on the incubator he was preparing for the historic specimen. She followed him. "Then the husband will carry the test tube with the fluid to me, and I'll use his sperm, which I'll collect here, to fertilize and incubate. In a few days, the husband will carry the test tube with the fertilized egg or eggs back over to Sweeney. It's ingenious. I will get to fertilize an egg that will actually be implanted."

This endeavor was fraught with disaster. "I suppose you've run this by the chief?" Shettles ignored her question as he had ignored the chief's prohibition against human experimentation.

She opposed the objections to human experimentation; the time for animal experimentation with rabbits was past. She did object, however, to

Shettles not informing the women when he took their eggs. Her protests didn't sway him. He threatened her with expulsion from the lab. This was too important. And this time was different. The informed woman had signed waivers.

Shettles put a clean white coat over scrubs. "This could be the world's first test-tube baby. Both aspiration and transfer will take place at Sweeney's hospital, not here. I'm in the clear. Perhaps you shouldn't be involved. The stain, you know. I'll be in touch." He waved her off.

She walked to the door and paused with her hand on the knob. "I'll risk putting my career on the line, for this." He didn't call her back. He ordered her to leave the lab.

CHAPTER 29

Vile Loss

All they wanted was what millions, billions, of couples took for granted — their own baby. On September 11, 1973, the Floridians, John and Doris arrived at New York Hospital on the Upper East Side of Manhattan. Anxious to undergo an experimental procedure, their last chance to have a baby of their own, they signed the scribbled waivers presented by their infertility specialist, Dr. William J. Sweeney III. Hospital personnel recorded that Doris was admitted for a gynecological surgery. Not her first. That day, she settled into her private hospital room to prepare for surgery the next morning.

Dr. Sweeney had treated Doris in New York ever since her marriage to John in 1968. At twenty-five, with a young daughter, Doris had married John who himself had two grown children. After the marriage, however, she suffered a complication that blocked her fallopian tubes.

Surgery in 1970 resulted in a pregnancy, but ended in a miscarriage. But the couple was committed to having a child of their own. The following year the couple experimented with the theory that artificial insemination could bypass the fallopian tubes, but the attempts failed.

As a last resort, Dr. Sweeney showed them David Rorvik's 1971 *Look* article trumpeting Dr. Landrum Shettles' IVF research. The experimental method of fertilization outside the body in a glass Petri dish, in vitro, would allow fertilization to bypass Doris' blocked tubes. Since she had been on fertility drugs for almost a year for her earlier procedures, she was prepared and anxious for this surgery.

In the hospital operating room, at 8 a.m., September 12, Dr. Sweeney aspirated the follicular fluid from Doris' ovaries. Even as Doris lay on the operating table, the doctor sent a nurse with two test tubes of fluid to the pacing husband in the waiting room, who placed them in his jacket pocket, nestled close to his heart.

John rode the elevator to street level and raced to York Avenue for a cab. He released the first one he hailed to a woman on crutches. When another approached, he swung the door open before the cab came to a complete halt. "Harkness Pavilion, 180 Fort Washington Avenue and an extra fifty if you get me there through this traffic in fifteen minutes or less." The cabbie shot up York and onto the FDR Drive.

At the destination, John paid him, happily including the tip, exited the cab, and, skipping steps from the sidewalk down to the lobby doors, hastened to his meeting with Dr. Shettles. Dr. Sweeney had shown him a picture of the doctor, but Dr. Shettles was the only man in the lobby in a physician's coat and thick black glasses. "I've got the test tubes." John patted his chest.

"I'll take those," Dr. Shettles said. No niceties. He reached for the bubble-wrapped vials, exchanging them for a glass container that almost slipped from John's sweaty hand. "Take this to the men's room." He pointed down the hall of the narrow wood-paneled lobby. "Do I have to tell you what to do?"

"Sweeney explained everything." John hurried to the men's room. Despite the unpleasantness he encountered, surprising for a hospital — the graffiti, an overflow of used brown paper towels, the smell — in a private stall, John manually expressed seminal fluid into the container. He tackled a sudden bout of nausea. Red-faced, he surfaced from the men's room and handed Shettles the repository, his last hope, wrapped in brown paper towels.

"I'll get these to the lab," Shettles said. "This is a ground-breaking day for all of us." He explained that if fertilization were successful, it would take those test-tube-enclosed fluids three to four days in the incubator for the cells to multiply to the blastocyst stage, which would then be ready to implant into Doris' uterine wall. "You can go," Shettles said. They didn't shake or say goodbye. Two vials and one container all filled with hope.

That afternoon John peeked in on his sleeping wife in the hospital. He reflected on the previous day. In her room before the surgery, she had taken his hand. She had his fingers trace all the scars from the many surgeries on her belly. She cried that all she had to show were scars. No baby. Now, all the pieces of their last hope were housed in an incubator in a lab far from him and his wife. He let her sleep. A few days and one last surgery to go — the implantation.

Meanwhile, back uptown, Shettles, after executing the fertilization and containing and incubating the mixture at 37 Celsius, couldn't contain himself. He boasted to a colleague that he was brewing a test-tube baby in the lab. Word shot to the chief.

In the morning, Shettles was summoned to the chief's office. It wasn't until after 2 p.m. that he appeared for the showdown. He expected to be berated. What he hadn't expected was the sight of the test tube on the desk, its dark contents no longer at 37 Celsius, but at room temperature. Lifeless. He hardly heard his chairman. Not sterile. Lawsuits. Federal regulations. Hospital liability. Clearance.

It was over. The end. His life's work, begun prior to WWII, finished. He charged from the office to call Sweeney.

The following morning, John arrived at Doris' hospital room overlooking the East River, the swirling waters an inviting view by day, but it was too early for daylight to have filtered into her room. The blinds were drawn. As John looked in, artificial light entered from the hall through the crack of the open door. It was sufficient to illuminate the white sheets Doris had ensnared herself in. Without disturbing her, John, his hair unkempt, entered and sat in the chair beside the bed and rested his head on its edge. He wanted his face to be the first thing Doris saw upon awaking. The tips of his fingers skimmed the back of her hand, where he placed his lips. He flicked the wet hair from her face, exposing her swollen eyelids.

Doris opened her eyes. "Dr. Shettles called me last night," she said. "Tell me how a stranger could have deprived us of our last chance to have our baby."

At Columbia, the chief locked the lab. Shettles resigned in disgrace.

CHAPTER 30

Nexus

Morning through late afternoon, there was no pause. Life moved. Lives changed. Lives began. Lives ended. The emergency room, like the aquarium in Shettles' lab, with nooks, coves, and spaces for its denizens, to dart in pursuit of its objectives: ambulance drivers rushing the injured and ill to doctors; nurses and physicians streaming en route to delivering medicine, machines, expertise, and babies; patients on gurneys heading for the operating room or, for less drastic intervention, accompanied to a treatment bay; med students, guppies, schooling from bed to bed, abreast of their attendings.

She was finished with pediatric rounds for the morning, and Candy's lab coat pockets were weighed down with reference books, notebook, stethoscope, ballpoints, sterile gloves, reflex hammer, penlight, alcohol pads, scissors, lubricant, disposable suture kit, tape, gauze, even a blue hippo finger puppet for the current four-week pediatric module, the puppet to be switched for a gestation wheel during the obstetrics module the following month. Clipboard in the crook of her arm, she had sprinted to her volunteer service in the emergency room where an open spigot of cases continually flowed.

At one treatment bay, she approached an unattended young woman in denim bell-bottoms, wet and frayed hems too long for her chunky-heeled shoes, her jacket, purse, and dripping umbrella hanging on a chair. "Has anyone seen you yet?"

The patient stretched the sleeves of her sweater over the fists she pressed into the sheets. "A nurse told me to wait here. I'm so embarrassed. Are you a nurse? I'd rather have a woman examine me. I've never been to a gynecologist."

Candy stepped back and jerked the green polyester curtain closed for privacy. "I'm Candace, a med student. So you have a gynecological complaint. Let's begin with your name."

"Jenny Nash." She handed Candy the crumpled intake sheets she had stuffed into her purse and stared down toward the dots of dried blood on the linoleum floor as the water from the umbrella flowed into them. "That's not my blood." Her voice broke, rose, and broke again. "I'm not bleeding. Am I?"

She approached the girl and, like a parent, felt her forehead. "You are warm. We'll be able to help you once you tell me what brought you here, but I don't think that's your blood." Candy blocked Jenny's view of the floor as she took the paperwork, then perused Jenny's written answers. "Can you talk to me about what brought you here today?"

With both hands still fisted in her sleeves, Jenny swept the hair away from her eyes. "I'm only nineteen. I don't want to die." She stared at Candy and grabbed at her arm. "Please help me."

Candy placed her hand over Jenny's, and leaned against the edge of the exam table. "What makes you think you might die?" Despite the background noise, she spoke in a soft voice to counter Jenny's anxiety.

"I have a tumor. It's got to be cancer. I should've had it checked sooner." She took the pillow from behind her, put it over her abdomen and hunched over. "I didn't want to show it to a doctor. I hoped the lump would just go away, but it's gotten bigger."

Candy wondered if she could be talking about a pregnancy. When she drew a ballpoint from her pocket to begin her notes for the chart, the finger puppet flew out with the pen, which made Jenny laugh.

"Pediatric rounds. Take it," Candy said. Jenny looked so young she could have been a peds patient. *Such innocence.* "Keep the puppet as a reminder to visit the doctor. Where's this tumor?"

Jenny slid a hand under the pillow and between her legs. "It's right here." With her other arm, she wiped her nose with the sleeve of her sweater.

"Is it painful?"

"Yes. And itchy. Sometimes I scratch until I bleed. I don't think it's bleeding now. This is too embarrassing. Can I leave?"

"You're here and in pain. Let's get you the answers and treatment you came for." She held on to Jenny's hand. "Getting here was the hardest part. I'll be working with a doctor, who'll probably be a man. I hope that's all right. We'll take a look after I get you into a gown. Try to relax. Be right back."

She backed out through the crack between the curtains into the emergency room flow and onto an unsuspecting foot. "Sorry," she said as soon as she felt the impediment. An attending, Dr. Walker, whom she hadn't worked with since the previous semester. "Would you have time to do a gyn assist on a patient in here?"

"Everybody's in a hurry. No harm, but I'm glad you're not wearing your stilettos," he mocked as he drew his hand along his brow. "Narrow escape."

He was a good-natured guy, so she took no offense. "I had to part with heels for practicality once I started clinical." She lifted her foot to show her wedge. "Quieter too. Do you have a moment?"

"Before I check my next patient." He pointed to the closed curtain. "In here?"

She dragged it open. "Jenny, this is Dr. Walker. He'll assist me." Candy handed him her clipboard on which a nurse had recorded Jenny's vitals. "I'll get you a gown," she said to Jenny.

Walker took the clipboard and pen. "I'm surprised you don't have a gown in your pockets. They look loaded." As he approached Jenny, Candy left.

When she returned, she handed Jenny the gown, and took the clipboard. "We'll leave while you remove your clothes, waist down and put this on, open to the back," she told Jenny. "Say 'okay' when you're ready."

When they returned, Candy pulled the curtains tightly closed with a sharp tug, hoping Jenny would feel secure. "Please lie down, knees up, feet flat on the table and close to your bottom." She took a package from her pocket, slipped on the sterile gloves, and covered Jenny with a sheet. "I'm going to palpate this small mass," she said as she examined the labia and reported to Walker the presence of an egg-shaped lump on the left labia majora. "An inflammation of the Bartholin's gland. Trapped mucous causing a cyst."

"Is that bad?" Jenny asked, still prone and staring at the ceiling, sucking nasal mucous into her throat.

"You can sit back up." She stroked Jenny's arm and said the relatively small cyst could be treated without surgery.

Walker, standing near the curtains, raised his eyebrows and shook his head. "We could get rid of this right now. No interim measures."

"Oral antibiotics and topical antibiotic cream should take care of the infection. Sitz baths will help, in lieu of surgery."

"That's the conservative approach," he said. "We don't have to baby her. If we did surgery, she wouldn't have to come back."

Candy scrutinized her frightened patient. "I'd like to try the conservative approach first," she said to Dr. Walker, "since she exhibited a fear of the hospital."

She said to Jenny, "Dr. Walker will write the prescriptions I mentioned, and I'll provide instructions for the baths. We'll begin there and you can schedule an appointment for a re-check in a week. That's not so bad, is it?"

"It's not cancer?" The puppet still on her finger, Jenny pushed her sleeves up to her elbows under the gown.

"You'll be fine, if you follow our instructions," Candy said. "Report to our clinic immediately if pain occurs or a fever spikes. That would be urgent."

"Thank you." She wiped her nose with the back of her hand.

Candy gave her a pack of tissues from one of her pockets. She wrote out the directions for a tub sitz bath and an over-the-toilet sitz. On Jenny's way out, Candy asked her if she needed a birth control prescription, and Jenny said she'd like one.

Walker wrote the prescriptions. "It was lucky you finally came in. It could've gotten worse. Get dressed. We'll be right out there."

Walker prodded Candy, "What will you do if she worsens?"

"If it becomes abscessed with severe pain, she'll require hospitalization and I'd take cultures to begin intravenous therapy with the appropriate antibiotic. If the infection didn't respond, she might require a marsupialization."

"I'm so relieved," Jenny said. She handed Candy the pack of tissues and the puppet.

"Keep them. Make regular gyn visits. You can come to our clinic. Don't ever feel embarrassed to care for your health. You can fill the script in the hospital pharmacy. Follow the signs." She pointed to the corridor and handed Jenny the page of instructions. "Read this. Any questions?"

Jenny took the paperwork, reached around Candy with both arms and hugged her.

"No more embarrassment, okay?"

Jenny released her grip on Candy, waved at Walker and left.

"Quick study, grateful patient, a win," Walker said.

"Heavy studying. Dewhurst's new ob-gyn text is great."

"If you can leave the ER, would you like to visit my breech patient?"

"Of course. I'm doing peds this month, but if you can, I'd like to do an ob-gyn preceptorship next, with you. I had signed up for a random match."

"I could arrange it. Let's see how the rest of the day goes." They walked the institutional green corridor to take the central bank of elevators to the fifth floor of the adjacent building. Walker rested both hands in his lab coat pockets, then took out a pack of gum and offered her a stick, which she declined. He asked about her work with Shettles.

"I was his research assistant. His fearlessness finally brought him down." She pulled the notebook from her pocket. Taped to the cover was the photo of sperm fertilizing an ovum. She passed the notebook to Walker. "In addition to everything he taught me, which I would never have learned anywhere else, he gave me that photo and a copy of his little green book."

"The man's brilliant, a bit of a maverick." He handed the notebook back. "But I do think the chief acted rashly in removing the test tube from the incubator."

"That poor couple," Candy said. "What a leap forward it will be when medicine can help women with destroyed fallopian tubes."

Walker raised his eyebrows. His forehead furrowed. "You knew Shettles well. Do you think he wanted to help the couple conceive with IVF, or did he want to be the first in the world to achieve an IVF birth?"

"Hard to judge. He started work on egg physiology and fertilization before World War II." She slipped the notebook into her hip pocket. "Although he wasn't always aboveboard with his patients, his resignation and departure are a monumental loss. I miss him."

"I don't think Shettles can go anywhere now." When the elevator stopped on five, Walker exited and Candy followed. He took the gum wrapper from his pocket and put it to his mouth to spit the gum into it.

Fertility had become a ripening field as researcher John Rock had predicted back in the forties. By 1968, there had been over half a million visits to doctors for problems with infertility. And now, in 1973, an unanticipated outcome of *Roe v. Wade*, only eight months earlier, was the significant number of women opting for legal abortions, which left fewer adoptable babies for infertile couples. A need for in vitro had become manifest. She was ready to pounce into the field of IVF, until the devastating event with Shettles shut down research.

"Speaking of procedures," Walker said, "I have an early trimester abortion scheduled after I check my breech. Join me if you have time."

"I'm here as long as you'll let me shadow you. This has been an ironic year with the legalization of abortion and a near in vitro." As she made the matter-of-fact statement, she considered the legalization's impact on women. How different her life could have been. The hairs on her arms stood on end.

"And it's possible you could assist in both an abortion and a delivery today," Walker said, "depending on Helen's progress."

En route to Walker's office, they strode along a section of the hallway with floor-to-ceiling windows offering a view of the garden surrounding the chapel outside. Rain hit the glass and slid down in long streams. "The leaves in the courtyard were at peak color yesterday," Candy said. "Now they're disappearing." A thought of the twisting oak leaf outside the consult-room window of Staten Island Hospital pierced her memory and shattered there, but didn't release her. How unnecessary all of that pain was. Seven years too early.

"I don't notice the weather or the seasons anymore." Walker's black tassel loafers stopped with a squeak at the open door to Helen's room. "Rubber soles." They entered and greeted Helen before washing their hands; he dropped the gum wrapper into the waste bin.

As they dried off and pulled on sterile gloves, she wondered when he'd introduce her. She turned to Helen and spoke up. "I'm Candace, a med student, and I'll stay if it's okay with you."

"A young woman. What a pleasant surprise. Please stay."

"Thank you for helping me learn from your experience," Candy said. They took positions at opposite sides of Helen's bed.

"The baby's kicking up a storm," Helen said. "I hope he, or she, is about ready to come out."

Her banged bob emphasized her ruddy cheeks. Her large belly mounded the white sheets. Beyond that mound, hung opposite the bed, was a bucolic landscape featuring a weathered farmhouse and a wide, apple-laden tree with farm animals grazing beneath. Nature didn't change.

"So, your baby is determined to be different, coming in breech." She leaned over to whisper, "I was born in a toilet in the middle of the night. That was different." Both women laughed.

"Is that what got you interested in gynecology?" Helen asked.

"That's a long story for another time. I'm going to examine your abdomen." At Helen's side, she pulled the sheets down as far as the pudendum, then lifted Helen's nightgown to expose her bare, veined abdomen. She felt the baby's head, arms and legs by sweeping her palms over Helen's belly. "Feels like a Frank breech, not kneeling or footing," Candy said over her shoulder to Walker.

"Intuitive hands," Walker said.

Hand on her upper abdomen, Helen said, "I knew this was the baby's head."

"What's your plan?" Candy asked Walker.

"You tell me. She's thirty-six weeks."

"That's an optimum time to turn the baby, unless Helen wants to schedule a C-section. What do you think, Helen?"

"I would prefer the delivery room with my husband, no C-section. What's involved? Can it hurt the baby?"

"It would only take a couple of minutes." Candy said, then looked at Walker. "But it could be painful. There are risks to the baby if there isn't enough fluid; the cord could wrap around the baby's neck." At Helen's abdomen, she moved her hands in circles to demonstrate the possibilities. "Membranes could rupture; the placenta could pull away from the uterus; the baby could move back. Weigh your options."

"Please do it. Dave and I prefer natural childbirth. I don't want drugs or surgery. We went to Lamaze classes." She sat up and clasped Walker's arm.

"We'll go ahead with the ECV, external cephalic version, to turn the fetus," Walker said. "Candace, give me an assist here. Have you done the maneuver?" He settled Helen back to a fully prone position.

"I've studied it," Candy answered. "Helen, do your breathing. It'll be practice for the big moment. We'll apply a little gel to your abdomen to ease the massage." She asked Walker to get some gel. "It'll be cold," she said as she applied a coating of the gel to Helen's abdomen. "Relax the best you can. This might hurt a bit, but it won't take long. Ready?"

"Ready," said Helen. She closed her eyes and clasped her hands behind her head.

Walker put his hands just above the pudendum and said to Candy, "With my hands here around the baby's bottom I'm going to push up." While he did, he instructed Candy to place her hands around the head, under Helen's breastbone. They massaged the baby by degrees, counter-clockwise all the way around until the head was downward, facing the cervix.

"That wasn't too bad, Helen, was it?"

"No," Helen said. "Good job."

"Candace, you can assist at the delivery, if it's okay with Helen."

She asked Helen, "Would that be all right with you?"

"Of course. And I hope I have a little girl who could grow up and be anything she wants to be, like you."

"Fine job, Helen," Walker said. "Let's hope the baby stays in this position. I'll check in on you later."

Candy and Walker removed and disposed of their gloves, washed their hands, said good-bye, and left; Candy was pleased with the procedure.

On the way to the elevator, Walker stopped and touched Candy's arm. "Good assist in there. I'll contact you at delivery to see if you're available."

"I'm always around. I may live at the dorm, but I'm never there. I don't have time to sleep."

"Are you still interested in the abortion?"

It was hard for her to believe that a mere three years ago, Jane Hodgson had become the only American physician ever convicted for performing an abortion. A female doctor in Minnesota, she had performed a therapeutic abortion on a married mother with rubella, in a hospital, but they pilloried her anyway. Exonerated after the *Roe* decision, she opened a women's clinic in Duluth for legal abortions because so many women had gone to her practice for care after botched illegal abortions. Candy could have worked there if she had followed Jonathan to Minnesota. She tugged at both ends of the stethoscope around her neck. "I want to give women what they need."

After a long wait, the elevator arrived, and they took it down to the first floor and continued their conversation as they made their way through the warren of halls, past the closed doors of restrooms and offices marked with physicians' nameplates, a reminder of the nameplate on her private room in Staten Island Hospital.

"I agree. Why limit the procedures you offer your patients? More procedures, more income. What other motivation do you need?"

She had learned to choose her battles and bit her tongue after that deplorable comment, as if she were doing this for money, really? When he unwrapped another stick of gum, she asked for one.

"Today, I'll be doing an in-office procedure. If it were less than seven weeks since my patient's last menstruation, what procedure would you suggest?"

"A menstrual extraction, removing what would have been expelled in menstruation, hardly noticeable as an abortion."

"With my patient, it's been eight weeks."

"You could perform a suction abortion with local or general anesthesia."

Walker opened the door to his office. The receptionist sat behind a sliding window opposite the entrance. He introduced Candy as a med student.

""I'm happy to meet the rare female med students," June said. "Wish I could do it." She pulled patient files as Walker went to the door of his suite of exam rooms and opened it for Candy.

Walking down the narrow hallway, he informed Candy that the patient had opted for local anesthesia so she could go home within two or three hours. The procedure itself would take only fifteen minutes. "Is this your first abortion?"

"My first assist." Memories of her ordeal crashed over her like an avalanche rumbling into a valley, but she maintained her composure.

"Anita's had an injection of ergotrate. You know what that does?"

"It causes uterine contractions, but can cause nausea and vomiting."

"Abortions may be legal now, but they're not without pain." He discarded his gum.

"Not only physical pain," Candy said as she followed him and discarded her gum.

Walker stopped at the closed door. "She's waiting in here." He took her patient file from the plastic pocket outside the room and knocked on the door.

She surveyed the room and Anita. Except for the en-suite toilet, it was typical. Anita was about thirty-five, attractive. She wore a wedding ring. Already in a hospital gown, she was propped up by pillows against the raised back of the examining table and under a sheet with empty silver stirrups sticking up on either side. Candy couldn't help but remember José's rough hands thrusting each of her feet into the stirrups. She had to learn to confront her past, when it popped up like a frightening jack-in-the-box, without an overt show of emotion. Anita was reading *Ms.* magazine. Women had rights to their bodies, and she'd be instrumental in serving them, not for the money. She clenched her jaw. Would she be able to restrain her emotions, or would she blow it and lose all she could learn from Walker?

"Hello, Anita. This is my colleague, Candace, a med student who will be assisting, if that's all right with you."

"Thanks for asking. A young woman, of course."

"Did you opt for the Demerol?" he asked.

"I did. I'd be lying if I didn't admit I'm nervous, but I'm ready." She tossed the magazine to the table.

Walker removed the pillows and Candy leveled the inclined back of the bed. They washed their hands and slipped into the gowns, gloves, masks and caps June had placed on the cabinet. He spoke quietly, "I've already done a pelvic and checked her blood type for Rh." Walker wheeled the electric suction pump over to the foot of the table where doctor and student rolled their stools, and Walker placed his foot near the machine's pedal.

"Anita, slide down to this end so you can put your feet in the stirrups."

"Socks," Candy said, "simple, but brilliant."

"June's suggestion, also the *Ms.* magazines." Walker said.

"I like June," Candy said.

Walker told Anita she'd remain conscious during the procedure. "If you have any questions, don't hold back."

Candy quietly asked Walker if subsequent pregnancies would abort if Rh-positive blood and Rh-negative blood mixed during an abortion.

"Yes. But you do know I was asking Anita for questions. However, ask away if you have any."

"I'm here to learn," she said.

Walker inserted the speculum to view the cervix. Next, he washed the cervix with antiseptic solution. He had Candy place the tenaculum to keep the cervix in position.

"I feel something," Anita said. "Cramping."

"Did I do something?" Candy asked.

"No," Walker said. "That's normal, Anita. Let me know if it becomes unbearable." He injected the local anesthetic into three places in the cervix. "Once the cervix is numb, I'll begin dilating." He inserted and removed dilators of increasing size, then the cannula from the machine into the uterus, moving it back and forth to suction the pregnancy tissue as he pressed on the machine's pedal. "How are you holding up, Anita?"

"The cramps are pretty bad right now. And I'm nauseous, but I can take it."

"Do some deep breathing," Candy said. "Let us know if you need a tray to vomit into."

Walker asked Candy, "Can you look in and see the suction tip loosening the fetal tissue from the uterine wall and aspirating it?"

"Yes." Then she looked up to check Anita, whose eyes were closed. Her hands were crossed over her chest, and she was breathing normally. She had not asked for the vomit tray.

Having aspirated the tissue, Walker removed the cannula, wiped the vagina, checked for bleeding, and removed the instruments. The tissue was caught in gauze in a stainless basin. "We'll check the basin later to assure that we got all the pieces so there will be no lingering signs of pregnancy."

Candy stared into the basin and reflected on her illegal abortion. The pain. The trauma. The irreversible consequences. This is how it could have been — should have been. Why did women have to struggle for the vote, for property rights, economic freedom, the right to choose careers, contraception, legal abortion, and fertility measures? She hadn't marched with placards, like Brenda, but she'd play a role in delivering women their rights.

After Walker checked with Anita, Candy wiped Anita's forehead. Walker said, "You can rest here until you're ready to leave. You'll feel cramping while the uterus contracts and empties, and you'll experience contractions for a few days, and bleeding for up to two weeks. You'll have to rest." He held her hands over her belly. "You must contact me the minute there's heavy bleeding or elevated temperature. Lie back now. June will come in and give you written instructions."

"My husband's coming to pick me up," Anita said. "I have to call to confirm the time."

"June will help you with that. Make an appointment with her for a follow-up. I'll leave the birth control prescription we discussed. Your period will return within four to eight weeks."

At the sink, Candy scrubbed her hands red as fury and elation raged within her pulsing blood. She was furious that in recent times women had to suffer, even die, needlessly and bear the shame of the scarlet "A" of illegal abortions. She was elated that doctors could now keep women in need safe. After Walker moved away from Anita and to the sink, she stepped over to

Anita. "You were able to exercise your choice in a safe environment. You're fortunate."

Anita clasped Candy's hand. "I was thinking about that. Thank you both." When June entered, Walker and Candy left.

Back in the hospital corridor Walker rubbed his hand across Candy's back. "Good job in there." She squirmed away. "Let's stop in the break room for coffee and recap."

"I might have to get back to the dorm."

"I'm expecting to hear from Helen soon. Thought you wanted to assist."

"I do, but I want to set personal boundaries. I'm your student."

"My hand on your back? It didn't mean anything."

"As long as we're clear."

Walker glanced down at his waist when his pager beeped. "It might be Helen. Are you in or not?" He used a wall phone to check his page. Helen was ready to deliver. Her water had broken. He had his office alert delivery.

They went back to the elevators where an elevator was waiting and open. "Another first," Candy said. "Well-timed, my happening upon you today." She risked adding, "Still I would have been remiss if I didn't make myself clear on personal boundaries. I'm glad you're not holding it against me." When the elevator stopped, they dashed out and sprinted to Helen's room.

Helen's husband stood at the bed tending to her. In a business suit, covered by a blue gown, he coached Helen through a contraction while timing her breathing, mopping her forehead with one hand, and with the other, he placed a can of tennis balls at her lower back. "Lamaze tricks I learned. Every little bit helps her, doc," Dave said. "Contractions are closer. I think the baby's ready."

"This is Candace, Dave. She's a clinical med student shadowing me today."

"Helen mentioned you," Dave said. "The baby, doc?"

"Let's check the cervix." Walker and Candy approached the foot of the bed and sat on the two stools to assess Helen's progress. He lifted the sheet.

"Cervix is nine and effacing." He felt her abdomen. "Baby still in proper position. We did a good job with that ECV."

"Baby got the idea," Candy said. She stood and observed Helen's discomfort across the sheet.

"Let's roll her to delivery," Walker said.

They wheeled Helen, panting, to the center of the room under bright lights, instrument trays prepared, three masked nurses waiting. Again, Walker and Candy, wearing scrub caps, went directly to the sinks and washed up. In delivery, a nurse helped each gown up. They returned to Helen. "Ready to meet your baby?" Candy asked.

The head of the table was inclined to a ninety-degree angle. Dave stood supporting Helen, holding her upright, massaging her back as he coached her through the he, he, he breathing with each contraction. Finally, Helen grunted and groaned and screamed with a push. "It hurts. It's coming. Breathing's not working. I feel it coming out my backside." She bent forward. "Glad I had that enema. I'm never doing this again."

"Breathe, Helen, short, quick breaths," Dave said.

"Go away, Dave," Helen shouted.

"Keep going. Rounded back, chin down," Walker said. "Push with the contractions. Don't strain from your face, Helen. Crowning." He turned to Candy. "Can you name the baby's position?"

"Anterior, facing Helen's back. This will be easier for her," Candy said. "So much blood. *Origin of the World*, through the open doors of the labia majora." As hard as birth must be, I would have done it a dozen times, she thought, without voicing the sentiment.

"What was that?" Walker asked.

"Anterior," she repeated.

"Take it from here. I'll hold this cloth beneath the baby's head, and you hold the head. Head's out, now shoulders. There it is. A girl," Walker announced. "I'll suction the airways. You dry her." After clearing the airways, Walker clamped the umbilical cord in two places. He handed a scalpel to Candy. "Wait a minute, then do the honors and cut the cord."

Candy cut the cord and couldn't help thinking how she had cut the cord of lineage that had kept her family's women connected for a thousand years. She patted the Janus coin under her gown and scrubs, pressing it against her chest, her personal scarlet "A."

"I'll give her to Helen and Dave," Candy said, "for a few skin-to-skin minutes before the Apgar. Then we'll warm the baby while we deliver the placenta." She positioned the naked newborn against Helen's bare chest.

A baby against Helen's chest. A two-thousand-year-old coin against hers.

Dave leaned over and embraced Helen and the baby. Beads of sweat fell from Helen's hairline across her ruddier-than-ever cheeks, dotting Dave's blue gown and spilling down to the baby's hand. "She's perfect."

"Shall I wait for the afterbirth to present?" Candy asked Walker.

"After I take the baby for her Apgar, wait for one last contraction, then press down hard on the abdomen." Having given the new parents several minutes with their baby, Walker lifted her and put her on the warming table in the room. The pediatrician had entered and was waiting to assess the newborn.

At the delivery table, while the baby was tested, Candy pressed hard on Helen's abdomen, flushing the placenta out with enough force to send it off the table across the floor. Candy found the smell fetid. A nurse collected the discharge. Candy withdrew to the scrub room to remove her protective clothing.

Finding the baby to be in good health, a nurse wrapped her in a blanket, put a cap on her head, brought her back to the mom, and braceleted both with matching wristbands. An attendant wheeled Helen to recovery. Dave followed.

Outside the room, Walker caught up to Candy. "Another good job. Congratulations on your first baby." As he started to reach for her back, he withdrew his hand, as though he were about to pet a rattlesnake. "Has the experience changed your mind about having one of your own?"

"I knew what to expect, but participating did leave an impression. I'd do it a dozen times over." She was glad he refrained from touching her and considered it a victory — the whole day, in fact, gave her release in an adrenaline rush. In her darkest hour, in Staten Island Hospital, she had made the right decision to enter medicine, and then gynecology. Her regret right now was the locking of Shettles' lab and the end to in vitro.

Walker spoke up. "Why don't we meet up in an hour or so and go to the diner for a drink to celebrate?" He pulled out another stick of gum. "We can discuss the preceptorship."

She deflected. "Do you think Helen would accept a gift from me?"

"How'd you manage a gift?"

"I've crocheted afghans for years," she said. "A calming pastime. I have quite a collection in my dorm. Guess that shows how tense I've been." She laughed and asked Walker for another stick of gum. "I can put the afghans to use as gifts for new moms. I'll bring a pink one to Helen's room tomorrow."

"And the drink?" They got back on the elevator and took it down to the ER where they had met that morning.

"I could use a drink," Candy said. "A toast to new life and the gifts of medicine. Give me an hour."

"I'll meet you at the dorm, at the lobby entrance," Walker said.

They pushed the swinging doors out to the ceaseless activity in the passageway.

CHAPTER 31

Exposure

"Been waiting long?"

"You're right on time," Walker said.

For the short walk to the diner from the safety of the dorm lobby, into the pounding rain, each opened an umbrella — Walker's black, oversized, Candy's from the museum gift shop, burgundy, printed with cabbage white butterflies, *Pieris rapae,* with the two charcoal spots of the female (not the single spot of the male), on each forewing, appearing as eyes.

"My umbrella's plenty big for both of us," Walker said. He reached out to her waist, but she jumped back. "Close yours and walk with me," he said. "I'll even run yours back to the lobby while you wait here under mine."

"I'm good with my own." She also liked her own space and the ability to define herself apart from him. Feme decovert. *Feme sole.*

The buffer created by the umbrellas and the beating of the rain rendered conversation difficult as they avoided splashing through water collected in potholes. "A bad night to come out," Candy shouted over to Walker, "but preferable to one more meal alone in the communal kitchen." She didn't care about the meal, but was anxious to nail down her preceptorship with Walker, a mentor in high demand, after a good day working together. They vaulted a final puddle, more of a moat guarding the curb. The roiling darkness reflected the blinking neon sign above the rain-streaked window of the Star Diner.

At the double door, Candy said, "I love the coziness of diner booths."

"And this diner's name couldn't be more appropriate," Walker said. "You were a star today."

"I'll take the compliment, but I did what any med student could have done. No need to pander. Fulfilled by the day's good outcomes, I'm ready for the days when things will go south." She closed her umbrella, twirled the rain from it and clasped it shut. Walker yanked his umbrella closed and pulled the door open for her. Walker's thick black hair, flecked with gray and coated with a men's hair-care product that smelled like Bay Rum, had captured globules of rain and resembled the morula stage of an embryo.

They placed their umbrellas against a stand, already filled beyond capacity. Whatever the weather, the diner was popular with hospital personnel. The acoustics were terrible, with the noise from the open kitchen wafting into the music and murmur of voices pervading the room. She hoped the noise wouldn't interfere with their planning session.

Near the entrance rotated a dessert display case flaunting foot-high lemon meringue pie, equally inflated banana cream pie, along with other temptations. Having indulged in one or two of these desserts in the past, she had found, tall as they might be, they didn't rise to expectations. As she and Walker passed the exposed brick walls under the lofty post-and-beam ceiling and unconcealed ductwork, everyone who knew Walker called out to him.

One woman, whom she recognized as Helen's nurse, said to Walker, "Nice job turning that baby, doc." She shook Walker's hand and then stared at Candy. "I know you," she said. "You were at Helen's delivery. Out and about with him, are you? And in this weather."

"Nasty night," Candy answered. *Nasty comment.* What would the staff make of her being out with him? She hadn't anticipated gossip. Even women objected to female doctors, few as there were, working closely, let alone socializing with, the male doctors.

Walker jumped in. "It was her first delivery assist. Just a drink and a bite, Louise, and planning for the preceptorship." They moved on.

As he stopped Walker, a doctor in green scrubs said, "Hi, Curt. What got you out of the hospital on an inclement night?" They slapped each other's backs. Walker explained that weather wasn't an issue for him.

Candy spotted an empty booth. Before they reached it, a man at a table with three others invited Walker and Candy to join them.

"Thanks. A booth just opened up, and we have some planning to do," Walker said.

The booth had a tabletop jukebox. "I was hoping we would be able to plan for the preceptorship. By the way, I'm buying in appreciation of a rewarding day," she said. The last time she had offered to treat a man was at Serendipity with Jonathan. She felt foolish then; this would be different. This was professional.

They hung their coats on the booth's hooks and slid across their respective benches. "I'm supposed to get to know my students well. From what I observed today, you're skilled, careful, prepared, generous, thoughtful, and empathetic." He grabbed her hand as she unwrapped her cutlery.

She recoiled at the physical contact, but hid it with a toothless half smile.

"It'll be easy to get to know you. It's part of my final assessment. We'll be working together very closely through the process. It's all part of the final assessment."

She pulled away and pressed her head against the seatback. "When I signed up, I didn't indicate a doctor preference, but after today—" She had worked closely with Shettles with no hint of physicality. This should be the same. She hadn't heard any rumors about Walker, but he usually worked with men.

He unwrapped his cutlery and placed the napkin on his lap. "It's in your best interest if we get along. An eighty-hour week, plus the heavy reading load I'll be giving you before we start. It'll destroy your social life."

"I don't have one. I'm excited to dive in."

Despite the crowd, a waitress came by within seconds and placed menus on the table. "Drinks?" she asked as she filled their glasses with water.

"Stoli martini, up, stirred, dirty," Walker said.

The waitress jotted his order and asked Candy, "And for you?"

"White wine."

"C'mon now. Be a man. I'll order for you."

Wayne and the apple juice.

"Vodka, shaken, twist," he said.

She could be wrong. She had to overcome her fear of becoming a victim. A deep breath. Jaws clenched. Manufacture a smile. Her solitariness created barriers to fun. She could relax and allow herself an evening with a colleague without guilt and fear.

"You did well with the ECV. And not to diminish your ability, but, absent complications, babies practically deliver themselves."

She opened up a bit to let him in. "A butcher delivered me, or more precisely, saved me from drowning in the toilet." She flicked her napkin and smoothed it across her lap.

"Don't leave me hanging. Did he botch the delivery, or was he literally a butcher?"

She allowed herself a laugh and related her birth story.

"Your toilet story, the one you mentioned to Helen. You had a head start in gynecology, so to speak," Walker said. "And it won't be long before you'll be creating pregnancies and delivering the babies."

"An ambition I was devoted to. Although now that the lab's been locked, my prospects look dark."

The waitress carried their drinks over. "Feed my disappointment with a bloody, thick burger," Candy said.

"I always order the same thing," Walker said. "Stuffed pork chops, mashed, baked beans with bacon." The waitress left with their orders and Walker continued, "You haven't tried your martini." He lifted his glass to her, careful not to spill from the shallow bowl.

"What got you into medicine?" she asked.

"My congenital hemophobia." He pulled a lighter from his pocket and placed it on the table. "As a child, when I'd scrape a knee or get a bloody nose, the sight of the blood was worse than the pain. I'd get light-headed, suffer vasovagal syncope, or wretch." He stirred the speared olives in his glass.

"I didn't notice any reaction today." She pushed the lemon twist from the rim of the glass into the bowl.

"I'm getting there. In ninth grade, my best friend and I were playing tennis before the courts opened. He came to the net, slid on the clay, and hit the fleshy under-part of his chin on the post, and boy, did it gush."

"I'm told at two or three," she said, "I fell from the monkey bars, and the blood from my chin turned my white rompers scarlet." She put her martini down and lifted her chin to display the scar.

"Barely noticeable," he said. "To wrap up, when I ran to help him, I fell to the ground beside him and almost passed out. I stared forever, it seemed, but finally got myself together, got my towel, wiped his chin, and applied compression, all with my eyes shut." He crushed his napkin in both hands. "Turned out having to help someone was what I needed. After that, I started volunteer work in the ER. The more blood I saw, the less of a reaction I experienced, and I discovered I liked medicine."

Maybe he was a good guy. Would it ever become easy to avoid becoming prey? Was that why the female cabbage whites had two "eyes" on each wing?

Above the clattering of china cups, plates, and voices, Paul Simon sang "Kodachrome" through the tabletop jukebox. "Great lyrics," Walker said. "Do you think everything looks worse in black and white?"

"I think nothing is black and white except maybe cabbage whites, butterflies." The waitress delivered their food and eyed the empty glasses. "Another round?"

"No thanks."

"You said you liked vodka. Just one more." He ordered another round.

She held her burger with both hands and bit in. He cut each bite of pork with his steak knife. The second round of drinks arrived as they cleaned their plates, which the waitress cleared after placing their martinis.

Walker reached into his jacket pocket, pulled out a pack of Camels, and tapped out the filter end of a cigarette, which he removed from the crumpled pack with his lips. He squinted toward her.

She considered asking about the date engraved on the lighter.

"Nothing like a smoke and a martini after dinner," Walker said. "Casablanca—now there's something that looks great in black and white. When I smoke, I think of myself as Rick in Morocco."

"Not so black and white," she said.

"How so?"

"Right and wrong. Was Rick a good guy or not, living outside the law, using Ilsa to justify his cynicism, murdering Strasser?"

"Of course, Rick was a good guy," Walker said. "He helped people. He didn't know Ilsa was married, and he sacrificed for her in the end. Strasser got what he deserved. It was Ilsa who cheated on her husband."

"When Ilsa was with Rick in Paris, she believed her husband was dead, so she wasn't cheating on him," she said. "Not so black and white."

"You really dig into old movies," he said.

"My father, at eighteen, before he was my father, took part in the Normandy invasion. Idealistic, but it destroyed his life even though he survived. I like movies that make me think." She finished her drink.

"That's too heavy for two martinis and a long day. What else do you enjoy?"

"Crocheting, you know, and volunteering. At one time, there was shell collecting, entomology, ice skating, dancing."

He reached into his pants pocket and brought out a handful of change, which he sorted through. "Three quarters. Select some music from our jukebox, but there's no dancing here. We'll get one more round of martinis." He gestured the waitress over and ordered another round.

Candy flipped the pages with the lever under the jukebox. "'Will It Go Round in Circles' and 'Right Place, Wrong Time.' I'll leave the last for you."

After she let go, he took over the lever. "Got one. 'Diamond Girl,' for you." He scooped up his change, then removed another cigarette from the pack.

There was a lull in the conversation. A third drink might be too much. They sat back. Walker lit up and inhaled. He blew smoke across the table at Candy. She waved it back. Her first song played.

The waitress dropped off their drinks. "Bring the check," he said.

"Too bad there's no dancing here. One of those underappreciated pleasures that falls by the wayside without notice." She and Wayne had fun when they danced. That was real. "I have a wedding coming up on Sunday. It's short notice, but it's a place we could dance. Purely professional, in a 'getting to know you' way."

"One downside of obstetrics," he said, "is that it's hard to plan."

"We haven't done much planning for the preceptorship," she said.

"I've done so many. I've got it covered. You're in gifted hands."

By the time their third martinis arrived, she had difficulty focusing, but with little conversation, drank it much too quickly. Walker had chain-smoked nearly the whole pack of Camels. "I think it's time for us to leave. Almost everyone is gone." He put the cigarettes and lighter back in his pocket, took out his wallet and left several bills on the table with the check.

She had forgotten to ask about the lighter. No matter. "I said I'd get the check."

"You're a student. I earn a living. I'll get it," he said.

When she stood, she had to hold onto the table. "Wow, I'm a bit tipsy. I didn't realize—"

Walker helped her with her coat and slipped into his. He put his arm around her waist. "Got your back." They walked to the door and collected their umbrellas. "No need to open yours. We'll both fit under mine."

Even with all the time they had spent in the diner, it was still pouring. Under his umbrella, she stayed close to Walker. As they moved on, she glanced down to avoid the puddles. When she felt quite a bit of time had passed, she peered out from under the umbrella to see they were not headed for the dorm. "Where are we?"

"You're in no shape to go home alone. Since I can't go to your dorm floor. I'm taking you to my apartment."

"I don't think so. I'm not that tipsy."

"I pegged you for a modern woman, sex without strings. A risk taker. Bold. Stay with me tonight. You might even enjoy it."

Although unsteady, she pulled away at once, opened her umbrella, regained her bearings, and headed home.

"Bitch," he shouted and continued walking.

Feme sole.

CHAPTER 32

Autumnal Fall

The earth's imaginary axis, straight up, produced a singular brightness. Day and night were nearly equal. Lingering traces of summer's warmth commingled with enough of a chill to warn of impending winter and a plunge into darkness. Not a stasis, like the solstices. No stopping. Only change spinning forward, earth a celestial carousel. The fire of the autumnal forge, proclaimed by the blazing trees in Central Park, was primed to mold new forms of the malleable clay figures gravity kept earthbound.

This September twenty-third wedding date assured that Brenda was neither a June bride, more appropriate for the young, nor the winter bride she and Rick had envisioned. Brenda and Simon, equals in their partnership, viewed the Libra equinox as the ideal juncture for their union, propitious for the two redheads.

Following the nuptials in the Lady Chapel of Saint Patrick's Cathedral, wedding party and guests proceeded up Fifth Avenue to the reception at the Sky Gardens of the St. Moritz On the Park, with a view of Central Park in its autumnal glory. For their first dance to "You are the Sunshine of My Life," Simon and Brenda skimmed the dancefloor, after which he danced with Brenda's mother, freeing the bride to rescue her maid of honor, whom she had seen conversing with her mother.

Gloria held Candy's, stroked her hair, maternal gestures, and told her, as she had over the years, how proud she was of her drive to become a doctor. But she always followed with the inevitable "Are you keeping company with anyone?" question. "You're still wearing Grandma's necklace," she said. "Does that mean you plan to honor our family legacy in spite of your choice to work?" She stared into Candy's eyes, then threw down her daughter's hands as if they were hot. She drew a pack of L&Ms from the handbag on the table. "This should be your wedding." Her hands shook as she struck several matches. "You need to have children soon, even if there's no January baby. Make time for a man in your life. You're not nineteen anymore."

She wasn't prepared for the burn of this onslaught of guilt. When Brenda swung by, Candy burst forward and cocked her head toward the balcony. *Get me out of here.*

"I promise I'll bring her back," Brenda said.

"The last time you took her, she never came back. She's not even the same girl," Gloria said. "To think I used to trust you with her care."

Bride and maid of honor fled the cacophony of the banquet room, passed through the French doors, over the threshold, which snagged the bridal gown. "We need a quiet moment to catch up," Brenda said. She examined the tear at the hem. "Remind me to hide it in the pictures." They leaned their elbows on the balustrade of the balcony thirty-three floors above the park. "You have to learn to open up. I'm always here for you."

"Husband, children. The necklace," Candy said. "I'm such a disappointment to my mother. My bad choices."

"There's nothing you can do, and I'm not sure you can tell her," Brenda said. "You're doing important work."

"That's all fallen through too, after the Shettles debacle and now Walker."

"Walker? Even though I'm not in the next room anymore, you call me."

Not long after Candy had moved to Columbia's campus, Brenda had relocated to D.C. to be close to Rick in Arlington, and Simon had followed. The apartment where they had shared so much lay vacant. Right now, Candy felt empty, having lost Shettles, possibly her dream, and now the preceptorship with Walker. She plowed her fingers through her hair and tugged at her curls.

Wayne had long ago caught her. Trapped her in a loveless glass jar from which she clearly observed the love of others like Brenda and Simon, but a love like theirs would never be hers. Her best efforts to join the world of romance had left her wings beating and beaten. Frayed to powder. As happy as she was for Brenda and Simon, she hoped Brenda couldn't read her deep envy and resentment. "I wish your skill for making good choices had rubbed off on me."

"Workload? Lack of sleep? Shettles?" Brenda handed her a champagne coupe from the tray of the passing waiter. "You'll come up with something to get back in that lab. Shettles gave you all his secrets."

"As did my grandmother, and look what I did with that. I can't get out of my own way."

"It takes time." Brenda freed the envelope that she had tucked in her bra. "I've never totally let go of Rick. Remember the letter his mother gave me at the funeral, urging me to move on? His parents declined their wedding invitation." She folded it back into her bra. "It's my 'something old.' I visit the grave weekly. Simon isn't threatened."

"I'd love what you and Simon have. Forgive me for thinking about myself on your big day."

Brenda took a glass of champagne for herself at the waiter's next pass, and another for Candy, hers already empty. "Celebrate with me." She explained how Simon had accepted a position with the Department of Health, Education and Welfare and she'd developed ties with the White House, thanks to Helen Thomas. She said she was anxious to cover the end to the war and Watergate. They'd bought a house in D.C. "Use the Manhattan apartment whenever you'd like. We're keeping it as a pied-à-terre."

Simon appeared at the balcony doors, then joined the women. Brenda took his hand and held it against her chest, over the envelope, a corner jutting out from her bra.

"I hope you didn't get to the best part without me," he said and winked at Brenda.

"What's that?" Candy asked.

"I'm pregnant with twins," Brenda said. "Can you believe it?"

"I can't believe you kept that from me the whole time we've been talking." Would the muscles of her face betray her? Could she be deceitful enough to hide her sheer pain? She was overjoyed for them as they looked forward to a joy she'd never have. She said to Simon, "Now, that's the way to deliver babies."

What he didn't say was that she owed it to her poor choices. "I envy you." *That was honest.* "Twins. How will you manage it all?"

"Rick and I had discussed my being a working mother on our last night together," Brenda said. "We never arrived at an answer, but I wouldn't do it alone." She put her arm around Simon.

"There's some great dance music going to waste in there," he said to Candy. "Let me spin you around the dance floor till you're dizzy." She was already reeling with her conflicting emotions, and perhaps the champagne. Simon walked between the two women, an arm around each, and they went back inside.

Unlike Brenda, she was going it alone, as it was her solitary challenge to break out of her glass prison. She wanted more than a Helen Gurley Brown sex partner, like Jonathan was, although she didn't want her personal life to remain barren. She had busied herself with work in the hospital and in the free clinic, obsessed with helping as many women as she could reach with compassionate care, contraception, safe abortions and fertility. The light was just beyond those two millimeters of glass.

The memory of Wayne and his Cheshire Cat grin had become all-enveloping, like a spider web she'd walked into, its sticky silk having ensnared her. She twisted. Gravity got the best of her. Wings folded, she lay on the bottom of the glass jar.

CHAPTER 33

All That Glitters

This last day of 1978 she awoke with difficulty in her two-person suite at the dorm. After Dr. Thompson had alerted her that Jessica, the candy striper of twelve years earlier, would be back in New York from California for a residency at Columbia, Candy reached out with an invitation to be her roommate. Jessica's perennial optimism would keep her from cracking. Although in different departments — gynecology and surgery — they'd be able to connect during the day.

Jessica had arrived in June, a month before the destroyed test-tube case finally went to court that July, five years after the Shettles debacle. That same week, thanks to the tireless efforts of Drs. Steptoe and Edwards, Louise Joy Brown, the world's first in vitro baby, had been born in England. And five long years after the chief had destroyed Doris's embryo, Doris won her case against him and Columbia. Because of the new positive news coverage, in vitro, IVF, gained favorability with the public, with Americans asking, "Why wasn't the USA first?" And for five years, the chief repeatedly refused Candy's demands, entreaties, negotiations, challenges for admittance to Shettles' locked lab. For five years, from her illusory glass prison, she had fruitlessly prevailed upon him for access to the lab and the research rotting in there. And the once-glistening glass slides, vials, Petri dishes, syringes, waiting.

She argued that access to the data, which she had helped compile as Shettles' assistant, belonged to her as well and could prove priceless, especially at this juncture, in the field of reproductive endocrinology. Confident in Shettles' procedures, she sought to review his materials against the research she had been studying from Dr. Steptoe, the gynecologist who favored laparoscopy for egg retrieval, and his partner, the embryologist, Dr. Edwards. The chief was stone-faced indifferent. Her fists tired of pounding glass walls.

Back in 1973, would Shettles' destroyed test tube have produced a baby? She believed it would have. She hypothesized that Steptoe's use of the laparoscope was a determining factor in his success. She couldn't budge the chief, but she continued to speak up. She refused to let a man stand in the way of the dreams of those American women who had no choice but to conceive with in vitro. Georgeanna Jones was doing her part pioneering in vitro research with her husband at Eastern Virginia Medical School, as they had at Johns Hopkins. Candy didn't care who succeeded first in the U.S., but contemporaries of Shettles, the Joneses, were well on their way, with a working lab and bespoken funding. Frustrated, she kept abreast of Georgeanna's hundreds of scientific articles. By the time Jessica had arrived, Candy's wings were all but powder.

She didn't hear any noise in the suite, and assumed Jessica was already up and out. For the moment, she could face the day, brew strong coffee, shower, dress, and head to the hospital where she was better at helping others than she was at helping herself. Struggling, she lifted her head from the pillow. She threw off her layers of blankets. Getting out of bed was a measured ritual this morning. After rolling over and sitting on the edge of the mattress, she placed both feet on the floor, then pulled them up with the shock of the cold. When she stood, stooped over, feeling as if she carried an elephant, she realized it was the Janus coin around her neck weighing her down, a look-back, a reminder of her failures.

Her mother had recently died with the family legacy unfulfilled. Though Candy had made it home to be with her, Mother hadn't recognized her. The final cord with her family had been severed. Stuck at the bottom of the jar for five years, since Brenda's wedding, there was no way out of this silken web that had engulfed the remnants of her wings. She was nauseated.

Anxious to wash away the failures of the setting year, as well as years past, she craved an ablution. She reached for the robe on her chair and slipped into it, leaving the belt uncinched. Now acclimated to the cold floor, she trudged to the bathroom where she passed her hand between the shower curtain and the wall and touched the lever, which broke off in her hand.

After pulling a towel from its hook and pulling her sash tight, she walked out of her suite and down the hall, knocking on successive doors without responses, her hair reaching out in all directions as she repeatedly raked through it, her heart pounding, as she grew light-headed. At the end of the corridor, she opened the exit door to the stairwell and ran down a flight of stairs.

Pushing past the red-and-black "Men Only" notice with both hands, she gained access to the hallway to find a series of locked rooms, until she came upon a row of partially-open curtains on shower stalls in the men's communal bathroom. Not even considering that any men might be present, she threw open the first curtain she saw and turned the faucet. While waiting for the water to flow hot, she dropped her robe to the floor outside the stall, and then stepped in.

As she lifted her face to the water from the showerhead, she twisted in the tight space and lathered with the soap from the tray. The brown-stained grout between tiles triggered a memory. By the time a man's hand reached in to turn the water off, she lay crumpled over the drain, the water no longer pelting her face.

"Ma'am, are you okay?" Her eyes angled up to the voice. "Can you stand?" He picked up the robe and held it out between the two of them. "Let me help you." He knelt on the lip of the shower's threshold and thrust his forearms beneath her armpits to lift her high enough to slip her into the robe from behind.

Once out of the shower, he helped her stand, but she fell to the floor, where she sat with her chin on her raised knees. "All I wanted was a shower," she said. "I couldn't find a shower. Where am I?"

After he shooed away an incoming man, he said, "You're in the men's residence. Are you visiting?" He pulled a towel from a peg on the wall, covered her hair, and sat with her.

She reached up to the towel and rubbed her hair. "What's my punishment?"

"Punishment?"

"For being on the men's floor."

"Do you know how many women are sneaked up here? Don't worry."

"I need time." She towel-dried her hair for several minutes before attempting to stand. "Walk me to my room."

"You live here?" He stood, and when she reached for his hand, he helped her to her feet.

"I'm a resident. I've got to get to work."

"You need a day off. You must be upstairs."

She tied her belt. "Up. Women only," she said. She leaned on him. "I'll make an exception for you." Her knees wanted to cave.

"I've seen quite a few flu cases at the hospital recently," he said. "Maybe you caught it."

"It's not the flu."

Together they walked up the stairwell, she leaning on him, and reached a door with a "Women Only" notice posted. They laughed. He accompanied her to her suite, and sat her at the kitchen table. He lifted the teapot from the counter, filled it, and placed it on the burner. "Tea always helps," he said.

"Thanks."

"Mind if I join you?" he asked and sat with her after she nodded. "I'll stay until I pour your tea."

When Candy explained how the broken shower handle initiated the events, he offered to inspect it. "That happens around here a lot. I think I can fix it if you have a screwdriver."

She directed him to the tool kit under the bathroom sink. She trusted him. He was gone only a few minutes when she heard water running. The teakettle whistled and she got up for a teabag and a cup. "Would you like tea?" she shouted into the bathroom.

He came out. "No thanks. I've got to get to the hospital if you're okay." He walked to the door, and she followed. He shook her hand. "Jim, cardiology. See you at the hospital."

"Candy, gynecology. Thanks." She closed the door and went to the table for her tea, composed herself, dressed, and left for the hospital.

She was late for the first time, but other residents had covered her patients and the world hadn't fallen apart. She stepped into her routine. Jessica soon arrived in the department and took her aside.

"I've been searching for you for the past two hours. No one had seen you. You look awful. What happened?" Jessica asked.

Candy led her to the lounge. "I wasn't feeling well."

"I can see that."

Candy went to the percolator on the counter and poured herself a cup of coffee. "Missed my cup this morning. Had tea instead."

"Are you okay now?" Jessica asked as she lifted a paper cup from a stack. She poured herself some coffee and sat at the table.

"Fatigue, maybe." She sat opposite Jessica. "I'm fine. Do you know Jim in cardiology?"

"No," Jessica said. She blew on the coffee, had some, and placed the cup on the table.

"He helped me out this morning, fixed our shower, made me tea. He lives a floor below us. Why did you need me earlier?"

"Our shower was broken?"

"Why did you need me?"

"Are you well enough to attend a New Year's party?" Jessica asked. She pulled an envelope from her pocket and passed it across the table. "Open it. It's intriguing."

Candy took the envelope and removed the metallic square, engraved in script. Some glitter seeped out. "Studio Fifty-four cordially invites you to turn over a new leaf on New Year's Eve." She handed it back. "Where'd you get this?"

"A patient, Robert, with a head lac requiring fifty stitches. Fell off a ladder. He's the party planner for the club and had to be there for a delivery of four tons of glitter for tonight's event. He was grateful I worked quickly, so he invited me and a friend. Can you imagine four tons of glitter?"

"You've been in California too long," Candy said. "That club has a reputation for hedonism and drugs. The moon and the spoon and all that. Cocaine. What would two introverted doctors like us do there?" She finished her coffee, stood, and disposed of the cup.

"Speak for yourself," Jessica said. "I date. I'm on the pill. You've got to get out too. You could do what everyone else does there, but without drugs. Escape reality, indulge in fantasy, let off steam. Robert made it sound exciting while I sutured his laceration. He even signed the invitation for two to guarantee us admittance."

"You're not thinking of going?" Candy approached the door to leave the lounge. "I'm behind on patients. I've got to go."

Jessica sprang up to block her at the door. "It's New Year's Eve. Please go with me. We'll turn over a new leaf. It's one night."

"This morning I was thinking that I'm glad you're here. You're right. It's one night. It might be what I need."

"You won't regret it. But we only have till ten to find something spectacular to wear."

"Brenda still has fabulous clothes at her apartment," Candy said. "We can take the subway downtown after shift, find something to wear, and taxi to the party from there."

"I'll catch you at home," Jessica said. She tossed her unfinished coffee into the trash near the door, waved to Candy, who went in one direction as she walked down the hall in the other.

At Brenda's apartment that night, Candy decided on a floor-length, red taffeta skirt and a sheer ivory shirt with strategically placed pockets. Jessica chose a vivid Pucci mini-dress. "I can't imagine Brenda in this," Jessica said. All the clothes in the closet carried Brenda's signature scent, L'Air du Temps.

"She never wore that dress. The tags are still attached," Candy said. "It's great on you." They put on their own evening shoes, slipped back into their coats, and headed to Fifth Avenue for a cab uptown. Arriving at West Fifty-fourth, the mass of people in the street prevented the taxi from getting close to the club. They got off on the corner of Eighth Avenue and walked the grimy sidewalk past industrial buildings, beckoned by the bright light of the 54 Marquee overhanging the sidewalk and a portion of the crowd. With spectacularly outfitted men and women outside the velvet rope vying for passage to the coveted side, the scene was chaotic. "I'm doubting the wisdom of this," Candy said.

At the rope Jessica handed the invitation to the gatekeeper; he was allowing passage to celebrities and selecting common folk dressed to his liking. "Robert wrote a note on it when I treated him at the hospital this morning," she said. Jessica gave him the entrance fee for both of them. He refused it.

"Robert told me about you two. You don't look like any doctors I ever met," he said. He lifted the red velvet rope.

Beyond the major hurdle, through one set of smoked glass doors to another, down a mirrored hall, like being inside a kaleidoscope, they walked under a baroque vaulted ceiling dangling chandeliers from the venue's opera theater era, the faceted crystals now hit by futuristic green lasers that punctuated the blasting bass beat, rattling Candy's senses. On the dance floor, pulsating strobe lights — red, green, blue — bathed writhing bodies, arms waving in the air, to the disco beat of Gloria Gaynor's "I Will Survive."

After checking their coats, Candy and Jessica went to the bar and ordered champagne. Drinks downed for courage, they were fueled to step down to the dance floor onto the glitter, the four tons of glitter, which was at least four inches deep. "This is what four tons of glitter looks like," Jessica said. Agitated by motion, glitter flew from the floor into the air, sparkling in the strobe light, like stars in the solar system, mincing reality. Everyone danced in the sparkling cosmos. The cavernous galaxy exploded with undulating light and music.

Some revelers were elegant in evening wear; others were topless, naked, or wearing only a thin coating of body paint; some indulged fantasies in flamboyant costumes of feathers, togas, the uniforms of Roman soldiers. Shirtless waiters' bare chests boasted satin-lapelled white boleros with white bow ties, and the men flaunted white short-shorts and knee-high stockings.

Tubes of floating red and blue lights dipped and rose. Pink, yellow, and green lasers clashed. Glittering disco balls spinning overhead reflected the colors. Except for the beat of the music, everything, including the heaving theatrical dance floor, was in constant flux. Alcohol for most, and drugs for many, magnified the surreal effects. Above the fantastic universe, the hanging crescent moon engulfed the spoon.

Truman Capote smoked a cigarette and, under his Panama hat, surveyed the scene from the mezzanine balcony. Grace Jones danced on stage in little more than a metallic "V" attached to a matching bikini bottom. Bianca Jagger posed with Andy Warhol. Liza Minnelli, Diana Ross, Halston, Debbie Harry, Jerry Hall, and Paloma Picasso sprawled on the banquettes. Candy and Jessica added their bodies to the momentum, everyone dancing in a free-for-all, the common people, except for "bridge and tunnel" people, his way of mocking people from the outer boroughs, of course, joining the celebrities, and the exhibitionists. The surroundings were ephemeral, even without the mind-altering effects of drugs or alcohol.

"Good choice on the outfit," Jessica shouted to Candy as they danced. Jessica shook Candy's arm and pointed to Diana Ross wearing the exact skirt Candy had on, with a different top.

Candy leaned into Jessica. "Continue dancing. Restroom."

She maneuvered among the dancers, through the ever-snowing glitter. In the unisex restroom, among people engaged in various sexual acts or snorting cocaine, she had an urge to cast off her inhibitions too. Slipping her bra straps down her arms, she slid the bra off under her shirt and hurled it into the trash.

"Go girl," a stranger shouted.

Released from a vise imposed by polite society, she closed her eyes, inhaled a whiff of second-hand cigarette and marijuana smoke. Renewed, she left to reunite with Jessica on the dance floor. The stroke of midnight unleashed an outpouring of jubilant physical contact, and the music never skipped a beat.

When Jessica and Candy hugged, Jessica pulled back. "I didn't notice because of the pockets, but what happened to your bra?"

"I needed to breathe. This seemed like the perfect place to liberate myself."

That first morning of 1979, Candy and Jessica emerged from the Hall of Hedonism and the night's excesses. "You've always been a good influence on me," Candy said. "Should we go home or to Brenda's?"

"Home," Jessica said. "I'd like to begin the new week and the new year there."

"I did turn over a new leaf last night." Like Janus, she looked forward.

On their way to the avenue to hail a cab uptown, they passed a newsstand. The *Post* and *Daily News* both featured front-page photos of celebrities at the party. Jessica picked up a copy of the News. "Would you like a memento of the event?"

"I'll take the *Post*," Candy said. They stepped off the curb to wave down the first cab they saw. After giving their destination to the cabbie, Jessica held up her paper and said, "Diana Ross is in your skirt on the front page."

"It's Brenda's skirt." She put distance between herself and the photo. But there it was, Wayne Woods, that Cheshire Cat smirk of his, celebrity quarterback, with his arm around the singer in the photo, both shaking glitter from their hair. Candy ran her fingers through her hair, and glitter fell out. "I wonder how long it will take us to get this stuff out of our hair?" she asked. Like the glitter, she couldn't seem to shake Wayne's presence with her in the universe, especially in New York.

"We may have to wear scrub caps outside the OR as well, so we don't contaminate our patients," Jessica laughed. "As surreal as the party was, we have empirical proof we were there."

Candy was relieved she hadn't noticed Wayne at the club. How did he manage to haunt her? First, only flashes of memories, and now a photo. The same glitter in her hair as his. She wished him away. She flipped the pages of the tabloid and stopped at an Air France ad for a romantic weekend in Paris.

"You're so quiet. What are you reading?" Jessica asked.

Candy was back to holding things in, even though Jessica was one person who would understand her distress. "An ad for a long weekend in Paris. I've never taken a vacation. Until this morning, I've never even been late. I think I can arrange a trip in time for my birthday. Join me?"

"Can't do it. I just got to Columbia. It may not be wise to go by yourself. You've never been out of the country. Do you even have a passport?"

"I'll get one. Romantic Paris is probably the last place one should go alone, but I'm going to do it," Candy said. "I need a change of scenery." She'd put the Atlantic between herself and Wayne.

PART IV

Off with the Lid

CHAPTER 34

L'Étranger

Paris, 1979

Escaping her demons in New York City, Candy arrived in Paris. The drive from Charles de Gaulle Airport to the city deepened the inner gloom she had hoped to elude in the City of Light. Gray was abundant in the sweeping sky above the low profile of the buildings — constructed of the limestone bedrock on which they stood — their profile a contrast to Manhattan's soaring edifices, which eclipsed the sky. As they drove, a tinge of pale yellow perforated, and then overpowered, the gray. Along the route, naked trees endured the absence of leaves. Their outstretched black arms, silhouetted against the backdrop, appeared to be in supplication of more light.

New Year's Eve, three weeks earlier, had been a break from her disciplined routine. The extravaganza temporarily liberated her. She enjoyed a moment of action without consequence. That long-lost freedom of gliding on ice. Or the thrill of reaching the peak of the roller coaster, about to plunge. The play of youth. Actions without consequences. Although she had left that bra in the trash, needing a bra was confirmation that she was an adult. Her actions carried consequences. She didn't trash, or burn, her other bras.

The searing memories, which Wayne's front-page photo lit, fueled this impulsive decision to travel to Paris, although the realist in her knew distance alone, not even the Atlantic, could extinguish the memories. She was foolish to think she could flee Wayne and the trailing guilt and pain ensnaring her, even if it was imaginary. As usual, second thoughts overcame her, and she would have asked the driver to take her back to the airport, but her ineptitude with French stifled the urge, although she knew he spoke English.

At the airport, she had given him her destination — "Hotel Bersoly's St. Germain, vingt-huit Rue de Lille, près de la Gare d'Orsay," as she read the phonetic pronunciation from her travel agent's cheat-sheet.

"Oui, madame. I know it," he had said.

Her French had not fooled him; however, it had given her a small sense of control. She couldn't retreat this soon, before daring the uniqueness of the moment — the unbounded sky, her solitariness, days without work or structure — to become familiar, if only for a long weekend.

Enveloped by her thoughts and the view whizzing by, she was surprised how soon the cab stopped in front of a quaint building resembling all the other quaint buildings on the street. Each window of the white façade flaunted a planter of hanging greens. An unpretentious awning over the entrance displayed the hotel's name on the scalloped valance.

"Madame, we've arrived." The driver retrieved her suitcase while she stepped to the narrow sidewalk, waited beneath the awning, and took her wallet from her purse. After exchanging several pretty bills for her bag, she entered the hotel. Upon learning that Candy loved history, the travel agent had chatted up this venue as an intimate seventeenth-century building of sixteen rooms, each decorated in the palette of a French Impressionist, a perfect mix of art and history, and it was reasonable.

Traversing the timeworn stone floor to the reception desk, she noted a fireplace toward the far end of the lobby, near a wood-paneled bar, and beneath the vaulted ceiling, tables set with white cloths and small vases of fresh flowers. She introduced herself to the concierge.

"Madame or mademoiselle?" He leafed through papers on his desk.

"Doctor," she said. An attempt to reassert her identity.

In fluent English, he welcomed her, introduced himself as Maurice, asked for her passport, and said her room was ready. After he came around from the counter and picked up her bag, he led her to a door that could have been a janitor's closet. "The elevator." He pushed the door open. "Room for one, you see. I'll meet you upstairs. Push button four. When it stops, exit right." A winding staircase beside the elevator tempted her.

"Merci," she said. He placed her bag inside. The elevator, as slow as the wheel bug, *Arilus cristatus*, finally stopped with a thud. Next time she'd walk. When she stepped out, Maurice was waiting at her room. Ensured she was pleased with the accommodations, he accepted a tip and asked if she had plans for her first night.

"I thought I'd settle in." She put her wallet back in her purse, tossed it to the bed, and placed her suitcase on the luggage rack.

He stood near the open door. "Forgive me. Don't waste even one night in Paris. You can easily walk from here across the Pont Royal, just steps from the hotel, and visit the right bank. For a destination, I suggest the Ritz." He produced a brochure from his jacket, along with a map.

"Merci. I'll study these."

"If you want to relax, may I add that a guest raved about the facial at the Ritz spa. They take the last client at eight. If you decide to go, I will be pleased to make the arrangements." He handed her the key. "Is there anything else?"

"When is sunset?"

"A little after five." He checked his watch. "Less than an hour," he said before leaving and adding, "You may wish to adjust your watch to the clock."

She took a minute to survey the Monet room, an aqua-based palette to match the water lilies prints over the twin beds. The bathroom with shower was about the size of the elevator, spare, but adequate. She peered out the window to the surrounding roof tops, walked over, closed the curtains, and felt more at ease, the room not so different from her suite at Columbia.

She picked up the brochure and map, sat at the table, read about the spa, and penciled a route to the Ritz on the map. Why would she hesitate? A brisk evening walk and a luxurious facial. She had promised Brenda and Jessica she'd call. She'd miss sunset. Her first call was to Maurice to book the appointment. Then she placed calls to Brenda and Jessica, saying she'd arrived, and all was well.

Unpacking, she fit the little she had brought into the armoire and its drawers. She showered and changed into slacks, a sweater, and a spritz of Brenda's maid-of-honor gift of L'Air du Temps (it was Paris after all).

No one had warned her how cold Paris would be. She had in mind all the songs about Paris in the spring. On her walk toward the Seine, she covered her mouth with her scarf and followed the path she had set. Crossing the Pont Royal, she stopped to view the Eiffel Tower. The clouds engulfing it, once the tallest structure in the world, retained a hint of the yellow she had seen from the cab. But pink from the sunset she'd missed upstaged the yellow, nothing a photo could capture. It's no more possible to preserve rare delights than it is to unshackle torment. The past never leaves. Other pedestrians, inured to the beauty of this view, she surmised, rushed across the bridge. Despite the cold, she was content to remain near the center, to breathe in the spectacle and the scent of the city, making it a part of herself.

The Louvre, to her right, was not far from the foot of this bridge or the next. She'd go in the morning and spend the day with *Mona Lisa*, *Winged Victory*, and *Venus de Milo*, among other notable women. The day after, she'd tour Napoleon's tomb at Invalides, homage to the man whose rebellious spirit Schweinfurt had lashed to hers. Painful moments clinging like glitter. She'd confront them.

Resuming her walk, she arrived at the Right Bank, her route leading her to the Ritz. The spread of the hotel's exterior, even in comparison to New York's structures, impressed. The mansard roof, with its own floor of rooms, capped the three stone stories below. Pillars and Roman arches at street level created an arcade along the length of Place Vendôme. Four lighted awnings marked the hotel's entrance. She walked beneath one into the lobby, then descended the marble staircase to the lower level health club. Early for her appointment, she managed a peek at the sumptuous pool, the classic Roman beauty of pale stone and marble enclosing the azure water.

After checking in, a uniformed aesthetician, Monique, accompanied her to a room of yellow wood lockers stenciled with blue and white laurels and wildflowers. There she traded her clothes for a peach robe with the Ritz monogram. After several minutes, Monique arrived to escort her to a private room where Candy removed her robe and lay on a heated hydrotherapy table under a soft sheet and light blanket, her neck resting on a warm pillow that exuded the relaxing scent of lavender. Maybe laboring mothers-to-be would appreciate the scent during delivery. Classical music played in the background. During the extravagant indulgence, her first facial, she relaxed, the last trace of feeling a stranger in a foreign country dissolving along with the exfoliated cells of her skin. She must have dozed off. The aesthetician shook her gently and said she'd wait outside the door, after which she led her through a maze of halls back to the lockers.

In the dressing area, a mirrored wall backed a marble make-up bar boasting myriad beauty products to embellish the blank canvas of a stripped face. For her, there was no need to enhance; stripped was fine. She'd walk back to Bersoly's in the dark, a scarf covering most of her face, return to her room, and sleep away her first night in Paris, happy she had ventured out.

Assured she was the last client of the evening, she dropped her robe and, in front of the mirror, surveyed the etching the years had wrought. Breasts more pendant than perky. Face chiseled by emotional pain and fatigue. Poor eating habits, combined with hours of sedentary studying, researching, peering through a microscope, had wrought their handiwork. Had she ever surfed or skated or danced? A stranger to herself, she dressed and covered the damage.

Upon opening the spa doors to the polished white marble floor of the antechamber, she walked out and admired the center medallion at the base of the bifurcated staircase. Until this moment unaware of anyone nearby, she collided with a man who must have exited the men's locker room opposite the spa. In dark shorts and a white T-shirt, he wore a towel wrapped around his neck as she'd often wear her stethoscope. Drawn to him, literally, she extended her hand. "Entirely my fault."

"American?" He raised both hands, but didn't reach for hers.

Awkward, she withdrew her hand. "Oui."

"Enchantée. Charles," he said. "Forgive me for not shaking your hand. I'm sweaty from the gym."

"Quite all right." The heat of a blush rising on her face, she backed away to walk up the stairs.

"Still full of energy after your workout?" he called after her. "There's an elevator." He slid the towel from his neck and dried his hands. "Your face. It's glowing."

"A facial, not a workout." She walked faster, but found herself still talking. "I flew in from New York this afternoon and decided to unwind." Revealing information to anyone, let alone a stranger, was unlike her. She had let her guard down, more relaxed than she thought. "Taking in Paris for a long weekend, my first vacation ever." Having revealed even more information, she fled up the stairs. Out of her element.

Charles raced after her. "I love New York. I travel there often on business. Are you staying at the Ritz?"

She stopped. "A place on the left bank, Bersoly's." Was she brave, or foolish, or normal? As they approached the landing, she tugged her hat on. He pursued her to the lobby. "I know the hotel. I don't see a wedding ring. What do you do in New York?"

A bit aggressive. Again, she dared to assert herself. "I'm a doctor." She couldn't keep herself from giving information to this man. He reminded her of Fritz. The silver hair, the smile. Knowing better than to engage a stranger, she persisted in her attempt to part ways.

He drew her back. "Incroyable, a doctor. So young. I am intrigued. Are you meeting someone?"

"I'm going to enjoy a brisk walk back to my hotel." She tied her scarf and pulled her gloves on. It was time to pull back, hard.

"Please, allow me to walk you. I would like to know you better."

Wayne, that first time on the beach, wanted to know her better. And here she was, hoping to escape that cascade of horrors. Not a path she wanted to retread. "Absolutely not, thank you. I'm happy to walk alone." *Always trying to be polite.* She waved goodbye. When he reached up for her hand, she withdrew, as though his hand were afire.

Disarming, he practically laughed as he spoke. "You are correct. I should know better. A beautiful young woman like you. I am a stranger," he said. "Meet me here tomorrow morning, and we won't be strangers." He followed her. "Is eight too early? I'll be in the lobby in that Louis XVI chair." He indicated a chair in the corner opposite the reception desk. "Sleep well on your decision."

She stopped. "Before I even entertain it," and she was startled that she did, "I must know if you're married." Again, awkward — asking a presumptuous question, incroyable, indeed, but having learned Walker was married—

"No," he said. "Pas marié. And I believe you aren't either. Bien. You already want to know more about me. Tomorrow. Bonne nuit."

Following the intrusion, she fled the Ritz to Place Vendôme, toward the Pont Royal and home. Smiling beneath her scarf, she took in the lights and the fresh air, tempted to accept Charles's offer. Rather than linger on the bridge, she, like the many inhabitants accustomed to the view, whom she had she had noted earlier, hurried to the hotel where Maurice greeted her and she thanked him for his suggestion. Comfortable in her blue room, she prepared for bed.

Under the covers, however, her mind spun, and sleep eluded her. She regretted not bringing her crocheting to calm her. After Helen, she had begun gifting afghans to mothers whose babies she delivered, or helped deliver. She got out of bed, sat in her reproduction Louis XVI chair, picked up the *Where Paris* magazine on the table, and read through, committing some sites and directions to memory. Mind cleared, she settled into bed and slept.

CHAPTER 35

Les Âges

Light filtered through the curtains and woke her hours later. As she showered and dressed, she reviewed — brushing her upper teeth, the pros, and her lower teeth, the cons — of meeting Charles. She'd prevent trust issues from paralyzing her. The researcher in her, having run through her list, decided, in the curious light of a Paris morning, to meet him and learn more about him, if he showed — no commitment to either of them, after all.

She took the stairs down to the lobby's breakfast nook and found an empty table among a few couples and a family with two children. The little boy took a flower from the vase on his table and handed it to her. "Merci," she smiled. Italian, German, and English melded around her as she poured a cup of coffee, and then sat alone with her extra flower, at a table for two, before setting out for her rendezvous.

Following the path of the previous night, she enjoyed the daylight view. It was easy enough to follow through on her idea to visit the Louvre if the meeting with Charles fell through. Fashionably late, she entered the lobby of the Ritz. A woman in a fitted sheath and stilettos occupied the chair Charles had pointed out the night before. Had he invited another woman? The guests in the lobby were a disparate group in jeans, slacks, dresses, coats, their casual attire a juxtaposition to the formal background of marble pillars, crystal chandeliers, antiques, and oriental rugs. Not seeing Charles, she conceded disappointment.

The silver hair caught her attention, long on the collar of his full-length dark coat, his back facing her as he stood at the reception desk. When he turned, she waited for him to make the first move, and he walked her way.

Within arm's length, he reached for her hand and kissed it, reminiscent of Maurice Chevalier in *Gigi* or *Love in the Afternoon*, romantic movies she had enjoyed with her mother, who had often escaped into matinees.

"I'm honored you chose to meet me." He released her hand as she stood. "Now you have a friend in Paris, as I hope I have in New York."

Having invited her to breakfast, he walked her toward the revolving door of the rue Cambon exit and told her of Coco Chanel's history on this street. As they pushed through the revolving doors, he secured his scarf under his collar. "The hotel is too fussy. I know a little place around the corner." After a brief walk, he led her through unoccupied sidewalk tables into an unassuming café, and to a booth in the corner near a window.

Across from the café loomed a structure resembling a Roman temple, or the Supreme Court. "That building, perfect classical architecture, doesn't seem to fit in the Paris landscape."

"How quickly you've found La Madeleine, a church. Magnifique, no?" He slid into the seat opposite her, his back to the window. "Not yet two hundred years old, but a testament in stone to our ancient heritage, a history reflected in the soil of Château Madeleine, my vineyard, as well."

When the waiter brought menus, Charles ordered café crème, coffee with milk, he explained, and she nodded. Charles raised his hand. "Un moment, s'il vous plaît," he said to the waiter, who then left. When Charles suggested

Candy try the pain au chocolat, she agreed, but the waiter was nowhere in sight in the busy wood-paneled café of bistro tables and booths beside cafe-curtained windows.

With the monogrammed handkerchief he pulled from the flap pocket of his jacket, Charles leaned across the table and scooped the air between them toward his face. "Everything in France has a history. L'Air du Temps, oui?"

Amazed that he recognized her perfume, she rubbed her neck. "I never thought of a perfume as having a history. This very name, as I interpret it, the air of time, is ephemeral and the essence of fragrance, quite the opposite of history."

"I fear you will think me ancient, but I will relate, in any event, that I remember when Nina Ricci, non, her son, created the fragrance in Paris after the war." With a gesture for her permission – she held her scarf out of the way – he dabbed the handkerchief at her neck to transfer a bit of the scent. When he brought it to his nose, he closed his eyes.

An intimate gesture for strangers, yet her shoulders shuddered with chills that ran to her feet. She was missing so much in life. And the smell of espresso and baked goods comforted her with memories of Caffè Reggio and home.

"The perfume was intended to capture the renewed spirit of the post-war era," Charles continued, "the passion of a refreshed generation, as much as it was to metaphorically overcome the nightmare of the occupation." He cupped her face in his hands, the gaze of his pale blue eyes penetrating hers.

His gentle touch and the stare relaxed every vertebrae in her spine, softened her further, and she slouched, forearms on the table.

"As a woman, who has chosen to be a doctor," he said, "you represent that new generation."

"You give me too much credit." She sat up straight again and interlaced her hands on the table.

"You are cutting new paths." He nestled the handkerchief into his pocket. "A souvenir," he said and patted it. "I admire you."

"You don't know me." *Did she know herself?* Did his flattery have an agenda? His demeanor caught her off-guard. Maybe familiarity was a French trait. He wasn't an enemy. Perhaps Jessica had been right about her not knowing the mores of France.

Despite doubts, she clenched the hand still touching her cheek, and brought it to the table. "I don't see how a perfume does all that." Curious to learn more about him before revealing more about herself, she asked, "Why would a man know so much about a perfume?"

"Oui. You question me." He brought both hands up and propped his chin on clenched fists. "First, I am a *French*man. You will trust me. I will open up. I was married back then, to an American. You remind me of her. She loved the new fragrance."

"Married?" She wasn't sure she wanted to know, or to hear he was still married, which he had already denied.

"Only a few years into our marriage, Emily contracted pneumonia and died. We never got to have children."

The hairs on the back of her neck stood. She crossed her arms over her chest and sat back. "Where is that waiter?"

"We have time. And that's what we thought, my sweet Emily and I." He steepled his fingers, pressed them against his lips, and shook his head. "We didn't know what was important. Young, we wanted to have fun first, and suddenly, poof (he snapped his fingers), she was gone." He shook his head. "After a long period of grief, I admit I became a bit of a playboy. That's two bad things I have told you." He slapped one hand on the table. "I vowed never again give my heart to anyone. Even with many affairs, I've kept it bottled up. But I am no more le playboy."

Perhaps he was as imprisoned as she was. Her release lay in in vitro, within the glass of the Petri dish. "I'm sorry for your loss," she said. Despite the anger, or because of the regret she saw in his gesture, she stroked his hand as she did when she delivered bad news to a patient. She and Charles had each endured grief. Like she and Wayne. *A red flag?* Why was she thinking of Charles in a romantic way? Paris. His gentle touch on her face.

"You know about me, and I know little about you. Are you ready, at least, to exchange last names?"

She laughed at the oversight. They didn't even know each other's names. She was way ahead of herself. "Krzyzanowski," she said.

He attempted a pronunciation, which she adjusted, and then he passed her a pen and paper. "And mine is easy, Madeleine, like the church."

"Quite a coincidence. And the name of your château, if I remember correctly."

"And the champagne produced in my vineyard." He crossed his hands over his heart. "Ah, it's a good sign that you are listening attentively."

She took her eyes off him and the church visible above his shoulder and looked around for the waiter. "Training," she said, denying an interest in him the credit.

"But without heirs, as I have told you, I have failed my family."

His agenda?

He told her about his vineyards outside the city, in Reims, beyond the suburbs, bordering the forests. For more than four hundred years, generations picking grapes together had produced the finest wine with great patience. He told her of the unique terroir: the climate, the history, the human and natural elements sunk into the earth; the footprints of Caesar's troops marching through Gaul; the blood of the dead; the droppings of the horses; the rotted leaves, the eroded stones, the cleansing rains. Fine wine coming from death, destruction, and waste. And time. He said no other place on earth had exactly that mixture of accumulated history that could be imbibed in the globes of his grapes, in the bubbles of Champagne Madeleine. And now, no generations to pass it to. All past. No future."

Although she recognized the ache, she didn't understand it in a man. He had choices. She choked on a swallow. An involuntary reflex, she clutched the coin on her chain. Was he interested in her youth because he wanted her to give him children? Incroyable, impossible. They had just exchanged names. A few stories. Was it too soon, or pointless, to tell him of her plight? It was something she didn't share. She recalled Jonathan. "I know the sadness," she said. He had been a font of information, and she enjoyed their conversation. Though they hadn't had more than coffee, she decided it was time to part ways. She stood and buttoned her coat.

He sprang up beside her. "Please, stay a little longer. Your pain au chocolat. What have I said to alarm you? I'm sorry."

It was no one thing, perhaps just her own thoughts. He seemed a lonely man who wanted to share stories. Because he was charming and even more handsome the more she studied him, she rolled her shoulders and sat back down.

"Ma chère," he said, "We don't have to eat. We can explore, beginning with La Madeleine if you like." He left money on the table.

CHAPTER 36

La Madeleine

"I haven't seen the inside of a church since high school. I don't know which of us might burn up."

"I assure you, made of stone, it has stood almost two hundred years. Your presence will not burn it down. And neither will you." He laughed.

That deep engaging laughter. Even without it, it was the depth of his voice that vibrated chords deep within her. Was it his voice, both strong and gentle, that kept her engrossed and here with him past their non-breakfast? Was it blasphemous to mix the sensual with the religious, his physical draw, to accompany him into the church? Diminished in the enormity of La Madeleine, its sixty-foot columns making it appear more a Roman temple than a French church, she ascended the steps to the great bronze doors, followed by Charles. At the threshold, he bowed his head. Then he explained that Mary Magdalene, for whom the church had eventually been named, had left the Middle East after Christ's resurrection, to convert the French. After the French Revolution, Napoleon had his architect design this monument to honor his armies.

She dared to enter, hoping to find —

She bowed, or ducked, covering her chest with crossed arms though the pediment depicting the Last Judgment was at least sixty feet above her, and she hurried past the enormous open bronze doors depicting the Ten Commandments, a gauntlet of sorts. When would she be judged? Guilt riddled her. "It's odd," she said, "that a church, especially one named for a woman who through the ages has been stigmatized as a prostitute, was built as a monument for soldiers, or that a church was named for her at all."

"Napoleon didn't provide the name. He had ordered construction of a Temple de la Gloire de la Grande Armée, a monument to honor his armies, on this plot, but he later moved the construction of that monument," Charles said, "from this site to another, and built the Arc de Triomphe."

Occupations, revolutions, wars. Appropriately, in a temple, she thought, her mind flashed to the coin resting on her chest, she now felt, with the tightness of a heart attack, Janus, the god of beginnings, doorways, transitions, endings, whose temple doors were opened in times of war for citizens to pray for positive outcomes, and closed in times of peace, which in Rome were rare, to keep the wars within. Her war was within herself. She had fled to France for an escape, but felt her burden heavier than it had been in New York. "I really must leave," she said.

"But you are Catholic, no? You will appreciate this, I promise." He held her hands and brought them to his chest. With a worried expression, he said, "Why are your hands clammy? This is a good place."

She pulled her hands back and turned to leave, even if it meant leaving him.

But he persisted. "After Napoleon's demise, two thousand years after Mary Magdalene's death, this site became a church, the name a veiled message to any remaining revolutionaries, it is believed, that if they repented, like Magdalene, all would be forgiven." Charles made an abbreviated sign of the cross. "Even a former playboy is still a Catholic. A male Magdalene of sorts, oui?"

Forgiven. Candy stopped and turned to Charles. Perhaps he had a point. The story of Mary Magdalene, how she had washed Christ's feet with her hair, how that story inspired the Magdalene Laundries in Ireland. Even on this cold day, she felt sweat dampen her skin. Fallen women, discarded women, women with minds of their own, orphans, unmarried girls and their babies, babies stolen, sold, left to die. Forgiven? Hardly. Not even guilty. The girls, their identities lost to them as they served out their sentences, mostly life long as slaves to the nuns. They washed, not Christ's feet, but dirty laundry, as their penance, until they died or somehow escaped the institution. In that part of Ireland, she, herself, might have succumbed to such a fate. She explained to Charles the story an Irish patient of hers had told her of her incarceration by her parents in a Laundry because she had become pregnant without marriage, and her subsequent daring escape, but without her baby which had been sold.

"Mon Dieu, I have never heard of such things. This could never happen in France. Is that why you are so agitated, sweaty?" He used his handkerchief to dab her brow.

"If not in the laundries, society has long diminished women, especially those who make non-conforming choices." Her own desire to become a doctor opened her to pain delivered by men who judged women unworthy, unequal. But the stories of these fallen women were about sex, rape, unwanted pregnancies, even sex appeal. For those crimes, she had discovered, women were enslaved and tortured, many for life. She grimaced. Her clothes were soaked in sweat. "Perhaps we should go elsewhere."

Charles pursed his lips. "Don't be concerned. You will see a great triumph inside, a tribute not to armies, but to women. I know it will please you."

In contrast to the stern exterior of the church, the interior was opulent, soft, dimly lit, with the light and shadows of the domes, the globes of chandeliers, and the deep jeweled tones and gold of the religious frescoes and mosaics covering the walls. Rather than expose sinners, the interior seemed to give them cover. At the far end of the aisle triumphed the symbol Charles had alluded to. The centerpiece of the altar, a towering sculpture of Mary Magdalene, lifted heavenward by angels, dominated the church. From her great height, eyes downcast, the long fingers of her open hands welcomed the imperfect, as well as the faithful, to join her en route to heaven. Magdalene was empathetic, kind, non-judgmental.

Entranced by the vision, Candy walked toward it. In the churches she had been in, such prominent a statue had been of the Virgin Mary. Virgins and mothers deserved honor, not women who didn't know how or when to portion out sex. Her mother, the nuns had warned her. But here it was the triumph of Mary Magdalene. As she digested the difference, the homage here paid to a woman maligned for two thousand years, a sense of forgiveness flooded her veins, heart, and arteries. It pounded toward her brain, down to her feet. She recognized her years of pain not as emanating from society, or Wayne, but as self-inflicted. She seized the power of the moment to forgive herself for her youthful choices. She saw their impact not as punishment, but as a new beginning opened to her. She stood, as weightless as Mary Magdalene, though sculpted of tons of marble, appeared to be, wafting heavenward toward the oculus. She, too, with her own tons of solidified guilt, suddenly lightened, experienced the illusion of floating upward, even as she fell, knees hitting the unforgiving floor. She lost perception of time and place, forgetting Charles, until his hand on her shoulder grounded her.

She rose from her kneeling position to join Mary Magdalene, standing with the angels, strong in her stance, invincible to the slights of society. The blood ceased pounding in her ears, replaced by Charles's voice.

"Are you all right?"

"Strangely," she said, "never better."

CHAPTER 37

Fontaine des Mers

As they exited the church and stood on the landing overlooking the plaza, Charles reached for her hand. "Again, your face is glowing, like the night we met."

"Last night, you mean." Either because of, or in spite of — it was hard for her to distinguish — her sudden lightness, she pulled away from Charles. Raising her brow, she glared. "You don't know me. If I were to reveal my true self, you'd run."

"You are talking to le playboy," he said. "Why haven't you run?" Although he smiled, he withdrew his hand.

Perhaps she should. He'd mentioned this playboy thing more than once, she thought as playful banter, but it may have been an actual warning, like swarming army ants, *Dorylus*, which will devour anything, even humans, not prudent enough to flee. If she made another poor choice, in light of his warning, she'd again be devoured after her miraculous restoration in La Madeleine. He, on the other hand, would be guilt-free of having cunningly preyed on a naïve American out of her depth. She'd keep her distance and enjoy his company, warily.

With his rejected hand, he pointed out La Place de la Concorde, the plaza of peace and harmony, laid out before them, its striking obelisk, taller than the church's columns, flanked by two monumental fountains. "An ironic name, Concorde," he said, "the obelisk marks the placement of the guillotine which, in the Revolution, executed thousands, including Marie Antoinette." They ambled toward the obelisk.

More talk of war and death. Destruction, part of a cycle always at hand. In the shadow of this enormous phallic symbol. "This gift of Egypt is over three thousand years old," Charles said.

Men and their testosterone. She slid her hands into her pockets. "I'd like to enjoy the mist of those remarkable fountains." She walked in front of him to circle the basin of the south fountain.

"La Fontaine des Mers. Ah, I am a good tour guide, oui?" He looked at her pockets and pursed his lips, making a smacking noise.

She ignored him. She would have found the plaza on her own, but not La Madeleine. She owed him that. The fountain was peopled with larger-than-life painted bronze statues, the figures loosely dressed in robes and loin cloths. One male, standing in the water holding a spouting fish, wore a scallop-shell necklace, the sight of which softened her shelled-in mood, her shelled-in heart, and brought a smile to her lips. She turned to Charles, and his eyebrows lifted in anticipation. "When I was a child," she said, "I loved combing the beach for the most perfect scallop shells, and when I had enough of just the right sizes, I made necklaces exactly like this. As often as I looked, though, I never found an entire shell hinged together."

"How extraordinary, to imagine you a sweet child delighting in simple pleasures." He maintained his distance.

She didn't want to be seen as a child. (Perhaps it was the language difference, but, at least he didn't allude to Candy and sweetness, as so many had done. Her mother had cursed her with this name.) Her mind flooded with images of children — her children who would never be — beachcombing, plinking their perfect shells into white tin pails. She'd teach them to pick up all shells, cracked and chipped, and she'd give them pails tarnished with rust from the salty ocean air.

His expression was wide, waiting for a response.

She looked away from the fountain, turned toward him, and stopped at arm's length. The fountain splashed them in the breeze, and she faced him with her truth. She hedged. With the sounds of the water and the traffic, he might not hear her. "I must come clean with you," she said. "With my first love, I was naïve and got pregnant."

His sucked in air.

She placed her hand over his mouth. He had heard her. She had to continue. "The father wasn't ready for a child, and he convinced me to have an abortion, illegal at the time, but after we married, he promised, we'd have children."

He moved her hand and clasped it between both of his. "I can understand how that could happen. It must have been painful for you," Charles said. "And I'm sorry you suffered it."

"But you don't understand." She didn't want him to think that because she was young, she could give him the children he seemed to want, heirs, what Jonathan's mother wanted. "Forgive my audacity in thinking this would matter, but there's never a good time to raise the issue. Sooner is better. In order to save my life, doctors performed a hysterectomy. I can never have children."

She had never told Jonathan her secret, even after two years together. She knew Charles a day and blurted it out. She owed this man nothing. Perhaps that was why. She wanted to see how it felt to put it out there, to deliver the death blow out front. Watch him run. She could have been the sly one, could have trapped him with her youth, only to deliver the bad news when it was too late — after he had fallen hopelessly in love, even after they were married. Listen to herself. She was so far ahead of reality. But it didn't matter. She had told him. It was an experiment. After the hysterectomy, she never expected to be like everyone else, to fall in love, to have a family. If marriage seemed to be a possibility, how would any man she loved react when he learned the truth? When should she say something? This was a good trial run. Whatever Charles thought of her, her complete freedom was, this moment, consummated. When she realized he had not let go, she squeezed his hand.

Charles drew her close and wrapped his arms around her. Rather than resist, she let her head relax on his shoulder. In an embrace, they remained as one figure outside the fountain, *The Kiss*, Rodin's statue. Whispering in her ear, he said, "I can't imagine how you feel, but none of this affects my feelings and respect for you. Consider what you've done, for yourself, for your patients."

She took a step back to study his expression. "Thank you." She pulled a Kleenex from her coat pocket, dabbed her eyes, blew her nose, and stuffed the crumpled tissue back into her pocket.

"Would you like to go to your hotel?"

"No. Let's walk."

"You give me too much credit," she said. "My pursuit of medicine was selfish. I cloistered myself in studies as a strategy for forgetting my pain and avoiding men, hopefully helping women. When abortion became legal, I was grateful to keep others from repeating my botched experience." Feeling the darkness cast by the shadow of the obelisk she asked, "When is it okay to take a life? When your country calls? When you are desperate not to have a child? When you are desperate for a child? Is it even my decision? These are the dilemmas I grapple with daily."

"You are too hard on yourself. I have a thought. I'll explain later. Over dinner this evening, if you're willing."

"I'd love to spend more time with you." Still enclosed in his embrace, she kissed his cheek.

"For now, I know a place on the Left Bank that might interest you. Do you mind walking, not too far from your hotel? You're not too cold?"

"Lead the way." They entwined arms and walked to Pont Royal where they crossed the Seine and walked along Quai Voltaire with the wind blowing off the water, the air smelling fresh.

Charles steered her along a more protected route to their destination on Rue de l'Ancienne Comédie and through the double doors of a long black façade. He escorted her into the seventeenth century, into Le Procope, the oldest coffee-house in the world, he informed her. "With your interest in history," he said, "you might appreciate this restaurant. The original décor has been maintained through the centuries."

She stepped into the ornate red and gold interior, incandescent with history everywhere. The maître d' led them past portraits and tributes to Benjamin Franklin, Robespierre, Voltaire, Balzac, and Napoleon, among others, who had met here. She mentioned to Charles that she perceived the café as a lab for the incubation of rebellions.

"True." Charles stopped at the display of a familiar hat encased in glass. "Napoleon left this here as a pledge to return to pay his bill, so it's said. And it's still here."

"Looks like he never redeemed it." They continued down a long corridor, then up some stairs. "I knew of the rich history of Paris, but to actually be at the places where significant history occurred is electrifying. History here is set in stone, yet alive, enduring, in the DNA of humanity. I must return, but for a longer stay."

"Perhaps you'll leave a trinket with me as your pledge to return."

"I'll have to think of something."

He kissed her cheek. "Your face is still cold. You'll warm up in here."

Charles suggested tea and madeleines — scallop-shell-shaped sponge cakes. "Juxtaposed to the span of time chronicled in this restaurant, and France," he said, "the perfection of madeleines is fleeting, and they are best enjoyed straight from the oven, as they serve them here." The maître-d' sat them. "When you told me about the scallop shells of your childhood, I thought these would please you. And wait till you taste them."

She found Charles considerate and attentive. Having let her guard down earlier, she trusted him. When the madeleines arrived, they were warm to the touch and released the fragrance of oranges. Their scalloped edges were crisply browned. The heat of the oven had incubated the ingredients and made them perfect, as her day had been.

"You have a choice," he said. "I can walk you back to Bersoly's, and you can sleep there, or you can accompany me to my suite, freshen up, and who knows. Either way is acceptable. I am a gentleman."

With a warm madeleine about to touch her lips, she froze. From the moment she first met Charles, she desired to make love to him. Now that the fantasy could actualize, she stopped to allow the rational to overtake the emotional. Her experiences with Wayne and Jonathan restrained the enthusiastic "yes," as powerful as Molly Bloom's in James Joyce's *Ulysses*, pounding to escape over the madeleine. Is sex with a stranger how she would celebrate her release? Tarnish her guilt-free feeling when she was going home, when it would be fruitless? Defile that white-wedding-gown feeling she'd been wearing since La Madeleine? Maybe she still wasn't free.

"This isn't a test," Charles said. "Whatever makes you comfortable. But I would be lying if I didn't say that I want you."

CHAPTER 38

Au Revoir

Her swollen feet throbbed in her now too-tight boots. Two days of covering the sights required more sensible footwear. Next trip, and there would be one, she'd be better prepared. Nevertheless, she chose this longer route to the Ritz, rather than the direct one she had mapped on her first night, in order to relish Fontaine des Mers on her own. The water had slowed her heart, softened her jagged edges, the way it does as it trickles over rocks.

Though the water was now shut off and the fountain drained, she imagined it as she had seen it with Charles. He had told her they were lucky to have seen it in operation. She lingered at the empty basin. Lighted at night, and without streams of water and spray obstructing the view, the circular shape and bold colors reminded her of a carousel and children's laughter. She was worthy of being loved, even if she couldn't have children. Even if the fault was hers. Water will flow again.

On reaching rue Cambon, she glimpsed Charles leaning against the wall of the building outside the revolving door. Then he walked toward her.

He swept her up. He kissed her on both cheeks. Minus a coat, scarf, and gloves, his cold fingers brushed her face when he slid her scarf down to uncover her lips. "You should have let me come for you at your hotel."

"My last walk over. Time alone was what I needed, but this is what I want. We're together now. I missed you." After removing her scarf, she stretched for his lips and they enjoyed a long, slow kiss.

His hands moved from her cheeks to cup her head, remove her hat, and nuzzle her hair. But a couple was exiting. She and Charles squeezed into one compartment of the revolving door and pushed through, into a corridor of the Ritz.

As they walked, Charles said, "Please don't remind me this is your last night. These past few days, you have been my raison d'être." He opened the door beneath the overhanging sign of Bar Hemingway. "I hope you enjoy my little treat. Bon. Right this way."

All the leather barstools were occupied, and the cushioned wingbacks surrounding glass-topped tables were taken by couples and groups. Only the pink settee, with a cocktail table in front of it, was available. After Charles helped her with her coat, he led her by the hand to the settee. The room, unlike a bar, radiated the intimacy of a friend's parlor, with the Old World charm and glamour of wood paneling, antiques, and framed photographs. Charles sat beside her, their hips and thighs touching, as though attached. He reached over the back of the settee and rested his hand on her shoulder. "Are you comfortable?"

"Happy. It's been a long time." She reached up to interlace her fingers with his.

The bartender, Peter, came by and set coasters on the table. "The usual?"

Charles nodded.

"How do you know I'll like what you ordered?" She released his fingers, and her hand went to her lap. Wayne, Weaver.

Charles was quick to reach over to caress her hand. He distracted her with a question. "Are you familiar with the legend of the coupe?"

"I'm not sure I even know what one is."

"The champagne glass," he said. "It's said to have been formed on casts of young Marie Antoinette's breast as part of her campaign to encourage noblewomen to breastfeed rather than depend on wet nurses. I tell you because you're an obstetrician and because I ordered champagne."

"A noble intention on Marie's part," she said, "but I'm not sure how the coupe and breast milk have anything to do with champagne."

"Bien sûr, the doctor, scientific and logical."

Peter returned with two coupes, which he placed on the table, a white orchid secured to her glass; he opened the bottle with modest fanfare, poured the bubbly, and slipped away.

Charles handed her a glass, raised his, then entwined his arm with hers, forcing them closer as they sipped.

Unable to swipe away the image of the coupe from which they sipped as a breast, especially in this intimate embrace, the pose aroused long-dead surges that vented in tears, the thought of him kissing her breast. They dallied in the position long past its usefulness, pressed their lips together again, and placed the half-filled glasses on the table. She vaguely recognized the sensation. When she had lost her uterus, she assumed she wouldn't experience such intense pleasure again. She never experienced anything with Jonathan. She shuddered to imagine how explosive sex with Charles could be. She was fully invested. She wanted to run out of here and up to his room. It wasn't the champagne. She watched the bubbles effervesce up the coupe's hollow stem only to dissipate. *Time is fleeting. I can't make this mistake again.* "Perhaps you'll show me around your vineyard on my next trip."

"So, there will be a next trip?"

"What was the idea you mentioned at Le Procope yesterday?"

"It's about the legacy for my vineyard."

"I told you, I can't give you heirs." She had confided in him. All this time, she thought he understood. Was it a language barrier?

"Oui, oui. I listened about the Magdalene Laundries too. Those poor lost girls. Perhaps I can help a few."

His smile was broad. His eyes glistened. Where was he going with this?

"I have a proposal." With his hands on her shoulders, he turned her toward him. "I'm excited about this. I don't know all the details, but I will find such young women here in Paris, in Reims, and open my château to them. They would have a wonderful home, a paying job, and health care for themselves and their children for as long as they wanted, or as short, in a communal setting. What do you think?"

He was a good listener. "It's extremely generous. I love it." She wanted to add, I love you. I could love you, but restrained herself, still protecting herself from hurt, especially in the throes of lust.

"Here's the essential ingredient. I'd like you to be the doctor in the plan. You would be key in helping the women, their babies, their young children. The laughter of children in the château again, generations working together, as they had for centuries." With his gesticulations, champagne dripped from his coupe. "I couldn't imagine it without you. Would you consider it?"

Her jaw dropped and locked. He was asking her to move to France? Unable to close her mouth, she placed her glass on the table, then enclosed his hands in hers. Her professional life, her goals. "I have a life back home, with patients and commitments, and breakthroughs in fertility. This isn't a complete 'no,' but a 'not right now,'" she said. "I never expected anything like this. We've just met." And he could still hurt her. He could be a smooth talker who sensed her vulnerability, like a recluse spider, *Loxosceles gaucho*, which can find the weak spots in even heavily armored prey. She wouldn't give up everything for a man, not even Charles, who was after all a stranger. He was too familiar with Peter and this bar. Drinking was one of Wayne's traits that she had consciously ignored. And here, Charles produced alcohol. And he admitted to having been a playboy. He had been married. Maybe he still was, like Walker. Would she never learn?

"It could be too soon for this," Charles said. "but that won't stop me. I'm presenting my thoughts out of order." He reached into his jacket pocket to remove a wrapped package and handed it to her.

"A gift?" She pulled one end of the velvet ribbon on the box, releasing the embossed paper and the tissue beneath. After opening the box, she worked through the shredded tissue, and reached the buried scallop shell, about the width of a coupe. "A complete scallop shell. You did hear every word I said at the fountain." He had listened, and he cared enough to make this poignant gesture. "You thought of my recollection at Fontaine des Mers, of my not being able to find a complete shell, but you did, in Paris, in a day."

"Not so difficult, I cannot lie." He mopped his brow with his handkerchief. "They sell scallops at Le Procope; that's why I took you there after the fountain. I bought the shell there."

Was it that simple? She decided to be more trusting. "Incroyable, indeed."

"That means you like it?"

"It's perfect." As she fingered the shell's ridges, the crenelations that gave the fragile form the strength to survive the ebb and flow of tides, and predators, she found a clasp opposite the hinged side of the shell.

"It opens," he said.

She lifted the top to find more shredded paper, which she worked through to discover, nestled within, a diamond ring.

Charles slid from the settee, down to one knee in front of her. "I never thought I'd fall in love again. I wouldn't let myself. But you are unique. Marry me."

For a moment, she processed the image of Charles kneeling before her with a ring — this man she didn't even know days before. With both hands, she held his face and bent to kiss him. "I haven't felt as close to anyone as I feel to you. I want to marry you." The "yes" she had held back at Le Procope buzzed out.

"I love you." Charles slid the ring on her finger. "A family heirloom, but it was close at hand. Choose another if you like." He sat beside her again.

"I treasure tradition, and you." She clenched her Janus necklace with her newly adorned hand and the heirlooms struck one another. She wished she hadn't made that rash youthful choice under the stars, but it had led her, somehow, to Charles. It was impossible to compare whether she had loved Wayne, with all the fun they shared, as she loved Charles. It was as though she and Wayne had been mere grapes, and she and Charles, in such a short time, had fermented into a singular wine.

"The ring links our families and that's what's important." She wanted him and she wanted her work. She'd have both. "That said, I can't abandon my work in New York when we marry. Can you accept those terms?"

"I understand. As long as we're committed to joining our lives, we'll handle the details. What gave me the courage tonight is that Hemingway, the bar's namesake, asked Mary Welsh, his fourth and final wife, to marry him on their third meeting." After Peter came by to fill their coupes, Charles raised his glass. "À votre santé." The couple touched glasses and sealed their engagement with Champagne Madeleine and kisses on both cheeks. "Champagne Madeleine for all," Charles said.

Peter walked through the room placing coupes and pouring champagne. When he completed his rounds, she and Charles raised their glasses to the surrounding patrons, who tipped theirs to the couple.

"I know I said I plan to live in New York, but how can I possibly leave you in the morning?"

Charles pulled her close "Tonight, we celebrate." He advised her to follow her schedule as though they had never met, which she said was impossible. He added that he'd take care of the paperwork and details of the wedding.

"I don't even know how weddings work in Paris. Since I'll live in New York, I'd like to marry here."

"We marry first at the mairie, the town hall of my château. After that we may marry in a church."

"La Madeleine, don't you think?"

CHAPTER 39

Candy and Goliath

Three doctors in their white coats stepped into the empty elevator, the women first, followed by the Chief of Obstetrics and Gynecology. Like a bulwark, he stood between them and the door. Leaning against the back rail, Candy covered her mouth and twittered as the chief reached over to push the elevator button. "Someone pushed all of them," she said.

"I don't have time for this. I agreed to open the lab for you, but I don't have the patience for tomfoolery." He tossed his ring of keys into the air and hit the open button as the door was closing.

Unlike her to defy the chief, she thrust a hand out to reach for the keys mid-air. "I've pleaded for years, since Shettles resigned, to get back in. Give me this five-minute delay, or if you must be elsewhere, I'll take the keys."

She was startled by the insistence in her voice, firmness bordering on irritability. He caught and kept the keys.

It had been hard for her to part with Charles in Paris the previous day, but the wedding would be soon enough. Without intending to, and never mentioning it, Charles had tempted her to abandon her long-stalled IVF research. This could be her last opportunity to haul the chief to the lab before she was sidetracked by her impending nuptials. She wasn't going to let a button-pushing prankster stand between her and the quest she had joined in with Shettles, as his research assistant, when she was a med student. She was not about to be shy in letting the chief know how determined she was. Although Jessica remained pressed against the back wall, she gave Candy a gentle nudge of approval.

"If anyone opens the lab, it'll be me. I'm in charge here." He pressed the "close doors" button. "It would take even longer if we waited for the next car," he said. "Let's get on with it." In silence, they continued their interrupted ascent.

Back in pre-med, Schweinfurt had heinously tried to discourage her from entering the medical profession. And just this weekend, Charles could have inadvertently derailed her from following through on her stalled professional goal, luring her away with a vision of helping women in a more immediate way. And with love. And marriage. What almost everyone else had. What she had wanted in the first place, then thought she'd never have. Charles had lulled her into that sweet spot where she floated, one with him, oblivious to the world. No struggling. A vision of a life without friction. She wanted to stay in Paris with him, open the château to women who had no options, set her goals there rather than in New York.

But New York was where the real mystery and challenge lay dormant, within the lab. She hoped to force the chief to permit her to continue experiments with eggs and sperm, in vitro and embryo implantation, to yield the key to a successful birth like that of Louise Joy Brown's only months earlier. In that birth, the quest had become flesh — incarnate, no longer theoretical — and within reach for her to launch IVF in New York, even if the Joneses in Virginia should succeed there first. If the first test-tube baby hadn't yet been born, she might have moved to Paris, abandoning a possibly futile professional pursuit. But she saw Shettles' mission of IVF, the Holy Grail, within her grasp. She would have it now. She hoped she wouldn't have to sacrifice Charles on that altar.

Not the joyful option of her unanticipated relationship with Charles, not sixteen elevator buttons, not the pompous chief, nothing would stand in her way. In parting with Charles, she found new strength and resolve to accomplish her goal. She'd learn to compartmentalize. She and Charles would love and support each other wherever they were, whatever they were engaged in. Here, she would focus a team on successful embryo implantation, pursue her fellowship in reproductive endocrinology and infertility, and, hopefully, share a life with Charles.

Having swept Jessica along for moral support, she hadn't said a word to her since entering the elevator, but she reached down and took hold of her fingers. "Thank you. We're almost there. Almost at the breakthrough. We had fertilized so many eggs in that lab. All we need is one successful implantation with a willing woman." Solving the endless variables of in vitro was her passion, though not Jessica's.

After the doors opened for the final time, she raced out to the locked door. The chief called after her, "I could have come up here without you. I should never have left Shettles to his own devices. I want to be clear that I'm in control if I let you back in there." She stood at the lab door, panting breathlessly, almost to the point of fainting. She had her hand on the doorknob, waiting for him to place the key in the keyhole, anxious to throw the door open.

"Stop." He put his hand over hers. "You will execute my protocols, secure clearances. So I know you understand me, tell me you will execute my protocols before you open that door."

She ignored his bluster. "Clearances, yes. You don't know the IVF protocols, do you?"

"Wait till you see the lab, Jessica. History was made here first, though few realize it." She opened the door, remembering the last time she had had her hand on the inside knob, telling Shettles she'd stay, not knowing it would be the last time she'd see him. In her memory, the lab was monumental, but the door opened to a cramped space. And musty. Neither the chief nor Shettles had removed all the dead tissue. Perhaps her dream had dissipated in the dark and would never yield fruit. Faced with this reality, her enthusiasm flagged, but she led Jessica to the Zeiss phase-contrast microscope and blew the dust from it. "It's not much now, but this lab is everything. This is the stage where I witnessed sperm fertilizing an ovum, the stage on which Shettles took the first photograph of that historic event prior to my ever being here. And where I observed blastocysts grown from fertilized ova."

"Can you replicate the experiments?" Jessica asked. "I'll volunteer to help set it all up again."

"As soon as the chief gives me the green light." She surveyed the familiar room. "The photographs are all gone." She glared at him. "Did you take them down, or did Shettles?"

"It wasn't me," he said. "They were his babies. There's not much here to work with." He opened the slats of the blinds. Dust motes flew at them on the entering light. They covered their faces. She sneezed, again, and again.

At the desk, she fondled the notebooks and flipped through pages of scribbled comments, diagrams, and symbols. She rubbed the covers. "He left these for me, I'm sure." She batted at resilient spider webs spun in corners and over the upright test tubes and rows of Petri dishes. All the glass and instruments on open shelves were gray with dust. Within the cabinets, all was stored as she remembered. It was all in place, waiting for her.

"We'll need to assess the equipment. We might need new wiring, a generator, controls for air quality, a plan for patient volunteers' informed consent. We'll draw up a list." She walked around the room. "It's never been so quiet in here." She regarded the clocks. "All of the clocks have stopped ticking, but I'll reset time." She examined a few. One was unplugged. She wound the next. There were too many to go to now. She stared down the chief. "This is the silence you've met patient requests for IVF with. Time is fleeting."

"All work product here belongs to the university," he said. "And you're not the only one in this hospital interested in IVF." Close behind her, he paged through the many notebooks and put one in his pocket.

"There are others in the department who are interested. Good. We need a team — an embryologist, techs to handle sperm, nurses, surgeons, an anesthesiologist, a geneticist. I can't do it alone." After handling so many grime-laden articles, she drew her hands down the sides of her white coat, leaving long gray streaks behind. She took a tissue from her pocket and mopped her brow. Her stomach was unsettled. She drew a deep breath. "Shettles taught me how to select the best eggs. He said that that ability was my true gift, but I can teach the techniques. I can explain the notebooks and the protocols. The more input, the better. There are countless variables to explore."

"But there is no budget. Shettles did it all alone, and with you," he said. "There's still no government funding available for human experimentation. If you want to use rabbits and mice, that's different."

"And you know to pursue human success, we've moved far beyond animal experimentation. That was Miriam Menkin working with John Rock in 1939, almost half a century ago."

"It'll take time to get funding," he said, "before the success of Louise Joy Brown's birth in Great Britain really translates into international rivalry giving rise to federal funding here in the U.S., if that ever happens."

"If it does, Columbia will be ready. I'll make sure. Do you think the Joneses in Virginia are waiting? They're pushing on, and close to success from what I've read."

"Where are you getting your information?" he asked.

"Despite the fact that you wouldn't give me access to the lab, I've kept up with the literature available — *Lancet, Nature,* and Steptoe's own 1967 book on laparoscopy. While Shettles didn't believe in laparoscopy, I do. Maybe I should join the Joneses and head to Eastern Virginia Medical School." Of course, she felt a kinship to Columbia, but the idea of leaving wasn't a total bluff. However, it was her hope to bring IVF to her hometown.

She dusted the notebooks with tissues from her pocket. Jessica took a handful of Kleenex and helped. They began arranging the books by date on the shelves, oldest on the higher shelves. "We'll get this lab organized," she said, "and we'll find volunteers. Until the day we procure NIH funding, we'll solicit private funds like other researchers do. Or we can fund IVF from abortions like Steptoe did." She turned and pointed a finger at the chief standing behind her. "You must have some wealthy patients interested in IVF. They'll donate. One patient of the Joneses gave the them millions."

"In the past few months," the chief said, "I've fielded questions about IVF, but human experimentation could endanger the funding of the entire hospital. Some of my infertile patients demand to know how Oldham, a small town in Great Britain, beat out a prestigious New York hospital, all U.S. hospitals in fact, with successful IVF. Why do you think I'm here? Patient needs. I'm planning to get up to speed now that there's a baby born of in vitro. Let others make the mistakes before I step in. What's your driving interest?" He eyed the incubator. The door had remained open all these years. He closed it.

"Unlike Shettles, I'm not driven to be first," she said. "My involvement is personal. I had a hysterectomy at nineteen. Jessica was only a candy striper then, but that's when I met her in the maternity ward of Staten Island Hospital, and she played an important role in my recovery." She put her arm around Jessica's shoulders.

"She fought her way back," Jessica said. "And she'll fight till she succeeds with IVF."

"Each and every day since," Candy said, "I've experienced that ache of women who want, but can't have, biological children in our mother-centered culture. I feel daily what Doris felt that June day her baby could have been born." She backed away, then faced him with hands on her hips and feet firmly planted and widespread. "Because of your ruthless action, we'll never know if the embryo was viable, if Shettles succeeded."

The impenetrable force he was, he ignored her. "I froze that test tube, by the way," he said.

"What did you say?" Nose-to-nose now, she felt his breath on her face. "I assumed the test tube was discarded — by you or Shettles. We should see if it fertilized, or if it even contained eggs, although we'd never know if it would have implanted successfully and given Doris her baby." She walked to the incubator. "We do know, however," she said, "on that 1974 June day in Florida, Doris crumpled to the floor with an armful of baby clothes in a department store. Her visible pain humanized the abstract test-tube-baby controversy and stripped in vitro of its stigma. I expect you will secure funding to continue Shettles' research."

She didn't know how her words flowed. She hadn't anticipated bringing up the sore point of the lawsuit the chief and the hospital had lost only months earlier, the same month Louise Joy Brown was born. "Perhaps you'll take that test tube out of the freezer and see how far along the embryo had developed, if an embryo, if indeed viable. Shettles will be vindicated, or is that what you're afraid of?"

Jessica coughed. "Are there any clean glasses in here?"

"In the cabinet near the coffee pot and the Maxwell House coffee can," she said.

"I'm a big enough man to admit you're right. You're finally showing the passion I needed to see." He removed several notebooks from the shelf. "As I said, I never got involved with Shettles. I'd like you to review these with me in my office. Follow me now." He added the book from his pocket to the pile and handed them to her. He removed a key from the ring and laid it on top of the pile of books in her arms. "Lock up *your* lab."

CHAPTER 40

Take Two

Manhattan, 1983

Her hands firmly on the door handle, one over the other, Dr. Madeleine pulled on it from her stance the waiting room, ensuring it was completely and utterly closed tight, shutting out all possible intrusion of memories and lingering pain. She staggered to the counter June had left to go find Dr. Reed. With elbows on the cold marble, she hunched over, supporting her head, heavy in her hands. The parachute jump, the roller coaster, the carousel, all in one, rising, dropping, going around in circles, finding a destination, ending here, back at the beginning, as most rides do.

But the door creaked open. She had pulled it closed tight, but couldn't lock it from this side. "I'm sorry ma'am, I mean doctor." The door closed again, and footsteps clacked toward her. "We don't have lady doctors in my hometown of Red Boilin' Springs. You're the first one I ever met." She rubbed the doctor's back.

Beneath her white coat, she stiffened. "There aren't enough anywhere." She covered her mouth, and uttered a muffled, "How can I help you?"

"I had to save up, money and courage," Brooke said, "to come to New York from Tennessee. I'm glad I did because I never would have met a big man like Wayne back home." With the mention of Wayne, still just on the other side of the door, Dr. Madeleine began to heave.

Brooke scrambled behind the counter and brought her the wastebasket. "My, you really are sick. Poor thing. Should I do something?"

Dr. Madeleine shook her head and waved her hand, then looked up. She took tissues from her pocket and wiped her mouth. She prayed the resurging memories were all out of her system. She had thought she had purged them at La Madeleine, then at the fountain, but deep down, she knew it wasn't over, couldn't be over until a physical face-off. Yet she never imagined it would happen like this. Now. She had forgiven herself. She had shared her truth with Charles and learned she could be loved, and married. Still, there was this one step. This one rending. Although forgiven, there was no one to blame but herself, for it was she who had forged the path to this encounter. That this moment of confrontation should intersect her moment of her triumph was a cruel nightmare. Perhaps, that New Year's Eve, she should have gone back into Studio 54 to look for Wayne to confront him there, instead of fleeing to France. But what she would have missed. This was the price.

Brooke sat her in a chair, got her a paper cup of water from the cooler, and helped her sip it down. Then she sat next to her and gripped her hand in her lap.

How did Wayne deserve such a thoughtful girl? Like acid reflux, her choices burned their way down her gut and up again. It was her professional duty. She had taken an oath. Do no harm. *Seek no vengeance?*

She could send the couple to Virginia, doing no harm to them, or herself. In Virginia, after all, Georgeanna Jones's idea of using certain fertility drugs had increased the number of oocytes for harvesting and had already resulted in a healthy IVF baby in 1981. Already a success, that was an excellent option for this couple. She liked Brooke. Candy's driving force had been to help women. Duty. Principles. Self-sacrifice, not necessarily.

Her mind spun. *There was simply no way she could give him the baby he had long ago denied her.* She fought to rationalize. *Stupid, stupid.* Although she could challenge the most complicated problems, she thought she might go insane thinking this through. She faced the closed door, the final shield between her and her demon. Or the doorway to her final escape? Whatever it took to go back into *her* office and confront him. Did he even realize it was her? She had vomited the past into a green metal wastebasket. She had to focus on the present.

Her hand still in Brooke's lap, she looked up at her. "You should go to the Joneses in Virginia. They've already had a successful in vitro birth." *Truth.*

Brooke sighed. "Husband doesn't want to leave New York. And now that I've met you, I want you to be the one to help us."

"Georgeanna Jones is a female doctor."

"Nope, it has to be you. I trust you with our family. Let us be your first successful in vitro birth."

That thought spun her. With her thumbs on her cheekbones and her fingers on her forehead, she shook her head. *This can't be happening.* The realization of her big dream nearly four years in rebuilding the lab, in trials, in battling the chief, in setting up the clinic, had brought her here. She gathered her inner strength, her confidence in her professional success, and in Charles's love for her. She dipped a tissue into the little cup of water and dabbed her face, the way Wayne had at that outdoor café, when he was afraid she might change her mind about the abortion. She stood, tall, wiped her stiff, sweaty, open hands down her new, white coat. Her identity sewn in gold thread. Girded for confrontation, like the *Allegory of Fortitude* Brenda had emulated. Fortitude is what she needed. "Brooke, could you please wait here while I go back into my office?"

"Of course, ma'am, doctor." She got up to get a magazine, *People*, from the table and sat back in a waiting-room chair and crossed her legs. "If you're okay."

Dr. Madeleine touched the doorknob, and a bolt of electricity surged through her body. She pushed the door open.

Wearing that constant grin, he narrowed his eyes and stared, as if burning off the mask it had taken her seventeen years to mold. Choking her name up on his vocal cords, from wherever he had buried it, in a hushed and sputtering tone, "Candy?" he asked.

Her heart pulsed in her stomach, as she realized he was seeing her for the first time today, really seeing her. This was her last chance to find a path to "no." It would be her professional death if she turned him away. The truth would out. But her own psychological death if she didn't. She choked on it. Spin it, spin it and spin it, until she could create a way to live with it, *if* she did what they wanted, what she was here for, after all. Like a kaleidoscope, she turned the end of the dark tube and shook it, the bits of glass cutting her soul with every twist. Everything changed, but nothing changed. There was no if.

"Candy?" he asked again before she replied.

Becoming a different person had taken over a decade of molting, growing, renewing. She cleared her throat. She caught the depth of his stare and shot back. "Dr. Candace Madeleine." She wanted to slice off his pasted-on Cheshire-cat grin.

He walked up close, his warm breath on her skin, touched her cheek with the back of his hand.

She jumped back. "I'm not that girl. Keep a professional distance. Now that you know who I am, do you still want my help?" She steepled her fingers in front of her chest. "I've given your wife the option of going to a successful clinic in Virginia." She skirted past him to stand behind her desk, putting it between them.

He followed. "Why would I go to Virginia when you're right here?" He shrugged his shoulders. "I don't care what Brooke chose. I choose you. Why wouldn't I? Nana always loved you, and asked about you. I told her you left me. You'd do it to give her a grandchild." He made the motion of rocking a baby in his arms. "Wouldn't you?"

However he managed it, his fiendish grin widened. Every inch of her skin was on fire, as though she had been bitten by red ants, *Solenopsis invicta*. As he held her gaze, she concentrated on her breathing, like a birthing mother using Lamaze, and she found her voice again. "Did you ever go to the hospital and ask about me after you dumped me there?"

"Who do you think paid your bill?"

"And that letter."

"I didn't want you ruining my chances with the pros. I threatened you to frighten you to stay away. And look at me now, a big shot, even after I retired. I paid my dues. I took care of you."

"More like you left me for dead."

"And look at you. A doctor. Head of this whole operation." He skulked around to her side of the desk. "I'd say I gave you the push you needed. You would have ended up like my wife — or my wife, exactly." His grin vocalized in a laugh. "I saved you."

"Saved me?"

"Saved you from me." He ran his finger over the name on her breast pocket.

She jumped back. She had once loved his touch. She picked up the letter opener on the desk and raised it.

He crossed his forearms, shielding his face and chest in a self-defense posture, stepped back and laughed. "Why so unfriendly? You must have married. I remember an impossible name with a 'k.' Without me, you would have ended up a bug lady in that museum, or a science teacher on Staten Island. Look at what I made of you."

"That's it. Leave before I call security."

"You owe me, doll."

She knew her strength. He was here wanting something from her. If it were not for Brooke, she would have called security. Instead, again concentrating on her breathing, she inhaled deeply, puffed out her chest, and stood taller than she was, mimicking the deimatic bluffing behavior of the *Phasma* butterfly, with its dramatic wingspan flash. His fate, his legacy, was in *her* hands. Although she acknowledged her part in the abortion, before her stood the man who led to the obliteration of her dream for a family, and the end of a thousand years of family tradition. She was the end of the line. But he wanted his line to live on. She laid the letter opener on the desk.

She marshaled her better angels, like the marble statues in La Madeleine, to lift her, to guide her to the right choice. The hubris of him. She wanted to throttle him. To put her healing surgeon's hands around his neck and squeeze till he turned blue. Having forgiven herself, she had to forgive him. But did she have to give him a child?

Still behind the desk, she took the key from her breast pocket and opened the bottom drawer. She brought up the cigar box. "My grandfather gave this box, once full of Cuban cigars, to my father to take to the hospital, the Stork Room of Manhattan Lying-in, the night I was born. I saved it after he died and put a little lock on it." With a click, she unlocked it. "First, I hid my grandmother's 'secrets' in it, oral tradition at first, handed down a thousand years, well before humans even understood pregnancy — methods to assure an April pregnancy, strategies for having a girl, and such things that had helped my family have January baby girls for centuries, to pass the Janus coin on to for generations." As her eyes welled up, she turned away from him, then spied him from the corner of her eye.

Relaxing from his guarded position, he slouched closer, tilting his head, opening his hands. "C'mon, doll."

Now she would make herself vulnerable by telling him this truth. "When we were dating and I thought you might be 'the one,' I wrote letters to my babies yet unborn. I folded the notes and tucked them in here. Because of the hysterectomy, to save my life after the abortion, I will never have those babies, and here you are asking me for a baby."

For a second, his eyes looked questioning and his grin disappeared. He shook his head and squeezed his eyebrows together. Had she reached him?

"I never knew. But how does that change anything?"

"Not to disappoint the little ones waiting for you and Brooke, not to disappoint Nana, or my better angels, maybe even the soul you and I were meant to have, we have a clean slate." She wiped her eyes with the back of her hand. When he approached, she held up one hand and pressed it against his chest. "Step back. This is my duty." She locked the box and tucked it back into the drawer.

"Does that mean I won you over?"

There wasn't a sigh deep enough. "Get Brooke, and come back in." She walked him to the door. As he lifted his arm to open it, the smell of sweat wafted her way.

CHAPTER 41

Light in March

Seated at the desk in her Park Avenue office, she tilted her head back and stretched her spine. Exhausted after a long day of surgeries, she inhaled deeply, filled her stomach with air she held and then expelled forcefully. On the wall, in her line of sight, were photographs of nearly a thousand babies, all born of successful in vitro, at the Columbia Center and here. But her eye always fell upon that one baby boy, her first success, Brooke's baby. Except for the photo, for nearly twenty years since that birth she had been Wayne-free.

Her cell rang. She sat up straight and fumbled across piles of papers to find it. A French accent, but she didn't recognize the voice. "Docteur Madeleine?"

"Oui."

"Madame, je suis vraiment désolé...." The phone slid from her hand. Its glass face shattered on hitting the stone floor. It must be a mistake. Although fluent in French, she must have misunderstood. She had been in Reims last weekend. Maybe something happened in the vineyard. Charles was perfectly fine, happy, and charming, as always. She pulled her landline close and phoned him directly. She had to clear this up. In her trembling hands, the handset missed the cradle, and, dangling on its curly long cord, bumped against the side of the desk as it blared its annoying signal, which vibrated in her brain. She ignored it as she ran out to June.

Denial had never been an effective strategy. She booked the next fight to Paris, informed June, and had her call Brenda and Jessica to meet her in Paris. Without baggage, she had a taxi race her to Kennedy Airport. This was no time to have damaged her cell.

At the château, she made a beeline to their suite. There was Charles, still on their bed, just as the doctor who had called told her he had left him, under the covers. She sat next to him and scooped him into her arms. And wept. His cheek was cold when she leaned to kiss it. He was so beautiful, his silver strands framing his face, his sea-blue eyes permanently closed. A union so perfect couldn't have lasted forever.

The doctor and some staff inched in close to the bed. "So sorry, Madame. We didn't know you had arrived. We left everything, as you requested." The doctor stepped closer, hands on her shoulders. "I will arrange everything once you tell me your wishes." He, and the little group, all wiping their eyes, bowed and stepped back, out of the room.

She lay on top of the blankets beside Charles for a while, until the doctor returned to tell her it was time. After she pulled herself up, she noticed an envelope addressed to her on Charles's nightstand. He must have known, but didn't warn her, didn't call. In the note, he wrote that having happiness he believed he'd never experience again, he wanted her to celebrate his life, with Champagne Madeleine, of course, and to invite everyone they knew in France and abroad, have the funeral at La Madeleine, and bury him at the château. He urged her to be grateful for their decades of happiness and to go on doing great things, even enjoy love if she were fortunate, as he had been, to find it again. No. Never. Charles was the rarest of men. She wouldn't sully his memory.

After she left the doctor to care for Charles, she had his driver, Adrien, take her to Paris, to the Ritz, where she tripped over her own feet running down to the spa level. She sat on the marble floor, on the medallion where she had first bumped into Charles. She sat there, cross-legged, hunched over, sobbing without check. People walked around her. An attendant she knew from the spa, Monique, came to her and helped lift her. In a darkened room, she comforted her and settled a lavender-infused towel around her neck, placed cold cucumber slices on her eyelids. And sat with her.

Although Brenda, Simon, their sons, and Jessica were probably waiting for her at the château, she couldn't go home just yet. They all knew where their suites were, and they'd be taken care of. Instead, she decided to follow the path of her first walk with Charles along the Seine to Le Procope, where she ordered scallops and madeleines, but barely laid either on her tongue. Both, however, gave her an idea for her next step, after her last parting from Charles. He was still supporting her. Smiling, she placed a hand on her shoulder, as though it were on top of his, as though he were standing behind her. She rejoiced and finished one warm madeleine in his memory.

At the end of a week of rituals, more like a wedding — champagne, macarons, and madeleines — than a funeral, she was the last to leave. She enclosed Charles's note in her bra, next to her heart, as Brenda had done with Rick's note. She would lock it away in her cigar box when she got back to the states. But she didn't go there. Instead, she boarded a plane to Florence, Italy.

Intent on enveloping herself in the ancient and eternal art of Florence, and the city itself, she booked a hotel near the Uffizi with its unmatched art collection and purchased her ticket even before settling into her hotel. The following morning, the first day of spring, she had been among the first to enter the Galleria degli Uffizi.

Like melting snow filling a swollen river, the morning light of spring's first day spilled from the window above the landing of the stone staircase she climbed. As she clutched the banister carved from the wall, she found the ascent arduous, as though the gravity of centuries, palpable on these steps that had served for over four hundred years, exerted its pull. She imagined the Medici who built this edifice, generations in their Renaissance robes, brushing this very stone on their way to their offices, the uffizi, and their art collection.

The madeleine that had warmed her lips and found its way to her tongue at Le Procope had reminded her of Botticelli's *Birth of Venus*, the scallop carrying Venus to her destination in society, painted in Florence for the Medici four hundred years ago, and still here. An air of fate and permanence. It had been her fate for the winds to blow her to the shores of medicine, to France to meet Charles, despite all obstacles, starting in Schweinfurt's anatomy class. The delicate-looking Botticelli had the strength to withstand the vagaries of time and cultural revolutions.

She looked across the staircase toward the elderly woman who gripped the banister of the opposite wall as she too mounted the steps with difficulty.

"La tua prima visita?" the woman asked.

"My first visit, yes. But I don't speak Italian."

"I come every year on the first day of spring," the woman said. "Walking the four flights, my penance. *The Birth*, my pilgrimage. I'm Anna."

"Candace." She waved. "I can't wait to be face-to-face with Venus." She crossed to the other side of the step and offered her arm to Anna. "May I give you a hand?"

"Grazie. I will accomplish it alone. There's an elevator, but I don't take it."

Candy continued alone and arrived at the entrance to the Lorraine Atrium, which would take her to the Botticelli rooms. She didn't expect the first piece she saw to be the life-size painting, *Fortitude*, which informed Brenda's philosophy on clothing, the picture she had kept tucked in her bureau mirror.

From the antechamber, Candy entered the vast rectangular gallery, home to *The Birth of Venus*, the first this day to tread the earth-colored tiles to the thin black rail along the perimeter of the room. It warned, "Go no closer." This was hallowed space.

The painting, five feet tall and ten feet wide, was large enough to study at a distance. But she couldn't resist being as close to it as she could, and she leaned against the rail. Through the painting's Plexiglass shield, she could see the lines of the brushstrokes; the V-shaped waves playing against the phallic-shaped reeds; the weave of the two linen canvases and the horizontal seam connecting them; the breath from Zephyr's puffed cheeks; the air escaping Chloris's parted lips; the fall of the pink roses against the pale blue of the sky; the subtle movement of the translucent blue-green waters that carried the ridged scallop shell bearing the life-size Venus, her blonde hair tangled by the breeze pushing her toward shore, toward the billowing robes society, in the embodiment of one of the Horae, the goddess of spring, held open to capture her on the last moment of her naked innocence. Candy held her breath, and like Chloris, pushed the air out in one puff. A work of beauty and hidden eroticism. She felt Charles behind her.

Anna tapped her arm, startling her. "You too are a prisoner of its beauty." She made the sign of the cross, kissed her fingertips, and sent the kiss to Venus. "See the roses. They're not pink. They're white, tinged with Venus's blood." Anna lifted her glasses and wiped her brow. "Venus will prick her heel on a thorn as she runs barefoot to her dying lover, Adonis. It's already here, written into her destiny, before she even touches shore." She turned toward the benches behind her. "I must sit down."

Candy followed and sat beside her. "Did you choose to visit this first day of spring?" She reached for Anna's hand and held it as she would have held her grandmother's hand. "For me, visiting today was mere chance."

"You believe in chance?" Anna asked. "In the painting, I see the breezes blowing away the past, the debris of winter. I see light, the brightness of new growth. This is a rebirth, for me, maybe a redemption." This time, she raised the glasses on the bridge of her nose and wiped away tears. "Spring after spring, year after year, I begin another cycle, and I release tears of joy."

"The gods don't steer us," Candy said. "We control our fate, adjust our sails, regardless of what fate has painted on our canvases. The image adjusts." She put her arm around Anna's shoulder. As a stream of visitors entered the room, Anna said goodbye, urged her not to miss the caffè, then left the room. Candy remained to study the other works, mostly Botticellis, then circled around to bid farewell to Venus, then *Fortitude*. She exited to the Eastern Corridor to walk among Medici ancestors, their statues, busts, and portraits lining the halls. She sat on the ledge in front of windows that afforded natural light to the hall and panoramic views of the Arno River and the Ponte Vecchio, the old bridge, the one too beautiful for even Hitler to destroy. She then followed the Western Corridor of the U-shaped museum and peeked into the many art-filled rooms on her way to the terrace caffè Anna had suggested.

In memory of her grandfather, she ordered a cannoli and an espresso with lemon rind. How wonderful it would have been to experience the museum with him, in his native Italy, or with Charles and a child they had conceived. Her grandfather had done the next best thing to taking her to Florence in introducing her to Caffè Reggio with its Medici bench and authentic espresso, the flavors of the coffee beans pushed out under intense pressure. She should have taken time from work and come here with Charles, even without a child.

She paid the cashier with a euro banknote and dropped the change into her coat pocket. While the cashier prepared the order behind the counter, she made small talk and asked if she had visited the *Birth*. Her sole reason for the trip to Florence, Candy answered.

"If you sort through your change, you will see I gave you a ten-cent euro coin. It shows a detail from the painting — the head of Venus with her wild hair."

When she reached into her pocket to retrieve the coins, there it was, the face of Botticelli's Venus. "Mille grazie." She opened her purse and saved the coin in a zippered compartment before taking her tray to carry out to the terrace. Using her elbow to close the door, she noticed a poster announcing "8 Marzo Festa della donna." After claiming a table near the door, she left her tray there, and retraced her steps to read the poster.

She had missed Day of the Woman. On the announcement was a poem, in English and in Italian, attributed to a Giuseppe: "Without women, the world would end; there wouldn't be sweetness; there wouldn't be the love of a mother; there wouldn't be the smile of a girl; there wouldn't be the desire to live. Thank you, women." *Perhaps the Italian rhymed.*

She went back to her table, which had been set for two, to enjoy her treats. She missed Charles's touch, his company, his open and generous nature. The museum was attracting ghosts of her own.

The waitress appeared at her table. "I saw you reading this. You may have it," she said, handing her the poster. "We should've taken it down weeks ago. No poet, Giuseppe."

Her grandfather's name, Joe, in Italian. "Mille grazie," Candy said. Decorated with blooming mimosa branches, the article below the poem encouraged men to give women the golden blossoms, a tradition. She recalled seeing countless such trees as she traveled through Tuscany to Florence the previous day. Mimosa trees in containers graced the perimeter of the terrace. She finished her espresso and walked to the balustrade fencing in the balcony.

She pulled her guidebook from her purse. Nearby was the crenelated tower of the fortress, Palazzo Vecchio, the old palace, the town hall. A little farther north soared the imposing Il Duomo, Brunelleschi's dome atop Santa Maria del Fiore, Saint Mary of the Flower, the conception and construction of which paved the way for the social and cultural revolution of the Renaissance. It loomed above the terra cotta roof tiles undulating over the buildings, ubiquitous throughout Italy.

She took a cut mimosa branch lying across a clay pot. She carried it to her table and placed it there acknowledging that Charles, the romantic, would certainly have engaged in the ritual and given her one. She felt his hand on her shoulder.

The waitress returned to ask if she'd like another espresso. "We precut twigs so people won't damage the trees. Enjoy." She slipped her a creased magazine article from her pocket. "You might enjoy this, also from Festa della donna. You must come next year."

"Grazie, and yes to another espresso." She unfolded the article. "The Fate of the Uffizi in the Hands of a Woman." It was the story of Anna Maria Luisa de' Medici, the final scion of the Medici, the end of the long-powerful family. Candy was in good company, being the last of her long line as well.

Early in Anna Maria Luisa's marriage she had suffered a miscarriage, and later contracted syphilis from her philandering husband. Despite their twenty-five-year union, Anna Maria Luisa was unable to bear children. At the death of her brother, she inherited the vast wealth and collections of the Medici. But she had no heir. Fearing the collections in the Uffizi and the Medici castellos would be dispersed by the Lorraine branch of the family to France, Austria and elsewhere, Anna Maria Luisa negotiated a family pact, signed by Francis Stephen I of Lorraine, future father of Marie Antoinette, decreeing all Medici possessions be bequeathed to him provided they remained in Florence, always available to the public in the Uffizi. With her last breath, "an oppression on the breast," in 1743, the Medici line expired.

Anna Maria's story resonated. The lot of women. The strength of women. The long-reaching impact of their decisions and actions. She had inherited Charles's fortune, and there were no other heirs. She'd have to consider his legacy, maybe the home for women he had once envisioned. She tucked the folded article into her bra, near her heart and her Janus necklace, the legacy she had failed to continue.

Bearing the weight of unexpected emotions, sweating, her knees buckling, she reached the balustrade and leaned over for a parting view of Florence from the heights of the terrace. A sudden strong breath from Zephyr and Chloris blew at her back, tangled the curls in front of her eyes, and scattered golden mimosa blossoms from the nearby trees swirling around her feet, like gilded snowflakes, funneling upwards, gathering around her, embracing her.

Feeling as light as the blossoms engulfing her, she believed she had made the best of the life path she had followed, assured that her ancestors approved. Yet again, she felt Charles's hand on her shoulder.

She turned, as though she'd see him as she did. Instead, she saw a stroller hidden beneath the tilted white umbrella shielding the diners from the setting sun. She caught the edge of a pastel afghan, like the thousands she had given her mothers, attached to the stroller. She made her way over to peek under the umbrella, to see if she recognized the family.

"Dr. Madeleine," the woman said, "what a surprise to meet you in Florence." She stood to greet her, as did the man whose hand was on the stroller. The family stepped away from the umbrella and pulled the stroller with them.

"A wonderful surprise," Candy said. "I don't keep up with all my families, especially since I stopped delivering the babies, but this little one has the afghan, and your blue eyes."

"And, thanks to you, I have her," Dorothy said. She reached for the man's arm. "This is my father whom I'm visiting, Joseph Vespucci. He is a native Florentine and still lives here."

"A great pleasure, he said. He drew closer to Candy, heart-to-heart; he brushed her left cheek with his, and then the right. "My granddaughter has been a great gift. Molte grazie."

"My honor and joy," Candy said. She put her finger near the baby's hand, and the baby curled her little fingers around it. Candy paused and stood. "Would you mind if I gave her a gift?"

"The afghan was more than enough, and of course, the baby herself." Dorothy pretended to take the afghan from the toddler, who held tight. The grandfather laughed.

"She may grow to appreciate this gift even more, a link to her heritage." She unclasped her Janus necklace and showed it to Dorothy. "May I?" She gestured toward the baby and handed the heirloom to Dorothy.

"If you're sure, I'd be honored to have a personal possession of yours." Dorothy took it, turned it to see both sides. "It appears to be quite old." She passed it to her father.

"An authentic Roman coin?" he asked. "How could you part with it?"

"My grandmother took it from Italy. It's two thousand years old, and fitting I should return it here. Time to let go."

Dorothy handed it back it to her. "You should be the one to bestow it, parting with a family heirloom."

As she approached the stroller, the baby held onto her blanket and waved her arms, just like the baby on the plane, Cynthia, so many years ago. "Such innocence," Candy said. "The necklace comes with no obligation but to enjoy it, a link to your Italian roots." She fastened it around the child's neck and kissed her on the forehead.

Dorothy dipped in, lifted the baby from the stroller, and handed her to Candy. "You've been part of our family," she said, "as you are of all of the families you've helped create."

Candy cried and held the baby close. "I didn't even ask her name."

"Hope."

THE END

ACKNOWLEDGMENTS

After reading the first draft of my novel, then discussing changes, Cara Santos presented me with a mug that reads, "I write, therefore I rewrite." That was early on. I have so many to thank for their assistance as I progressed through countless rewrites.

My appreciation to the South Walton Writer's Group, the tireless organizer, Ronald Larsen, members, and my first editor, Jenny Bowman for their feedback.

Authors at the annual Seaside Writers' Conference in Florida encouraged me to apply for the Taos Summer Writers' Conference, which I did, despite having only eight months to submit a completed manuscript.

My weekly canasta group was polite enough to listen to me outline a plot. Margaret Schmidt read each chapter as it was created. Thanks to beta readers Cate Barber and Robin Wiesneth who read after many rewrites.

At the week-long Taos Conference, mentor Kent Nelson and fellow writers, Nancy, Ro, Peter, Matt, and Shirley ripped the draft apart and offered suggestions to rebuild.

Work with agents in Writer's Digest workshops sharpened my vision of characters, plot, and setting.

The four-day St. Augustine Author-Mentor Novel Workshop suggested a new title and a new structure that greatly enhanced the manuscript. I especially thank Paula Munier. And I must acknowledge Robert Olen Butler for his wise words and the inspiration to continue that shot from his hand to mine in a farewell handshake. More rewriting.

I wish to credit the Women's Fiction Writers Association, which offers ever-expanding resources to writers of women's fiction. It was through their webinars that I discovered AuthorBytes to whom I owe the final push of birthing this novel, especially their awesome design team.

Tanya H. Lee, copyeditor, deserves kudos for adding her magic touch to my work.

Great appreciation is extended to Norman Assad, M.D. and Marelyn Medina, M.D. who enhanced the medical information of the novel's time period beyond that which I had gleaned from my research.

Since it took many years to write this novel, I also want to thank those I don't specifically mention here. Very special thanks to my children for their feedback and unflagging support.

ABOUT THE AUTHOR

Linda M. Habib was born and raised on the island of Manhattan, the setting of her debut novel. After teaching English in New York City public high schools for more than thirty years, she retired to an island in Florida with her Shih Tzu, Genghis Khan. Her children maintain her connection with Manhattan. Visit her online at lindahabib.com